Flight

K.G. RING

Get Access to Free Books and Exclusive Material

One of the best things about living in the future is that authors can build relationships with their readers. I occasionally send newsletters with details on new releases, special offers, and other news related to my writing.

To begin our relationship, sign up for the newsletter at KennethRing.com or scan the QR code below.

Newsletter Link

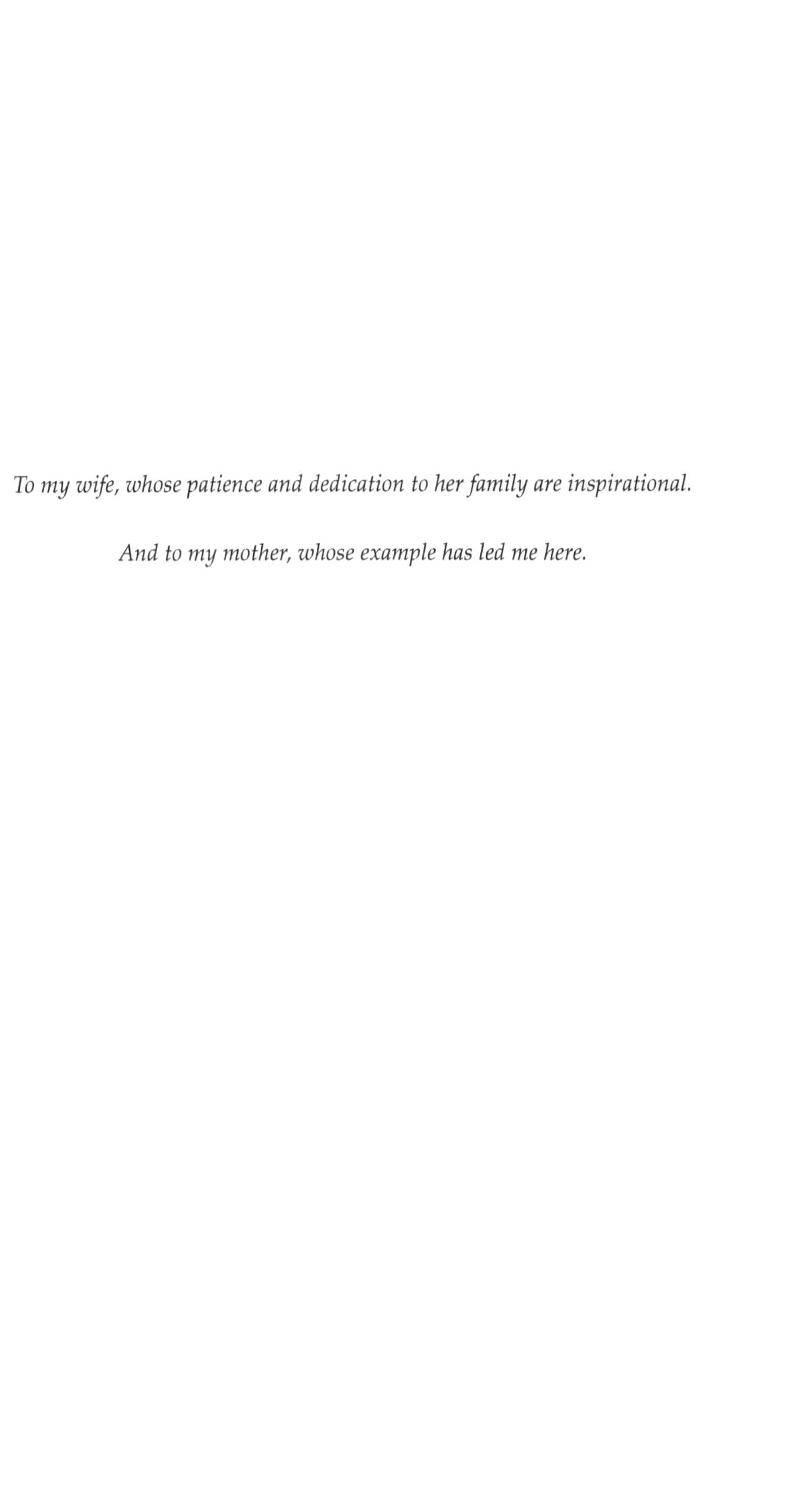

To my wife, whose patience and dedication to her family are inspirational.

And to my mother, whose example has led me here.

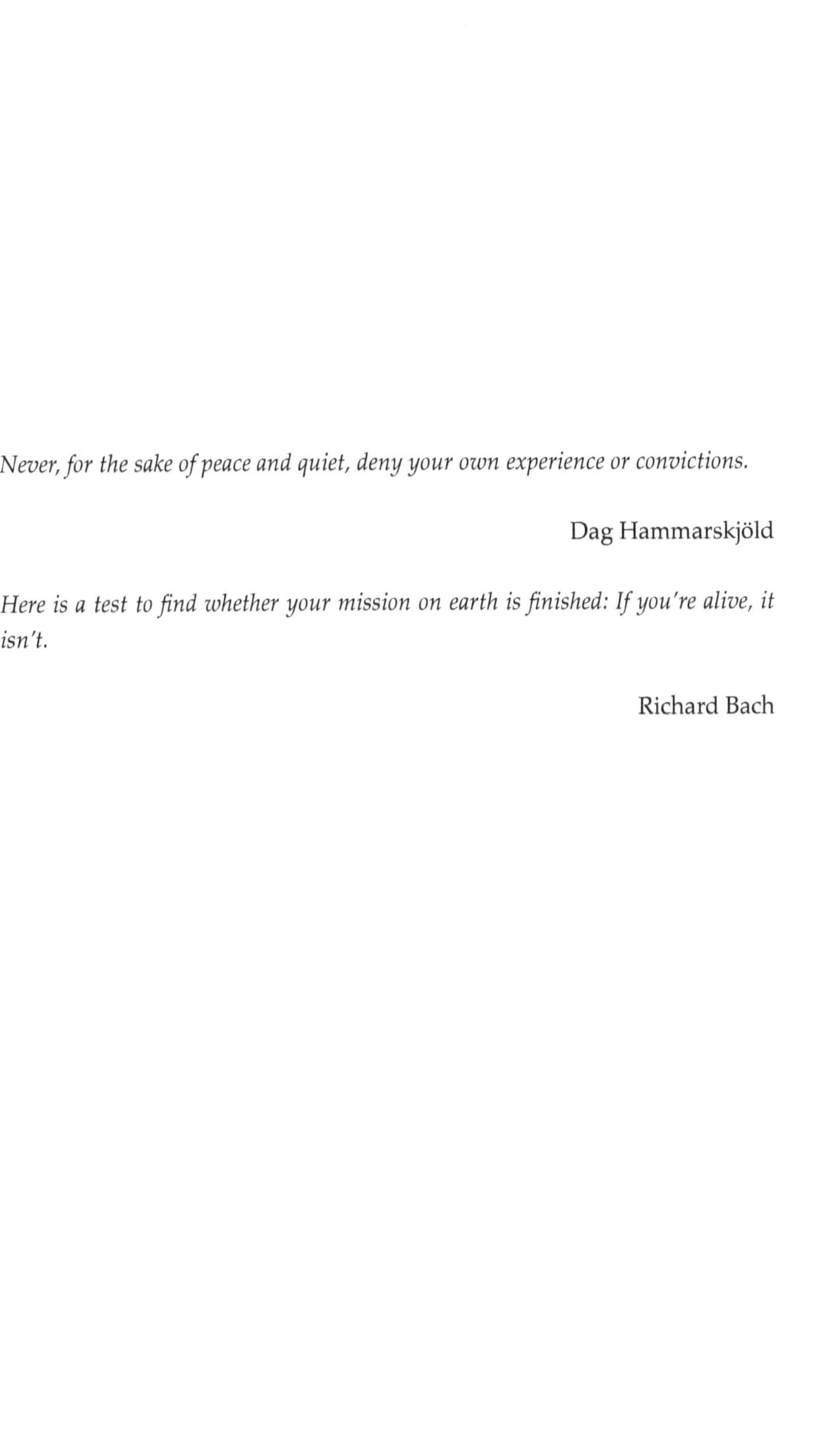

Never, for the sake of peace and quiet, deny your own experience or convictions.

Dag Hammarskjöld

Here is a test to find whether your mission on earth is finished: If you're alive, it isn't.

Richard Bach

One

APRIL 16, 2026

I came in from the fields looking forward to dinner with my parents. As I entered the barn and headed to my apartment on the second floor, I noticed cars in the driveway. People often stopped for vegetables, even if we didn't have the sign out. Some part of my brain registered the coincidence that all three of the cars were black SUVs.

Visitors meant I had time for a shower before dinner. I was unbuttoning my shirt as I walked through the door but stopped short, surprised to find my living room full of people.

"Who are you?" I asked, pausing in the doorway.

"Olivia Donnelly?" A large man in a suit asked from across the room.

"Yeah, that's me. What's going on?"

I glanced around the room.

"Where are my parents?"

"Ms. Donnelly, I'm Anthony Graham with the U.S. Marshals. We need to ask you some questions. Will you have a seat, please?"

He phrased it as a question, but it came across as a command.

"What? Where are my parents?" I asked again, my stomach knotting.

A woman, younger than the man, stepped in from the kitchen.

"Your parents are fine, Ms. Donnelly."

I heard her, but didn't respond. Delicate features and dark brown skin distracted me momentarily, but she was a strange person in a team of strange people going through my stuff.

"Um…identification. Let's see some ID."

Graham spoke, but the woman stopped him. She held her ID card from the chain around her neck. I leaned in to read it and caught a whiff of perfume. Something with vanilla. The card said that she was Agent Stefanie Tucciarone, Federal Bureau of Investigation.

Well, crap, I thought.

"FBI?"

"Most of us," she said, gesturing to the large man. "Graham is with the U.S. Marshals."

"Again, Ms. Donnelly," he said, "Will you take a seat?"

He was 6'3" and solid. I had sparred with guys like him in martial art tournaments, learned to throw them and to be thrown.

Still, I would not like to tangle with this guy, I thought as I entered.

"You'll tell me what this is about?"

"We have some questions about your recent activities," Graham said. I noticed a bit of a southern accent. Not heavy, but there. Georgia, maybe?

"Activities?" I asked, hoping my voice didn't squeak. I had done nothing strictly illegal, but I was nervous. I get nervous when a cop pulls me over for having a headlight out. FBI agents in my living room? My hands were shaking and my voice quavered.

"Ms. Donnelly," Agent Graham said, "Can you tell us everywhere you've been in the past six months?"

I needed a minute to think and ground myself.

"Look, I was headed to the bathroom. Can I go in there and pee? Before we talk?"

I glanced at Agent Tucciarone.

She nodded at another agent who went into the bathroom. I heard him check the medicine cabinet, toilet tank, and the shower door. He came back out thirty seconds later and nodded.

"No window, solid floor and ceiling," the agent said.

Graham gestured magnanimously towards the bathroom.

"Thanks."

I avoided the agents' eyes as I walked to the bathroom. After I finished, I washed my hands and face and took my hair down. I combed it with my fingers and remade my ponytail. My shirt was still open, showing the undershirt below, so I buttoned it back up.

Standing in front of the mirror, I took a moment to meditate. When people think of meditation, they usually picture someone sitting quietly for a long time. That's the way you start, but when you get good at it, you can meditate anywhere, anytime. Dr. Wayne Dyer described Zen as being the space between two thoughts. That's where I went. I stopped thinking, watched my body and breath. Calm and self-control descended and enveloped me like my grandmother's old quilt.

When I stepped back into the living room, I offered the agents something to drink.

"Ms. Donnelly, we're not your guests. I need you to sit down and answer some serious questions," Graham said.

"Nothing for you, then. Anyone else?" I asked, looking around.

"No, thank you," Agent Tucciarone said. "We really need to do this, ma'am. Then hopefully we can get out of your hair."

"Hallelujah."

I got a glass and filled it with water from the cooler, then sat down. Graham gazed intently at my glass as I drank, and I suspected he was thirsty. I took a long swallow and smiled as best I could.

"I'm all yours."

"Your whereabouts for the past few months," Graham reminded me.

"Right, let's see," I counted on my fingers, "April, March, February...?"

"Let's start with October," Graham said.

"Oh. That's a long time ago."

I don't enjoy lying. I'm no good at it, but I couldn't tell the government what happened outside of St. Louis.

"Give it a shot," Graham said.

Two other agents sorted through books and papers on my kitchen table.

"Well, I live here, of course. That's one." I said weakly, trying to see what the other agents were doing.

Graham blinked.

"Um, I'm not in school this semester, so...not there," I said, stalling.

"What school would that be?" Another agent took notes, and Agent Tucciarone set a digital recorder on the coffee table.

"You're recording this?" I said, "Is that even legal without my permission?"

"Ms. Donnelly, I'm done being polite. We're here on an issue of national security. You may not be aware, but we have a lot of latitude in situations like these. Now, will you cooperate or not?"

"Agent Graham," I said, anger at his bullying threatening to break through my calm, "have I refused to cooperate?"

"What school?"

I told him.

"Go on," he said flatly.

I listed all the places I could think of, including my martial art school, yoga class, library, grocery, feed shop, hardware store, and department stores.

"Have you been to the dentist, Ms. Donnelly?" another agent asked.

"What? Oh...yes." That caught me off balance, which was probably the point. How much did they already know?

"What about the courthouse?"

"Yeah..." I said, remembering the tax forms I filed for my parents.

"What about online purchases, Ms. Donnelly?" the first FBI agent asked. What was her name? I couldn't remember. Stefanie something.

Graham said nothing, just stared at me.

"Online purchases? Um, yeah, you know."

"Why don't you pretend we don't know," Graham said.

"I could check my eBay and Amazon history if you want a complete list," I said. Something about this man was infuriating me.

"How about you give it your best shot without the computer?"

I sighed.

"I bought an old-fashioned aviator's helmet and goggles."

Graham nodded.

"And a silk aviator's scarf. And a leather flight suit."

"Anything else?" Agent Stefanie asked.

I swallowed hard.

"I bought an emergency parachute."

"Are you a pilot, Ms. Donnelly?" Graham asked.

"No, not yet."

"Then why would you need an emergency parachute?"

No answer could make this any better. I leaned forward, elbows on my knees, fingers steepled.

"For emergencies," I said.

Agent Stefanie smiled and turned away.

"Emergencies," Graham said, glancing at her. "Ms. Donnelly, have you been out of the state in the past six months?"

"My car's not the greatest," I said, sitting back again.

"I didn't ask about your car," he said, his attention focused entirely on me again.

I took a deep breath.

"I visited Illinois recently, but I don't remember the details."

That was accurate enough. I wasn't in a town and couldn't pick out the field where I landed on a map.

"Don't remember details? Maybe I can help. Do you remember this?"

He glanced at one of the other agents and nodded. The agent set a folder on the coffee table and made a show of opening it. Inside were still photos that he arranged in front of me. They were video captures that showed the back of a gigantic blue and white jet in flight. The first showed something that wasn't much more than a blob at the top of the vertical stabilizer. The second showed the shape of a person in a leather helmet and goggles. The third showed an indistinct ball streaking past the right side of the camera.

"I do not remember taking those pictures," I said. The attempt at humor was spoiled when my mouth went dry and my voice cracked.

"Ms. Donnelly, again, you are being questioned on a matter of national security, one which has implications and repercussions, the likes of which you cannot imagine."

He stared at me, his gaze granite hard.

"Olivia Donnelly, is this you in these photos?"

All anger and humor were gone. Only fear remained.

"Yes."

The Federal Bureau of Investigation headquarters in Indianapolis is a newish building on the northeast side of the city. It's three stories tall, has lots of parking, a guard gate, and a black chain-link fence around the perimeter.

I was kind of impressed.

The SUVs drove to a secure entrance in the back that wasn't visible from public streets. We drove through two gates topped with razor wire before they helped me out. Things didn't look good.

Three agents escorted me through the building to a room with a table and several chairs. I had seen enough *NCIS* to know it for what it was - an interrogation room. I sat down and waited while they attached my cuffs to a bolt in the floor. After a long day working on the farm, I was tired. When the agents left, I sat back and put my feet up on the table, hoping to catch a quick nap.

"Feet off the table," a voice said.

"What?" I asked, opening my eyes.

"Take your feet off the table," the amplified voice repeated.

The table was new, but just steel and Formica. My work boots wouldn't hurt it.

"I just want a quick nap so I can be fresh to answer your questions."

"Take your feet off the table, Miss," the voice said.

That "Miss" sounded like an insult.

"Why?"

"You are in federal custody, and we do not allow you to put your feet on the table."

"Let me go then, and I'll put my feet up on my bed," I said, no longer impressed.

The voice went away, and the door opened. Marshal Graham and Agent Stefanie came in. She dropped a folder on the table, and they both sat down.

"Hi agents," I sighed, sitting up and putting my feet down.

I was nervous, but also tired and hungry. For the duration of the hour-long car ride, I had meditated and worked on centering myself. Now, I tried to maintain that calm.

"What are we talking about now?"

"Ms. Donnelly, I understand you're not a criminal. Aside from driving too fast, you seem to be a pretty good person," Agent Stefanie said.

"Okay," I said, wary of the compliment.

"The...situation appears to have changed," Graham said.

"I'm not sure I follow you."

"Frankly, I don't know where the law begins and ends with people like you."

He was silent for a moment, and my jaw fell slack. I sat up straighter.

"People like me? What do you mean? There are others?"

Graham said nothing, just watched me.

I glanced at Agent Stefanie, then back to Graham.

"Okay then, where do we go now?" I asked.

"That's what our bosses are deciding," he said. "For what it's worth, you will not gain any points for yourself with petty rule breaking."

My calm fractured and rage propelled me to my feet, but the cuffs chained to the floor prevented me from standing up straight.

"Petty rule breaking? I'm being treated like a criminal. An animal!"

Graham looked at me with narrowed eyes, but otherwise made no move to do or say anything.

I closed my eyes, sat down, and took a deep breath. I shook my head and shoulders and opened my eyes. Have you ever tried to calm yourself with adrenaline rushing through your veins? It's difficult.

"We understand," Agent Stefanie murmured, "and, for what it's worth, I apologize."

Her eyes were sincere, and I sat back in the chair and nodded, breathing deeply to control my temper.

"I'm not the sort of man to cage an animal," Graham said, "let alone a person who doesn't deserve it." His southern accent was more pronounced now. Was he trying to sound sincere?

"Tomorrow, we're taking you east. Probably to Quantico." He paused for a moment before saying, "Ms. Donnelly, this is a big deal. You understand?"

I shook my head.

"Not really, no."

Agent Stefanie leaned in.

"Look, we can't go into details, but it's…important. You'll probably meet people," she paused. "Well, people you've seen on the news."

"Will they put me in a lab?"

"It wouldn't surprise me — among other things," Graham said.

"Let me tell you something," I said, leaning forward and speaking very low so hopefully only they could hear me. "This won't work. They can do whatever they want, but they won't be able to figure it out. They can take me apart atom by atom, and they won't find any answers."

Graham turned his head, glancing at the camera, then back to me.

"What do you mean?"

From my very first levitation experience to the present, I have kept a digital journal of my experiences. I started writing once I knew I wasn't crazy or hallucinating. When I began posting online, I kept the story on my blog about a year behind the actual timeline. I needed time to process events and discoveries and frequently edited articles before they posted, as I came to understand things better.

I considered for a moment before I responded.

"I've written about this. It's not something they can turn into a weapon," I said. "It won't work like that."

"Don't be too sure," he said.

"I *am* sure. It works by becoming peaceful, a better person. By becoming, I don't know, spiritual, for lack of a better word."

I was uncomfortable saying that word out loud.

He looked at me quizzically and then smirked.

"God DAMMIT!" I yelled, trying to stand again. I looked at the camera. "Haven't you guys even read my blog?"

I had posted answers to these questions months before.

"Of course we've read it," Graham said.

"Then you think I'm an idiot? That I don't know what I'm talking about?"

Graham pushed away from the table. "We think you might be…hasty in your conclusions."

"'Hasty,'" I repeated, falling back into the chair. "Great. 'Hasty.' I'm being interrogated by freaking Treebeard."

Agent Stefanie snorted a laugh.

"Your blog has attracted attention," Graham said, standing. "Lots of attention."

"From who? Almost nobody reads my blog."

Graham looked at me as if I were an idiot.

"I'm not talking about page hits or shares. Not your followers, or community leaders, or whatever. I'm talking about governments, corporations, political organizations."

"What? You mean they want it for military applications? I've already told you, that's not possible. I'm not worried."

"Well, you should be. They're not just interested in military applications. They're interested in a group of people for whom passports and border crossings are no longer an issue. Smuggling and espionage and…"

"Freedom," Agent Stefanie said, looking up at Graham.

He paused, raising his eyebrows at her. He finally sat down and sighed.

"Maybe," he said, throwing his pen down onto the folder in front of him. He scrubbed his face with his hands and pushed his hair back.

"Look, I won't sugarcoat anything. You're in danger. The U.S. government has its issues with you; Defense and Homeland both want you. My job is your apprehension and protection. The FBI's job is finding and catching the bad guys."

"Bad guys? What bad guys?" I asked.

"The ones who are coming for you," Agent Stefanie said.

They left me alone for an hour before Agent Stefanie came back into the room.

"Listen," she said, leaning over the table. "Tomorrow morning, a helicopter will land outside. We'll take it to the airport and then fly directly to Quantico."

"Okay, what—"

She cut me off.

"Get some sleep. You have a big day tomorrow."

And that was it. Agents moved me to a small cell with a cot; I was uncuffed and offered microwaved food from a box. I declined but took all the water bottles they would allow me to have. Then, I did my best to sleep and meditate.

Early the next morning, I was doing Sun Salutations when the helicopter landed. By the time the agents opened the door, I was tying my boots. They let me use a bathroom where I washed my face and did my best to clear my mind.

Four burly male marshals escorted me through the facility. Agent Tucciarone (I had gotten her name from one of the other agents) fastened a bulletproof vest around my chest, giving me another whiff of vanilla as she did. I was grateful when she tightened my ponytail after strapping a Kevlar helmet to my head.

I started to ask a question, but she shook her head.

"Remember, they're keeping you safe. That's their job."

My heart felt like it was climbing up my throat. I forced myself to be calm. I needed to breathe and be meditative.

Fear and tension faded, and I centered myself in that moment. No thoughts of the future or the past. I was here now, and I loved who I was, what I was doing. I was free and in control. The feeling of oneness that I had felt at crucial times in my practice returned. I felt a deep connection with Agent Stefanie and the marshals.

When they led me through the door, the bright sunlight caused me to squint. Suddenly, we were hurrying across the lawn to the helicopter. I had never been in a helicopter.

The certainty that I wouldn't be in one today either flooded through me. I was in light meditation as they jog-walked me across the yard. The agents had cuffed my hands behind me, but my feet were free. I felt, or more precisely, I *knew* something significant was happening. The marshal in front of me was in danger, and nobody saw it but me. I had to help.

You know how sometimes, when you are holding your breath, suddenly you realize you have to breathe? Like that, I had to kick the marshal's legs out from under him. I watched myself step up with my left foot and sweep my right leg to catch him in the ankle and push both feet to the left. He started falling just as the marshal behind me put his hand on my shoulder and pulled.

I let the momentum of my sweeping kick turn me around, and I kicked the Marshal behind me. I put my right big toe squarely into his left hip joint. He folded over, and I took a fraction of a second to hope he wasn't seriously injured. They hit the ground simultaneously, just as the others were turning.

I shot into the air and heard the crack of a shock wave from the sniper round that passed under my feet, right between the two standing agents. The shouts and cries of a half-dozen people followed me into the air, quickly drowned by the roar of 150 mph wind buffeting my head as I shot through the clouds.

So…hi.

I'm Olivia and I can fly.

And that was how I escaped from the U.S. government the first time. But how did they find me? And how *can I* fly? *And who's trying to kill me? And, and, and….*

We'll get to all that.

But first: the photographs. Six months before the feds introduced themselves in such a friendly way, I attempted my first long cross-country flight. It did not go as planned.

Excerpt from the blog: *Griffin's Flight*

NOVEMBER 24, 2025

"Environmental Lapse Rate" is what meteorologists call the decrease in temperature with altitude. It varies, depending on things like humidity and how much the air is moving, but it's about four or five degrees Fahrenheit per one thousand feet of altitude. That means if it is 40° on the ground, then it will be around 30° when you are 2000 feet above the ground. This can be significant, and even life-threatening, especially if you are flying without the benefit of an airplane.

So, during the planning stages of my first long cross-country flight, I purchased several pairs of thermal underwear and began dressing in layers whenever I practiced. I wore insulated boots with room for thick hunter's socks, and a barn coat big enough to cover several turtlenecks. Layering helped with the cold.

That Sunday in October, I was up early. The plan was to fly to St. Louis, Missouri, and back, a round trip of close to 1000 miles. If all went well, I would be home by lunchtime. It was warm that morning, so I wore fewer layers than usual. The temperature on the ground was almost 70°, which meant it should be around 40° at my altitude. As long as I kept my face covered, I would be good.

I headed up as the sun was rising. The sky was hazy, and there were clouds to the west.

I don't use the ground-based navigation aids that pilots use. Why? Intuition. When I need an answer, it's usually there. But not always, which is why my phone was in a rig on my left forearm. I could check the GPS if I needed to. Studying weather was on my list, but I hadn't gotten far. Again, I trusted intuition to guide me.

But, it doesn't hurt to have a backup, I thought.

I headed west and a little south. I would follow I-70 almost all the way. If I got there early enough, I could fly through the Gateway Arch. If there were too many people around, I wouldn't try it.

Just past Indy, I noticed there was a layer of clouds about five hundred feet above me. I stayed alert for other traffic and flew well below them.

A small airplane began closing from my right. I changed course to avoid him, but he kept getting closer.

My coat has to stand out against the clouds.

Since I didn't want to be seen, I took a quick detour through the overcast layer. There was a risk of other traffic hidden in the clouds, but I had to take it. I transitioned to vertical flight and shot straight up, trying to pierce the cloud layer as quickly as possible.

I grew nervous as I continued to fly blind, higher and higher. The overcast layer was thick. When I came out on top, perhaps 1500 feet above my previous altitude, the sun dazzled me. It was like walking through a door into another world. Unfortunately, the humidity inside the clouds had soaked my coat and helmet. My jeans were heavy and damp and my goggles fogged.

It was a lot colder up here, too, and the air was thinner than I was used to.

I checked for other traffic. The top of the overcast layer resembled a starkly beautiful, if unadorned, landscape. The sun was still behind me, so I knew the general direction to go, but the air was wintry cold. I didn't want to fly above the clouds the whole way. Despite the beauty of the cloudscape, I was cold and needed to get below.

I took a southwest heading and flew. My teeth began chattering, and I was soon shivering. The next time I checked my phone, there was a layer of frost on my coat. My jeans were the same. I slowed down and hovered. I tried to remove my goggles to clear the frozen fog, but they had frozen to my face.

It was becoming impossible to stay meditative, which would mean that soon I wouldn't be flying, I would be falling. I headed down.

Mental note: Look into parachutes.

In the clouds again, the humidity was thicker than ever. The frost on my outer clothing turned to a layer of hard ice, and if I had depended on aerodynamics to fly, I would be in real trouble. I couldn't control my shivering now.

I broke through the clouds into a light drizzle and quickly checked for traffic.

Nothing. Get to the ground.

I was flying over small fields and vast wooded areas. I landed hard and stumbled to my knees, my legs cramping from the cold. When I could move, I stumbled to my feet, went into the trees, and sat on a log to rest, think, and cry, not necessarily in that order.

Remember, when flying, I have to be in light meditation and that shuts off the logical left side of the brain. So, while I was flying, I hadn't registered how much trouble I was actually in. Even though I was now safe, retroactive fear flooded over me for a few minutes.

But, eventually, gratitude arrived, and I may have shed a few more tears as I sat there. I was alive. The weather sucked, but I was in a beautiful place. Peaceful. The trees were bare, and there was a thick carpet of leaves. I gazed around and relaxed. The air was warmer, and the drizzle had stopped.

After I had my emotions back under control, I took my coat and helmet off. The clothes underneath were damp, but not frozen. Since I was alone in the middle of the woods, I took my boots and jeans off, leaving on the long underwear. I slipped my boots back on and spread my things out to dry as best they could in the weak sunlight. Starting a fire would be ideal, but too risky.

I practiced martial art forms to get my muscles warmed up and try to dry out my thermal underwear. I didn't want to break a sweat and make my clothes even wetter, but I needed to get my blood moving.

By this time, it was close to 9:00 am.

Every so often, I shook out my clothes and turned them over. When I checked my phone, the weather forecast had changed. It was going to stay warm, but get cloudier and wetter.

As long as the rain holds off, I'll wait for an opening in the clouds and then pop up through the overcast and head home.

I stayed there at the edge of the woods for more than an hour. When my clothes were as dry as they were likely to get, I got dressed.

Finally, a long thin gash appeared in the ceiling to the south. I could fly down there, pop up over the clouds, and fly back home, relatively dry.

When I get home, I'll drop through the clouds and fly right down into the barn.

That was the plan, anyway.

I put my phone back in its rig, donned coat and gloves, helmet and scarf. I checked for both air and ground traffic, stepped back into the trees and lifted off under their cover.

I climbed until I was so close to the clouds that mist formed on my goggles, then dropped a few dozen feet and flew fast. In less than 15 minutes, I would be above the weather.

When the sky lightened up ahead, I descended 100 feet to get a better view. On the ground to the west, patches of sunlight crept across the fields like spotlights. I turned towards them.

That's when I felt the vibrations in my stomach that meant a plane was close. I slowed and looked all around, but could see nothing.

The vibration intensified, making me anxious. It had to be descending through the clouds. Rolling, I dived, head down, rocketing toward the surface. At about 1000 feet above the ground, I hovered, waiting. I couldn't see anything, but I could hear the engines as the plane passed overhead. Just as I resumed my trip toward the break in the overcast, the airplane dropped below the clouds. It was massive! No wonder I felt it so long before I ever saw or heard it.

It was a Boeing 747, mostly white, but blue at the front with words along the fuselage. Each of its four engines was bigger than my bathroom. It had a huge wingspan, and the vertical stabilizer was maybe four times as tall as me.

I turned west to follow. The jet was so loud and so close I couldn't even hear the air rushing past my ears. The 747 continued to descend slowly. Up ahead must be an airport. Surely we weren't that close to St. Louis yet.

Without thinking, I flew through the massive airplane's turbulent wake, enveloped in the sweet scent of burning jet fuel. I removed my right glove and touched the trailing edge of the rudder with one finger. A shudder ran through me at the feel of the cold metal. I backed off a few feet, pulled my glove back on and turned - just in time to see two fighter jets breaking through the overcast, following a few thousand feet behind the huge aircraft.

Why are military jets escorting a 747?

I had no time to think. I was flying backward behind the 747, still buffeted by turbulence. Still, I was close enough to the escorts that I could look the pilots in the eye.

Am I camouflaged by the huge plane behind me?

Regardless, as soon as you move, they'll see you for sure, I answered myself.

Suddenly, a beam of sunlight struck me. It scared me at first, but I jumped at the opportunity. I pulled myself into a ball and reversed direction as fast as possible, shooting directly between the two fighters.

When they whooshed past me, I unfolded and shot straight up through the break in the cloud ceiling. Hopefully, the pilots would think I was a high-flying turkey vulture or something. I flew straight through the hole in the clouds into the bright sunlight on top. It was dazzling and frigid after the humid gray gloominess under the overcast layer. I pulled my scarf up over my nose and mouth and fastened my collar around my neck.

I headed home as fast as I could fly. Streamlining my body, I tucked my chin into my chest, pulled my arms back alongside my body, and pointed my feet directly behind me. I thought about home and speed and flew like a rocket. The wind hammered at my ears, even through my helmet. I was going faster than I ever had before. I looked for other traffic every so often the best I could just by moving my head. There were jets ahead of me lined up to get into Indianapolis, then they were past.

And, without even considering the question of the fighter escort, the answer popped into my mind.

I just touched Air Force One. The President of the United States of America was on board that plane.

Crap.

A fter escaping from the FBI *(Holy CRAP, I just escaped from the FBI!)* I flew to Mom and Dad's, knowing the Feds wouldn't be far behind. It was about fifty miles as the crow flies, but I was sure there were local agents, even state police, nearby. I closed my eyes most of the way and got there in about fifteen minutes. I landed in the yard, not worrying about secrecy, and started calling out as soon as I landed.

Mom came to the door with her hand on her chest.

"Livvie? What happened?"

Yes, my mom calls me "Livvie" when she's worried. I was 12 when we shortened it to "Liv," but she forgets when she's worried.

"I'm okay. Where's Dad?"

He came out right behind her.

"I need help," I said, running to the workshop. It was awkward with my hands cuffed behind me. They both followed.

"Dad, can you get these open? Or off? We've only got a few minutes. Mom, can you get some clothes together for me? Maybe some food? And money?"

As she hurried away, I added, "We've got *maybe* five minutes." She nodded and hurried up to my apartment.

"To save time, why don't I break the chain and send a hacksaw with you?" Dad said.

"Awesome."

He cut the handcuff chain with bolt-cutters.

"You found a vest, I see," he said.

"Yeah," I gave him a half-smile, "You like it? A helmet too."

I hugged him, apologized, and ran up to my room.

"I think they took all of your flying things," Mom said.

"Not all. I have a spare helmet and goggles in my car."

I grabbed my keys and ran downstairs, got the bag from the trunk, and ran back upstairs. I put as much into my duffel as I could. The FBI had my parachute and flight suit. I would make do with my winter coat and long underwear.

Mom went to get some food together. I was heading downstairs when Dad came up.

"I've got some cash here," he said. "We had good sales this fall, and not a bad spring. I was going to take your mom on a cruise. It's about $6,000. I don't know how far it will go, but take it."

My eyes misted up.

"Dad," I tried to say, but my voice got stuck in my throat.

He just shook his head.

"No time."

I recovered my voice and said, "No. Look, you need to know this. The FBI was trying to protect me. Someone shot at me."

His eyes got huge.

"Are you sure?"

"Yes. You can tell mom when I'm gone."

He nodded slowly.

"Is there somewhere you can go?"

"I don't know…" he said, drawing the words out, "Look, don't worry about us. We'll be okay. It's you they want."

"Yeah."

I hoped so.

Back in the yard, we stuffed my duffel bag with food and clothes. Mom's iPhone was in my pocket, Dad's money was in a hidden pocket of my coat, and my helmet and goggles were on. I kept the bulletproof vest. I hugged both my parents, kissed my mom on the cheek, told them I'd be in touch, and took off.

As I was flying away, the Feds were coming down the road. Four black SUVs pulled into the gravel yard in front of the barn and skidded to a stop. Agents poured out and swarmed over the farm. They handcuffed Mom and Dad and put them into separate vehicles.

That was hard to watch. It was my fault. I shouldn't have come home.

My phone rang. Unknown number. I answered it, curious.

"Hello."

"Hi, Ms. Donnelly," said a female voice.

"Hi," I said, "Who is this?"

"This is Agent Tucciarone."

"Oh. Hi," I said.

I had never tried talking on the phone while flying. Dividing my concentration made it terrifically difficult.

"Hang on."

I landed in the woods, in my old practice area.

"Are you okay?" she asked.

"Yeah. How are the marshals?"

"Alive."

"Did you get the sniper?"

"No. The noise from the helicopter made it impossible to tell where the shot came from."

"Great," I said. "Do I have to throw this phone away?"

"Look, Ms. Donnelly, we're not your enemies."

"No? No, I suppose not. Still, I've done nothing wrong. I can't live locked up."

"We want to protect you," she said.

"I have work to do. Somehow, I don't think your bosses will allow me to do it if I'm in custody — protective or otherwise."

"Hard to get any work done with a bullet through your heart," she said.

There was no arguing with that.

"Gotta go, Agent Stefanie," I said, forgetting her last name again. "Glad your guys are okay. I'm turning this phone off now."

"Ms. Donnelly — Olivia. Be careful."

"It's just Liv, and, uh, I will. One more thing. What are you doing with my parents?"

"With you on the run, they'll be questioned and placed under surveillance. Agents will be around, if not on the premises."

"Good enough. I'm sure we'll talk soon."

I ended the call and turned off the phone. I flew up above the trees and watched two SUVs head up the road toward the highway.

I had unprecedented freedom, for a while at least. I brushed an icicle off the end of my nose while I levitated. One thing I knew for sure, I needed to head south.

It was late morning when I landed at a truck stop along the Mississippi River. I discovered I was near New Madrid, Missouri. There wasn't any food there I wanted to eat, but I got a shower and some water. I flew to the roof and risked turning on my mother's phone.

I opened an anonymous browsing session and began looking for small independent restaurants with wireless networks or even computers. I noted the addresses of several, then turned off the phone. After checking for government cars, I had fruit and water for breakfast. I needed a nap, but first I had to get the handcuffs off. Hiding them inside my coat sleeves was becoming annoying. I took out Dad's saw and went to work.

I woke up from a nap, having been only half asleep, and knew exactly where I was. I was still alone. It was 10:00 pm, fully dark, and I was hungry again. I ate some of mom's beef jerky. This batch had red pepper flakes and orange peel, which was a strange combination.

Afterward, I headed to the store to use the restroom and then to the restaurant where I ordered tea and plugged my phone in. I checked the newspaper, thinking that a shooting at an FBI office would be national news.

There was nothing.

For the past few months, Mom and Dad have been helping me with my blog and social media. The blog has gotten more popular, and it's sometimes difficult to keep up with the comment moderation.

I assumed the FBI had probably swiped their computers. Once they replaced them, I was confident that my parents would take care of that side of things for a while. We automated everything except the comments. Mom could keep up with the Facebook page and other social media, but I was the one who interacted personally with people in chat rooms and one-on-one.

I had a decision to make. On the one hand, I could publish all the posts and videos I had in the queue. That would drop a tremendous amount of information on my site at once. It might confuse people, but it would get the entire story, as far as it went, out.

On the other hand, I could do nothing and allow my posts and the timeline of the site to remain a year behind what was actually happening.

Maybe I should write an article about what's going on now, I thought.

If the government would not allow my story into the news, I could force the issue. But I wasn't sure if it was the right move or not.

I closed my eyes for a moment and cleared my mind in a flash-meditation. I asked the Universe for guidance and opened my eyes.

The server came by, and I asked for lemons and honey for my tea. They didn't have honey. They had packets of "honey-flavored syrup."

"Just the lemons," I said.

I put the phone down and looked around the truck stop dining room, allowing my mind to wander. It wasn't busy this late at night. Dolly Parton sang about the travails of office work. Several men sat at the counter eating and flirting with the servers. A few couples sat in various booths, and one tired-looking family sat at a curved booth in the corner. The father had bags under his eyes, and the mother struggled to feed chicken nuggets to a toddler.

One man sat alone at a table near me. He might have been Native American or Asian. I wasn't sure. He caught me looking at him and nodded, taking a sip from his mug.

I nodded back, wondering if he might be from the government, or even an assassin?

He set his mug down and glanced at his bill. He took out some money and placed it under his cup as he stood and began winding his way through the tables in my direction.

Crap, I thought. *Crap crap crap.*

I moved, but I was still trying to free my legs when he stopped at my table.

"Mind if I join you?"

I looked up at him and didn't answer.

"I'm harmless, I swear," he said, smiling and holding up a hand as if making a solemn vow. His voice had that slow, careful pronunciation and slight accent that I associated with Native Americans. I sat back in the booth. If he was an assassin, I doubt he would want to sit down with me.

"Um… no, help yourself," I said, sitting back down and gesturing across the table.

He sat.

"It's a little of both, actually," he said, scooting to the middle of the seat.

"I'm sorry?"

"It's both. Asian and Native American."

What?

"It can be confusing," he said. "Some people even think I'm Hispanic."

"Oh."

"Kim," he said, holding out his hand.

"Liv," I said, shaking it. His handshake was firm but soft at the same time.

"Liv, what are you going to do next?"

"Pardon me?"

"Someone shot at you barely 12 hours and 400 miles from here. Someone wanted to kill you… end your existence. What are you going to do?"

"How do you know that?" I asked, sliding the phone into my pocket despite my shaking hands.

He smiled and held up both hands, palms out.

"I'm not your enemy, Liv. I wouldn't say we're friends yet, but I'm definitely not an enemy."

I thought about bolting…thought *hard*. I could kick the table into his lap, pin him to the bench and fly out. But…I hated the idea of fear controlling my actions. That, and I wanted to know who this guy was.

"Okay," I said, forcing my body to relax and clearing my mind, "So, who are you?"

"You and I," he said, gesturing to us both, "we're kin. Kindred spirits, anyway."

He had a curious habit of ducking his head to emphasize certain words. He did it with the word 'spirits.'

"I'm not sure what you mean."

"You're going to find that we don't all come in the same flavor," Kim said, laughing. "Never mind. That's not what I want to talk about. I'm neutral, okay? I want you to be informed - to have the information you need when you make a choice. You understand?"

"Okay, but I don't really know what you're talking about."

He waved my statement away with a smile.

"So, here's what you need to know right now. Obviously, you're right about your technology. You can't trust it. The government knows every time you turn it on, every time you email or text. They won't necessarily *act*, but they have it. Don't trust your technology yet."

"Yet?"

He laughed.

"The dark side clouds everything. Impossible to see, the future is..." he said in a horrible Yoda impersonation. "Still, there might come a time when you can trust your tech again."

"Wait, you're saying that the government knows where I am? Right now?" Panic began rising in my throat.

Kim smiled.

"Not just them. Much worse!" He grinned.

"Christ..." I muttered. I glanced up, trying to see through the glare of the windows to the parking lot. Were they surrounding me even now?

"Relax, Liv. I wouldn't be here if there were any danger."

"So, why *are* you here?"

"I told you. I don't like to see people manipulated, even by my...well, by anyone."

"How is anyone manipulating me?" I asked.

"You already know. The Feds are using you as bait. They're allowing you to run because it forces anyone who wants you to scramble to keep up. That will make them easier to find."

"Will it?"

"Sure. People call the cops when there's shooting. What's important here is that they're happy to let you get yourself caught. Or killed."

I sipped tea with shaking hands while Kim smiled at me.

"So, what about the guys trying to kill me? Who are they?"

I couldn't help scanning the restaurant as we were talking, scrutinising everyone who went through the doors. My voice shook nearly as much as my hands.

"Oh, there are lots of people who would like to control you. Only a few of them want you dead. Too much to get into."

He leaned in and became serious.

"Here's what's important. You're not the first they have come after. This… Alliance. It's been around for a while. Members come and go, and none of them really get along. But they put aside their differences for the hunt, and they all have their own reasons."

"The 'hunt'?"

They're hunting me? I'm being hunted?

"Well, yeah. Remember the sniper?"

"Yeah, I just…I don't know. It kind of brings it home, saying it that way."

"Yeah, it does," he said, ducking his head a little. "Okay, so let's recap. One: Don't trust your tech. Two: The good guys are using you to find the bad guys."

I sighed, and my breath caught in my throat.

"Okay. I'm with you. What else?"

I clasped the mug in my hands to keep the shaking to a minimum.

He looked toward the windows for a moment and seemed lost in thought.

"There's another group," he said, and paused. The humor seemed to leave him.

"Another group?" I prodded.

"Yeah. They're…not bad. You're not in physical danger from them, but I'm not sure they have your best interests at heart. It's complicated."

"Complicated," I said. "Okay, well, as long as this group isn't trying to kill me, I can deal with them. Death and prison seem to be the more pressing matters to me, don't you think?"

"I agree," he said, shaking himself and smiling again, "but what do I know?"

He shook my hand again and rose to leave.

"Wait. I have, like, a million questions. How are we related? Can you do…things? What's going on? Why can I…."

My voice trailed off. He had said nothing about flying yet.

"Why can you fly?" he asked, grinning, and then shrugged. "Better to ask why more people *don't* fly. There's nothing different about you, Liv. You're no more special than anyone else."

"That's what I keep saying!"

"Keep practicing," he said, and turned and lifted a hand in farewell.

He walked away toward the doors. When I lost sight of him, there wasn't a crowd. He didn't turn a corner, and he didn't go through the door. I was watching him one moment, and the next I wasn't. It was like the windows in the background moved in front of him somehow.

I'm just getting tired, I tried to tell myself.

But I didn't believe it.

Good guys and bad guys alike already knew I was here, so I took out my phone and wrote a blog post. I re-read it and meditated briefly, listening to my emotions and my body, waiting for Guidance.

I learned during martial art training that my body usually knew when I was performing a technique or form correctly or not. I felt balanced and stable when it was right, out of balance and weak if it was wrong. Likewise, when dealing with people, I could feel in my belly when I was doing the right thing, going in the right direction. The more I listened, the stronger that sense became.

If I stayed calm and listened to those parts of my body, they could lead me in the right direction. Earlier that morning, right before the assassin shot at me, I had received a message from my body that all was not right. I listened and lived. I may have saved other lives as well.

That thought made me smile. I was glad the agents had all survived. As I read over the statement I intended to post, I "checked my gut." When it felt right a few minutes later, I logged in to my blog and Facebook page and posted the message. I put everything away, threw a five on the table and headed for the door, keeping an eye out for Kim.

Right outside, leaning against a roof support, was a large bald man in a short navy blue pea coat. He wasn't looking at me, but in his hand were the remains of the handcuffs I had left on the roof.

Not good.

On one hand, I was glad I had brought all my other stuff with me. On the other hand, it loaded me down and made me clumsy.

Clearing my head, I took a half breath, deep into my abdomen, and released all thought and misgiving.

Checking my body, I asked myself: *What now?*

The cashier was watching me talk to myself, so I started patting my pockets. I found some small bills in my shirt pocket and impulsively walked over to her.

"Can I get a lottery ticket, please?"

"Sure. You got in just under the wire. Sales shut down at 11:00."

"Lucky me! Hey, do you have maps here?"

She tilted her head to the side.

"Yeah," she said, drawing out the word, "Pay for this first, then you can look at the maps."

"Okay," I said. In my peripheral vision, Pea Coat Guy walked into the store. I didn't look at him, but I was sure he knew who I was. He knew I was aware of him, too. This guy didn't look like FBI or even Homeland Security. My stomach clenched.

Looking down at the counter, I made up my mind.

"How much is the most expensive atlas over there?"

"What? Geez, just go get it, and I'll scan it."

"How much?"

"$24.99."

I gave her two twenties.

"It's going to get scary here in just a minute. I'm not stealing the atlas."

"What?" she asked, looking scared. "Are you crazy?" Her voice was rising, attracting attention.

In my smoothest voice, (which, you know, not that smooth) I said, "Look, I'm one of the good guys."

I smiled. She remained unconvinced.

"Maybe you should just call the cops."

I took my lottery ticket and put it in my pocket.

I turned, and Pea Coat Guy was right behind me.

Clearing my mind, I said, "Hi, nice coat. Is that real wool?"

I tried to step around to his left, but he reached out and grabbed my arm with his right hand. Without thinking, my arm circled up and around his, lifting the elbow and arching his back. His other arm was reaching into a pocket, presumably for a weapon. My right hand shot straight in, becoming rigid, turned and struck the side of his neck hard.

The man's eyes rolled up, and he dropped to the floor in a heap.

I turned to the girl.

"Call the cops," I said, my voice tight.

I reached into his pocket and found a sap, a kind of leather bag filled with metal beads. I tossed it onto the counter and reached into his coat. There was an automatic handgun, probably a nine millimeter. I didn't know. I put it gently on the counter.

"You should hide those until the cops get here. The atlases over here?" I asked, gesturing toward the door.

She nodded slowly.

"Thanks." I pointed to the phone. "Cops."

She shook her head and picked up the phone.

So, how did this all start? It's kind of a long story. Here's the very first article from my blog, where I tell the story of moving back home. Think less origin story, more rationalization.

~

Excerpt from the blog: *Griffin's Flight*

JULY 14, 2023

I'm an ordinary girl. Woman. Whatever.

I'm 20 years old and already a failure at life. They booted me out of school for being academically bored. I lost my job because I lost interest in serving angry, frustrated people. My girlfriend gave up on me because I gave up on myself.

When I couldn't afford my apartment any longer, I swallowed my pride and talked to my parents. Of course, they invited me back to the farm. What else were they going to do? Allow their only child to become homeless? I did a lot of thinking that week. Vowed to make changes.

Mom and I talked as she made meatloaf that night, my childhood favorite. Dad was his usual mute self. She didn't push, but we talked about how hard it is for people to change. We talked about how she quit smoking. She told me she replaced smoke breaks with quick walks.

"It's not enough to get rid of bad habits, Liv," she said. "When you do that, it leaves a void in your life. You need to fill the void with something good."

The food was good. Mom could cook, I would give her that. Mom and Dad had moved here from town 30-some years ago and started farming conventionally (corn, soybeans, fertilizer, herbicides, etc.). But Mom had researched organic farming almost right away.

She was a science teacher, and Dad was an industrial technology instructor at the community college. Farming was a part-time job for them, a hobby that sometimes paid the mortgage, but usually didn't.

When I was in middle school, they left the farm fallow for several years until they could go organic. They grew a lot of vegetables and raised animals, mainly for their own use. The past couple of years, they had experimented with grain.

By the time I got to high school, I spent mornings and afternoons working on the farm. I baled hay and stacked it in the loft. I cleaned stables, turned compost heaps, fixed fences, and did pretty much anything that Dad showed me how to do. As a result, I was strong and pretty good with my hands. Both Mom and Dad had taught me life skills. I could make cornbread from scratch as easily as I could change the oil in the old Ford tractor.

After doing the dishes, I hugged Mom goodnight and went to bed. Changing my schedule from a night-time pizza delivery driver to a farm-hand would be rough. In my old life, I would be at work for another four hours before going home and putting in *a* video game.

I straightened my room, changed into pajamas and lay on the bed with a library book. The library was one perk of city living I would miss. My card would be good for a while, and I planned to take advantage of it. I had visited the self-help section that afternoon on my way to the farm. The first book I checked out was Eckhart Tolle's *The Power of Now*. It was about quieting the ego, being present here and now, and learning to live and not judge.

During my time away, my bedroom had become a guest room. It was no longer the blue *Monsters, INC.* themed room of my childhood. Mom decorated it with wooden hearts and broom straw. I didn't judge, but I couldn't see myself staying here for long. I finally got to sleep around midnight, bathed in the scents of cinnamon and orange rind.

At 6:30 the next morning, after consuming copious amounts of bacon and eggs, Dad and I sat at the breakfast table and did not chat over our morning coffee. He didn't read the paper, and I had left my phone in my room. In my teens, it might have been a small slice of hell. Now, I was too tired to think. Eventually, Dad said he had something to show me, and we headed out to the yard with our coffee.

In farming parlance, they call our barn a "bank barn." That meant it was built into a hill, or bank, so that two floors were accessible from ground level. The top of the hill was level with the second floor, and the bottom with the first.

We walked in the front to the second floor. My stuff was mostly still in boxes on the horse trailer parked on the floor beneath us. Dad unlocked a door that I had never seen before and opened it.

We walked into a modestly furnished studio apartment. Apparently, my parents had built it last winter, anticipating the need for live-in help.

"I think you'll be more comfortable out here, don't you?"

"Well, yeah. But how much do you want for rent? This is really nice!"

"Nothing. We already talked about your salary. This is a perk, I guess."

"Dad…I don't know what to say."

The stress of losing my job, moving back home, and missing sleep was getting to me. My eyes became watery, but crying always made Dad uncomfortable. Knowing that didn't stop tears from rolling down my face.

"Hey, now. None of that," he said, folding me into a one-armed hug. "There's no crying in farming," he said into my hair, intentionally misquoting a favorite movie of ours.

I laughed and continued there for a moment, allowing him to comfort me. Finally, I wiped my eyes, and we separated. I glanced around at the kitchenette, built-in bookshelves, table, and furniture. I would have privacy and comfort, but access to family when I wanted. It was perfect.

Three

I walked out of the truck stop door. My hands were shaking again from the adrenaline dump. I needed to leave, but if I didn't clear the energy coursing through me, I wouldn't be able to think. I lifted off and landed back on top of the building. When I hit the roof, I dropped my bags and shook like a dog coming out of water. I took a couple of deep breaths and blew them all the way out.

Once I felt better, I slipped back into the straps of my bags, launched, and headed south. I needed a place I had never been and had no connection to. Camping would be cheap and anonymous, but I needed access to technology as well.

I remembered my yoga instructor telling me about a campground on the north shore of Lake Pontchartrain. It was directly across the lake from New Orleans. It sounded good. I didn't know if I could fly into a city undetected, but I would find out.

I could find Lake Pontchartrain with no problem. Just follow the Mississippi to the Gulf of Mexico. I could land anywhere dark, wait for daylight, and then check my very expensive atlas. I already had the address of a cafe in New Orleans.

By the time the sun came up, I was resting on a piling of the Lake

Pontchartrain Causeway. Idyllic, if not for the roar of morning traffic passing overhead.

When it was light enough to read, I opened the atlas and began searching the shores of Lake Pontchartrain for the campground. I found it in no time. Fontainebleau State Park was right in front of me. I packed everything away and headed out over the water.

This early there was no one on the beach. I was exhausted and needed a nap. Using my duffel bag for a pillow, I stuffed my helmet and goggles into my pack and laid down. It was around 60° here. Not warm, but not the 40° I left in Indiana. I was so tired it wouldn't matter. I wrapped up in my coat and dozed off.

~

I woke several hours later with the sun in my eyes and sweat running down my face. It had warmed up a lot. My head felt like it was full of cotton, and my stomach was empty. I gathered my things and started walking. As I was heading to the campground, I realized I should have paid to get into the park. I have no receipt, or even a tent to camp in.

So, I hid my duffel, put my wallet and goggles in my pocket and left. I needed to find a sporting goods store, and then come into the park the right way.

An hour later, I had purchased a backpack, sleeping bag, and tent, along with other lightweight camping supplies I might need. The clerk was an avid backpacker and showed me the best way to pack everything. Once I got the gist of it, he pointed me towards a couple of books that would help, and I bought them, thinking that I could give them to someone else when I had read them.

When I asked about natural food stores or farmer's markets, he gave me directions to a place a few blocks away. It only took ten minutes to walk there and another thirty to stock up on fresh produce and enough meat for the night and morning. A big, hot meal and a long sleep sounded blissful.

I headed back to the campground and went through the front gate this time. I was on foot, and it felt good to stretch my legs. My midsection, though strong, was going to take some time getting used to the pack. It would also affect me in the air, decreasing both speed and maneuverability.

No matter. I would carry the entire pack only when I had to. I rented a camping spot, set up my tent, and retrieved my gear.

Back at the campsite, I started a fire. I made beef stew with grass-fed beef, carrots, sweet potatoes, coconut flour, and rosemary. I drank bottled water. Wine would have been good, but I needed to stay focused.

I was cooking the beef before the sun was even down. Soon I added sweet potatoes and carrots and was cleaning greens for a big salad.

The smell attracted comments from other campers. Some stopped to chat, but most just smiled or commented while walking by.

A young couple, Mitch and Teri, stopped to talk.

"You know," I said after a few minutes, "I'm not used to cooking for just me. I made way too much. Would you like to join me for dinner?"

"It smells amazing," Teri said. "I'll run to our site and grab some water bottles. Don't start without me!"

Teri was a slender black woman, dark complected with curly black hair and a musical voice. Her husband, Mitch, was tall and slender with fair skin and red hair.

A few minutes later, she was back with water and a loaf of French bread.

"I don't have a bread knife, so we'll just have to tear chunks off the loaf."

"Thanks, but none for me," I said.

"Watching your figure?"

I laughed.

"Not really. It just doesn't agree with me."

I told the story of how I had changed my diet and lost a lot of weight. I left out the bit about flying, but otherwise, I told them about my martial art and yoga classes.

"Mitch has been in karate since he was a kid. I just started the year before we got married."

We ate and talked for more than an hour. They were a young couple spending a few weeks exploring up and down the Mississippi, visiting tourist sites and Native American sites. I was yawning for the second time when Teri stood.

"I think it's time for us to go. You need rest."

I didn't argue. They said good night and went off to their campsite, thanking me for dinner.

I lay in my sleeping bag that night and wondered what was going on out in the world. I hadn't seen my parents for a couple of days, and I hadn't heard from them.

Am I a fugitive?

I turned over. That thought hadn't hit me before.

I'm a fugitive. That's weird.

Of course, it changed nothing. I had done nothing wrong. Nothing changed, but somehow I felt different.

I was exhausted and soon fell into a deep sleep. When I finally climbed out of my tent, it felt late. I looked up. The sun was just clearing the trees on the east side of the campground.

Maybe not so late.

I made my way to the showers and spent half an hour there. In the movies, fugitives always change their appearance somehow. Cutting or coloring my hair might be a good idea.

On my way back, Mitch and Teri were outside their tent and I waved to them.

"Coming over?" Mitch called.

"Sure! Let me put my things away," I said, holding up my toiletry bag and towel.

I left my tent up but packed my gear just in case I needed to make a quick getaway. I smiled briefly at the thought, but sobered again when I thought of the sniper in Indy.

At any rate, I was soon sitting down with Mitch and Teri. They prayed over their pot of navy beans, then dished them out. I had a cup of hot coffee beside me.

"Since it's breakfast…" Mitch said. He picked up a can of cinnamon.

I must have made a face.

"I like it in my beans in the morning," he said defensively.

"Really?"

"Sure. Brown sugar or honey too, but you don't eat that stuff, right?"

"No. Sometimes honey."

"Campers eat some weird things," Teri said.

"We knew a guy on the AT who would make tea in his soup cans, so he got every bit of nutrition from his dinner," Mitch said.

"AT?" I asked

"Appalachian Trail. It's a long trail that begins in Georgia and ends in Maine. Hikers come from all over the world to hike the trail. Some try to do all of it in one year; others do a part of it every year."

"Cool."

"It's very demanding," Teri said. "We've talked about doing it, but it's hard to get away from our jobs."

"Do you guys have plans for the rest of the day?" I asked.

"I think we're hiking some trails and then having dinner across the lake," Mitch said.

"Nice," I said. "I have some work to do. Maybe I'll catch you tomorrow."

"Maybe," Mitch said.

Two hours later, after a quick swim and a change of clothes, I flew into the city. I landed in a lonely cemetery and found a pawnshop where I bought a laptop for $300, then made my way to the cafe. After my talk with Kim, I worried that any work on my website might bring the Marshals, the FBI, Homeland Security, or worse, someone from the Alliance down on my head as soon as I tried it. I sat there looking at the screen for a long time, my finger poised over the Enter key. I had my username and password already typed into the fields, just waiting on one more keystroke to log me in.

There was no choice. I finally made myself do it. I logged in, created a new user with admin privileges, and logged out again. The new user was a fictitious name attached to a brand new email address. I then restarted the computer and logged back in with the new account.

When I was in, I set all the queued blogs and videos to post at 4:00 p.m. that afternoon. A year's worth of posts, give or take, went live all at once. I had explained the situation briefly in my Facebook post from two days ago. I explained how I had written them in the past year. Until I could fix them, the dates would confuse some people, but the story itself was true.

I had warned my readers it would be hard to believe and people would say I was a fake or crazy or an attention whore. The fact of the matter was, I had kept the timeline private to keep myself and my family safe. Now it seemed nothing could do that. I would have to post the blogs and let people decide for themselves.

~

The next morning I was back at the cafe. I sipped coffee and logged into the site.

Several months ago, someone had jokingly referred to my small group of early subscribers as "followers." I hated that. I didn't want followers. Anyone brave enough to open their mind to something as crazy as what I was sharing was a leader, not a follower. I posted a blog banning the use of the word "follower." The idea caught on.

Traffic on the website had blown up overnight. Despite several hacking attacks, the site stayed up. Leaders volunteered to store back-ups on their machines. Some were moderating the forum, and we mirrored the site on servers around the world. We occasionally shared a list of the mirror sites on my social media, just in case my site went down.

Of course, there was discussion about whether the videos were real or not. Skeptics were testing the videos and would return with the truth, but it would take time.

Typical of the internet, there were a lot of arguments and name calling. Software handled the worst of the language. Mom was probably having a tough time keeping up with the spam and comments.

There was speculation about what had forced me to change my timetable. I wasn't talking, and lots of people were worried. Some suggested that was my intention all along, that it was a publicity gimmick.

Most of the Leaders were good about not engaging in the bickering taking place on the site. It wouldn't do us any good and would hinder their practice. And practice was the whole point of the blog. I shared my experiences and provided a place where people could share theirs as well. I fully expected people to share their own levitation videos soon.

I browsed the comments to see how people were reacting to the new articles and videos. Responses were mixed, but many people accepted the story. I could divide the disbelievers into two rough camps.

First were the trolls who just wanted to argue. Second were the people who seemed to be interested in discussion but were adamant the laws of physics were immutable and not open to reinterpretation.

As I browsed the forum, several names came up again and again. Some were trolls, but others were regular people. BlueEyes_90 didn't give advice or force her opinions on people. She corrected facts, usually with links to back herself up, and she gave alternative points of view. When she commented, she was the calm voice of reason.

I wanted to talk to BlueEyes_90 but remain anonymous. Maybe I wanted to get a feel for the person she was. I sent a message with a chat request.

While I waited to see if she was online, I continued to browse through comments. My mother was online again, and new comments kept showing up. Even though I couldn't talk to her, I knew she was safe. That was comforting.

An icon popped up at the bottom of my screen, signaling BlueEyes_90 was available to chat. I clicked the link. My screen name was Edmond_89.

BLUE EYES_90

Hello there.

EDMOND_89

Edmond_89: Hi, thanks for accepting.

No prob. Got a break at work.

Chatting at work?

If I'm careful... lol.

My day off.

Nice. What do you do?

(Crap! What can I tell her?)

I'm a fitness instructor.

What brought you here?

A friend.

Nice. What do you think?

Not sure.

Really? I thought everyone had an opinion.

I'm still making my way through the site. Not sure what to think yet.

I've been on here for a while. Griffin seems like an honest person.

Griffin was my pseudonym, my persona as the author of the blog. I used "Edmond_89" to lurk. For obvious reasons, I kept my identity secret.

Oh?

She used to be on the site sometimes. She chatted with people.

Did you ever chat with her?

Yeah.

This surprised me. I didn't remember chatting with her, but I chatted with many people.

What do YOU think?

Again, she seems sincere.

What about the whole "attacked by the government" thing?

It sounds fantastic, I grant you. But I'm inclined to believe her.

What do you think they'll do to her if they
catch her?

Lock her up, I assume.

Just for flying, though? How come?

National security. Whatever that means.

Seems like they should have given a good reason.

Yeah, well, maybe they had one they couldn't
share.

Like what?

No idea, really. Could have been anything.

Well, what have you learned here?

I've been meditating. Not a lot. I'm a busy girl.

What's that quote about meditation and not
having time?

I know, I know. ;P

I read the other day that might not be the case.

Do tell.

Yeah. Meditating for 30 seconds might be as
good as 30 minutes.

Interesting.

Maybe. Might be true. Might not.

Why do you doubt?

Lol! I doubt everything. Don't you?

I want to believe. Don't you?

> What do you mean? Either you're a believer or not.

Well, I mean, I want to believe in God, but I'm not sure about the evidence. I want to believe in Griffin, but the evidence seems suspect.

> I see. You want to believe in an afterlife....

Right. That's the idea.

> Good luck figuring that out.

Thanks. I should get back to work. Good talking to you.

> You too. I hope we can do it again.

:-)

She wasn't sure whether to believe in me. I thought the new videos would be a slam dunk. Apparently not. I spent the next hour looking over the comments on the videos themselves. Again, it was a mixed bag but ran more to the negative.

With all the special effects in movies and all the times videos on the internet had fooled people, they had become jaded and were unwilling to believe what they were seeing. I could relate to that.

How do I fix things, though?

That was a good question.

I had been hiding for so long that it became second nature.

What if I did the opposite?

I needed a friend, someone to talk to.

That evening, Mitch and Teri's camp was still there, but they weren't around. It was fully dark by the time I got back. Maybe they were in bed already.

My campfire was dead. There was still wood and quick-start charcoal, so I had a fire going in no time. I boiled water, cut up some beef jerky, threw in a handful of kale and in a few minutes had a hot, savory stew.

It felt good to sit by my little fire and enjoy food that made me think of my parents. I enjoyed being alone, but I still needed to talk to someone. Someone who knew the entire story.

Then it hit me. I had an idea.

I finished eating, cleaned up, and grabbed my helmet, goggles, and my jacket. I might be gone for a while, and didn't want to be unprepared.

It was midnight when I stepped out to the beach. I watched for several minutes, but I didn't see anyone. Gently, I lifted into the air and flew out over the water. I stayed low and flew towards the Gulf of Mexico. There were bugs, lots of bugs. I wished I had a shield that I could hold in front of me to block my face. My mind wandered wordlessly as I flew, imagining shapes of shields and how I would angle them as I flew.

Suddenly, I noticed that fewer bugs were striking my goggles and scarf. I slowed and stopped, and immediately a cloud of the critters enveloped me. When I started moving again, I felt them striking my head and face. I imagined a shield, and I felt a buffer come up between me and the bugs. I imagined they were being channeled safely around my body.

As soon as I felt safe, I climbed up to about 2,000 feet above the water. The sky was clear to the horizon, but I still couldn't find what I was looking for.

I climbed up to about 10,000 feet. I had to watch for planes, but prayed I would see and hear anything coming long before it got to me. At this altitude, everything was traveling quickly and could be on me in a heartbeat.

I flew south for a long time, ignoring my chattering teeth.

Finally, east of Houston, I found it: a cruise ship. I dove until I was hovering right above it. Landing near the antenna array, I found a spot at the top of the bridge.

I took out my phone and turned it on. It took a moment, but it eventually connected to the shipboard cell system.

I called my parents first.

"Hello?"

"Hi Dad, it's Liv."

There was a rustling sound, and he called Mom.

"Liv! How are you doing? Is everything okay?"

"I'm good. Still hiding, but I'm okay. How are you guys holding up?"

"Don't worry about us. Here. You're on speaker."

"Liv? Honey, how are you?" Mom said.

"I'm fine. Glad they let you two go."

"They said they wanted to protect you. Are you sure you're doing the right thing? Someone shot at you?"

I sighed.

"Yeah, Mom. Someone did. But believe me, they wouldn't let me continue blogging or sharing video if I were in custody. They wouldn't let me tell my story."

Mom didn't respond. In her eyes, not blogging was worth people not shooting at me.

"Look, I don't have much time. Any time I use electronics, they can find me. I just wanted to let you know that I'm safe. Thank you for keeping up with the website. That helps me more than anything else."

"We'll do it as long as we can," Dad said.

"I can't tell you where I am, but I'm okay. I'm just trying to decide what to do next."

"Anything we can do?" Dad asked.

"No."

My voice caught, and I almost lost it. I cleared my throat.

"It's just…good to hear your voices. I needed to know you were okay."

"Don't worry about us, Livvie," Mom said. "You do what you need to…so you can come home."

We said our goodbyes and hung up.

Since the FBI had kept things out of the media, the public hadn't heard their names. Nobody was camped on the lawn. That was something anyway.

I was done sobbing into my scarf by the time Agent Stefanie called.

"Hi, Liv. How are you?" she asked.

"I'm well, Agent Stefanie. How are you?"

"Fine, thanks. I didn't expect to talk again so soon."

"I wanted to let my parents know I was okay. How many bad guys do you catch that way?"

"Talking to their mothers? A few. Even bad guys love their mothers."

"Yeah. Actually, I wanted to talk to you, too."

"Really?" she said, sounding surprised.

"Really. I have a problem and want your advice."

"I'm not sure that's a good idea."

"Why? I mean, besides our being on opposite sides of this thing, of course."

"Isn't that enough?" she asked. I thought I could hear a smile in her voice.

"Well, maybe. It's not like I'm a criminal, though."

"I'm afraid escaping from federal custody makes you a criminal."

"Are you kidding? Even though I did nothing wrong?"

She was quiet for a moment.

"That will not be the story, Liv. Officially, you were involved in a money laundering scheme."

It was my turn to be quiet.

"Money laundering. I barely know how to launder my clothes, let alone money."

She laughed. She had a great laugh.

"Well, you would probably say something like that if you were guilty, wouldn't you?"

"But—never mind. You know it's not true."

"Regardless of the truth, we have seized your accounts."

"My accounts? You mean my $300 savings? And my $75 checking? Curses. Foiled again."

I waited, listening to a party happening somewhere inside the ship.

"What about my parents?" I asked.

"Not yet, but if you refuse to come in, they're next."

"I can't believe someone like you would allow this to happen."

"*I* have nothing to do with it, Liv. My job is to study you. We're talking right now because Graham thinks you have a thing for me."

Her bluntness surprised me. Was more going on than I realized? I looked around, but nobody seemed to know I was here — no boats rushing in, no helicopters on the horizon.

"Am I safe?"

"We're not coming for you on a cruise ship, if that's what you're asking."

"Um, yeah, that's what I'm asking."

"Not a bad idea."

"Thanks."

"Listen, I want you to stay safe. I'll hold them off your parents if I can." She sounded sincere.

"Arresting or harassing my parents will not increase the likelihood of my helping you."

"I know. I've already told them that. The alpha males disagree with me."

"Will they go after my website?"

"Eventually, yes. The videos are everywhere. Your blog is slowly being reposted all over the world. We could probably still stop it, but the alphas seem to think it will die out quicker if we leave it alone."

"They might be right. General opinion seems to be that I'm faking it all somehow."

"I'm sorry," she murmured.

"Er, thanks. Here's something to tell your alpha males. If they move against my parents, there won't be any doubt. I'll see to it."

"Not a good idea, Olivia."

"Tell them."

"They're listening right now."

"Oh."

Given how she had been talking about them, that surprised me.

"Ah," I said. "Well…then…yeah. You guys do anything to my folks, and I'll start granting interviews."

"Olivia, don't be an idiot," Agent Stefanie said.

"What do you mean?"

"As soon as you go to the news, people will know who you are. Your parents won't be safe. Right now, they're anonymous. That's the only reason they aren't in custody. We've protected you as much as we can."

"Protected me? How have you protected me?" I glanced around, realizing how loud I was being.

"We've protected you by cleaning up your cyber-footprint. We've helped keep you anonymous. If not for us, you *and* your parents would be dead."

Suddenly, despite the subtropical warmth, I was cold. There was no way to know if what she said was true, but I believed her.

"Okay," I said. "Okay, I get it. Still, leave my parents alone." I sounded like a child, and I knew it.

"We're trying, Liv. If you want us to leave them alone, we need to take you into custody."

"There's no way I'm coming in with a charge of money laundering or drug dealing or whatever the hell else hanging over me. That's just not an option. I might consider protective custody with no charges, but even that...."

My voice trailed off, and she was quiet for a few moments.

"Think about it, Liv. Nobody here wants you in jail. What we want is to protect you and the public from these bad guys." She sounded sincere, but she was going for the hard sell.

"Agent Stefanie, it's been nice talking to you," I said with a sigh. "I'd like to do it sometime without the alphas listening in."

She laughed.

"I'll see what I can arrange."

"Okay. Well...."

How does one end such an awkward conversation?

"Look, Liv, I'll look out for your folks as much as I can. Really."

So, I didn't really learn *to levitate. It just sort of happened. What I really had to learn was how to transition from levitating to flying. These journal entries high-light that process.*

∽

Excerpt from the blog: *Griffin's Flight*

MARCH 01, 2024

Now that I can levitate with my eyes open, it's time to practice control. So far, I've been focusing on getting off the ground. I need to learn to control my altitude. The problem is, I don't know how.

MARCH 03

I began my afternoon session, levitated, and thought about going higher. As before, whenever I allow a thought to form, such as the word "higher," my meditative state dissolves and I fall to my cushion. Something happens inside the meditative state that allows levitation.

APRIL 2

The sun was bright and high overhead when I sat down. I tucked the blanket around my legs, and when I levitated, it came up with me. Despite this being my first time practicing with eyes open outside, I had no trouble. I kept my gaze neutral and unfocused and levitated about three feet above my cushion.

My goal this time was just to raise myself higher. Last night I realized that since the key to levitating was the sensation of levitating, the key to moving might be the sensation of movement. I imagined swooping vertigo in my stomach again and immediately shot up about nine feet higher into the air.

As it happened, the first branch of the tree above me was about 12 feet off the ground. I had gone whooshing up and smacked my head on the lowest branch in the clearing. I probably don't have to say that both medi-tation and levitation were over for the moment.

When I smacked my head on the branch, pain exploded in my head and my eyes slammed shut.

"God DAMN it!" I shouted and immediately started falling.

I realized I was falling at the same time my hands made it to my head. I had no time to prepare for my fall except to round my back.

I hit the side of my cushion and caromed off it to the right. I tucked my elbows in, and my right shoulder slammed into the forest floor. My hands holding my head kept it from snapping down towards the ground. I lay there for a moment, dazed, then another while I contemplated my condition.

I wasn't breathing much. There was pain, but nothing severe. I tried to roll onto my back, and that hurt a lot. The pain made me gasp, which sent more pain shooting through my right side. My feet had gotten tangled in the blanket, and I had a claustrophobic, panicky few seconds.

I forced myself to stay calm and took shallow, slow breaths, not allowing my ribs to expand nor my shoulders to rise until I found out where and how severe the damage was.

I used my left hand to extricate my legs from the blanket and stretched them out.

"Aaah!" I exclaimed. The stretch hurt, but it felt strangely good at the same time.

With my legs straightened, I rolled onto my back. It hurt slightly less this time, but I still hissed with the pain from my shoulder and ribs.

On my back now, I started testing my breath. No sharp pains. That was good. Luckily, there had been no rocks or sticks underneath me. I was probably just sore.

My shoulder was another matter. Now that blood flow was restored, I could tell something was wrong. It hurt a lot. I couldn't move my arm without pain.

I stood up slowly and took a deep breath. Things in my spine shifted and ground as they settled back into place. It didn't hurt exactly, but it didn't feel great either.

Tilting my head to the left, there was tension in my right shoulder. I allowed it to flow out. Leaning forward, I let my arms fall freely. I swung them around in gentle circles.

No serious pain. Maybe I had only stressed the soft tissue in the joint, and it would be okay soon.

After resting for a few minutes, I tied the blanket into a kind of sling to hold my cushion and threw it over my left shoulder. I divided my stuff between my pockets and the sling. My right arm hung down, relaxed.

I found I had a small goose egg on the top of my head. I had almost forgotten about it after the much more painful injury in my shoulder. When I started bending over and picking things up, the throbbing pain in my scalp reminded me. Thankfully, my hair was pretty thick, and there was no blood. It was going to hurt for a few days, though.

On the way back home, I reflected. I had controlled my altitude, kind of. If I weren't so beaten up, I would celebrate right now. At least I had another clue. Or rather, I relearned an old clue.

At any rate, the key appeared to be sensation.

JUNE 14

I meditated in the woods (just meditated) for several days before I was ready to practice directional control. In the middle of the clearing, I sat on my horse blanket and began. I levitated about six feet off the ground. My eyes were open, my mind was clear, and I was ready to go.

Vertical movement was all about feeling the movement in my stomach. So, cautiously, not wanting to skewer myself on any horizontal branches, I thought about lateral movement. I imagined the lurching feeling of a car as it accelerates.

Nothing.

I tried to feel myself moving forward.

Nothing.

I relaxed for a moment, floating in mid-air. Levitating while I pondered the problem was possible, as long as I didn't get too far away from my meditative state. The less I thought, the better I did. Or, to put it another way, the less I involved my verbal, logical, left brain, the easier it was to levitate.

So, I thought in pictures and sensations. I tried to solve the problem at the level where it existed. This was a feeling problem or a sensation problem. I had to feel the right feeling. It was tricky.

Still, it didn't matter. Nothing happened. I stayed in place, anchored to a spot in the very center of the clearing. As I gave up trying to move and hovered, I felt joy at being able to levitate. I was consciously enjoying every moment I existed in the clearing.

Butterflies fluttered around the edge of the clearing. The yellow flash of their wings caught my eye. I experienced them, floating, looking for flowers. Unbidden, the phrase "Tiger Swallowtail" came into my mind.

I stayed meditative and watched the butterflies. Their jittery flight, the way they could fly high and then glide down several feet and then start fluttering back up again, entranced me. Extending my hand, I brought it underneath the nearest butterfly. I caught it for just a second, but it took off almost immediately.

Butterflies probably didn't have to think about flying. It was instinctive, and they just flew. I thought about this in very basic concepts, not words exactly. Butterflies fluttered around the honeysuckle on the other side of the clearing. They were alighting and feeding on the flowers.

Suddenly, I realized I was watching them right in front of me. I was no longer in the middle of the clearing. I began falling, but I unfolded my legs and lightly dropped to my feet.

"Well, how about that?"

JUNE 18

I spent the week rereading books like The Secret and other so-called "self-help" books, trying to find something that explained what I was experiencing. Nothing I've ever read prepared me for today's session.

I sat in the clearing and began meditating and then levitating, as usual. This time, I wanted to try something different. I levitated toward a tree branch overhead. As it came within reach, I grabbed, pulled, and swung to another branch. I caught it and swung through the tree branches around the clearing.

My hands were filthy and sticky from sap as I went all the way around the edge of the clearing. I had been climbing as I traveled, so I went one more branch, intending a controlled descent to the ground.

Catching the next branch, I pulled myself up. I had a little speed to bleed off, so I pictured myself swinging around the limb, one-handed, like a gymnast.

My weight and momentum were too much for the branch. Just as I was at the apex of the swing, it snapped, pulling upward. One second I was swinging in a graceful arc around this tree branch, the next I was shooting up towards the canopy feet first. The motion lasted less than a second as I was jerked rudely to a stop by the branch's remaining connection to the tree. I held there for a moment, upside down, palm sore, afraid I was about to be catapulted above the treetops.

That particular exercise, flying above the treetops, was scheduled for later in the summer or early fall. I was looking forward to it, but not just yet. Keeping my grip on the branch, I pulled my feet back down toward the ground and tried to allow gravity to pull me down.

No luck.

Everything else looked normal, but for me, there was no gravity. My feet were floating back toward the sky, and it felt like I was being pulled skyward. I almost let go, just to see where the feeling would take me. Before I released the broken branch, I thought better of it. Using all my strength, I gave a tremendous pull and felt myself moving down toward another set of limbs, almost as if I were in the ocean and fighting my natural buoyancy. I kept pulling myself from branch to branch, and almost down to the ground.

Again, I heaved my feet toward the ground and let go of the last branch. My feet touched the ground and began gently floating back up.

"No!" I tried to say.

I sounded like a sleepwalker.

Is my brain asleep?

Talking seemed to help.

"Stop flying," I said, since I couldn't think of anything else to say.

The upward pull diminished, and I could descend. I was nearly overcome with gratitude when my feet settled back onto the ground.

Everything felt strange. My hands and feet were buzzing as they do when I wake unexpectedly in the night. It could have been adrenaline, but I didn't feel it in the rest of my body. I sat and gazed around the clearing.

I needed a moment to return to consciousness. My body felt as if it had been in intense, still meditation. I felt disconnected and half asleep. I picked up the camera, turned the screen around and began filming myself.

"Butterflies don't think about flying, they just…fly," I said. "Just because we can describe their flight mathematically and physically doesn't make the fact of their flight any less mysterious and natural to them." I paused and thought for a moment.

"Butterflies fly because it is in their nature to fly. I flew today because it is in my human nature to fly."

This thought triggered powerful emotions. Tears welled up in my eyes and rolled down my cheeks.

"I flew!" I said to my image on the camera screen. My image smiled back at me, tears shining softly in the afternoon sun.

Four

I sat amongst the ship's antennae and mulled the conversation over. One question kept returning.

Had the FBI lady been flirting with me?

I wasn't sure how to feel about that. Of course, I was never sure how to feel when someone flirted with me, so that was nothing new.

Still, was she flirting in the line of duty, or was it real? Was it that she didn't care what her colleagues thought? Eventually, I left it alone. There wasn't enough information.

Since I was on a cruise ship, I considered sneaking downstairs to find an open buffet before I left, but that would be dishonest. I didn't mind stealing some bandwidth, but stealing food felt wrong. Back in the air, I headed towards the campground, and tried not to think about Agent Stefanie.

I flew straight up for a bit, took my bearings from the stars, and headed north. Before long, New Orleans was brightening the horizon. Eventually, I saw a couple of jets on a long final approach into the Louis Armstrong Airport, across the lake from where I was staying.

I skirted the city to the east and flew in over Lake Ponchartrain. The campground was easy to find. I checked in with my intuition before I dropped and landed on the beach.

I was taking my helmet and goggles off when someone to my left said, "Liv? Is that you?"

My head snapped around, and my jaw dropped. Mitch was standing there underneath a mangrove tree with his hands in his pockets.

I froze. I didn't know what to do. My instinct was to leap into the sky, but with my heart hammering like it was, I wasn't sure that was possible.

I decided to play it cool, a strategy foreign to me.

"Hey, Mitch. How's it going?"

"What? How's it going? Where the hell did you come from?"

"What do you mean? I came from the beach."

"Yeah, before that."

"My campsite?"

He looked at me, confused.

"It was like you just dropped out of the sky. One second you weren't here, and the next, you were."

Remember me and lying?

"You didn't see me walk up here?"

"No, I just walked up here myself. I went to the bathroom and came out to look at the stars. Then bam! You appear on the beach!"

Fear was causing both the volume and pitch of his voice to rise.

"Look, Mitch, let me explain."

"You're that girl?" he asked, his fist punching his empty hand. "I knew there was something…."

"What? What girl?"

"That girl in the videos." He dropped his voice and looked around. "The one who can fly!" He whispered the last word.

I dropped my gaze to the sand that was creeping up around my boots. What was the worst that could happen?

"Let's sit down."

There were some picnic tables nearby. My heart was pounding. I hadn't yet confided in anyone outside my family.

Well, unless you counted the FBI.

And I didn't.

Mitch seemed like a good guy. I really, really hoped he wasn't an assassin.

The moon was coming up over the trees and helped us find the tables. I sat on one side, Mitch on the other. I unzipped my jacket. He was in a t-shirt and shorts.

I crossed my arms on the table and looked at him. I couldn't read his features in the gloom, but I could make out the rough outlines.

"Mitch…I'm the girl. Woman. Whatever," I said, shaking my head.

"Ho-*ly* shit," was his response.

I felt a surge of emotion. It was a relief finally to tell someone.

"Yeah," I said, "That was pretty much my first thought."

"You really can…fly?" Again, he whispered the last word.

"Yeah," I said, "I don't get it either."

"But…you…can fly!" he said.

"Yeah," I said, smiling.

"Dude."

"Yeah."

He sat quietly for a minute.

"What are you thinking?" I asked.

"I was trying to figure out what you say to people who can fly. What do people say when you tell them?"

"I've never told anyone. You're the first, except for my parents."

"Yeah? How did that go?"

"Rough," I said with a little laugh. "They were troopers, though. Nobody passed out. It was a close thing."

"No doubt."

We sat in silence.

"Okay, look," Mitch said, apparently all business now. "I haven't read your blog or been to your website. Someone posted a video on Facebook. I thought it was fake. Didn't I hear that you're in some kind of trouble?"

"Um…yeah."

"What do you need?"

Just like that. No further conversation needed. Just *what do you need?*

"Mitch…" I was close to tears. This guy barely knew me, and he was offering to help.

"Look, I don't know what you're into, but I've gotten to know you a little these past few days. I don't believe you did anything too wrong."

"'Too wrong'?" I asked.

"Well, you may have pissed in the wrong pool," he said, and I could tell he was smiling, "but I don't think you did anything serious."

"I touched Air Force One. While it was flying. With the president inside."

"You…touched…."

I told him the story. I also told him about the DOD having footage of the incident.

"Whoa. Whoa!" Mitch reached one hand across the table and grabbed my shoulder and shook it.

"Dude, that is SO cool!"

"Yeah, it was. Though apparently the military is less than amused."

"I don't doubt it. So what's going on? How can Teri and I help?"

"Mitch, I don't think you can," I said seriously. "I can't tell you how much it means to me, though, your offer."

"Why not?" he asked, sounding a little hurt.

"Mitch, there are other people after me besides the military and FBI."

"Who?" he asked quietly.

I took a deep breath and let half of it out.

"Bad guys. Very nasty guys."

I leaned across the table and whispered one word: "Assassins."

He had leaned in close, but sat up straight and glanced left and right, then back at me.

"Are you bullshitting me?" he asked seriously.

"No, Mitch, I'm not. I think it's safe right now. One reason the FBI wants me is to protect me. I don't think anyone else knows where I am."

"The FBI wants to arrest you, and someone else wants to kill you?"

"I think if the bad guys could, they would try to catch me, too."

"Okay, so again… what do you need help with?"

"I can't ask you and Teri to risk your lives to help me."

"Ah, it'll be fun. Besides, Teri will probably turn you in when she finds out, anyway."

I laughed, and Mitch joined in.

"Okay," I said, "do you have a laptop?"

"Yeah."

"Get online in the morning and read my blog. At least the last, say, 10 posts. That will give you an idea of where things are," I said. "We'll talk after that. To be honest, I was just thinking that I need someone to talk to."

"You got it," he said, standing. I stood up too, unthreading my legs from under the picnic table.

"I can't believe it," he said. "You're such a regular person."

I smiled.

"Yeah."

He put his left hand on my shoulder and held out his right. I took it, and we shook hands for a long time.

"We'll figure it out. I need some sleep and a shower. In the morning, we'll have coffee. Maybe bacon and eggs. Everything will be easy after."

"Thanks, Mitch. It means a lot to me you're willing to help," I said, still shaking his hand.

"You…" he started and then stopped and shrugged. "You can fly," he breathed.

I pulled him in close and gave him a one-armed hug. Two pats on the back.

But then I held onto him and turned towards his head. I whispered to him, "Want to know another secret?"

He nodded, uncertain.

"I think you can fly, too."

He pulled back, and he wasn't smiling. He looked down, then back up at me, and tilted his head to the side.

"See you in the morning," he said, his voice strange, and he walked back to his tent.

I woke up late. So late, in fact, that all the showers were available, and the water was hot again.

I stood in the shower and let the scalding water pour over me.

Living a meditative life was good for lowering stress levels. Being away from home, running from the law, and having your life and your parents' freedom threatened was enough to cause even me to feel stress. I am not vengeful by nature, but I was looking forward to bringing all this down on someone's head before long.

As I walked back to my campsite, I was looking forward to tea and honey. I still had some fruit that would work for breakfast.

Mitch was up and about as I walked by his campsite. I waved, and he waved back but didn't come over.

Awkward.

I put the kettle on and started cutting up fruit.

"Hey!" Mitch called.

I turned around and saw him and Teri coming over.

"Hey there!" I said. "Have you had breakfast?"

Teri laughed.

"Most campers are thinking about lunch."

I shrugged and went back to work.

"Yeah. I was…out late."

Mitch snorted but said nothing.

"There's plenty of water," I said. "Want some tea?"

They glanced at each other.

"Mitch wants to head to town," Teri said. "We *were* going to hit the road later, but…" and here she looked back at Mitch, "he wants to stay another day or two."

I looked at Mitch, who was watching me intently. He glanced at his wife and smiled. "I like it here. We're not on a schedule, are we?"

"No," she said, smiling, "Not really."

"Good. Then we can hit the road after the weekend."

Teri looked back at me.

"Can we get you anything?"

"Oh, uh…" I thought about it. When you had to carry everything yourself, you traveled lightly. "If you want to have dinner with me tonight, we could have roast chicken. Or a duck if they have any at the natural food store."

"Sure," she said with a smile.

I gave Teri some money and suggested a duck and some root vegetables.

After breakfast, I went to the beach and practiced martial art forms. There weren't many campers around. I took my t-shirt off and practiced in just a sports bra and martial art pants. I practiced for a long time. The sand dragged at my feet. It made it hard to move and cost more energy. It felt good.

I performed each of my forms 10 times apiece. It took about two-and-a-half hours. When I finished practicing, I ran down and jumped into the freezing water. I was hot, and it almost felt good. I stayed in long enough to wash the sweat off. When I got out, I pulled on my t-shirt and boots and started running.

I made a complete circuit of the campground on the road, then started on the sidewalks and trails. After an hour of running around the park, I took another quick shower and changed clothes.

Later that afternoon, I was writing on my laptop when Mitch and Teri came back and parked at my site. They unloaded my groceries, and I got to work.

They brought a beautiful duck that would be perfect for the three of us. After I built my fire, I borrowed a cast-iron pot from Teri and put it in the fire to heat. I seared the duck in the hot pot, just enough to brown the skin. I set it aside, allowed the pot to cool on the table, and got everything else ready.

When I could touch the pot again, I assembled carrots, sweet potatoes, and daikon radishes at the bottom. I cut an apple and an orange and put them inside the cavity of the duck, which then went back into the pot on top of the vegetables, and the lid went on the container.

I set it at the edge of the fire and reminded myself to turn it now and then. When the fire died down, I could put it inside the embers.

In the late afternoon, as the sun was going down, Mitch and Teri came over. We sat at my picnic table and chatted.

Eventually, Mitch opened his tablet. My heart started beating faster. He looked up at me and smiled.

"I read that blog today. The one we talked about last night."

Teri looked up at me.

"What blog?"

"I…well…."

"You've probably seen it online," Mitch said. "The woman who can fly."

"Oh, that. Have you heard of her, Liv? Everyone's talking about it."

"Yeah, I heard."

"Her writing needs work," Mitch said, "But she seems legit."

"Really?" Teri said. "You're always so skeptical. I didn't think you would believe it at all."

"I didn't at first."

He looked over at me. Teri looked from Mitch to me, puzzled.

I took a breath. Instead of talking, I put my hands on the table and got up to rotate the pot in the fire.

"Liv convinced me it's for real," he said.

There has to be a better way to tell someone than just saying it. What if I just did a double front flip and kept walking like no big deal? Would it freak her out more?

When I sat back down, Mitch and Teri were both looking at me.

"Teri, the blog is mine. I'm the woman."

"You're…the woman?" she repeated. "The woman? *That* woman?"

Her voice was getting higher, but not louder. It worried me.

Mitch interrupted her.

"Honey, yeah. She's the one."

"You…saw. Her. You…saw…her?"

"Fly," he breathed, "Yes, I saw her fly. Well, land actually, but still…I saw her."

Teri looked away. I leaned forward to touch her hand, but she jerked them away.

"No!" she said, her voice tight. "No. Sorry, but…." She was shaking now. I looked at Mitch, worried.

"Honey, it's all right. It's okay, honey!"

She looked at him, her eyes bright with fear.

"I want to…I mean…."

She finally looked at me. Even in the gathering darkness, her eyes were so wide the whites showed around the irises. Her face was pale.

"You can fly?" she whispered.

I looked at her, calm and focused, and nodded my head once.

Picnic tables are not good places to be if you feel faint. Teri tried to get up, but her feet tangled in the legs and struts. Mitch tried to get her to put her head between her legs, but there was no room. Then she said she felt like she would be sick.

I grabbed my trash bag, just in case, and Mitch tried to get her feet untangled.

Ten minutes later, after a walk to the beach, they came back. I had turned the pot again and was sitting at the table. Mitch put my trash bag back where I kept it, and they sat.

Teri looked embarrassed.

"I'm sorry, Liv."

"Don't be. I reacted the same way."

She smiled.

"Actually, Mitch is the one who has taken it the best. Besides my parents, you guys are the only ones who know. And the FBI, I guess."

"The FBI?" Teri said.

"That's why we're staying, sweetheart. I offered to help her."

She looked back at me, concern on her face.

"I haven't done anything wrong."

"Except for molesting the president," Mitch said, laughing.

"*Basically*, I haven't done anything wrong," I said, smiling.

"Then why is the FBI after you?" she asked.

"Two reasons. One, the U.S. Government doesn't like the idea that their walls and fences might be meaningless. Two, it turns out that *other* governments, corporations, and churches feel the same way. There are teams of people trying to find me and catch me. Or, failing that, kill me."

Teri's eyes got huge, and she sat up straight. Her breath huffed through her nostrils. She looked at Mitch with both hands flat on the table.

"It's okay," he said. "Nobody knows where she is."

"It is NOT okay. You cannot just go around killing people because they can do something you can't!"

She looked back at me, furious. Her anger on my account brought tears to my eyes. I cleared my throat.

"Even though the FBI wants me in custody, and is being pretty nasty about it, they are helping to keep me safe and anonymous."

Teri relaxed slightly.

"How do you know they are trying to kill you?" she asked.

"I was in the FBI's custody last week. They were going to take me to Washington."

I stopped. I didn't know how to tell the next part.

"I got a sense something was happening. As I walked out to the helicopter, surrounded by U.S. Marshals, I knew what I had to do to survive. I dropped the agent in front of me and the one behind me and flew off in, like, less than a second. As I was flying away, there was a rifle shot. I think it barely missed the agents I knocked down and me."

"Were they okay?" Mitch asked.

"Yeah. I might have hurt one of them with my kick, but the sniper's round could have killed all three of us, I think."

"I'm not sure I understand," Teri said. "Why did you knock them down? Why not just fly away?"

I hesitated before answering.

"I just...knew what I had to do. I didn't see it or imagine myself doing it. I just knew it and did it."

"So you got some kind of, what, Divine Guidance?" she asked.

"If you like. I haven't tried too hard to define it, to be perfectly honest."

"Tom Brown talks about that," Mitch said. "Have you heard of him?"

"No."

"He grew up in the Sixties and met his friend's grandfather, an old Apache scout, one of the last ones alive — kind of cross between a hunter and a holy man," Mitch said. "Anyway, he taught Tom and his friend how to be at home in nature and to listen to its voice."

That sounded interesting. Nature's voice.

"I need to find his book," I said.

"There are several. I have some field guides with me, but there are others that might be more what you want. More of the spiritual stuff," Mitch said.

"Good."

I opened my laptop and made a note of the name.

Mitch got up and checked the fire for me. He moved the pot into the middle of the coals and lifted the lid to check on the contents. The aroma was incredible.

"Smells good!" he said, coming back to the table.

I checked my watch.

"Should be ready soon. Half an hour or less."

"Good, I'm starving," Teri said, smiling.

"So, what's your plan?" Mitch asked.

I told them about flying to the cruise ship, how I had talked to my parents and the FBI. I verbally sketched what the FBI wanted from me and how they were applying pressure.

"I can't believe it," Teri said. "How can they just make things up? They… they are making it up, aren't they?"

"Yes, they are. It's funny, though, that I didn't commit any actual crimes until they arrested me for a crime I didn't commit."

"Hilarious," Mitch said, looking at Teri.

"Congratulations," she said. "You're an honorary black person."

We talked until dinner was ready. It took a while for Mitch and Teri to get their heads around the situation. That was understandable, since I was only just beginning to understand. People wanting you dead is a fairly difficult thing to get used to.

Of course, they had to get used to the whole flying thing at the same time. I at least had a decent handle on that after the past few years. I wasn't mentally ready to bring it out to the public yet, but the bad guys and even the good guys were forcing my hand.

We ate dinner together. Mitch pulled out some organic wine to have with the duck. If you've never had vegetables cooked in duck fat, you're missing out. I hoped there would be some left for breakfast so we could cook sweet potatoes and eggs.

The duck was practically falling off the bone, and the vegetables were stewing in the fat. Mitch and Teri had never eaten duck and seemed hesitant at first, but the way the flavors came together erased their doubt.

"This is heavenly!" Teri said after her first bite.

"Where did you learn to cook?" Mitch asked.

"My mom. Dad too, sometimes, but mostly Mom."

We took our time and talked little during dinner. We were all hungry and ate well.

Afterward, we moved the picnic table closer to the fire so we could feel the heat and see each other while we talked. My back was to the fire, so I sat sideways. I had some apples my mother had dried and brought those out to nibble on as we talked.

"I said last night we would help you," Mitch said, glancing at his wife. "Maybe I should have waited to see what Teri thought before I committed us, considering the danger."

"Maybe," she said, "but I agree." She looked from her husband to me. "Most people probably like to think they are special somehow. We go through our lives wanting to show people who we really are, what we can do." She looked back at her husband. "We're just regular people, doing the best we can."

Mitch nodded.

Teri looked back at me.

"But this is a chance to be the people we like to *think* we are. Helping you is the right thing to do."

Again, the emotion in her voice was touching.

"Thanks," I croaked out, "I can't tell you how much I appreciate your offer. But I have to ask, are you sure it's worth the risk? Do you have kids or other family members to worry about?"

"No kids yet," Mitch said, "and yeah, we have other family members, but they're good people. They'd help you if they were here."

"I don't know how dangerous it will be," I said.

"You're not the one making things dangerous," Mitch said. "You don't have any excuses or apologies to make."

"So, enough of this talk," Teri said. "Where do we start?"

I gazed into the fire.

"I suppose we should begin with moving."

"Moving?" Teri asked.

"The FBI knows I called from a cruise ship in the Gulf. They had to have tracked my computer usage in NOLA. If they wanted me, they would be here by now. It wouldn't take a huge stretch of the imagination."

"Okay," Mitch said, "should we leave tonight?"

"No. It doesn't feel right. Maybe tomorrow…the day after."

"Feel right? You're talking about Divine Guidance again?" Mitch asked.

"I'm trying to listen to my instincts, my intuition, internal guidance, God, whatever you want to call it. We all have it. I'm trying to listen to it. I don't have all the answers, and I make mistakes. But if I pay attention and try to stay close to the…well, the path it lays out, I think I'll do alright."

"You told me last night…you think I can fly, too."

Teri looked at her husband.

"Really?" she said. Then she looked at me. "Really?"

"Yeah. Well," I said, smiling, "It's just…I'm not special. Lots of people can probably do this. Or something else like it. I think if you follow your Guidance, you'll figure it out."

"So you *don't* think I can fly?" Mitch asked, seeming crestfallen.

"I don't know, Mitch. Before long, other people are going to post flying videos on YouTube. Real ones. Why not you?"

"How will I know?" he asked.

"When you do it, I guess. That's a crappy answer, but it's the only one I have."

"How do I train? Can we start now?"

"I'm still figuring it out. For me, it has something to do with meditation and getting free of the ego. It also has to do with my diet. Too much sugar and things don't work so well. The quieter my digestion is, the easier flying is."

"Is that why you don't eat bread?" Teri asked.

"Or beans, or dairy. Butter and cheese once in a while, maybe some yogurt, but that's about it."

"Are you allergic to milk?" Mitch asked.

"I wasn't. But after I cut bread and dairy out, I became really sensitive to them. Now when I eat grains or regular dairy, it causes all kinds of problems: stomach aches, gas, bloating. Not fun."

"So, don't eat dairy if you want to fly?" Teri asked.

"Not necessarily. I feel better if I don't eat it. That's all."

"So," Mitch began thoughtfully, "if I want to get started, I should stop eating…what?"

"You should follow your instincts. Not your thoughts, but your gut feelings. Lots of people eat crap and say they're following their guts. They're following their addictions and their ego. There's a difference."

"How can you tell the difference?" Mitch asked.

"Ego and addiction are loud and easy to hear. Guidance and intuition are quiet and easy to miss. Ego is a voice in my head, while Guidance is a feeling or an idea. Learn to meditate, and you'll probably learn about Guidance."

"Do you receive Guidance when you meditate?" Mitch asked.

"I receive Guidance *because* I meditate. I receive Guidance when I'm quiet. Most people never get quiet enough to hear it."

We all sat for a moment, lost in our thoughts.

"So, meditation and diet," Mitch said finally. "That's it?"

I laughed, "Not really. Exercise is important too."

"Really? You need to exercise to fly?" Teri asked.

"Landing takes strength. Falling too. I've had some pretty amazing accidents while learning to fly."

"You look okay," Mitch said.

"I never broke any bones or lost appendages, but I've had my share of cuts and scrapes, bumps and bruises. And mild hypothermia once."

"Yike," Teri said.

"I took a bug-strike in the eye recently. That's when I bought the goggles. Two pairs, actually. The FBI has my favorite pair."

"But," said Teri, "going back to just learning to fly: why are diet and all of that important?"

"I can't honestly say. There's something about being conscious of what you're eating that's important. I don't think it means being a vegetarian, vegan, paleo, or whatever. You listen to your body and give it what it needs."

"How do you listen to your body?" Mitch asked.

"Come here," I said, and I got up and walked away from the fire. They both followed me.

"It's dark out here, but there's nothing around to hurt ourselves on. Now, grab my shoulders."

Mitch took hold of my t-shirt with one hand and my entire shoulder with the other. He was a big guy, about three inches taller than me, and his hands were huge.

"Now, I won't hit you or kick you. At least not very hard," Teri laughed. "But you defend, okay?"

"Okay."

I shot a front kick toward his left knee, nice and slow. He raised his leg to block the kick and then hooked my left knee, taking me down on my back. I broke my fall by rounding my back and slapping the ground with my arm.

"Dude! I didn't say to counter!" I said, laughing.

"Sorry!" Mitch said, helping me up. "It's just habit."

"Well, it makes my point anyway," I said, brushing the sand off me. "How did you know what I was doing?"

"I could see you a little," he said. "Your balance shifted. I felt it too since I was holding you."

"Right. You paid attention to what your senses were telling you."

"Yeah."

We walked back over to the table.

"Listening to your body is like that. Not just your physical senses, though. Listen to your body's intelligence and wisdom."

"You mean like when animals know how to eat some plants and not others?" Teri asked.

"Exactly! They're in touch with something that we have lost contact with."

"Instincts," Mitch said.

"Kind of. Maybe 'wild intelligence' is a better way of saying it. It's a nonverbal knowing, a kind of intuition divorced from intellect, that tells you what your body needs. And those needs might change from day to day."

"It sounds exhausting," Mitch said.

"It sounds that way to the ego. No offense."

"What do you mean?" Mitch asked.

"The ego wants to be in charge. There's a quote from Einstein I see all the time: 'The intuitive mind is a sacred gift, and the rational mind is a faithful servant. We have created a society that honors the servant and has forgotten the gift.' Ego is part of the rational mind. It's always talking to us, always telling us what we think. We forget the ego is just a tool. It's not really *us*."

"Yeah, I get that. I've felt that before."

"I don't have a clue what you mean," Mitch said. "It sounds like you're talking about a split personality."

We were sitting at the table again. I leaned my elbows on the table and said, "I don't think you're far off. I wonder if some mental illnesses are just an awareness of things that not everyone has. Another quote: 'There are more things in Heaven and Earth, Horatio, than are dreamt of in your philosophy.'"

"I'd be pretty silly to argue that point with the woman who can fly," Mitch said, laughing.

We talked for a long time. I told them about one of my favorite authors, Eckhart Tolle, and how he thought the ego was insane. We talked about spiritual books like *Conversations with God* and *The Celestine Prophecy*. We talked about God and creation, genetics, and physics.

In the end, we decided not to make any firm plans. We might leave in a day or two, and we might head west. Nobody was on much of a timetable, and we weren't rushed.

Before Mitch and Teri headed back to their tent, we meditated sitting at the picnic table. They had meditated before and knew the basics of how to get to the point between one thought and the next. Neither of them felt like they were "good" at it, but they understood the concept.

We did a quick ten minute meditation and said goodnight. I hugged them both and thanked them for being friends and for helping me.

Mitch said, "You have something to offer the world. I'm excited to be a small part of it."

"And I'm lucky to be married to such a good guy," Teri said, holding Mitch's arm. "I'm glad he connected with you last night." She reached out and touched my shoulder.

Teri glanced down for a second, then up at Mitch.

"What?" Mitch said.

"I wasn't going to ask," Teri said.

"Ask...?" I said and suddenly realized.

"You want to see...."

She blushed.,

"I know it's silly."

When she looked back up, I wasn't there.

Mitch and Teri looked around.

"Liv?" they called.

"What?" I answered from 10 feet above them.

Teri looked up and screamed. I laughed and landed back in the same spot.

I looked at Mitch, and his face was white.

"That is just weird," he said.

"I know," I said. "You OK?" I asked both of them.

"So cool," Teri said, her hands shaking.

"Being conscious is the first step. Meditation is the second."

"Right," Mitch said, "I may go consciously throw up now."

I laughed. It would be fun traveling with these two.

The first time I levitated, I worried that I was losing my mind. I was seriously concerned that I was hallucinating. So, I started recording my levitation sessions. That's what this entry is about.

∼

Excerpt from the blog: *Griffin's Flight*

AUGUST 28, 2024

Some people find meditation boring. I get that. They either lack the discipline or the desire to sit quietly for any length of time. Most people would rather watch T.V. or listen to music than sit in silence with themselves.

If you are one of those people who find meditation boring, it's only because you have never watched hours of video of *yourself* meditating.

It's torture.

Around the end of July, I stopped watching the meditation videos. Maybe if I forgot about it, it would happen sooner. That lasted for maybe a week. I started watching them again, just in case.

To ease the boredom and save time, I've been fast-forwarding to double or triple speed. But watching this way is a little risky. The first time I levitated, I didn't realize it was happening until I tried to find my water bottle. It might have happened many times before, to a lesser degree, without me noticing. But, I'll accept the risk if it means I don't have to spend an hour or more every day reviewing videos of myself sitting on a pillow and going nowhere.

So, it's about four months since I levitated. I had already been eating better than before I moved back home. Recently, I've been working hard to make my diet clean and organic. No more weekend pizza runs. No stopping for cheeseburgers when I go to the farm store. I also cut all the processed sugar from my diet. I'll write about that in a separate post.

I began taking martial art classes twice a week. There is space in the barn to practice, and I try to do that four or five times a week. I take a yoga class too.

I enjoy the yoga and the martial art classes for different reasons. Yoga is relaxing but challenging. The class is mostly women. It's peaceful and I enjoy going.

Martial art class is different. It's not quiet or meditative, but it's satisfying on a different level. As in yoga, learning new skills is rewarding, but the ease of movement I've developed the past few months is surprising.

Growing up on the farm, I was healthy. But as I have stretched and learned to move my body correctly, I've gained levels of strength I didn't realize were possible.

In my free time these past few months, I've studied history. Specifically, historical figures who reportedly levitated. From what I've read, the people who did this for real were all religious devotees of some sort. While I think of myself as spiritual, I don't adhere to any religion or doctrine.

That said, in the past four months, I have studied and learned a lot about spirituality, meditation, physical fitness, diet, and physical training. Even though I'm not religious, I believe in an Organizing Intelligence in the Universe. I don't know what to call it or how to characterize it, but I know it's there and is intimately connected to what I experienced.

The spiritual traditions from around the world have more agreement than differences, which suggests to me that people access the Organizing Intelligence similarly all over the world, regardless of religion.

Stories of magical transformations have also fascinated me. Of course, we all interpret stories differently, but some suggest actual events. The tale of Icarus, for example, was undoubtedly allegorical. It was also possible that a young man somewhere was trained to levitate by a father or teacher, and had used this ability unwisely. There's no way to know, but it's fascinating to ponder.

I wonder about the mystical abilities attributed to fairies and other magical creatures, gods and superheroes. Throughout history, people around the world have fantasized about the ability to fly. Could they instinctively sense a potential they already possess?

Wouldn't it be interesting if all of humanity had this capacity to one degree or another? When I think about how it could affect society, my mind boggles. We could save much of the energy we used to travel to and from work. The simple experience of freedom might be enough to give us a new sense of purpose. Awareness of possibilities previously thought fantasy might be enough to provide society a compelling reason for going on, for settling our differences and cherishing the brotherhood of humankind.

Five

I woke ready to take on the world. It felt good to have friends to talk to, people to confide in.

I took a run around the park and, after a shower and coffee, I walked over to Mitch and Teri's campsite. I had seen them puttering around when I came back.

"Howdy, neighbor," Teri called.

"Hey there," I said.

"Any fresh destinations on your itinerary today?" Mitch asked.

"Nothing cool," I said with a laugh, "I need to find another cafe, but that's it."

"No sightseeing planned?" he asked.

"Um…no."

Truthfully, it hadn't occurred to me. Sightseeing was the last thing on my mind.

"Lots of voodoo stuff around here. Might be up your alley," he said, smiling.

"Eh, no thanks."

"Seriously, though," Teri said, "would you like to join us for dinner? We can make reservations somewhere nice."

"Sure. Not too nice, though. All my clothes are just…."

I gestured down at my canvas work pants and flannel shirt.

Teri winked at me and said, "No worries."

We planned for them to pick me up at the library, do some sightseeing, and then have dinner.

I used the next several hours for martial art practice and meditation. Afterward, I felt ready for another shower, but I ran to the beach and had a cold swim in the lake.

Just for kicks, I tried levitating in the water. I rose to the top as if I had become super buoyant. I quickly switched the direction of my intention and sank to the bottom. The lake was cloudy, and I wasn't wearing a mask, so I kept my eyes closed, held my breath, and flew underwater. I imagined a shield as before to keep fish and other things away from my face.

I surfaced a quarter of a mile off the beach, treaded water, and looked around. Way off to my right, the causeway bisected the lake. To my left somewhere, it emptied into the Gulf of Mexico. In front of me, barely visible, the New Orleans skyline was a hazy smudge on the surface of Lake Pontchartrain.

I turned and swam back to the beach. It didn't take as long as I expected. I might have been "helping" my mediocre swimming skills with my flying ability. It was hard to tell.

I rinsed off in the shower (fully clothed so that I wouldn't have to wash my clothes), changed for my day in the city, and found a place in the woods to take to the air.

Midday in New Orleans is busy. I couldn't remember what day it was, but judging from traffic, it was a weekday.

Once inside the library, I connected to the wireless network and logged into the website. Before I had time to do anything else, I noticed a message waiting for me.

Griffin:

We don't know each other, but I like what you're doing here. Before long, the FBI is going to take your website down. It happens all the time. I can help keep things running if you like. I offer my services as a web security consultant.

We can arrange a meeting in person, or if you are concerned about your physical safety, we can set something up online.

Let me know your wishes. Of course, you may have already prepared for this possibility.

Again, I'm excited about your project. Keep up the good work!

S

W ell, I knew that the government killing the site was a possibility. I hadn't thought of it as inevitable, but maybe it was.

They had sent the message earlier that morning. I looked at active accounts and saw that the sender was online. His username was ST. I sent a chat request.

GRIFFIN

Hi there. Thanks for your note.

ST

You're welcome!

It's been a concern of mine for a while.

I'd love to help. Just give the word.

I'd like to meet in person first. Where are you located?

I'm sure you know that if the government targets your site, everyone involved will become targets as well.

Sure.

Then you won't be surprised that I want to maintain anonymity as well.

Okay. So how do we proceed?

> I propose we meet someplace neutral. I'll be in Chicago soon. We could meet there.

> I'll let you know.

I could see why he might not want to share his name online, but the exchange made me uncomfortable. Even though I was using a fake name myself, his use of only initials was off-putting.

After some housekeeping, I logged off, restarted my computer, and logged into my other account. I looked around the forum and read some conversations. There were no more posts from the enigmatic ST.

I read and wrote for an hour until it was time to meet Mitch and Teri. Outside, I leaned against a tree and meditated while I waited for them to pick me up. I checked in with my body and felt no direction, no nudge to change anything. Good news, I supposed.

They picked me up, and we walked through an old cemetery, then drove to the French Quarter where we visited a huge farmers market, and finally sought the famous restaurant, NOLA.

The food was fantastic. I didn't work too hard to limit my diet, other than to avoid bread, even though it looked and smelled delicious. It was basic food, but with a lot of style.

"I could get used to a burger like that," Mitch said.

"You better not," Teri said.

We splurged and had dessert. I tried the banana pudding cake, but it was too sweet. I could only eat a few bites. Mitch finished it after consuming his crème brûlée.

I rode in the back seat for the hour-long drive to the campground. Not counting time with the FBI, I hadn't ridden in a car in a while, let alone in the back seat. The heavy meal, combined with the road noise and close quarters, lulled me to sleep in no time.

The next morning I woke up fuzzy-headed and congested. Interrupting my usual eating habits had left me lethargic, but it had been worth it.

It was Saturday, and the campground was full. There would be no martial art practice today, and any flying would be risky. I was sitting outside my tent sipping coffee when Mitch ambled over.

"Hey, neighbor," he said.

"Howdy. Want some coffee?"

"You mean the diesel fuel you drink?" he asked. "No thanks. I like my stomach lining."

"You don't like dark roast?" It hurt that he would insult my coffee. "You don't like real coffee?"

"Just a little strong for my taste."

"I could put some butter in it for you," I offered.

"Ugh."

"I like to add vanilla, but I don't have any with me."

"Anyway, we thought we might catch a movie or something. Maybe get a bite to eat. Wanna come?" he asked.

It was my turn to decline.

"Ah… no thanks," I said. "Still recovering from last night."

"It was good, wasn't it?"

"It was outstanding, but I'm paying the price today."

I looked around the campground. There was an uneasy feeling in the air that I couldn't put my finger on. I let my gaze bounce around the various campers, trailers, motorhomes, and tents. Nobody was watching or paying me the slightest bit of attention.

I turned back to Mitch, who was surveying the crowd as well.

"I had forgotten how nice campers are," he said. "The people I mean, not the vehicles."

"Yeah? You camp a lot?"

"Used to. Not much anymore."

I nodded and went back to scanning the grounds.

"Well, we're busy during the day. How about we get together for dinner?" Mitch said.

"Your fire pit or mine?"

"Why don't we cook this time?"

I spent a rainy morning hiking and the afternoon reading. I tried to write but kept having the nagging feeling that something wasn't right and got little work done.

Finally, I meditated to center myself and then walked through the campground. I stayed meditative, remaining alert without judging or analyzing anything.

I said hello to a few kids who were running around and greeted the campers in my vicinity, and chatted with the camp host. Nothing seemed off with any of them.

After Mitch and Teri returned, I ambled over to their site.

"So, what can I do to help with dinner?" I asked.

We talked food for a moment, and I jogged to my site to gather my hunting knife and meager stash of spices.

"Perfect!" Teri said. "I'll cook burgers, and you kids cut veggies. We'll be eating in 30 minutes."

As I cut carrot sticks, I kept looking around. I couldn't shake the feeling I was being watched, but I couldn't see anyone.

The sun had dropped below the clouds and was hurrying toward the horizon. The unease I had felt earlier had dissipated while working. It began creeping back, growing stronger as daylight faded.

"Here we go," I said, walking back into their camp.

We finished the prep just as the sun was sinking behind the trees, and I felt like I was ready to jump out of my skin.

"I'm sorry," I said finally. "Something's wrong."

"What?" Mitch asked. "What's wrong?"

"I don't know. I'm going to go up and look around."

"Bad idea, chica. It's not dark yet."

"I know. No choice. Sorry."

I dashed out of their camp, feeling like a trapdoor was about to open under my feet.

My first thought was to launch from the beach and fly at treetop level to have a look around. But campers crowded the beach watching the sunset, so I headed for the hiking trail leading into the woods.

Night had already fallen under the trees. I was searching for an opening in the canopy that would allow me access to the sky when I stumbled over a man crouching behind a tree. I wasn't running fast, but he grunted as I made contact. As I was falling, I saw he was wearing camouflage. He either had black skin, or he had painted his face.

I tucked my right shoulder as I hit the ground, rolled and came back up on my feet. Camo-Man swore and dropped something. As he was turning toward me, he made the unmistakable motion of drawing something from his belt, either a knife or a sidearm. I didn't let him finish drawing.

I stepped in close, pinned his arm to his side, and slammed my elbow into the back of his neck. He crumpled to the ground, dazed, but not out cold. My eyes were adjusting to the gloom, and there was a rifle lying on the ground at my feet. I stooped to pick it up and pointed it at Camo-Man.

"Who are you?" I hissed at him.

His only answer was to hold the base of his skull and moan.

"Who sent you?" I asked, jabbing the barrel of the rifle into his shoulder.

The man exploded into action, taking the rifle out of my hands at lightning speed and slamming the butt across my face.

I spun away but didn't fall. He put the rifle to his shoulder and took aim, but he didn't fire. He murmured something, but I couldn't make out what he said. It sounded almost as if he was mumbling to himself.

Almost immediately, there were footsteps behind me. I closed my eyes and tried to find my center. If I was going to survive, I had to fly fast.

The person coming up behind me said something in a language I couldn't identify, and Camo-Man responded with one word. My senses lit up, and I could feel the person behind reaching for me. My feet left the ground, and I spun to my right, around the second man, and struck him square on his back. He fell forward onto Camo-Man. I covered my face with both arms and shot through the canopy.

There were shouts and gunshots behind me, then screams and shouting from the campground. I curved down and around the campground, trying to see what was happening. There were several more gunshots and then nothing but confused voices of campers.

Who were these guys? Who did they work for? Had they seen me with Mitch and Teri? Were they *targets because of me?*

I began circling back around to see what the shooter meant to do, trusting my inner Guidance since I couldn't see. I had instinctively conjured a shield to protect myself from the bugs of a Louisiana night in the woods. The problem was humidity. The pressure change caused by my shield created a corona of mist in front of me as I flew. I could barely see anything.

As I circled, there was crying from up ahead. I slowed and descended a few feet. The campground was directly in front of me. I dropped between the trees and flew to the edge of the clearing.

One shooter was standing behind Mitch, pointing a handgun at his head. Teri lay sprawled on the ground, not moving.

Again, faster than thought, I was behind the gunman, putting him in a headlock, pulling the gun away from Mitch and thrusting it under the man's jaw. I figured the odds were about even that he would fire reflexively. He didn't.

"Is she okay?" I yelled.

Mitch turned and saw me, then dove for Teri. He moved her head and checked her pulse.

"Unconscious. Bastard hit her."

He stood and slammed his fist into the man's gut. Somehow, the guy kept from pulling the trigger, but he grunted and doubled over, nearly pulling from my grip.

"Get the gun!" I shouted as Mitch prepared for another strike.

He saw my situation and began prying it from the man's hand, taking care to keep it pointing away from my head.

The shooter was struggling. Now that I could use both hands, I tightened my choke until I felt his neck creak. He began sputtering and making inarticulate sounds.

Mitch stepped back and pointed the gun at the man.

He slumped in my grip, but I didn't trust him. I suddenly felt chills running up my spine.

"He's not alone," I said.

Mitch slugged the guy across the face. I released him, and he fell to the ground in a heap. I crouched, turning to scan the rest of the campground, but it was too dark to see into the trees. Other campers huddled behind and inside their cars, some peeking out to see what was going on.

"Let's get out of here," Mitch said. "Teri needs an emergency room."

"Yeah. Can you get her into the car? I need to find the other guy."

I jumped into the air and flew to my campsite, where I grabbed my goggles and scarf and shot back up. Staying about 15 or 20 feet above the ground, I swept around the campground, but didn't see anyone. I was about to circle over the trees when my left shoulder struck something hard. It snapped me around and sent me whirling in an uncontrolled tangle of arms and legs. I slammed into the side of a large RV and slid to the ground, clutching my shoulder and groaning.

I heard a voice to my right but couldn't make out words.

Another voice replied from my left. Running footsteps began converging on me.

My shoulder hurt so bad that I could hardly breathe. I tried moving my arm, and it worked. The pain was intense, but not sharp. I struggled to my feet.

"Mitch?"

"Heading out!"

Two car doors slammed, followed by the sound of an engine.

"Okay, guys. You and me," I murmured, the pain in my shoulder causing tears to well up in my eyes.

I jumped on top of the RV and tried to see who was chasing me. I could hear them running, but they were only shadows in the gloom. Sensing danger, I dropped to my belly on top of the RV, crying out again when I hit the surface.

There was a shot, and I heard the whiz of a bullet passing over my head. These guys were fine with killing me. Not FBI then. I rolled onto my back and breathed, attempting to calm myself enough to fly.

"Did you hit her?" one voice asked.

"Think so," the other answered, "Gonna check."

One guy sounded Australian, the other maybe Russian.

I felt the RV shake as one of them began climbing the ladder. I cleared my mind and rolled off the edge, hopefully away from the other one.

I didn't hit the ground, but hovered. Trying to stay five feet above the ground, I began moving, gaining speed and then climbing. I looked out over the park and tried to find Mitch, but lots of cars were leaving. They were lost in the headlights and taillights of fleeing campers.

I climbed higher and looked down. I was maybe 500 feet above the ground now. My shoulder and face hurt, but I was okay. I couldn't tell what I had run into, but I suspected it might have been a camper's flagpole.

What do I do next?

Bad guys are wandering the campground looking for me, and innocent campers are in their way.

Would they hurt innocent people?

Probably. They hurt Teri.

How can I keep the other people safe without putting myself at risk?

Can't be done.

Had Mitch tied up the first assassin? Taken his gun?

I had to check.

Staying as high as possible, I curved around the outside of the camping area until I got to about where their site had been, then dropped feet first. I landed in a crouch and checked for danger. The guy was still there, on his side. He was conscious, but his mouth was duct-taped. Mitch had bound his hands and feet with zip ties and passed another between the two. He had hogtied the guy.

I checked for the handgun and rifle but didn't find them. Mitch had them then. I patted through the assassin's clothes and found a revolver on his ankle. That could work.

I didn't want to kill anyone, but I wouldn't let the Alliance hurt anyone else. I launched and flew back up towards the RV where I had last seen the others.

Only now I couldn't see them, or hear them. Did they have night vision? Thermal? No idea. They could have me in their sights right now.

I flew higher and calmed myself, listening to intuition.

The bad guys would look for their pal. If the cops found him, he might give information about his cohorts.

I flew back around to the trussed-up bad guy. He was gone. I had been aware of sirens in the distance, but suddenly the red and blue lights of approaching police cars appeared.

The bad guys must have been aware that they couldn't hang around forever. I prayed that, having recovered their comrade, they were in full retreat. For now, I needed my stuff before the cops came. I landed and ran to my site. I pulled down my tent quickly, stuffed it into the duffel bag, and packed everything I could.

As strange as it sounds, I was famished. We hadn't eaten dinner, and I had eaten little since last night. I finished packing my stuff and watched the police pull into the campground. I went over to Mitch and Teri's site. There was no way I could take any of their gear. My things, hastily packed, took up most of the room in my pack. I had room for dinner, though.

I grabbed some foil and wrapped the burgers and veggies, stuffed my pockets with water bottles, and left. The beach was deserted and dark, and I took off.

I used my phone to find the closest hospital and landed in the parking lot. There was an information desk just a few steps inside the Emergency Department, so I entered and asked for Teri. Either they weren't here yet, or Mitch had chosen a different hospital. I doubted he would do that, so I waited outside. Ten minutes later, he pulled up.

"Hey," I said, waving.

"Hey!" he said, getting out. Teri was sitting up in the passenger seat. I grabbed a wheelchair from beside the door and rolled it over.

"Throw your stuff in the back," Mitch said. "Do you mind parking?"

As Mitch wheeled Teri into the emergency department, I parked the car, locking my belongings inside. I stowed the handgun in my bag. Security cameras must have already recorded me. I wouldn't stay long, but I couldn't leave without checking on Teri.

"How are you feeling?" I asked back in the waiting area.

"Biggest headache in the world," she said, holding a large ice pack to her face.

"He hit her with the butt of his rifle," Mitch said, rage shaking his voice. "Did the cops get him?"

"No, sorry," I said. "He had buddies. They got to him first."

"Will they be looking for us?" she asked, clearly scared.

"I doubt it," I said. "I mean, the cops? Yeah. But the bad guys are probably only concerned with me."

She took my hand with her free hand.

"What about the guns?" Mitch asked. "Should we turn them over to the cops?"

"Probably," I said, "I don't know. We may need them before this is over."

"Turn them over," Teri said. "You've got your handgun in the car. There's no telling what they've been used for."

"You've got a gun?" I asked, surprised.

"Yeah," he said, "Lot of good it did me tonight. It's always locked in the car."

"Teri's right," I said as I calmed myself. "Let's not give in to fear. You've got a weapon. Leave it at that."

Mitch didn't look convinced, but he nodded and turned his attention back to Teri, smoothing her hair back from her forehead.

"I'm okay," she said, glancing up. "It's over. We're safe now."

Mitch looked at me, and I could tell he didn't really believe Teri any more than I did.

Of course, I eventually recorded myself levitating again. That's the one that went viral. Not a big deal anymore, right? To me, it was huge. *It meant I wasn't crazy. I'm not sure you can fathom the depth of my relief at that moment.*

Naturally, now that I wasn't crazy, I had to decide what to do next.

Excerpt from the blog: *Griffin's Flight*

OCTOBER 9, 2024

The first thing I thought about today was the video. What should I do with it?

The idea of posting it online is tempting. It's also ridiculously scary. I'm not ready for the psychological trauma that social media will inflict. Also, there will be real consequences for releasing this video. I'm not ready for those either.

Copying the video to my computer was obvious. I don't want the video to get out 'into the wild' yet, and I don't want to risk losing it either. I copied it onto an SD card and hid it in my paperback copy of *Jonathan Livingston Seagull,* by Richard Bach.

I thought about what to do next. There's no way around it. I have to practice. Lifting off the ground by myself during deep meditation was one thing. Before I let people know, I have to be good at it.

That the ability exists is incontrovertible to me. Many though will cry foul and dismiss it as fake. I would have done the same thing a year ago. For this to have the same effect on the rest of the world as it had on me, then I'll have to be much better at it.

I'll have to learn to fly.

The idea is daunting. I'm like a caveman seeing his fresh handprint on a wall and contemplating painting the Mona Lisa. I suspect it's possible, but I have no idea how to go about proving it. Also, it took eight months of meditation before I levitated, and another four months before it happened again. At this rate, I'll be entering middle age before I see any appreciable progress.

So, I'll keep this digital journal private for now. I'll save the daily entries and continue recording my meditation sessions. The more proof I have, the better.

I also need to experiment and try to understand the science. I've proven to myself that levitation is real. Now I have to prove it to others. I have to think about how to teach, too. What's the point of this if it's just me?

Once I'm comfortable with my abilities and the procedure, I'll share it with the world.

Six

They patched Teri's head within the hour. Karate training had given her the reflexes to dodge the worst of the blow, but she didn't escape a concussion. They bandaged her up and watched her for another hour before releasing her with the admonition to see a doctor when she arrived home.

"So, before you met me, where were you two thinking of going next?"

We were sitting in the parking lot of the hospital eating cold burgers and veggies.

"We were thinking of heading west to Sedona. Or maybe up to Cincinnati," Teri said. "There's an ancient Native American site I want to see."

"Which one?" I asked.

"Serpent Mound," Mitch said.

Serpent Mound is a tremendous "effigy" mound. It's made of rocks and soil piled into a very bizarre shape. It looks kind of like a snake swallowing an enormous egg. The body of the snake winds roughly a quarter of a mile across a hilltop in southern Ohio.

"My parents took me there when I was a kid," I said. "Have you ever been?"

"No, neither of us has," she said. "Would you like to go with us?"

I thought for a moment. I got no obvious nudge from intuition.

"Sure. I'd like that."

"Nobody will expect you to turn back towards home," Mitch said.

"Not in a car, that's for sure," I said.

I didn't ride back to the campground with them. If the police were there, I didn't want them to connect me with Mitch and Teri. And I really didn't want anyone to recognize me as the "Flying Woman." So, I sipped coffee and ice water and waited in a booth at a cafe up the road. Two hours later, Teri and Mitch pulled in. I left a five on the table and started out, but they met me at the door.

"Let's get some coffee before we hit the road," Mitch said.

"Okay."

We all sat in the booth I had just vacated.

Mona, my server, came over with a pitcher of ice water.

"I thought you'd left."

"I thought so too," I said with a laugh. "Can we get a fresh pot of coffee?"

"Anything else?"

Mitch and Teri both declined, and she left to refill the carafe.

"So?" I asked.

They glanced at each other. Teri held up one finger as if to say, "Wait a minute."

I nodded, sipped my over-chlorinated ice water, and waited.

"Here y'go," Mona said, bringing the coffee, cups, and a fresh pitcher of ice water.

"Thanks, Mona," I said.

She left, and Mitch poured for all of us. I was patient and refrained from saying anything.

"Okay," he finally said. "Nobody said officially who those guys were."

"Officially?"

"Local police wouldn't answer questions at all," Teri said. "People were trying to leave, but the police kept asking questions, and they wouldn't tell anyone anything."

"Then there were the feds," Mitch said. "Again, they didn't say anything, but they let on that it was drug-related. They asked Teri a lot of questions, but she didn't tell them anything about you."

"Are you on their radar because of me?" I asked.

"Maybe," Mitch said, glancing again at Teri. "We tried to play everything down, but they took all of our information."

"Damn," I said. "So, did anyone say anything about me flying around?"

"Not specifically," Teri said. "They asked if we saw anything 'out of the ordinary.'"

"I said, 'You mean like evil men shooting at us with guns?'" Mitch said.

I laughed.

"They wouldn't go into detail," he said. "Just kept trying to get us to say why the guy with the gun attacked us."

"No photos or videos to identify?" I asked.

"Nothing like that," Teri said. "The FBI seemed more interested in information. Not like they were trying to catch anyone besides the terrorists."

"Hm. Well, that's good, anyway," I said. "Let's hope you're right."

"Should we get anything to eat before we hit the road?" Mitch asked.

"Here?" I asked. "Nothing for me, but feel free."

Even though we had just eaten, they split a sandwich, and Mitch had a piece of pie. We continued to talk and wonder who the attackers might have been. Eventually, the conversation drifted to Serpent Mound and other places they might visit.

"After Serpent Mound, we can head west," Teri said. "Have you heard of Monk's Mound and the Cahokia Mounds? They're right across the river from St. Louis."

"From there, we thought about heading to Sedona, maybe see some places people hike to," Mitch said.

"I've never been to Sedona, but I've heard it's beautiful."

"Have you heard what people say about it?" Teri asked.

"A little," I said. "Energy vortices and that kind of stuff. Healing, I've heard."

"Yeah," Teri said. "We'd both like to see it."

We left the diner and started driving before the sun was up. It was late afternoon when we found a hotel east of Cincinnati. The mound is an hour east of the city. We slept, showered, ate, and crashed without even turning on the television. I woke the following morning to the sound of CNN and the smell of fresh coffee.

"That does not smell like hotel room coffee."

"No, ma'am!" Teri said. "That's my favorite blend in Mitch's French press. Ready for some?"

"Absolutely. Thank you."

"Nothing about Fontainebleau," Mitch said. "I've been watching for half an hour."

"Have you checked the internet?"

"Not yet," he said. "I didn't want that search linked to my devices. They have a computer downstairs that I'll check when we go down."

Back in the car, we headed east again by 10:00. According to Mitch, there had been nothing on any news service about the attack in Fontainebleau. We stopped at Jungle Jim's, a huge grocery store with food from around the world, and restocked our produce and other supplies. We tried to hurry, but Jungle Jim's is not a place you can get through quickly. I had been here before (we were only about three hours from my folks' house), but Mitch and Teri had never heard of it.

I navigated using my atlas rather than the GPS, and we were pulling into the park at 11:15. It had been bright but chilly when we left the hotel. Now it was warmer, but the clouds were darkening and sinking toward us.

"Better not risk the umbrella," Teri said, looking up at the clouds.

"Nope, stick with raincoats," Mitch agreed.

We walked past an old house-turned-office and followed the road to the mound site. The grass was that vivid green that you see in April. The groundskeeper's mower had left muddy tracks in some places. Although the trees weren't entirely in leaf yet, the signs of returning life and newness in the air invigorated me. Maybe the intensity of the atmosphere magnified the smells of spring. I felt energized as we walked.

"It's beautiful," Teri said. "I can see why the Indigenous Americans wanted to build here."

Before long, we saw the mound in front of us and signs describing the building, excavation, and rebuilding processes. It was the middle of the week and school was in session, so we had the park pretty much to ourselves. The other two cars in the lot might belong to park workers. We saw nobody else.

I longed to fly up and see the mound from the air, but it was a bad idea. The park didn't look sophisticated enough to have security cameras, but there were houses and farmland all around. I resolved to keep my feet on the ground - until I saw the observation tower.

It looked ancient. Rust seemed to be winning over the paint in most places, but it seemed sturdy enough. We walked the path to the east of the mound and climbed the tower after listening for thunder.

"So, they think this is a snake?" Mitch asked.

"Seems to be the consensus," Teri said.

"It looks more like a sperm," he said.

"Really?" she said. "Really. That's your contribution?"

"Well, it does!" he said. "Come on, surely you can see it."

"Of course I can, and so can everyone else. We have more manners than to say it out loud, baby," she said.

"It can't be a sperm," I said. "The builders didn't have microscopes."

"True," Mitch said. "But the aliens did."

"Oh, for Pete's sake. Why are we even doing this if you're just going to poke fun?"

"What am I supposed to say? Look at it! It doesn't look like a snake!"

He waved his arm while he spoke, taking in the entire mound from the head, down the undulating body, to the coiled tail.

"No, you're right," she said. "It doesn't. The drawings at Nazca don't look like what they're supposed to be either. It's called 'stylization'".

"Eh, maybe."

I was off to the side trying to stay meditative while they bickered. It was difficult, but I had learned to stay "in the shallows" of meditation, to hear and process conversation without labeling, judging, or mentally participating.

In my imagination, prehistoric people toiled below me. But why? Was the site ceremonial? Was it religious or astronomical? What would they have done down there?

"We're going up to the head, Liv," Mitch said. "You staying here?"

"For a minute. I'll be along."

Talking is hard if you're meditative. It's almost impossible to speak and remain in the gap, even in the "shallows."

I stood on the observation tower for 10 more minutes. The wind picked up, and I felt a few drops of rain before I finally headed down.

It was pouring when we checked into the La Quinta near Cincinnati that night. We were still recovering from the stress of the attack, the interruption of sleep cycles, and the long drive north. Nobody felt like driving through the rain at night.

I gave Mitch and Teri some alone time while I hit the fitness center. Most of their kettlebells were ridiculously tiny, but they had a 30-pound one that was decent. I swung it for a while, did some snatches and goblet squats, then jumped on the treadmill for a few miles.

After turning the lights down, I watched the rain as I ran. I fell into the gap while running, not thinking, not even feeling, just resting there and allowing myself to bathe in the experience. Sometimes when I meditate, I think of a problem that I'd like guidance on.

I hadn't done that this time, but I began seeing myself meditating with Teri and Mitch. Then I remembered back at Thanksgiving I had told Mom my story. We were strolling through her garden, and she had asked me to "fly" with her.

I had been reluctant, but eventually we had meditated together, and when I levitated, so did she.

The door opened, and the lights came up.

"Oh, did you want the lights off?" the guy at the door asked.

I just waved and shook my head. My meditation was broken, but I didn't feel like speaking yet.

"Sorry," he mumbled and began setting up a rowing machine.

I finished my run, said goodbye to the guy on my way out, and headed back to the room.

Someone had propped the door open with the little sliding lock gizmo, which meant I was welcome. I still knocked and called out before walking in.

"It's okay. Mitch is in the shower."

Teri reclined against the headboard on the bed closest to the bathroom. The bed was made, but not as neatly as by the staff.

"How was your workout?" she asked, glancing down at my sweat-soaked t-shirt and shorts.

"Good. How was yours?"

She threw a pillow at me.

"It was *very* good, if you must know," she said with a grin.

I caught the pillow and grinned back.

"Tell me to make myself scarce," I said. "I don't mind."

"If she won't, I will," Mitch said, coming out of the bathroom. "Who's next?"

I let Teri get in the shower while Mitch and I put together dinner. We had smoked salmon and fresh greens from Jungle Jim's. We tossed them in a quick vinaigrette. For dessert, we shaved 95% dark chocolate over frozen blueberries and cream.

"I think I'm going to Cahokia with you guys. After that, I might head to a big city like Los Angeles. Maybe Chicago."

"Why a big city?" Teri asked.

I was drying my hair and eating salad.

"A guy messaged me in NOLA about meeting him in Chicago. I get weird vibes from him, but I might do it. Also, I'd just like to see how many people actually spot me. Do people even look up anymore?"

"It would be one way to get into the news," Mitch said. "Hard to claim you faked security camera footage you never touched."

"Right," I said, thinking.

If I came out of hiding, allowed myself to be filmed, the FBI might go after my parents. Or worse, leave them as bait for the bad guys.

Before we left the next morning, Teri wanted to meditate. There was already someone using the fitness room, so we went outside. It was too early in the year for the pool to be open, but the surrounding deck was accessible.

We took cushions from the deck chairs and sat in a patch of sunlight.

"Do you do anything special when you meditate?" Teri asked.

"Not really. Focus on breath, feel the sensation of my skin over my body, let conscious thought stop. That's about it."

"I don't know what you just said," Mitch said.

"It's okay. Your Neanderthal DNA probably isn't conducive to meditation," Teri said sweetly.

He squatted down and rested his knuckles on the concrete, tilting his head quizzically.

"Sit down, ape-man," I said. "It's easy. Start with your hands. Even if they're sitting in your lap, they have sensation. Pay attention to it. Work your way up your arms until you can feel your entire body at the same time. It takes practice, but it allows you to be in the moment without thinking too much. It's a balancing act."

They settled down, and we meditated. Teri was still. Mitch, not so much. After fifteen minutes, he gave up.

"I'm going to load the car and check out," he said. "You girls done in the room?"

After he left, Teri apologized.

"No need," I said. "It's harder for some people."

"Can I ask you something?" Teri asked.

"Sure."

"You said you levitated with your mother. Could you do that here with me?"

I hesitated, and she sat back, holding up a hand.

"Never mind," she said. "That's too personal. I shouldn't have asked."

"No! No, it's not that. I don't know how it works, is all. And we're kind of in a public place."

"You're right. Forget I asked."

She was embarrassed, and at that point, I would have done anything to fix that. I reached over and took her hand. It was cool, and her fingers were long and slender.

"Wait," I said. "Let's try, okay? Back into the gap."

We closed our eyes and meditated, hands clasped loosely on our knees.

I opened my eyes, saw no one, and lifted us both into the air. We hovered maybe four inches in the air over our cushions, and I squeezed Teri's hands.

She opened her eyes, looked down, and immediately fell. I settled down on my cushion as she covered her face with her hands.

"Oh my gosh," she said. "You did it. We were floating! I can't believe it!"

I laughed.

"Well, that's what you wanted, right?"

"Yeah, but…I don't know. I didn't…."

"Didn't what? Didn't think it would work?"

"Kind of."

She zipped her jacket higher, and shuddered.

"We lost our sunbeam," she said.

I nodded.

"Are you okay?" I asked.

"Yeah. I just feel a little weird, you know?"

"More than you know. Are you going to tell Mitch?"

"You better believe it! I'm going to be zipping circles around his freckled butt so fast…."

I laughed.

"Baby steps, grasshopper," I said. "No zipping yet. Give it time. You don't know how long it might take. Don't rush yourself."

May 3

"I can't believe you levitated by yourself!"

"I know!" Teri squealed.

"Did you get hurt when you fell off the table?"

"She was fine," Mitch said before Teri could speak.

"I still have a lump on my head," Teri said, giving Mitch a hard stare, "while recovering from a concussion."

"Yeah, but it was mild. She was fine," Mitch said.

"Mitch was just happy for you," I said, attempting to smooth a touchy subject. "But you were doing it!" I said again, grabbing her and folding her into a hug.

Yesterday had been an easy day driving from Cincinnati to Cahokia. We had camped overnight, and I had gone for a run early the next morning. Teri had sat on a picnic table to watch the sunrise and meditate. When Mitch saw her rise off her cushion, he let out a "Whoop!" of excitement that brought Teri out of meditation and sent her falling to her cushion, where she lost her balance and fell off the table.

We talked for a while, standing on Monks Mound across the Mississippi River from St. Louis. It is the site of a vast ancient Native American city. The "king" of the city lived in a house at the top of the large mound, the largest earthwork in the world. There are many other, much smaller mounds scattered around the complex. Archaeologists had rebuilt part of the stockade wall and extensively excavated and rebuilt much of the site.

The view from the top of the mound was impressive. To the west, we could see all the way to St. Louis, the Gateway Arch and the skyscrapers behind it. Looking the other way, it seemed like we could see forever. I tried to imagine what the view would have been like for the kings and priests who lived here.

"Any advice?" Teri asked.

"Practice," I said. "Are you going to upload your video to the site?"

They looked at each other, an entire conversation happening behind their eyes.

"We'll have to talk about it," Mitch said finally, sighing. "Of course, we want to support you, but the danger from these creeps…" his voice trailed away.

I could only nod. Eventually, we climbed down the stairway and back to their car, where we ate before heading toward the museum.

We returned to the campsite as night fell.

"What's next?" Mitch asked as I worked on a jerky stew.

"Lots," I said, "In a way."

"What does that mean?" Teri asked.

"Today I found out that there are other people with gifts," I said. "I already knew that, kind of, but this is the first time I've had proof."

"So?" Mitch asked. "How does that change anything?"

"She's not alone," Teri said, reaching for my hand.

"No," I said, my voice husky. I took her hand and waited for a moment before going on.

"I'm not alone, not special, and not crazy. From the very beginning, I've thought about how to share this with other people. It seemed obvious the way to do that was over the internet."

"Right," Mitch said, nodding.

"But what if there's something…important…something significant about sharing in person?"

"Like what? Like that guru we watched splashing energy on people?"

"Kind of, I guess."

I had been tempted to laugh, watching that video with them the other day. But who knew? Could I judge something that was entirely outside of my experience? How was I any different from the people calling me a fraud?

"Teri levitated after practicing with me. That's significant somehow. It can't be a coincidence or happenstance, rather."

"What do you mean?" Teri asked.

"In geometry, coincidence is the exact matching of two angles — everything coming together perfectly from an infinity of possibilities. Happenstance is a chance occurrence. That you levitated before people who have been meditating and practicing on the site for months means something."

"Means what?" Mitch said.

"Yeah…I don't know. Am I 'flinging' energy or something? Seems far fetched. Maybe…."

I thought about the time years ago when my mom got contacts for the first time. I was in middle school and sat in a chair watching as an assistant helped teach her how to put them in. It was pretty straightforward, but Mom kept blinking and losing the contact, or folding it.

Finally, the assistant had put them in for her. After that, there were no problems. She could take them out, put them in, whatever. No further resistance. It was like her body just needed to know it was okay. She needed to experience it firsthand before she could do it.

I nodded to myself.

"I'm not ready to say there's no such thing as energy flinging," I said with a grin. "But I think it's more about the experience. Experience is more important than knowledge."

"How can it be more important?" Mitch asked.

"It's somehow at the center of this. I need to know more."

"What are you going to do?" Teri said. "Go off by yourself again?"

"I don't know. What do you think?" I asked.

We all fell silent and watched the flames dance along the wood of the campfire.

"I don't know," Mitch said. "I don't want to tell you the wrong thing and then have it blow up in your face."

Teri nodded.

"I think I might try to meet this guy in Chicago. It feels right."

"What's he saying?" Teri asked.

"Says he can help me keep the site up," I said. "He mentioned offering other help, but I don't know what that will be."

"You don't think he's a bad guy? FBI or Homeland?" Mitch asked.

"No idea."

"Could be a bad, bad guy, too," Teri said.

"So…what? We have good-bad guys and bad-bad guys now?" Mitch asked.

Teri shrugged and began dishing out the stew that simmered over the fire.

We ate in silence. I stayed centered and meditative, thankful for my friends and the meal.

"Yes," Teri finally said.

Mitch and I both looked at her, waiting for more.

She finally broke her stare away from the fire and looked at me.

"I think you should meet this guy. Find out if he's for real and get some help. It won't be long before someone goes after your site for real."

I nodded and looked at Mitch.

"What she said."

"Okay," I said, "I'll go into the city in the morning, find someplace to dive into the internet. I'll make the connection and get away."

I thought for a moment.

"Speaking of which," I said, "you two need to watch yourselves. You'll be on the radar now, after New Orleans and especially if you post your video. Both the Alliance and the FBI are watching you."

"Already talked about it," Mitch said. "We're not going into hiding. We'll head back home and do what we can to help."

"There's already another video of someone claiming to have levitated," Mitch said. "Did you see it?"

"No!" I said. "Wow. Did it look real?"

"I guess. The real ones look fake, and the fake ones look real, though. I don't know how to judge."

The next day, they drove me to St. Louis, where we found a coffee shop in the suburbs. It was hard to say goodbye, not knowing when we would see each other next. We became good friends in a short time.

I set my bags on the sidewalk and hugged them both, an arm around both of their necks. We didn't say much.

After they drove away, I ordered coffee, found a table, and fired up my laptop. I figured if I were lucky, I would have five minutes before someone found me.

Before I connected to the internet, I wrote an email to my parents reassuring them I was still okay and thanking them for keeping the site up. I also wrote an article for the site. It outlined what I had learned recently and what I was working on. I would put that one in the queue for posting later.

I wrote a second article introducing Mitch and Teri and welcoming them as moderators. In it, I gave them my full confidence to run chat rooms, make comments, etc. Privately, I hoped they could keep the energy of the site up in my absence.

I connected to the cafe's wireless.

It took 30 seconds to cut and paste the email to my parents. Maybe 30 seconds each for the two blogs. I didn't take the time to tag everything the way I usually do.

It took two minutes to find the address for TS, the guy who said he could help keep the site up. I finally found it and dashed off a quick reply, accepting his offer. I hit "Send" and checked my watch.

Five minutes had gone. I glanced at the door. I didn't see anyone through the windows who looked suspicious.

The coffee shop was in a suburban shopping center with narrow, curving roads. My original thought was that it would make it harder for anyone to follow me. I realized that it would also allow someone to get very close without being obvious.

I refreshed my email; nothing yet. My heart was pounding, and my hands were shaking. I needed to leave, but I didn't know when I might check email again.

Would he reply quickly?

Did he check his email?

Ten minutes gone and still no suspicious cars that I could see.

I refreshed my email again. This time, it was there! I opened it.

May 10, Adler Planetarium, 1:00 pm.

I knew the place. It was near the Shedd Aquarium and Soldier Field in Chicago.

I emailed back.

See you there.

I didn't power down, just closed my laptop, stuffed it in my bag, and headed for the door. Just as I slid my trash in the bin, I glanced up and saw two men in suits exiting an ugly sedan in front of the coffee shop. I froze.

"Is everything okay, ma'am?" the girl behind the counter asked.

"Hm? Oh…yes."

The men headed for the door as another car sped into the lot, not bothering to park inside the lines. Three men and a woman got out. One man held a phone to his ear and watched the door; the other three fanned out, keeping watch in all directions.

"Um… restrooms?" I asked the girl.

"Around the corner," she pointed to my left.

I turned the corner. There were two restrooms and a door that said: Employees Only. I opened the "Employees" door.

There was no one, just boxes stacked on the floor, and shelves of paper products and cleaning supplies. I stepped to the end of the shelves and poked my head around. To my right, there was the back of the counter area; to my left, a desk, and more shelves. There was a green exit sign above the desk pointing to the right.

I dashed around the corner, sliding my arm through the strap on my duffel, and saw the rear entrance. Hoping that there wasn't an alarm, I began clearing my mind. I hit the crash bar and was airborne before I was clear of the doorway.

Shooting upward, I grabbed the edge of the roof and slid down over the short wall. I didn't hear an alarm. Gravel crunched under my hands and knees as I crept around the rooftop and looked out. The man by the car, an FBI agent, I assumed, was still on the phone. There were raised voices, and he looked right at me.

He pointed and began yelling.

"Roof! She's on the roof!"

Praying that these were only good-bad guys, I cleared my mind and jumped into the air. I shot up fast, right over the broken layer of fluffy cumulus just a few thousand feet above the ground. I headed west, away from the direction I wanted to travel. Earlier that morning, I had stashed my backpack near the showers at the campground. I would have to circle around and pick it up before deciding what to do for the next week until my meeting.

So, did the whole thing start with moving back to Mom and Dad's, or did it start here the first time I levitated? Or did it start when I was a kid and Mom gave me books on meditation to read during the week, and then took me to Sunday school on the weekends?

I honestly don't know. Anyway, here's the story.

∼

Excerpt from the blog: *Griffin's Flight*

MAY 13, 2024

People don't just levitate. It doesn't happen. Except, apparently, sometimes it does.

I walked to my meditation spot this morning at my usual time. I had to be in the fields by 7:00 am, so I was in the woods at 6:00. Sunlight burst through the canopy of leaves and streamed into the clearing. The trees are that shade of green you only see in late spring and early summer.

I found this spot last fall when chasing an escaped pig. He had led me through the fields and woods and finally became tangled in the undergrowth at the edge of the clearing. After I disentangled him, I looked around and marked the place in my memory.

I began coming when the ground dried up in the spring. There was grass, but no trees. Why? Deer, maybe. They might keep the grass grazed down. Not sure.

I carry a thick horse blanket over my shoulder on the walk through the fields and woods. I put it down on the ground and rolled it out. The grass wasn't tall, but it was too tall to sit in without getting covered in bugs. I shuddered to think of trying to meditate with spiders crawling over my hands.

The blanket is just enough. With that and a small pillow to raise my hips, I can relax. From my meditation spot to my left, I can just make out the sound of the occasional car. It's not a busy road, but it's only about a quarter of a mile away through trees and a field. To my right, the woods continue for a few thousand feet. Past that, there's another pasture and then more woods. I rarely hear anything from that direction.

Behind me, the hill climbs before it peaks and starts going down again. There's gravel under the soil, deposited by glaciers 11,000 years ago, give or take. Below me, the hill falls away to a small stream. That stream finds its way to the river, then to another river, making its way to the Ohio River, the Mississippi, and eventually the Gulf of Mexico and the oceans of the world. I thought about that today as I prepared to meditate. I was connected to the entire planet.

Settling down onto my meditation pillow, I began, as usual, by putting my attention on my breath. I'm used to letting go of my thoughts by now. Leaving my thoughts behind is as simple as shrugging off a jacket. I just let them fall away, to be picked back up later.

My eyes stay open a little, and I let my gaze fall onto the blanket. With my eyes nearly closed, I can usually stay awake. Sometimes I fall asleep, but not often anymore. I rest my gaze on the blanket, focus on the pattern of warp and weft, and my breathing becomes shallow and even. Sound surrounds me, and I meditate.

Without thinking in words, I slid my attention to my feet and hands, then up to my legs and arms, my head and my whole body. I felt it all at the same time. Birds and insects sang and hummed, while tree branches creaked in the light breeze. The creek at the bottom of the hill burbled over stones and around bends. Cloud shadows crawled over my clearing occasionally. Time passed, and I was barely me anymore. During meditation, I became connected to the woods, a part of the world, part of the solar system, galaxy, and universe.

My body is the universe. The same. I inhabit my body just as I inhabit the world. My identity fell away, and I almost felt like singing. Or maybe I was. Maybe every cell, every molecule, every particle of my being was singing along with the universe.

Eventually, I realized that my mouth was dry and reached for my water bottle, trying not to think about it. It was part of me, too, the water bottle. Just another part.

I couldn't find it. It wasn't there. Where was it?

That question, that thought, brought me slightly out of my meditative state, back into time and space. I inhaled and glanced to my right, where I knew the bottle was.

It wasn't. In fact, nothing was. Not "nothing" exactly, but nothing was right. Everything looked wrong, and my mind was not comprehending what my eyes were seeing. The interpreting left brain was turned off, not responding.

"Where," I croaked, trying to jumpstart my brain, knowing my meditation would likely end, "is my water…" I went on. About this time is when my left brain woke up and told me what it was seeing.

"…bottle?"

No way.

I saw the ground as if I were standing. Had I stood during meditation without realizing it? That would be weird, and somewhat disturbing. I looked at my feet, which were still crossed in front of me.

No.

I suddenly felt ill. As my stomach lurched, I felt like I was falling. The rushing-down feeling was familiar to me. It was like waking up from a falling dream, or a flying dream. Only I didn't wake up wondering who I was. My hips hit my pillow, and my legs hit the ground. I felt a jolt go through my spine, and I crashed forward into the grass.

I unfolded my legs, rolled over, and closed my eyes.

Deep breath in, hold. Deep breath out, hold.

Okay, what just happened? What did I see?

I opened my eyes.

Wait, did I just dream…was I asleep?

I looked at the trees, at the angle of the sun. Almost no time had passed since I began meditation. So, what the hell just happened?

I sat up and reached automatically for the water bottle beside me. It was there, right where it was supposed to be.

If it was there the whole time, either I was dead asleep, or…I was…was not… no. I wasn't. It's not possible. 'Asleep' has to be it, I thought.

I looked around my little clearing. This was an average second- or third-growth wood, not a "forest temple" of old-growth trees. I'm just an ordinary person, not a spiritual master or monk.

What the hell? People don't just…levitate.

I sat and tried to rationalize the experience for several minutes before trying to meditate again. There was a brief sense of connectedness like before, but faint, like an echo. I watched the feeling slide away from me like one of the cloud shadows over the field.

So here I am, sitting at my computer instead of starting my workday with my dad. I'm trying to rationalize something that doesn't make sense. There are two possibilities: either I hallucinated and am very unwell, or levitation is a real thing. I can go to a doctor to determine whether I am ill or crazy.

But if levitation is real, then it's repeatable, and I have to prove it.

Seven

MAY 6

I flew into the canyon from the south. Desert gave way to red rock walls, gorgeous striations, and wildlife. I had been flying and camping for two days, feeling drawn to the canyon. I wasn't sure exactly why, but I needed to be here.

On the whole, it's against the law for aircraft to operate in the Grand Canyon, but there are occasional exceptions. Helicopters fly there regularly, and sometimes photographers receive special permission.

So, I wasn't too concerned about air traffic, but the weather could be unpredictable. Air currents could push me up out of the canyon, against a rock wall, or even dash me against the floor of the canyon before I could react. I needed to stay calm and listen to Guidance.

I couldn't see much of the rim. If people were in the area, I doubted I would stand out in my green shirt and khakis. But I tried to stay in the shadows as much as possible. I flew lazily, allowing myself to take in the canyon's beauty, the stark aridity of some parts, the lush green of others.

I became willfully lost, allowing intuition to guide me.

Landing near a small village beside a brilliant blue lake, I left my bigger pack among some boulders and walked toward the water.

"Hello there," a voice said.

I turned and saw a young man walking toward me.

"Hi."

"Visitors need to register ahead of time," he said, holding out a hand.

I took it. It was firm and dry.

"Just, um, hiking around. Got kind of lost."

I was uncomfortable lying. He glanced at my boots and then back up at me.

"Okay."

I looked down and saw that my boots were too clean to claim that I was hiking in the Grand Canyon.

"Thirsty?" he asked as he turned and waved for me to follow him. "Come on. Gran wants to see you."

I followed, wondering who "Gran" was and how she knew I was there. He led me toward the lake, in the opposite direction from the village. We walked less than five minutes and came around a stand of cottonwoods. There sat a house between us and the lake.

"You should know this isn't public land. It belongs to the tribe. I'm Ethan, by the way," the young man said, climbing the steps to a porch that wrapped around the house. He knelt and dipped water into a metal cup from a stoneware jar and held it out to me.

"Liv," I said, taking the water. "Thanks. I didn't mean to trespass."

"No worries. You must have missed the signs hiking in. Grandmother!" Ethan called through the screened window. "Want us to come in?"

"I heard you walk up," a voice grumbled. "Just give me a minute."

"She'll be right out. More water?" Ethan asked, seeing that I had emptied the cup.

"Sure, thanks."

I turned and leaned on the porch rail. The view was beautiful. I was used to humid summers, corn and bean fields. The heat and dry air made the red rock vista stunning.

"What an impressive setting for the house," I said, taking the cup from Ethan with a nod.

"Thanks. The water view is over here."

I followed him around the corner and saw the ground slope gently away toward the lake below. The area was lush, contrasting sharply with the blue of the water and red of the rock walls behind it.

"Oh my," I said, stunned.

"It's something, isn't it?" the voice of the old woman asked from behind me.

"Breathtaking!"

I turned to greet her. She stooped slightly and walked with a cane. Her hair, once black, was now mostly gray, and her face, despite the deeply carved lines, was beautiful.

I hesitated and held out my hand.

"I'm Liv," I said.

Rather than shaking hands, she took my right hand in her left and led me to the end of the porch and two rocking chairs. She stood in front of one and motioned for me to take the other. Ethan sat on the floor.

"So," she said after we were situated. She rocked and stared at me for several moments.

"I'm Liv," I repeated.

"Yes, I'm old, not deaf. Just call me Gran. Everyone does."

"Gran. It's a pleasure to meet you."

"Likewise, likewise."

We sat in silence for several minutes. I watched what might have been eagles circling over the trees and fishing the lake. I looked back at Ethan, and he appeared to be observing me. It was a little uncomfortable.

I looked back at Gran, and she, too, seemed to be patiently watching me. I tried to go back to the scenery, but I couldn't get past the weirdness of being silently evaluated.

"Um, well," I tried to think of a graceful way to exit, "I think I'll get going now."

"Not yet," Gran said. Ethan smiled.

"Oh...okay."

"Don't start worrying. You're safe enough here. I want to get to know you, is all."

I set the empty cup down on the table between us.

"Okay," I said after a pause. "Well, I'm Liv, like I said. I'm from Indiana, where it's very flat, humid, and most farmers grow corn and soybeans."

"And what do you do?" Gran asked.

"I help my dad on his farm."

"Cool," Ethan said. "You have cows and stuff?"

"Yeah, cows, pigs, horses…" I said.

"No," Gran said, "I mean, what do you *do*?"

"Um…well, I'm a student when I have the time."

"What do you do?"

"I'm afraid I don't understand. My name is Olivia. I'm a college student who works on my dad's farm. I'm a martial artist and take yoga. There's not much else."

"How does a college student who does nothing get here with no hat, no jeep, and no dust on her boots or pant legs?" Ethan asked.

"Oh…well…I mean…." I tried to find something logical that didn't sound crazy.

"Ethan, for example, is a healer. He's new to his gift, but it's coming along."

"A healer?" I asked, looking from Gran to Ethan. He looked down.

"Gran is the healer. Not me."

"You're a healer?" I asked, turning to the old woman.

"I allow healing," she said and looked out over the water. "But you, Olivia from Indiana. What do you do?"

"I…I guess," I hesitated. "Um, I mean…I guess I fly."

Ethan's eyes opened wide.

"You can fly?"

"Yeah," I said. I was suddenly shy. It was a terribly hard thing to say out loud.

"I thought so," Gran said. "I can smell the hawks on you. How are you doing with it?"

"Oh, not so bad," I said. "I'm getting better."

"Are you listening?"

"Um…yeah. Yes, I'm listening," I said, confused.

"I don't mean to me," she said as Ethan snorted.

"I mean," she reached out and touched one finger to my sternum, "are you listening?"

Even though Gran had withdrawn her hand, I could still feel where her finger had tapped my chest.

"I'm getting better at that, too."

"Practice. It's more important than flying. You need to *hear* if you want to survive."

"I don't understand."

"If you don't understand, then you're not listening."

"Okay, well, I'm listening to you, Gran. Maybe you could fill me in?"

She smiled and leaned back in her chair, rocking gently.

Ethan shook his head and smiled.

"She does that to me all the time. Likes to be enigmatic."

"Like? It's nothing to do with like," Gran said, scowling at the young man. Then she scowled up at me.

"What happened to your face?" Gran asked, tilting her head to see the bruise on my cheek.

I raised my hand to it absentmindedly.

"Oh, a guy hit me with a rifle."

"Ouch," Ethan said, standing on his knees to get a better look.

"Yeah, hurt like a bi…I mean, it hurt a lot."

Gran just smiled.

"Have you been to a doctor? Had x-rays?" Ethan asked.

"No. Not really an option," I said.

"No," Gran said. "Not for most of us, either."

She raised a hand, taking in the village south of the lake.

"Come on over here."

She stood and waved to my right.

There was a sturdy table on that side of the broad porch, and I hopped onto it, butterflies dancing in my stomach. Gran stepped up and poked at my cheekbone. She surprised me by reaching for my left shoulder as well.

"Hm. You already took care of this one, didn't you?"

"This one? What do you mean?"

"Feels like a mended fracture here," she said, sliding two fingers over my left clavicle.

"I crashed into a flagpole or something the other night. I kind of forgot about it."

Gran lifted her chin, frowned, and grunted.

"Tell me how you fly."

"I don't know. It just started happening."

"No, *something* 'just happened.' You probably levitated. You didn't start out just accidentally flying across the country."

"Yeah. Right. I floated off the ground while I was meditating. Thought I was going crazy for a while."

She smiled and nodded.

"Meditation. Tell me how that works."

"I practice Zen. It's hard to explain. It starts with concentration, but ends with whatever the opposite of that is. You move from focusing intently on one thing to focusing on nothing."

Gran smacked Ethan with the back of her hand and pointed to me.

"That," she said.

Ethan sighed.

She traded places with him in front of me.

"Start with your breath," she said. "No thought. Give thanks for your intellect, then release it and breathe. Focus on your breath. While your intellect sleeps, remain thankful. Accept the perfection of the moment. Healing hides in the perfect now."

I looked from Gran to Ethan and said nothing. Instead, I closed my eyes and meditated along with him. Shadows shifted around us, but I didn't open my eyes. The breeze carried the scent of the lake and the sound of the eagles calling.

I felt fingers brush my bruised cheek and heard Gran humming.

"That will feel better soon," Gran whispered at last.

I inhaled and opened my eyes. It's a good idea to come out of meditation slowly, so I rolled my neck a few times and loosened my shoulders before I looked around. I reached up and found the swelling in my cheek diminished. The pain was still there.

"Thank you," I said, and practiced moving my jaw. It felt better.

"Which of you did that?"

"I could ask the same thing," Gran said.

"Me too," Ethan said.

"I don't know anything about healing," I said.

"Me neither," Ethan said.

Gran waved both hands at us in mock disgust and went back to the rocking chair.

~

E than and I walked down to the lake.

"So, are there many people who can do things here?"

"No. Gran's not Professor X. It's mostly about tourism here."

I smiled and nodded, thinking.

"So, healing. How does that work?"

His expression clouded.

"For me? Mostly, it doesn't."

He picked up a piece of the red limestone and threw it out over the water.

"I've been around Gran most of my life. She was a nurse in the army. The people she sat with, prayed with, they got better faster."

I nodded.

"When she came home, she kept helping people. That's what she does."

"And you?" I asked.

"I'm not as good at helping as she is. Like with you, Gran tells me to listen."

He looked at me and touched his chest.

"Yeah," I said.

"But there's nothing to hear!" he said, his voice rising, his hands sweeping up in a circle.

I looked for the eagles, but they were gone.

"Sorry."

He turned and made his way along the edge of the lake.

"Don't be," I said. "I feel your frustration."

I caught up to him.

"Gran probably does too."

"She's getting old," he said, his voice quiet now. "I don't know how much time I have left with her."

"We never know," I said. "Any of us could die in our sleep tonight."

"I know. But I think about it all the time. What if I don't get this by the time she passes over? Will I ever?"

I quieted my mind and breathed for a moment. Then I stopped and took Ethan's shoulder.

"What was that she said? *Allow healing.*"

"Yeah. That's what she says. Doesn't help."

I released his shoulder, and he cocked his head, looking at me.

"What about you? How do you fly?"

"The same," I said. "I have to be quiet up here," I touched my head, "and listen here," I touched my chest.

"And you just fly when you meditate?"

"Yes, and no. There's a little more to it."

I told him the story of how it had started, how I needed to remember the feeling to generate the motion.

"Here, watch," I said.

I levitated and moved a few feet out over the water. His jaw dropped.

"Whoah!"

"To move, I just think about moving."

"Does it work for anyone?"

"I don't know. I've never healed anyone. Does that work for anyone?"

"No idea."

I stepped back onto the bank, and we continued chatting. They had dodgy internet access on the reservation, but he promised to read my blog when he got the chance. I said I would come back and visit soon.

"I'll be here," he said.

"I need to be on my way," I said. The shadows were deepening, but there was still daylight up above.

"Can you tell Gran goodbye for me?"

"Will do," he said, taking my hand in his. "Take care, Liv."

I reclaimed my duffel and began making my way back east.

∼

Excerpt from the blog: *Griffin's Flight*

NOVEMBER 27, 2025

After Thanksgiving dinner, Dad and I sat down with Mom. We took the door off the wood-burning stove, watched the fire, and talked.

"What have you been up to lately, Liv?" Mom asked. "You spend a lot of time alone in your apartment."

"Mostly reading and writing. I started a blog about the things I'm studying. Spiritual stuff. You know."

"May I read it?"

Dad and I glanced at each other. Could it really be this easy?

"Mom, it's very personal. I mean, it's up on the web and everything, but there are things there that will be hard for you to read."

She considered me for a moment.

"I understand if you don't want me to read it. You can't share everything with your mother after all."

"Mom, I would *love* for you to read it. Dad's read some of it. It will just be hard. Okay?"

I was making a mess of things.

"Let me think about it. I need to do the dishes."

"Mom, no. I'll do the dishes. Dad can bring the blog up on your computer."

She spread her hands out on her lap and sat looking at them. She looked up at my father.

"Nothing to fear," he said. "You know your girl. There's nothing bad, just…unexpected."

She looked at me and cocked her head.

"You're still gay, aren't you?"

Dad laughed.

"Jesus, Mom. Yes."

"Okay. Let's get on with this."

I cleared the table and started washing dishes. Dad and Mom had the laptop in the family room. I had butterflies in my stomach again, waiting.

I had the kettle on in case anyone wanted tea. The table was clean, and I had replaced Mom's bowl of fruit. I was at the sink finishing the pots and pans when they came in. I washed my hands and turned around.

Mom was pale and sat at the table with her hands in her lap, not looking at anything in particular. Dad looked at me and gave a slight shrug. He sat down beside Mom. I got mugs, spoons, a box of chamomile, and honey. I put the kettle on a hot pad and sat down with them.

"So," I started.

Mom glanced at me and then fixed her gaze on the fruit.

"Tea?" I asked.

"Please," Dad said.

I put the tea bags in their cups and poured water over them. I slid the honey over.

Mom still said nothing.

I needed something to do, so I made myself a mug of tea.

Why isn't Mom saying anything?

Eventually, she came around. When she started talking, she was angry with me (and Dad) for keeping her in the dark. She was angry about reading it instead of us telling her. She was angry that other people had read it first.

"I'm sorry, Mom. Next time I have momentous news, I'll bring it to you first."

"I certainly hope so," she said, not a bit mollified.

When Mom's hands stopped shaking, I took them to the field behind the barn and gave them a little aerobatic show. Dad had seen the scar in the cornfield where I had crash landed before harvest. We said nothing about that to Mom, but I think she guessed.

I told them about touching Air Force One and nearly being seen by the jets. Told them about the emergency parachute I bought for long flights. I showed them my leather flight suit, helmet, and goggles. And I explained the training I was taking in aviation ground school so I could learn about navigation, meteorology, and aviation regulations.

I told them how careful I usually was, leaving out some of my more boneheaded mistakes.

I wanted to tell them everything would be okay, but with the near-misses and accidents I had already had, I couldn't do that. Instead, I told them how I had made plans for my blog to be updated with all the newer information on a regular schedule. I explained how I had backed it up just in case something ever happened to me. The information, all of my writing, videos, and photos, would be safe.

I hoped I wouldn't need the redundancies and precautions I was taking, but there was no sense in taking chances.

My heart melted a little when my mother shyly asked if I could give her a ride.

"A ride? Mom, I'm not Superman. I don't know if I can support your weight."

"Oh," she said. Nothing else.

Dad looked away and squinted. He didn't agree with something, but wouldn't say anything.

"It's okay, Liv," she said at last. "I saw you fly. I just wondered how it felt."

Something about the way she said that… it got to me. I choked up. I'd never been able to do something that my mom couldn't. Her acknowledgment of that was an incredibly deep kind of acceptance that meant everything to me.

"Okay," I said, "Look, I've never done this before, but let's try."

She said nothing, just waited, never taking her eyes off me. Dad stood back and crossed his arms over his chest, almost as if he were standing guard or something.

I held out my hands, and she took them tentatively. I lowered my eyes and allowed my thoughts to drop away. As I entered the gap, I became acutely aware of my entire body, but especially my fingers lightly touching hers.

Her scream snapped my head up. I felt my feet hit the ground with a mild thump. Mom stumbled back, and Dad caught her under the arms, keeping her from falling.

"I'm sorry, but that was the strangest feeling!" she said. "Walter, you try!"

"Oh, no. I'm just fine down here," my father said.

"Not even a little?" she asked.

"It's okay, Mom. You and I can keep practicing."

"Well, I'll think about it," she said. "I might be okay here on the ground, too."

"You sure?" I asked. "Your next trip to Chicago could be something special."

"Ha!" she laughed. "No, Liv. We'll leave that to you. I might practice meditating more, but I'm okay traveling the old-fashioned way."

Eight

MAY 10

Indiana, my home state, is famous for being flat and uninteresting. The thing is, it's not really. The area west of Indianapolis, which a lot of tourists fly into, is flat. Okay, and maybe a little boring. Much of I-65 from Chicago to Indy is relatively bland, too. But there are areas of rolling countryside tucked away that you won't discover unless you get off the interstate.

As I flew north toward Chicago, I was struck by how beautiful it was. Of course, I wanted to fly over my folks' house, just to see it again, but intuition (and logic) told me it was a bad idea. So, I followed the rivers up from St. Louis, and when I got to Terre Haute, I headed north like a good girl.

Hundreds of little lakes, ponds, and streams dotted the landscape. I flew above a broken cumulus layer to stay as dry as possible. I had learned that flying too fast, too close to clouds, caused me to leave a condensation trail, like the ones that jet fighters pull off their wingtips in high-velocity maneuvers. That sort of thing is counterproductive to stealth. I traveled slowly, took my time, and enjoyed the scenery.

After I escaped from the FBI the week before, I had been bouncing around the country, visiting caves, mounds, and other Native American sites. I still watched for other air traffic but found that intuition and my physical senses told me when aircraft were around. I was no longer obsessed with midair collisions.

Finally, Lake Michigan was ahead, and I could barely make out the Chicago skyline in the haze. I gained a little altitude so that I could increase speed and covered the distance in less than five minutes.

It was almost summer, and the lake was busy. Despite being a weekday, there were sailboats of all kinds on the water. So many, in fact, I wasn't sure I could make it to the lakeshore unseen.

I hovered a couple of miles offshore, just below the clouds. It was unseasonably warm, and the good people of Chicago packed the beaches. I could make out the Shedd Aquarium, Adler Planetarium, and to the south, there was a park.

That might be the place to stow my gear.

There was a stiff breeze from the south, and the water was rough. I dropped until I was just skimming the waves and flew toward the park. As I got closer, huge pink granite blocks formed a rough wall south of the beach area. I headed for those blocks and landed. There was nobody around.

I took my small bag with money, phone, computer, and a change of clothes, and stashed the rest of my stuff where it would, hopefully, remain safe and unseen. I stepped cautiously around the wall and made my way up the gravel bank.

To my right, there were chunks of concrete that made a breakwater. Farther inland was an area that looked wild and overgrown. Between the blocks and the overgrown area was a concrete walkway. I stepped carefully around the granite blocks and made my way towards it.

L ocked gates aren't a significant deterrent when you can fly. The one in front of me was exceptionally sturdy, fitted to a chunky post with a six-foot chain-link fence to my left, and to the right... nothing. The fence had come completely loose from the posts. I laughed, stepped around the gate and onto the walkway.

The path on the left wandered deeper into a reclaimed wilderness area. Under other circumstances, I would have gone that way, but for the first time in a long time, I had an appointment. I headed right, towards the city.

Staying close to the lake, I left the walk and passed onto a vast lawn bordered with trees and tall grass on the lakeside. The smell of burning marijuana and the sound of laughter filtered through the vegetation. Paths led through the brush, lined with paper litter and old beer cans.

I continued up the hill towards an outdoor concert stage. A path led to the right, between the stage and the beach. I walked along, wondering what it might be like during the winter. For now, though, people packed the park, and the beach was full. The sun and mild temperatures had apparently drawn the city dwellers here to relax and enjoy time together.

Farther ahead, the dome of the planetarium rose through the trees. Adler was an art déco building built a century ago, the first planetarium in the western hemisphere. Recently, they had built a modern steel-and-glass addition facing the lake. I wished I had time to go inside. I ambled up to the building and ran my hand over the smooth granite surface.

"There's something about touch, isn't there?"

I turned towards the woman speaking. She was older than me, perhaps my mother's age, tall and slender with short salt and pepper hair. She extended her hand, and I glanced at it before we shook.

"I'm Sheila." Her voice wasn't deep, but melted over me with the richness that travel and education seem to confer.

"Er, hi. I'm…" I hesitated, not sure if I should use my real name.

"You're Olivia," she said, releasing my hand.

I started in fear, almost took off right there.

"Touch," she repeated. "You can tell a lot by touching something."

She looked up toward the dome of the building.

"Or someone."

"Who are you?" I asked, hitching my bag higher on my shoulder in case I needed to move fast.

"What did your touch tell you?" she asked, looking back at me.

"What?"

"When we shook hands, what did our touch tell you?"

"Nothing."

"Then," she grinned, "you weren't paying attention."

Sheila turned and walked around the building toward the lake. I glanced around. No one showed any interest in us - in me. Sensing no immediate danger, I followed her out of curiosity as much as anything.

"Better," she said as I came up beside her. "You listen to intuition, at least."

"How do you know that?"

"Because I listen to mine."

I sighed. I kept walking into that line.

"So, who are you?" I asked again.

"I'm Sheila." She took a big step down from the grass onto the walkway that followed the perimeter of the building. I followed, hopping down with both feet. Sheila continued strolling around Adler toward the Shedd Aquarium, maybe a quarter of a mile to the west.

"Sheila, yeah. You said that, but I still don't know who you are."

"If you had paid attention, you'd know that I'm...like you," Sheila said, inclining her head toward me.

"Like me?" My gut tightened, and I thought about running again.

"No, that's not intuition. That's ego telling you to run."

"I know," I said, my mind spinning. Was she reading my mind like Kim? I thought back to that conversation and how he seemed to know what I was thinking before I did.

She walked along, hands in jacket pockets. I scrutinized her. She looked and sounded American, but spoke with that odd, nearly British cadence of Hollywood in the forties. She had a lean, wiry look of a distance runner.

"Can we sit down? Do you mind?"

"Not at all."

We sat on the wall and looked out at the sailboats. Sheila leaned over, elbows on knees, hands clasped. Occasionally, an airplane passed overhead, towing a huge advertising banner.

"So," I began, "like me?"

"Yes, I've been on the path a while longer," Sheila said with a smile, "but we're basically the same."

"And what path is that?"

"Discovery? Spiritual innovation? Life? Everyone has their own name for it. We all come to the path from different beginnings. Yours was levitation. Excellent job, by the way. Mine was business."

Business?

"I know," she said, holding up a hand as if to intercept my question. "I learned to create products, deal with people, and solve problems intuitively. Of course, when I was young, I worked the usual way, but I always felt empty. I had a husband, kids and my business, but life felt dull and uninteresting. Futile, I suppose."

I could relate to that, despite not having a family of my own. I nodded.

"Eventually, I learned about meditation and tried it. It provided me with something that prayer never did. Instead of just speaking to a hypothetical God, I was listening. It changed everything."

"So, you think intuition comes from God?"

Sheila turned, smiled, and gave a kind of sideways nod.

"God, Allah, Grandfather, Universal Intelligence, whatever term you like. I'm kind of *old school.*"

"I've met other people like me," I said.

Like us?

"Have you?" she asked.

"Well, not exactly like me, but other…special people."

I cringed internally as I said the words.

"You think you're special, do you?" she asked, a smile playing at the corners of her mouth.

"Okay, no. Not special, but I'm different from…" I swept my arm to include the other people enjoying the sunshine along the lakeshore.

"We're just people. All of us."

A man, maybe in his sixties, touched my shoulder and held his hand out for me to shake.

"Pleasure to meet you, Ms. Donnelly." He moved on, and a woman, again, maybe my mother's age, reached for my hand with both of hers.

"So nice to meet you," she said and held my hand close. Her hands were warm, despite the breeze. She smiled, and it felt like the sun got a little brighter.

I looked, and there were 15 or 20 people, all dressed similarly to Sheila. They were smiling; some waved. I frowned, lifted my hand and tentatively returned their gesture.

I glanced at Sheila, and the man and woman were gone. When I turned, the others I had seen were gone as well. My mind boggled.

"What…who were those people?"

"Just other ordinary people like you and me. People who are on the Path."

"But where did they go?" I asked, standing and looking around as if they might have hidden nearby.

"I don't know for certain. Wherever they like."

My hands were shaking, and my stomach was in knots. I felt like getting away from this extraordinary woman. She was nothing like Gran, who, despite being stern, had been gentle, or at least likeable.

"Okay," I said, trying to keep my voice from quavering, "Okay, I get it. We're not special."

"No, we're not. We have the same *potential* as everyone else."

"Okay, we put our attention on different things," I said, sitting again. "We practice differently from most people."

"That's it exactly! I wish I had studied a martial art sooner. It makes you a better student."

I felt my ego flare up at the compliment, then ignored it, and looked out over the lake.

"So, what business are you in?" I asked, looking back at Sheila.

"None. Not anymore."

"Oh, you look young to be retired."

She chuckled and said, "Looks can be deceiving, my friend."

I frowned.

"Well, maybe you're older than you look, but you still seem too young to retire."

"Maybe so. But I never said I'm retired. I'm a teacher now."

"Oh, here in Chicago?"

"No, not a schoolteacher. I am the unofficial principal of a school for people on the path."

"Really?" I asked, interested. "Where is it? What's it like?"

"It's not so much about a place, although many of us like the South Pacific. The school is nothing like you would imagine. The students are all older than you."

"Older? I'm not *that* young."

"No? Would it surprise you to learn there is no one in our school under 35, and few under 50 years old?"

"What? Why?"

"Because people must *live* before they understand that there is more to life than what we see."

She waved a hand toward the Chicago skyline on our left.

"These people, they get caught up in ego and never really get to work on their spiritual lives."

"There are spiritual people, though."

"Yes, there are."

"Well? What about them?"

"Tell me, at your martial art school, does everyone practice as much as you?"

I flashed back to my conversation with Teri and Mitch.

"No, I have more time than most."

"Maybe," she said. "Are there people who don't practice at all?"

"I don't know. I'm not with them all the time."

"Eh," she scoffed, "you know what I mean."

She was right. Some students rarely, if ever, practiced. They never improved. Their forms and techniques always looked the same, no matter how long they trained.

"So you're saying that spiritual people don't practice their spirituality?"

"Right. How can you tell?"

"Because they never change, never try anything new."

She sighed.

"An epidemic as real as any virus."

"What's that?"

"Belief. Specifically, the belief that we've arrived, and that we have the answers. That there's nothing left to learn."

She leaned forward and rose to her feet.

"Everything is here, at our fingertips. We just need to open our hands."

She reached out, opened her hand, and there was a small, perfect apple sitting in the middle of her palm, as if created in the moment she opened her hand. She held it out, offering the apple to me.

"How did you…was that…magic?" I asked.

"What? I thought you were a smart kid," she said, looking at me doubtfully.

"What do you mean?" I asked, almost offended.

"Oh, were you making a joke?" she asked. "Sometimes I can't tell with young people."

"A joke? No, I mean, you just…."

"Let me see your phone," she interrupted, looking around.

"My ph… okay," I said, standing and reaching into the inside pocket of my jacket where I kept my mom's iPhone. I held it out to her. "But it's not turned on."

"That's okay. Hurry! No one's looking," Sheila said, taking it and gesturing around us.

I turned. Everyone appeared to be looking behind us to the south.

"Here, fetch!" she said, giving a heave and throwing my phone far out over the lake.

"Are you crazy?"

I didn't think. I jumped out over the water, flew as fast as I could, did the *Harry Potter* thing and snatched my phone just as it was about to hit the water, then jetted back to stand beside Sheila.

"What the *hell* was that?" I hissed, looking around to see if anyone noticed.

She manufactured a look of mock incredulity.

"How did you do that?" she asked, grasping my shoulder. "Are you magic?"

"You know I'm not," I said, brushing her hand away. I wanted to walk away, wanted to collect my gear and get as far away from her as I could.

"How many laws of physics did you just break?" she asked in her normal voice.

"What? I don't know."

"A lot?"

"Yeah, a lot."

I stuffed my phone back inside my coat.

"So, those are the only laws that are breakable? We can't break others?" she asked.

"I…you mean…" I started, but several thoughts at once overwhelmed me. I sat down again.

Sailboats trundled along on the lake, oblivious.

What was she saying? Gravity, inertia, mass, conservation, thermodynamics… none of it mattered? That simply wasn't possible. My mind boggled, and I felt nauseous. Elbows on knees, I dropped my head into my hands.

"All of them," she said, sitting beside me, "We control everything. Everything that we want."

"How old are you?" I asked, raising my head slightly.

"Rude!" she exclaimed in mock indignation.

"Forgive me. Seriously, how old?"

"Nearly 90 years old," she answered quietly.

"You don't age?"

"We do, but age does not render us infirm. It simply makes us more powerful. The more we understand, the more we practice, the more control we have."

"Control? Did you 'control' people to make them look away?"

"Liv, no," she said, holding up a hand, "Control over our environment, over processes, *not* over people. They looked away because something interesting was happening. I sensed the synchronicity and tapped into it."

"So, the apple," I said, thinking out loud, "you just…willed it into your hand?"

"Eh," she lifted both hands palms-up, "sort of. What about levitation? Do you will yourself into the air?"

"Not at all," I said, thinking of Gran, "I allow myself to levitate. It's there. I just let it lift me up."

"Just so. Likewise, the apple was there. I *allowed* it into my hand."

I looked at my right hand and stretched it out in front of me.

Nothing happened.

For a long time.

"I need more practice."

"Indeed," she said, rising to her feet again.

I followed her around the edge of the planetarium and into a plaza. The planetarium and the park were on an island, and the plaza was on the causeway leading to the mainland. There was a long walkway towards the Shedd Aquarium lined with shrubbery, lawns, and monuments. Sheila walked through the courtyard, away from the lake, toward the city.

"So, why are you all older than me?"

"Life experience. I told you already."

"No, I mean, why are we talking? I assume you're here to invite me into your club or something. Right? Or am I too young?"

"There's no minimum age," she said, stepping around to the front of a larger-than-life statue on a pedestal. "Look here."

I walked to the front of the square granite column. The statue was of a man holding a globe and compass (for drawing circles) and read:

NICOLAUS COPERNICUS

(Mikolai Kopernik)

1473 - 1543

By reforming astronomy,

he initiated modern science.

"This is a reproduction. The original is in Warsaw," Sheila said.

"Huh."

"That's it?"

"Well, yeah. I learned about Copernicus in school."

"Oh. You already know?"

I thought about what she was saying. Was Copernicus important here? I looked back up at the engraving.

Reform. Initiate. Science.

"Reform is a strong word," I pondered. "Frequently violent. Not usually gentle."

"You're right."

"Science is a study. Our environment. Various disciplines."

"Yes."

"So, by getting people to consider that the Sun rather than the Earth was the center of the universe, Copernicus encouraged people to question what they thought they knew. He didn't change reality; he changed the way we looked at things, challenged our understanding of the cosmos," I murmured.

"Good. What else?"

"Modern science," I said.

"What about it?"

"We know Copernicus wasn't entirely correct. But he was as close as he could be with the tools that he had."

"True enough."

"But it's the same now." I was getting excited. "We're Copernicus!"

"How so?"

"We know science doesn't have it quite right! We're aware of more than they are!"

The words tumbled out of me, drawing the attention of bystanders. I stopped talking, hitched my bag higher, and took Sheila by the arm, leading her away from the statue.

"Are you telling me we're going to revolutionize science again?" I asked quietly.

"A revolution is coming, but we're not there yet."

"Why? What's stopping me from flying up here, making a couple of loops around the Sears Tower, and getting on the six o'clock news?"

"It's the Willis Tower now."

"Whatever."

We were almost at another monument, and I thought Sheila looked nervous.

"Revolutions are like puberty," she said. "They're uncomfortable for everyone involved."

"Okay. That's no reason to be frightened."

"We are not frightened," she said, turning to look at me. She stood tall and crossed her arms. "The fact is, you aren't ready yet. You're young and prone to anger, tempted too strongly by your ego."

Cold fury blossomed in my chest. I knew she was right, but I didn't like her condescending attitude.

"I agree my ego is still strong," I said, crossing my arms in imitation of her posture. "Looks like I'm not the only one."

Her eyes narrowed, and I wondered if she was thinking of conjuring a lightning bolt down on me or something.

Suddenly, she did that sideways nodding thing again, and said, "Yes, you're right, of course."

She took a couple of steps back toward the Copernicus monument. I stood still, turning my head to follow her movement. My gaze swept past her, and there was a man in a suit at the edge of the plaza, watching us. I turned, scanned the plaza, and picked out three other people who might be federal agents.

"Are you kidding me? How did they find me?"

"Look at your phone," Sheila said.

"My phone? What did you do?" I pulled my phone out, touched the screen, and it lit up. She must have hit the power button before she tossed it out over the lake.

"Why?" I asked, shocked.

"You've seen what we can do. We can protect you, teach you. Maybe when you have more control, a better understanding of things, the revolution can begin. Right now, you're just not ready. The world isn't ready."

I forced my angry response down. Ninety-year-old lady or not, I wanted to punch her. She was manipulating me every bit as much as these government agents were.

It was getting noisier. People were clustering around the shore, pointing toward the lake. Through gaps in the throng, there were white boats with a blue stripe down the side. Police boats. Three helicopters with the same paint scheme orbited this end of the island.

"You're wrong, Sheila."

"What do you mean? Please, come with me."

She held out her hand.

"Nope," I said, pushing my shoulders back and hitching my bag higher. "It's time to grow up."

I picked an agent and started walking towards him. I didn't see Graham or Agent Stephanie. This one would do. He started talking into his cuff, and I held up both hands.

"Don't do this," Sheila said, suddenly at my side.

"Leave me alone," I said, keeping my eyes on the man in the suit. "It's already done."

"Hi there!" I shouted to the agent, "Do you know me?"

"Please stop right there, ma'am! Lie face-down and put your hands behind your head!"

"I'm unarmed."

"Please lie down, ma'am," the agent repeated. He stood with his right shoulder and hand to the rear, but hadn't drawn a weapon yet. I stopped walking, hands in the air. People were staring, and the agent noticed. He was cool and didn't take his eyes off mine, didn't escalate.

Finally, he took a few steps toward me, holding his hand out, palm toward me. He came close enough that he didn't have to shout.

"Ma'am...Ms. Donnelly, this doesn't have to end violently. You thought you were helping when you assaulted those agents."

"Assaulted them? I saved their lives."

"You dislocated a shoulder and fractured a hip."

"Ouch."

I *was* sincerely sorry. I hadn't meant to hurt them.

"As you said, they're alive. Now, come with me, and we'll get things sorted out."

"I can't do that."

I looked around for Sheila, but she was gone.

"Um, anyway, I came to meet someone, but I think it was all a setup. So, I'll just be going."

"Don't do it, ma'am. The island is surrounded: air, land, and water."

I took a couple of steps closer.

"Do you really want to do this with all these people watching?" I asked.

He glanced around. There were about 30 people close by, trying to hear what we were saying. Maybe another 20 or more were watching from around the monument. Several had their phones out, presumably recording.

"Ms. Donnelly, don't do this. It's dangerous. You do not know who's after you. Let us help."

"Lots of people are trying to help me today. But I do better on my own. Can you tell Deputy Marshal Graham that for me?" I turned to look for a way out, but glanced back. "And say hi to Agent Tucciarone for me, would you?"

I lifted the strap of my bag and slid it diagonally over my head and across my chest. It looked like I would have to ditch my camping supplies and hopefully come back for them later. I had calmed myself while I chatted with the agent. I felt intuition prodding me forward. Through the trees on my left, there was a harbor with boats of all kinds bobbing in the water. I moved west, toward the monument I hadn't seen yet, then angled toward the docks through the grass. My bag was bothering me, sliding down and to the back. I pulled it to the front just as there was a whiff of air and a dart embedded itself in the bag.

"Tranquilizers? Seriously?"

Agents began closing in from all sides. The agent I had been talking to would be following. Maybe he was in charge, directing the others. I started running. The ground sloped down from the edge of the walk. I jumped, clearing a 12-foot hedge, and a 6-foot fence farther on, falling 25 feet to the concrete below.

There were several exclamations from behind me. The bystanders thought I must surely break my legs, if not worse, in the fall. I hit the sidewalk, rolled, and started running. There were shouts from all around, several voices calling out directions, giving orders.

I wasn't afraid, more annoyed than anything. I didn't think agents would open fire with civilians around, but tranquilizers were a different story.

Several cops rounded a corner on the sidewalk ahead of me, and then a police launch pulled into the harbor. There was nothing for it but to fly. I sped toward the cops, running all out, when suddenly, I was running faster than I'd ever run before, faster than humanly possible. With no time to think, I jumped, clearing the cops by a good 10 feet, and landed behind them, still sprinting.

I didn't turn to see the expressions on their faces. I was looking for the next obstacle. Just as I stopped, having felt a warning pull in my gut, there was the clicking sound of a taser. A cop had dropped to her knee behind the wall and hidden, waiting for me to come into range. I was lucky that I had been going so fast. She had been leading me, and the contacts sailed harmlessly past. Without aiming, I yanked the dart from my bag and threw it at her.

I jumped into the air, hopefully away from any more surprises. Hands by my sides, I flew over the boats and away from the launch. I went carefully, slaloming through the masts of sailboats until I reached the wall of the harbor. I turned and flew parallel to it, going fast, listening for the nudge that would tell me when and where to turn.

"Ms. Donnelly!" came a voice, distorted over loudspeakers. "Please don't make us hurt you! Come peacefully, and you will not be harmed!"

Maybe they did plan to shoot me down. Maybe I was in more danger than I thought. I looked around and saw an agent arguing with uniformed police. Perhaps they had different agendas. The cop was gesturing toward a police launch.

There were more whiffs of tranquilizer darts as I turned and flew down a lane between two rows of boats. I zigzagged down the aisle, trying to be unpredictable. Flying fast, I rebounded off the hulls of yachts, masts, cabin roofs, anything I could think of to stay out of view of the helicopters and whoever was shooting at me. There was a tug at my jacket as a dart nearly found its mark and I went back in among the boats, using my hands and swinging amongst the masts and lines, pulling them after me and using them like monkey bars to help change direction.

There were police on the bow of the closest launch with binoculars. I thought they might have lost me, so I dropped to the water level and raced past them. There was a thump, and I turned to see officers on the back aiming a water cannon at me.

I shot across the row of boats fast, grabbing the mast of one and swinging 270 degrees around in an instant. I landed on a yacht with the name Seacret Keeper and got my bearings. More helicopters hovered around the harbor now. There was another police launch out in the open water. I was tired of being shot at, and I was tired of hiding.

I had two choices. Either I went straight up, or I sneaked out along the seawall right at the waterline. Either way was risky. I didn't get a nudge either way from intuition.

My phone rang.

"Damn it," I said, pulling it out.

"What?" I shouted, seeing the number and mashing the green key.

"Make it easy on yourself," Agent Graham said.

"Look, you're really pissing me off."

"Understandable. I have that effect on criminals. Are you a criminal,

Ms. Donnelly?" His Georgia drawl was more pronounced and annoying than ever.

There was another whiff, and a dart embedded itself in the deck at my feet. I turned and saw an agent with a gun at his shoulder. I also saw a family standing on the deck of a boat, watching.

"Graham, you're going to get someone killed," I yelled into the phone.

"You can prevent that. Let us help you."

"Everyone wants to help me," I said, scrambling to put the cabin between the shooter and me.

"Who were you meeting?" Graham asked.

"Look, I will not chat. End this, or I'm heading into the city. You've got 30 seconds."

"Not going to happen, Ms. Donnelly. Just remember, if you do this, you're putting your parents at risk."

"You're putting *everyone* at risk, Graham!"

I hung up, hit the power switch, and jammed the phone into my coat. I took a deep breath. Could I fly with my body flooded with adrenaline? No choice.

I cleared my mind, zipped my coat tight, closed my eyes, and launched straight up. I went fast - could hear the wind roaring around me, felt my jacket flapping against my body in the gale. There was a ripping sound as one of the outside pockets detached.

I slowed, opened my eyes, and looked around. The entire city of Chicago was spread out below me, and a condensation trail from the harbor pointed at me like an arrow. It was already dissipating in the breeze, but I didn't hang around. I descended 2,000 feet to the top of Willis Tower and landed, holding onto an antenna. As soon as I landed, a wave of vertigo washed over me. I felt the height in a very visceral way that I didn't when flying.

Carefully, I sat with my back to the antenna, closed my eyes, and cradled my head in my hands.

I didn't want to put my parents at risk. I couldn't trust Graham. And what about Sheila? If she really was like me, why was she trying to control me? I thought back to the man named Kim that I had met at the truck stop. He had *said* that people would try to control me.

The pieces I had didn't fit together. Someone had tried to kill me back in April and again in May. Someone who didn't mind killing FBI agents and innocent bystanders. Now, the FBI was pulling out the stops to get me back in custody and paint me as a criminal.

It made no sense.

I had to clear my name, protect my family, and keep any more innocent people from being harmed. Obviously, the FBI would not help me do that. Apparently, neither would Sheila nor her school. I didn't want to involve Mitch and Teri any further if I could help it.

Sitting there on top of one of the tallest buildings in the world in one of the largest cities in the world, I felt, suddenly, completely isolated.

The month before I told Mom about the whole flying thing, I told Dad.
I didn't have a choice.

∼

Excerpt from the blog: *Griffin's Flight*

OCTOBER 8, 2025

I was fascinated by the subject of speed. I've never been into fast cars or anything. Maybe instead of speed, it was the idea of rewriting physical laws that was seductive. I had to learn as much as I could.

Mom and Dad were in Chicago for their anniversary, and I had finished the morning chores. I opened the door to the hayloft, donned my flight helmet and goggles, and launched out over the fields.

The day was overcast, and I had been considering practicing above the clouds. Flying that high would be risky, but I was eager to try. Cloud cover would cut down on some of the general aviation traffic around town, and I could predict a lot of the traffic patterns around the airport. I promised myself I wouldn't go far.

Before flying above the clouds, I had a theory to test. If there were no inertia when flying, then the only limit to speed should be my cognitive abilities and maybe air friction. I wanted to test the idea at low altitude over the fields, where I wouldn't kill myself (or others) if I messed up.

Helmet and goggles in place, I hovered over the cornfield behind the pasture. I pictured a field a mile and a half away and set my intention to fly there as fast as possible.

The ground below blurred. I couldn't see. I couldn't breathe. Then I was still, hovering in the field I had imagined.

"Whoa!" was all I could say, breathing hard from sheer excitement.

Looking down, I realized I had lost my right shoe somewhere. I hadn't felt it come off. I felt okay otherwise.

"That was...pretty darn cool!" I shouted to myself after I landed. I walked to a tree and sat in the shade. My hands were shaking, and my knees were weak.

After a few minutes, I tried again. I imagined the yard behind the main barn and started flying. I was going at my usual slow, careful speed.

Strange, I thought.

I turned and tried again. I pictured the yard behind the barn and getting there as quickly as possible.

Rush!

Again, my surroundings blurred for an instant, but then my face shattered in pain. I hit the ground, and blackness enveloped me.

When I came to, I couldn't move. Corn stalks and leaves tangled my arms and legs. I could barely breathe. Blood and bug parts coated the inside of my mouth, and drying bug juice covered my goggles. I began spitting out as much of the blood and exoskeleton as I could. I retched while lying on my side.

That hurt.

My right arm was relatively free, and I used it to pull my goggles up and take my helmet off. That was a little better. My saliva glands were working now, trying to clean my mouth of the gore that crusted it. I was able to clear my throat and begin spitting and clearing it out.

I had a bottle of water in the tool pocket in my jeans. At least I had before I crashed.

I reached down and found the bottle. There was no way to open it one-handed, and I couldn't drink lying on my back, anyway. I tossed the bottle to my left and set about extricating myself.

I was thankful for the corn. No doubt, it had cushioned my fall and saved me from being seriously injured. I hurt like hell, but nothing seemed broken. Still, corn leaves are like sandpaper, and my face, hands, and arms were raw and bloody.

I got my other arm free and sat up. I reached out for the water bottle, got the cap off, and tried to rinse my mouth out. As I hydrated the mess, however, the taste made me retch again, this time right between my legs.

The bile coming up from my stomach was so vile that everything else paled, or so I hoped. Once my stomach finished lurching, I rinsed my mouth as well as I could, then tried to stand.

My mouth was on fire. Apparently, I had hit several giant flying insects. Mating dragonflies or something similar was my guess. Shattered exoskeleton traveling at several hundred miles per hour had sliced the delicate tissue of my mouth in a hundred places, which stomach acid had then irritated.

I was shaking and in pain. Tears rolled down my face as I climbed to my feet. My mouth was still burning, and I spat blood. Everything else seemed, miraculously, to be okay.

Oh, I lost my other shoe.

I turned to look behind me, and my mouth dropped open. My path through the corn was obvious, beginning high and gouging a long wedge shape from the plants. It was almost 200 feet long and shallow. Anyone could tell something had landed and been injured. If they found my shoe, they would know it was human.

I was in pain. I needed to get home, bathe, rest, and hydrate.

Can I fly in my condition?

I cleared my mind, slipped into the gap, and felt myself lift off the ground.

My chest swelled with gratitude to God, or whatever was allowing me to explore this experience. I vowed not to waste it.

I flew to the barn and went inside to doctor my injuries.

I devoted the next two days to recovering. But even doing the minimum on the farm still took several hours of work per day. And though I wasn't seriously injured, my entire body was raw, sore, and bruised. It would be hard to explain to my parents.

The day they returned, I felt much better. I was catching up on neglected chores when I remembered my missing shoes.

I walked a direct path from the barn to the stream. Some of it was corn, and some was pasture. Halfway there, I came to the scar in the cornfield where I had crashed.

Some plants at the edges were bouncing back, but come harvest time, the scar would be noticeable. I tried to keep from doing any more damage while I searched.

I found a shoe close to my impact crater. Okay, maybe that's a slight exaggeration, but the ground was definitely torn up from my impact.

I had no luck with the other shoe after walking all the way back to the creek. I took one more pass from the air before my parents got home. Then I flew low and slow all the way out and back, with no luck.

Well, it would be awkward if someone found it, but there was nothing else I could do. I'd have to let it go.

I finished the chores and went into the house to start dinner. My face looked pretty bad. There were welts, and the side of my face was bruised and swollen. Scratches covered my arms. On top of all that, my voice was hoarse, which I assumed was due to aspirated insect fragments, dust, blood, and/or vomit.

Still, I was feeling much better, even if I didn't look or sound like it.

Mother, predictably, freaked when she saw me. I tried a story I had used before about falling off a gate, but it didn't work. I then upgraded it to a fall from a tree. Mom seemed to buy it, but Dad remained silent, apparently reserving judgment.

I stayed to eat with them, and we talked about the farm, and I heard all about their trip to Chicago. They had seen a play, visited museums, eaten at several excellent restaurants (they brought me a pizza from Gino's), and had a great time. Mom went to bed early, and Dad and I sat up and watched television.

Eventually, he seemed ready for bed, so I said goodnight and got up to leave.

"Wait a second, Liv," he said, standing.

"I appreciate your not wanting to worry us."

I said nothing, but nodded.

"Will you tell me what happened?"

I stick to the truth out of necessity as much as dislike for dishonesty.

"Dad, what I told you is basically the truth."

"You fell out of a tree, hitting branches all the way, without breaking a bone? That's 'basically' what happened?"

"Kind of."

"I'm not buying it. You look like you got the tar beat out of you. Or took a ride through a combine."

"Yeah," I said, thinking fast. I took a deep breath and made a decision.

"I don't know if you're ready to hear this or not," I said, "but I'll show you if you say so."

It was his turn to think. He looked at me for almost an entire minute, then looked away for nearly as long.

"Okay. I'm willing to listen. I won't force you to tell me, but I'll listen."

I got his laptop and fired it up. He looked at me quizzically, but I just held up a finger and navigated to my blog.

I brought up the post that had the first video embedded.

"Please read this. I'll go put the kettle on. When you're ready, we can have some tea and talk."

I left him and went to the kitchen.

Twenty minutes later, he came in. He looked pale and tired, but also concerned, maybe even frightened.

He came near, and his hands were shaking.

"Jesus, Dad. Are you okay?" I asked, scrambling to my feet.

He sat down slowly and looked at me with the strangest expression I had ever seen.

When he opened his mouth as if to say something, nothing came out. He gestured as if he were indeed talking, but he remained silent. Looking away, he shook his head. He slumped back in his chair and slapped his hands on his thighs.

"Dad?" I asked hesitantly.

His eyes snapped to my face briefly, but his head didn't move. He resumed staring out the kitchen window.

"I..." he started, but his voice was hoarse and cracked. He cleared his throat.

"I thought you were going to tell me you got beaten up for being gay or something," he said without looking at me.

I was straining to hear him. My mouth fell open. "Wha...?" I sputtered. "Dad!"

"I couldn't think of anything else. Why else would someone beat you up like that? And you, of all people? All of that running around and kung fu stuff."

Maybe I should have expected it, but it never occurred to me. I put some cookies on a plate and set it between us. I sat back down and looked at my dad.

"Dad," I started, but he interrupted me.

"You're saying you didn't fall out of a tree or off a gate. You fell out of the sky?"

I sighed.

"Yeah. That's about it."

He looked at me, took a sip of tea, and sat back.

"I'm listening."

"Did you read the entire article?"

"Read the first one, skimmed a few more," he said.

"That happened about a year and a half ago," I said, watching his face.

He cocked his head to the side. He looked down at the floor, then back up at me.

"This started right after you moved back?"

"Yeah," I said with a half smile.

"You didn't say anything."

"No."

"Jesus."

"Yeah."

"So, what's happened in the last year and a half to cause... this?" he asked, waving a hand at my face.

"Dad," I said quietly, "I can fly. Really fly. Not just levitate."

"But, Liv," he said plaintively, "how is that even possible?"

"I don't know, Dad," I said. I shrugged and lifted my palms. "No idea. I think meditation changes something in the brain, changes the way physical laws work. Gravity and inertia…I don't know."

"What are you saying?"

"That's how I got hurt," I explained. "I was practicing flying. Really fast."

"H…how fast?"

"Not sure," I said, looking at the floor.

He sat there, waiting.

"Best guess?" I murmured, "Probably around 300 miles per hour."

"Three…hundred…" he whispered.

"I should tell you, when I crashed, I took out a bit of your corn."

"I don't…corn…" Dad said. His face was white.

"Dad, here," I said, "put your head down between your legs." I helped him lean forward. He didn't fight me.

"It's okay, Dad," I whispered, "I'm here."

Nine

After dark, I left the Willis Tower, gathered my pack, and flew southeast toward Cincinnati. I had already warned my parents and the Leaders about this latest FBI ambush. I might have made them all targets, either by the good-bad guys (the police, FBI, and other federal agents) or the bad-bad guys (Alliance operatives and assassins).

It was a warm night, and after I got to Cincinnati, nicknamed "The Queen City," I camped atop the Great American building. The top of this building was inspired by Princess Diana's tiara. It's essentially a large cage of curving white pipes. When illuminated at night and seen from a distance, it's lovely.

It's also a particularly awful place to camp.

The rooftop was isolated, true, but there was too much light for me to sleep deeply. So, I meditated and dozed for about six hours. When the sun broke the horizon, I stood and watched. Southern Ohio and northern Kentucky are beautiful. The Ohio River snaked off toward the rising sun, mist rising and drifting among the trees. It reminded me of Serpent Mound, which I visited with Mitch and Teri recently. It was only a few miles away in the same direction.

My mind wandered to the prehistoric people who built the mound.

Had they considered that people in the future wouldn't understand? Was it a tool they used or had they cast it into the future, a puzzle for us to ponder? There was no way of knowing.

I dug some jerky and carrots out of my bag and ate as I gazed out over the waking city. After eating, I took 10 minutes to clean and repack my bags. There wasn't much trash, but I had a nagging feeling that someone might have found it yesterday and planted a tracking device. I found nothing, but that didn't make me feel much better.

There were several bags of sand on the roof. I piled them in front of the access door so that no one could surprise me. I worried about my family and friends - I needed to talk with them before leaving the fragile seclusion of my rooftop campsite.

There were no open networks within range of my laptop.

I turned it off, took out my mom's phone, and sighed. I wouldn't be able to use it after this. It was becoming too dangerous.

Swallowing my fear, I sat down and turned the phone on.

The news was silent about Chicago. That was both surprising and not.

My email looked like it was mostly dull, everyday maintenance stuff. One of my Leaders had forwarded a list of apps that she thought I might like. Maybe she didn't understand how dangerous it was for me to use my phone right now. I left it in my inbox without reading it.

As I was about to move to social media, I received an email from Mom. I opened it.

> Liv,
>
> You must be in trouble. Dad and I are fine, but we're hearing stories of Leaders being arrested. Please stay safe. Let us know if we can help.
>
> *Mom*

I had been half expecting this and dashed off a quick response.

> Mom,
>
> I'm no worse off than yesterday. I'm in Cincinnati, but who knows where I'll be tomorrow? There's no news about Chicago, but I haven't checked social media. There were several people in the crowd recording.
>
> Maybe you and Dad can go away for a while?

I love you!
Liv

I wrote a quick post telling some of what happened in Chicago. Without mentioning Sheila, I explained that law enforcement was arresting Leaders. I encouraged them to protect themselves.

Next, I called Mitch.

"Hello? Liv? Is that you?" Teri answered.

"Hi there. You guys okay?"

"Oh, sure. How about you?"

"Uh… I'm good. A little scared, to be honest."

"What's going on?"

"Too much to tell. Feds tried to pick me up in Chicago yesterday. FBI…Marshals…someone. I wanted to make sure you and Mitch were okay."

"Mitch's in the shower," she said. "We're back home, of course. He's going to work soon. He wants to send you more money. Don't tell him I told you."

I had no reply. I choked up.

"Sorry to ruin your trip, Teri," I said, my voice rough.

"Liv, you didn't ruin anything! I flew…a little."

I smiled at that, but it was still hard to talk.

"Well, take care," I said. "I have to ditch this phone."

"Okay," she said. "Write this number down so you'll have it."

"Already done." I had made notes of important numbers days ago, just in case.

"Hang on…" she said. "What's going on with the site?"

"Nothing that I know of."

"It's super slow," she said. "Maybe just traffic. Here's Mitch now. Hang on."

I heard whispering in the background.

"Hey," Mitch said. "How you doing?"

"Good," I said. "I hope you took the time to put on pants."

"Nah, just a towel," he said, laughing.

"Small favors," I said.

"Why is Teri banging on her keyboard?"

"The site's slow. Hopefully, Mom's working on it. Look, I had some trouble yesterday. There might be fallout."

"Okay," he said, suddenly serious. "What's up?"

"Long story, and I don't have much time. Turns out there's a group of people who can do stuff...."

"Mutants," he said helpfully.

"Whatever. Anyway, they want me to join them, hide with them, and I'm not crazy about the idea. That was about as far as we got before this... lady sicced the FBI on me."

"How?"

"She turned my phone on without my knowing it."

"That's it? The same phone you're using now?"

"Yeah, I know. I'm running out of time."

"Wait, Teri's got something."

There was a rustling sound as the phone switched hands.

"They arrested Monica in South Dakota. And I think the site's under attack." In the background, I could hear Mitch telling me to pack up and go.

Inexplicably, I felt calm.

"It's okay," I said. "Slow down and tell me. What's up?"

"Monica," I could hear the fear in Teri's voice. "Yesterday she said she had an idea and was sending it to you."

"What? What kind of idea?"

"I don't know. She wouldn't say. She asked where we went when we were traveling together."

"Hold on," I said. "Let me check something."

I put the phone on speaker and switched back to email. I found the weird email with the apps. It was from Monica.

"She sent me an email about apps I might like."

"What's it say?" Mitch asked. Apparently, their phone was on speaker too.

"It's just a roundup of some blogger's favorite apps. I've seen the name before."

"Anything jump out at you?" Teri asked.

"Uh...maybe." Chills went up my spine. There, halfway down the page, was a photo of Serpent Mound.

"Yeah, there's something here. I think Monica wants me to download an app called 'Geocaching.'"

"Don't do it," Mitch said. "Let me."

While he worked on that, I paged through the email. Nothing else seemed significant.

"Okay," Mitch said, "I've got it. This app is about finding hidden caches of stuff. This will be tricky. I'm betting she left you something at Serpent Mound. But you won't be able to use your phone to find it."

"Tell me what the app says."

"The cache is on a trail. Too bad we didn't have time for those. It's on the bank north of the mound, overlooking the river. Liv, these things are level-based, like a video game. They set this one to 'Hard.'"

Fantastic.

"Good, thanks. You two take care. I'll find this cache. Hopefully, she's left me another phone, and I can call you tonight."

"No," Teri said. "Don't do that."

"Why?"

"They'll track this phone. I'll buy another one. I'll make the number higher than this, but as close to the same as I can. Just start one digit up and keep calling until you find me."

"That could take a while," I said.

"Fun times," Mitch said.

I heard no sirens, but the sudden tension in my gut told me the Feds (or worse) were getting close.

"Hang on," I said, listening.

Was someone trying to get the roof-access door open? I could hear a metallic rattle.

"Hey, I need to go," I said. "The FBI is here."

"Talk to you soon! Be safe!" Teri said.

"Keep everyone calm," I said. "We'll get through this."

Something hit the roof door hard.

I hung up, hit the power button, and stowed the phone in my pocket. It probably wouldn't help, but I wanted to wipe its memory before I threw it away.

With the pounding growing insistent, there were voices on another level of the roof, further down. I kept my head low as I strapped into my duffel and backpack.

As I climbed through the white bars on top of the Great American Tower, my duffel snagged. I was just getting untangled as Agent Stefanie stumbled over the sandbags and onto the roof. I gave her what I hoped was a jaunty wave and leaped into the air, heading south over the river.

I don't litter. It's kind of a big deal for me. That's one reason it was so hard for me to drop Mom's phone. After resetting the phone, I popped out the SIM card. I finally dropped the phone into the river, and then the card a minute later.

I felt a little freer after watching it hit the water. They shouldn't be able to track me now. Hopefully, I could finally stay ahead of anyone trying to find me.

I checked in with intuition. If I were right, I was farther east than I should be. I turned northwest, adjusting my altitude to stay low while maintaining visibility.

From less than 1500 feet, the world was a sea of green. Most trees had leaves, and fields of corn and beans sprouted. I even saw what I thought were tobacco farms below me. I had heard that some still existed in southern Ohio and Indiana.

Logically, I would never find the site without a map, but nothing about my situation had anything to do with logic. I tapped into my emotions and what I felt to be true. I flew briskly, then slowed the farther I got from the river. The sun was climbing toward its zenith, and I should be able to see the mound soon.

I saw a creek winding through the trees, then the road. Surely that was… and then I saw the tower. Funny, with the sun climbing overhead, the shape of the mound was hard to make out. What caught my eye was the shadow of the observation tower, and since it was empty, I landed there.

I walked around the mound once again, taking time to thank the builders mentally for sharing their creation with me. Not just the builders, but also the cultures through the ages that had repaired and restored the earthwork as it became necessary.

Finally, I headed east, past the museum and restrooms, and toward the field where I would look for the trailhead. As I was walking, I grew warm and stopped to take my jacket and sweatshirt off and stow them in my pack. I lay back for a moment to bask in the sun.

The lack of sleep was catching up to me, and as I rested, I dozed.

I don't know what woke me. I wasn't afraid, but I opened my eyes and sat up quickly. A man sat nearby, arms around his knees, ankles crossed. He was watching me.

I rubbed my eyes, ran my hands over my hair, and cleared my throat.

"Um…hi," I said.

"Hi. Are you Liv?" the man asked, smiling. He was about my age and of Asian descent.

I was instantly wary. My shoulders tensed, but there was no warning in my gut. My intuition wasn't setting off any warning buzzers. The world knew me only as Griffin. Only the FBI, Sheila, and a few of the Leaders knew my actual name. Monica was one of them.

"Uh…yeah. Yeah, I am. Who are you?"

"I'm Tim. Your friend Monica is my sister."

"So I was right about the cache?"

"Yeah, only she didn't want me to just leave something. She wasn't sure that you would show up."

He stood, walked the twenty feet between us, and sat down again, setting his pack in front of him.

"Nice to meet you," I said and held my hand out to him.

"Likewise."

He took my hand tentatively.

Is he afraid of me?

"What has Monica told you?"

"I've read your blog," he said. "In fact, I'm the one who shared it with Monica."

"Cool. What do you think?"

"My first impression? 'Cool FX,'" he said, half grinning.

I nodded and smiled, but said nothing.

"I don't know. Seeing you here, in person, I'm inclined to believe. But I honestly didn't think you'd show."

"Things got intense yesterday," I said. I glanced around. Nobody seemed to be watching us. "What did your sister send me?"

"Here you go," he said, pushing the pack over to me.

"Thanks. Where do you live anyway?"

I opened the top.

"D.C.," he said.

I stopped and looked up at him.

"That's a long drive."

"Yeah, I guess. About five hours."

"Well, thanks," I said, digging into the pack.

I pulled out a smartphone, charger, battery pack, lots of dried food and a water filter. At the bottom were four bundles of $20 bills.

"Wow, Tim, you and your sister may have just saved my life."

He laughed a short laugh.

"Well, thank her. She sent me the money and told me what to buy. A friend was supposed to get the phone. Hopefully, they can't trace it back to us."

I powered it up. The cell signal here wasn't great, but it worked. I checked the news, but there was nothing remarkable. I checked my site, and it didn't load.

Tim saw my frown.

"What's wrong?"

"My site's not loading. One of my friends this morning thought that it might be under attack."

Tim took out his phone and tried with the same result.

"I'll see if Monica knows anything," he said. I watched as he entered a text message and pressed "Send."

We waited a while and chatted.

"She's not answering," Tim said, looking at his phone again. "She always answers right away."

He punched a few more buttons and held the phone to his ear. He smiled, then his expression fell.

"Who is this?…No, this is my sister's phone…what does the FBI want with…Hell no…put Monica on the phone!"

"Tim!" I hissed, trying not to be overheard. "Hang up! Hang up!"

I turned my phone off and pulled the battery while he continued to argue with the FBI. I stowed the food and gear, leaving the pack, and hid the money in several places around my person and bags.

"Tim! I've got to go," I said, standing in front of him.

He finally hung up in disgust.

"This is your fault," he said, standing and walking up to me. "What do they want with Monica?"

"I don't know. I understand that you're upset, but don't blame me. Some people are afraid. They don't want humanity to progress. Blame them if you have to."

He said nothing but continued staring at me obstinately, like he wanted to punch me but was afraid.

"Look. Monica will be okay. The FBI are good guys. There are guys chasing me who aren't so good. Be glad the FBI got to her. They'll protect her."

"That's supposed to make me feel better?" he asked, his face going white. "What about me? Am I in trouble for helping you?"

"Nobody knows you helped me. Go to the museum, ask questions, take some literature home. Buy a book about the Adena culture. Make this place your hobby, and no one will wonder why you came."

Tim looked around.

"Yeah, okay," he said finally. I grasped his shoulder.

"Thank you."

"Okay," he said, running the fingers of both hands through his hair. "Look, I loaded the Geocaching app onto your phone and saved your next cache. Tomorrow morning, that one will have instructions from someone else. They've got a plan to help keep you fed and sheltered."

I left Tim standing on the lawn, one hand shading his eyes as he watched me fly away. Could someone else have seen me? Sure, but he deserved to know that his risk had been for something real.

I headed south, looking for a place to regroup, meditate, and think. I could fly through the night if I needed to. In fact, it might be safer that way. In less than two hours, I found myself over the ridges and valleys between West Virginia, Kentucky, and Tennessee.

The world was trees with occasional farms carved from the forest. After searching, I found a small clearing near the top of a ridge that looked deserted. There was a creek nearby that seemed clean, but I used my new water filter to be safe.

I spread out as little as possible as I ate and rested. I opened my phone again to see exactly where I was, and to get a sense of the news. The cell signal fluctuated but never dropped below two bars. I desperately needed a nap, but I tried to find Teri's new number first.

In the end, I sent over 200 texts before I found it. I was deleting the flood of "no" texts when she called.

"You're safe?" she asked when I picked up.

"Yeah. You guys?"

"It's been crazy," she said. "We had just hung up with you and were walking out the door when the feds showed up."

"What? Are they there now?"

"No. Just listen, okay?"

"Sorry. Go on."

"We were walking to the car and this brunette in a power suit walks up. She flashes her badge and says that she needs to talk. Mitch asked what it was about.

"She says, 'Your relationship with Olivia Donnelly.'

"Well, we just looked at each other, but there were these other agents behind her and beside our car. We couldn't run, even if we wanted to.

"Mitch went to open the door of the apartment. Just as he put the key in, there was a loud crack, and one agent fell against the wall of the building."

"Oh, my god!"

"We're okay. Just listen. There was more shooting. A bullet grazed Mitch's shoulder. The agent — I can't remember her name — she grabs us and pulls us down behind some cars. The agents beside our car had their guns out, but they couldn't see anything to shoot at."

"Was everyone okay?"

"No," she said, "The first agent that was shot, he died. The other one isn't very good. He might not make it."

"Damn," I said.

"It's not your fault," Teri said.

"I know. I wish I knew whose fault it was, though."

"Anyway, we're in a hotel again. Protective custody. They didn't search us, and they don't know about this phone yet. I think they will before long, though. You won't be able to use this number again."

"Crap…okay. How is Mitch doing?"

"He's okay. They gave him some pain stuff that knocked him out. He's sleeping."

"What about the site?"

"It's down. The traffic went crazy this morning, and then there was a DDoS attack. It killed the server."

"I have everything backed up at home. I wish I had something local."

"Don't worry about it," she said. "We'll get it back up, but it might take a while."

"I'd better get off here," I said. "I'm glad you're okay."

"We are. It will be awhile before we can talk again."

"Give Mitch my best," I said.

"Take care, Liv."

"Hey, um, I love you guys. Keep practicing," I said, and hung up.

I was shocked that people had lost their lives and my friend was injured on my account. Logically, there was nothing I could have done, but I felt responsible.

Before I powered the phone down, I checked out Geocaching. I had a message to find a cache in Peoria, Illinois. There were coordinates, but they were in an urban area. It would be better to get there at night, and it was easily 500 miles away.

The stress of the past few days made really deep meditation elusive. Exercise would help, but I only had a few options. I could run through the woods, but this was much closer to actual wilderness than the woods around my home. I wasn't used to areas where bears and who knows what else might be lurking.

There were also places down here where the farmers grew "unconventional" crops. I didn't want to come across an aggressive farmer protecting his stash or his still.

So, I worked on martial art forms instead. There was plenty of room, and I needed the practice if I hoped to achieve my black belt one day. I spent an hour practicing, then went back to the stream and bathed.

When I reclined on my pack, sleep came so quickly it felt like falling off the edge of a cliff. I slept soundly until my bladder woke me several hours later. The new moon was setting as darkness fell.

After taking care of business, I ate again, then took out my phone and checked the route to Peoria. I would fly northwest, passing Lexington on my right and Louisville on my left. Cincinnati and Indianapolis were so far to the right that I probably wouldn't have seen them during the day. At night, the glow from the city lights would guide me. If I were on course, I would fly directly over Terre Haute, Champaign, and Bloomington, Illinois, before reaching Peoria.

There would be air traffic, so I would have to be careful. I packed and took off, setting my internal compass.

This story is about dumb luck. It turns out that making the wrong choices sometimes turns out okay.

~

Excerpt from the blog: *Griffin's Flight*

SEPTEMBER 1, 2025

The day was bright and clear. After meditation, I left the barn and thought about heading to my new practice field after it warmed up. Then I remembered the dragonflies and other large bugs. I glanced up at the broken clouds and thought again about practicing high above them. One day of practice might be worth the risk.

I went inside, got my helmet, goggles, and scarf. I left through the upper hay window and checked for air traffic. Seeing nothing, I climbed and accelerated to around 100 mph. The speed was a wild guess, but it was very windy, and I felt like I was moving incredibly fast.

The clouds rushed toward me, and then I was above them with nothing but clear blue sky above. It was indescribably beautiful. I didn't want to go too high. Oxygen deprivation could be a problem, and I had no way of knowing my altitude.

I regularly checked the sky for airplanes. There was nothing in sight, so I put the sun on my right and started flying fast! I was way above the vast majority of birds and bugs. I was more concerned with jets and other airplanes.

I flew fast with no sense of speed other than the rushing wind. Turning, I flew in an arc to my right and headed south at top speed. Just for fun, I spiraled like a corkscrew and felt dizzy with joy.

I hadn't expected the nearly intoxicating feeling of freedom!

I pulled my head up and flew in a smooth arc into an inside loop. When I got to the bottom, I snapped to my right and made a horizontal loop. When the sun came back around to my right side, I rolled and did the same to my left. What an incredible feeling! I had complete control and felt fantastic.

I estimated I was about 3,000 feet above the ground. I grabbed a sweatshirt before I took off, but still I was shivering and would need to go in soon.

I realized I did not know where I was. The clouds below me were getting thicker, but not entirely overcast. Or…undercast, I supposed.

Nothing between the clouds looked familiar. I was north of home, I thought, so I started flying south. My phone was at home and no use to me.

I had two ideas. I could fly higher to get a better sense of things below, or I could land and find a newspaper or something that would tell me where I was.

In rural America, water towers used to have the town name painted on them. What a boon that must have been to early aviators! No such luck around here. They were all plain white, or, stupidly, I thought, had the water company's name on them.

I noticed a kind of vibration in the air. I glanced down at my chest and arms, looked at my hands, and realized it wasn't coming from me. But I could feel it in the palms of my hands and the center of my chest — a deep, thrumming vibration. I could hear it now, too. Like a lawnmower, but more intense.

I knew what it was. I moved forward fast because I knew there was nothing there. As I picked up speed, I looked over my shoulder and saw it. A single engine low wing aircraft. It was so close I could see the pilot, which meant he could also see me.

With this much cloud cover, I thought he might be under Instrument Flight Rules (IFR). If that were so, maybe he wouldn't be paying attention outside the airplane. He might not see me.

Criminy, I thought, *he must have been almost on top of me!*

I was lucky again. Descending so his wing hid me from view, I let him get ahead of me. Then I climbed to 30 feet above his altitude, maybe 100 feet behind him. I was close enough that I could smell his engine exhaust, but he couldn't see me, even if he turned to look.

Again, I wasn't sure how fast we were going, but it must have been between 100 and 200 miles per hour. The air was already cool, maybe 50 degrees, and if you add the wind chill factor, it was probably not dangerously cold, but damned uncomfortable.

I followed the guy for 20 minutes, flying along with my hands in my pockets, kind of leaning into the wind. Flying horizontally and watching the plane was hard on my neck. Flying vertically created a lot of wind resistance. So, I angled into the wind, maybe 30 degrees above horizontal. It allowed me to rest without causing my neck to cramp.

For fun, I began creeping up closer to the airplane. I didn't want to interfere with the plane, and I didn't want him to see me, but I had never touched an airplane before.

I flew right up over the tail fin, "vertical stabilizer" they called it. There was a red flashing light on the top of it. I reached out with my left hand and touched the top of the stabilizer. I could feel vibration through the metal. It was cold and smooth. The plane was a kind of tan color with dark brown stripes.

Very pretty, I thought.

I moved off, back to my previous position relative to the plane.

Looking below, I thought I might be near home. There was a road where the clouds were breaking up. If that was the highway, that would mean if I looked to the southwest I would see… there! That was my old school.

Thank God!

I said a mental goodbye to my airplane friend and headed down.

It still took me forever to find my house. I thought I knew exactly where it was, but there were lots of streams, roads, farms, woods, and barns. And they all look the same at first.

Finally, ironically, what caught my eye was the scar in the cornfield where I had crash-landed the other day. I checked the house and the fields and didn't see anyone. Freezing, I wanted to get right into the shower. Instead of walking in from the fields, I flew to the hay window and right into the barn.

I was undressing when I noticed an email waiting on my computer. I glanced to see if it was important.

It was a note on my website from someone named Natalie. She wanted to know more about my flying experiences.

Hers was my first real (not spam) comment, so I approved it and replied we could chat soon. Then I stripped and jumped into a steamy hot shower.

Maybe things would start taking off now, I thought.

I had been meticulously careful to keep my website anonymous. There was just one video on the site, and I had obscured my face. If the site became popular, there would be crazy people contacting me. I wanted to protect myself and my parents from that. Though I did not know what we needed to be protected from.

Ten

I got used to moving from place to place and finding caches. But I never got used to learning about the imprisonment of friends.

It took weeks, but the FBI found most of the people who had been helping me, both with the site and keeping me in cash, phones, and company.

They took my folks into custody the day I found the cache in Peoria.

I stayed at a campground on the east side of the lake. My website was still down, but when I searched for my name, I found a half dozen sites that had copied it and were presenting it, usually along with personal commentary.

There were no comment sections or forums, but there was always news of the Leaders. The site that posted about my parents being arrested was marginally sympathetic to my cause. Her commentary of my parents' treatment was scathing and bitter. She had no compassion for the FBI, but didn't mention the Alliance.

That night, instead of getting much-needed rest, I stayed awake, my new phone plugged into an outdoor receptacle. I wrapped myself in my sleeping bag and kept searching for information.

Eventually, when nothing more materialized, I dozed fitfully. When morning finally came, I was stiff and hungry. The face looking back at me from the bathroom mirror was disturbing. I looked 15 years older. Part of that was my unkempt hair, but part was the ashen pallor, lines, and dark circles under my eyes.

Each week grew harder. Every cache had news of arrests, few of which made the news. Then there were the unexplained shootings. They didn't happen every night, but often enough that newscasters were taking notice. Unsurprisingly, the FBI denied any such uptick in shootings and labeled journalists who mentioned them "conspiracy theorists." They relegated the story to late-night radio shows and fringe news sites. I began following George Kemp, a reporter from Las Vegas who reported on subjects usually given a wide berth by the media. He didn't support me or come down firmly on either side of the debate, but he had my videos analyzed and asked good questions when he interviewed the technicians involved.

Eventually, there were no new caches, as my friends, most of them anonymous to me, were arrested or, I could hardly imagine it, killed. I had to know what was going on with the FBI and my people.

One night in mid-June, I flew to the roof of the same truck stop I visited that first night back in April. I sat with my back to the facade and made a call to Agent Stefanie with my oldest phone.

It took a while to get through. I talked to several screeners who wanted to know my business with Stefanie and my location. Finally, I had to resort to the truth. As I waited on hold, I readied my bags for a quick escape and stood to watch the road.

There was nothing suspicious, but I walked to the middle of the roof and watched the roads in and out.

"Liv, is that you?"

Finally, it was Stefanie's voice on the line.

"Yes, it's me."

She paused for a beat.

"Your parents are safe. They're in Dayton."

Relief flooded through me, but I didn't allow myself to rejoice for very long.

"Why Dayton?" I asked.

"They already attacked us in Indy. It seemed logical to keep them close, but not local."

"Why not D.C.? Or Quantico?"

"It's complicated," she said.

"Complicated how?"

"I can't say," she said. "It's just better this way."

Frustrated with her lack of candor, I pulled the phone from my head and walked in a tight circle, rechecking the perimeter and the roads.

"Liv? Olivia, are you there?" her voice called from the little speaker.

"Yeah, I'm still here," I answered finally, bringing the phone to my head. "What's going on with my people?"

"As we find them, we're bringing them in. As much…."

"For their safety. Blah blah blah," I finished for her.

"It's true," she said. "You know we lost agents in Illinois. Other places too."

"I know," I said. "Look, I'm sorry for those agents and their families, but what's it really got to do with me?" I asked. "If you had nailed these guys, there wouldn't be any danger."

"I can't be as forthcoming as I would like on the phone, Liv. You know that, right?"

"Why? Because it's being recorded? Monitored? Yeah, I figured. No way I'm meeting you, though. Can we just stop with the games?"

"No games. Not anymore. I just want you to know that you won't get the whole story anywhere. Not for a long time."

I dropped my phone, and thought for a moment, watching the sky.

"Okay," I said finally, raising the phone to my ear. "Okay, I get that. What can you tell me about the shootings?"

"Not a lot," she said. "Some of them have been your people, but some we're not sure about."

"What do you mean?"

"I mean…we're not sure why they targeted some of these people."

That made no sense. I started speaking without thinking.

"What do you know about someone named 'Sheila'?" I asked.

There was a brief silence. I imagined Stefanie looking at her staff for input.

Why had I mentioned her?

"Sheila?" she said. "No last name?"

"No."

"We haven't heard the name in connection with you. I'll have some people check it, though. Why do you ask?"

"She's someone I met recently. Actually, she's the reason you caught up to me in Chicago."

"She called in the tip?" she asked.

"Called in?" I asked and then paused as puzzle pieces started falling into place.

"Evil bitch. Probably. She also switched my phone on without me knowing."

"Why does she want you in custody?"

She didn't. She wanted to force me to go with her.

"What's that phrase? 'I cannot say at this time.'"

"But you can give me her name?"

"Yeah, for all the good it will do you. I don't think she's violent, just...."

"Just what?"

"I don't know. Not...bad. She's not an assassin."

"Her actions resulted in the death of federal agents, almost costing you your freedom," she said. "What do you owe her?"

"I don't owe Sheila," I grumbled. "I don't even know her. If you have video of that day, she's the one I was next to when I noticed the agents."

She covered the receiver, and there were several terse exchanges.

"Hang on," she said to me. "We're calling up camera footage."

"While we wait," I said, "can you tell me if you're coming after me right now?"

"Obviously, we know where you are. And, equally obviously, you can fly away whenever you want. We will not surround you again," Stefanie said.

Her voice sounded perfectly reasonable, but I *knew* she was lying.

"Not until I stop talking anyway," I said, looking around. Was someone hiding behind that trailer in the parking lot? Motion in the ditch by the highway? I took cover between an HVAC unit and a set of exhaust hoods.

"Okay, I've got the footage from Chicago. Where were you when she was beside you?"

"The whole time. I don't know where you picked me up. The Copernicus monument?"

There was another pause.

"I see you there, but no one else," Stefanie said.

"She was white, sort of tall, slender, dressed in black."

"Hm... nobody like that at all."

"How can that be?" I asked.

"I don't know," she said, confusion in her voice.

"I didn't imagine her. We talked for a long time."

"You seem to be speaking," she said. "Actually, you look like you're talking to someone else, but there's no one there."

Had I imagined her? The thought that I had hallucinated that entire conversation was disturbing. Then I thought of something she said to me by the lake. 'How many laws of physics did you just break? Are those the only ones that can be broken?'

No, Sheila had been there. I was certain.

"Listen, she's there. I don't know if you'll be able to see her, but she's there."

"I don't know what that means," she said cautiously.

"It means that the laws of gravity and inertia aren't the only ones that we can break," I said.

As I crouched there, my back to a vibrating steel panel, I felt my gut tighten and the prickling of intuition. I lowered the phone and closed my eyes, trying to listen to what it was telling me.

As I took a breath deep into my diaphragm, I remembered the faint whiffs of the tranquilizer darts they had fired at me in Chicago. Without thinking, I rolled to my left, dropping the phone. My right hand seemed to have a mind of its own as it snaked through the handles of my duffel bag.

I continued rolling, taking the bag with me. My left hand shot out and grabbed my backpack, and then I was airborne, spiraling up through the night like an out-of-control bottle rocket.

I flew west into the night. The strain of holding the packs was agonizing. After flying for only a few minutes, I aimed for a dark area and landed. As I maneuvered my packs around into the right configuration for flying, I found six darts embedded in them. I dropped them to the ground. Would they have trackers in them? Could they have left one on me?

I couldn't worry about it. I had to get back in the air.

It was a warm night with lots of bugs. Creating a shield of air pressure was second nature now, so I quickly accelerated to around 100 mph.

I flew west and a little north until morning. The air changed as I flew. It was cooler, crisper. The ground had been rising beneath me, and I had climbed with it. I was now approaching about 7,000 feet above sea level, judging by the chill and the thinness of the atmosphere.

As the sun rose behind me, the Rocky Mountains seemed to rise in front, the peaks rose-colored in the rising sun. Patches of snow reflected the morning light in a way that I had only seen in paintings. Seeing the snow on the peaks gave me an idea.

There were fields below, which seemed funny somehow. I had never thought of farming in Colorado. But there it was. From the patchwork look of the ground, farms of some sort ran right up the sides of the mountains.

I landed and realized that I was simply exhausted. I hadn't noticed in the air, but I was suddenly bone-weary. But I didn't want to stop, not for long. I took out one of my phones and checked my location, then went to a paper map and began looking for ski resorts. What I found was surprising. Wikipedia has an article on ski resorts in Colorado, and even (as if they wrote it with my needs in mind) had a section on resorts that were no longer in operation. I picked one at random, found it on Google Maps, took my bearings, and set off.

I discovered I was wrong about the farms. There were farms, but they tapered off. The closer I got to the mountains, which took longer than I expected, the drier the ground became. Circular green spots in the fields below told the tale of centralized watering. There were watering holes for horses and cattle and the trails the animals left as they came back and forth.

Fatigue dragged at me as I flew. My mind wandered. I was imagining the cabin that I hoped to find, how good it would feel to stretch out and sleep without fear. A hot shower was too much to hope for, but even a cold bath would leave me feeling better than I had in a while.

Suddenly, I found myself flying up the side of a mountain ridge, trees closer than I expected. My speed, usually hard to gauge from altitude, was very apparent as treetops went whipping by a hundred feet below my boots.

After long practice, it wasn't hard to keep my surprise from turning to outright fear, but it took focus. I breathed deep into my abdomen, relaxed, and tried to gain altitude over the ridge. I kept my eyes open for vultures, hawks, eagles, and other airborne obstacles.

Finally, I crested the ridge and there, in front of me, was a massive pyramid-shaped mountain. The woods fell away as I passed the ridge, and suddenly I was 1,500 feet above the ground again, speeding toward the mountain. It was then I noticed that only a gentle breeze pushed my hair around, not the 100 mph gale that I should have been bracing against.

Again, with surprising speed, I was flying up the side of the mountain. I had lost all sense of speed, distance, and size. As I gained altitude, the mountain below seemed to slide out of perspective and appeared no bigger than a piece of living room furniture. In fact, it rather looked like a chair if you ignored the grooves running down the face. As I focused on those grooves, the mountain instantly snapped back into perspective, and I knew I must be too high. Was I suffering from hypoxia? Coupled with sleep deprivation, it would be dangerous.

I thought longingly of my hypothetical cabin. If I didn't find it, I would have to camp in the open.

I was flying over treetops again, slower now, just a leisurely stroll in flying terms. There was a break in the trees ahead, and I descended. I had to clear my head. I slowed and drifted into the space between the walls of pine trees. There was a narrow gravel road, and I landed softly right in the middle of it. I dropped my bag at the edge of the road and stretched, easing the kinks out of my shoulders.

I was tired, maybe as tired as I had ever been. But I didn't feel hypoxic. I didn't have a headache. My hands tingled from being free of the bag's weight, but other than that, I felt fine. I even felt warm, which I should not have.

I looked at my hands. The fingers were pink and warm. I squeezed one and watched the blood fill back into the capillaries. Everything seemed fine.

To my right, a driveway tunneled through the pines. To the left, the pyramidal mountain rose over the treetops, barely visible. I hoisted my bags again and set off up the driveway. Intuition told me I would find my cabin at the end.

When I woke later that night, I was famished.

I had eaten a little before crashing onto the thin bed, but I was exhausted, and sleep was more important. After making my way back from the privy, I surveyed the cabin. There was no electricity, but there was a wood-burner and a woodpile in the back. A hand pump in the kitchen sink provided fresh water. The place was surprisingly well kept for an abandoned lodge. Someone still used it.

I heated some water and bathed the old-fashioned way. After starting a fire, I found a washtub on the back porch, evicted the spiders, and brought it into the kitchen. It took forever to heat enough water. Apparently, there was a trick that I wasn't aware of.

At any rate, by midmorning I was clean and was washing my clothes. I had a pot of water on the stove with some beef jerky and the last of my veggies stewing.

Once my clothes were clean and draped over tree branches around the house, I sat down on the porch to eat. The water from the pump was good. The metallic taste of well water reminded me of home.

I found the silence in the mountains nearly overwhelming. There were the occasional jets, and sometimes small aircraft disturbed the quiet, but most of what I heard were wind, bugs, and birds.

After eating, I checked my phone. I had a signal, but barely. I went online and checked my website. It was still down. I had new email accounts, but there was nothing there either. Had the feds arrested everyone involved with the site? Had they been murdered? Sadness so thick I couldn't breathe overwhelmed me.

I ached for my friends and family who were suffering. Intellectually, I knew it wasn't my fault. But there was no getting around the fact that people were dead who wouldn't be if I had kept my mouth shut. Others were in jail because they liked what I had to say. At best, their lives were on hold. At worst…who knew?

I took out my computer and started writing a blog post, even though I might never publish it. I wrote to get my sadness and frustration out, to pour my emotions into the words, but the stream seemed never-ending. There was no way to express my unhappiness.

It wasn't fair. I mean, I don't expect the world to be fair all the time. But I couldn't get over the injustice. I couldn't think of anything else. Why was I free when everyone I knew and cared about was being hurt?

Should I give up? Would they let everyone else go if I did? Would it help at all?

No, intuition said. *It won't help at all.*

When I walked outside, I looked up into the brightness of the early afternoon sky. A large raptor was circling overhead. I didn't know what kind of bird it was, but I slid the phone into my pocket and lifted off gently, soaring up to the bird's altitude.

If I surprised her, I couldn't tell. It was a red-tailed hawk, like we had back home, and she was beautiful. But she didn't like me flying formation with her and headed off to the south.

When she left, my sadness, temporarily displaced by curiosity, returned.

What should I do next?

I landed, powered off my computer to conserve the battery, and then checked my clothes. Some were still wet, but I folded and packed what I could. There was still water and stew. Tomorrow I would have to buy food.

How long can I stay here? Does anyone ever come in the summer?

Judging by the spider population, no one had been here recently, but the pump worked, and the firewood wasn't rotting. I decided to stay for now. While I was thinking about it, I pulled two $100 bills from my pack and put them under an oil lamp on the mantle to compensate the owner of the cabin.

Just as I replaced the lamp on top of the money, I heard the last thing that I expected. The sound of two footsteps on the front porch froze me in place. The three knocks that followed nearly sent my heart through the top of my head.

I couldn't see anything from this angle. Again, three knocks. I walked to the door just as someone called out.

"Ms. Donnelly? Are you there?"

I'm not proud of it, but my first thoughts were profanity.

I centered myself, stepped to the door and unlocked it, unsure of what I would find on the other side.

It was an Asian man about my father's age, dressed in plain black clothes of natural fibers. They reminded me of Sheila.

"Hello?" I said hesitantly.

"You're Olivia? Of course you are. Hello."

He held out his hand, smiling, and I took it. Despite his age and slender appearance, his handshake was firm.

"May I come in?" he asked.

I glanced from him to the yard, then at the room behind me, trying to decide.

"I'm alone, Liv. No one else is coming."

I shrugged and stood aside, allowing him to enter.

"Lovely."

He stepped inside and looked around.

"Rustic." He smiled at me as if sharing a secret. "I like it."

"What can I do for you...?"

"Oh, forgive me. You can call me Tseten."

Tseten saw my bowl and spoon in the sink. I hadn't washed up yet.

"Nothing left? It smells good."

"Er...no. I mean, yes. Sorry," I said. Why was I sorry? I wasn't expecting guests. Something about him made me think of my father, I suppose.

"Would you like some?"

"No, thank you. Water would be nice, though."

I pumped water into a pitcher, filled two cups, and handed him one.

"Well, you're wondering why I'm here," he said.

"Yes."

"Indeed." He glanced around the room. "Should we sit and talk here, or would you rather the porch?"

"Have a seat." I waved a hand at the table.

"Down to business then," Tseten said.

"So, first, I'm alone. No federal agents will join us. Second, neither will Sheila."

"Good."

"She's rather ashamed of herself," he said, smiling.

"She got people killed, and she's 'rather ashamed'?"

"Well, yes and no. That's one thing I'm here to talk to you about. Neither you nor Sheila were responsible for those deaths."

I listened, but I wasn't in a terribly receptive mood.

Tseten spoke, nearly singing a song of calm reason. He told me things I already knew about free will and intuition. I wasn't impressed.

Finally, I interrupted.

"Tseten, I can't argue with much of what you're saying. But you are neglecting a universal truth: actions have consequences. Sheila ignored it, and people died."

"Olivia, I understand why you feel that way, but the fact is that even though the deaths followed from Sheila's actions, she was not responsible."

"Explain that to me, please."

"As I've said, Sheila made choices, the FBI agents made choices, the Alliance operatives made choices, and even the innocent victims made choices. If we could call a cosmic do-over, reset the universe, the odds of everyone making the same choices, resulting in the exact outcome, are astronomical."

"By 'exact outcome' you mean the same people dying, not people in general dying."

Tseten frowned.

"I see your point," he said. "If we anonymize, speak only of innocent deaths," his voice trailed off.

He drained his cup.

"May I?" he asked, pointing to the pitcher.

"Please," I said.

"The water is delicious," he said. "Right from the heart of the mountain."

He sat back and sipped.

"Well, you're upset, and I *can* see why. As I've said, I don't believe that either you or Sheila is personally responsible. We have to lay this squarely at the FBI and the Alliance's feet."

"They wouldn't have been there if not for Sheila. And if not for me."

"Perhaps Sheila bears some responsibility," he said, sitting forward and setting his cup on the table, "but you cannot blame yourself. It would be the height of arrogance."

"Arrogance?" Being called arrogant by this smug little guy had just made me angry.

"You think arrogance is making me feel guilty? You think I'm being self-indulgent?"

"Olivia," he said, softening his voice, "I don't mean it in a bad way. I'm a teacher, and sometimes we have to be brutally honest with students."

"Please be as honest as you like," I said. "Just don't expect me to sit back and accept your interpretations."

"Challenge authority. That's good," Tseten said.

As with Sheila, he was trying to manipulate me. I didn't answer but sat back and let my vision go unfocused. My conscious mind quieted, and I sat in stillness. I listened to intuition.

Tseten sat back, too. He sighed and shook himself the way I did sometimes when trying to meditate.

"Are you listening now?" he asked.

"What do you mean? Listening to what?"

"You know what I mean," he said, his eyes closing briefly in a glacially slow blink.

"I'm listening to intuition to get through this conversation. Yes, I want to understand you, but I want to make myself understood as well."

"Yes," he said, with a slow nod. "Hold your intention for the best outcome for everyone. Not just you, and not just me."

"Of course," I said. I knew he meant that if I focused only on changing his mind, then I wouldn't be open to the greatest possible good. If I focused only on winning the argument, then I might miss something that could make a difference.

"Good," Tseten said. "Now, was this tragedy your fault?"

Yes, my brain said.

But I hesitated. My intent had been to help, to advance humanity somehow. I had made no choices directly responsible for death or imprisonment.

"No," I said. The weight on my chest lifted.

"Was this tragedy Sheila's fault?" he asked.

Of course! I wanted to rage.

But while Sheila may not have had the *greater* good in mind, her intent had been good. And even though good intentions didn't excuse bad choices, I couldn't blame the Alliance's choices on Sheila.

"No," I said again.

Tseten looked at me, smiling.

"But?"

"But I don't trust her," I grumbled.

"Not bad. That's why I'm here."

"You don't trust her either?"

"It's not so much a matter of trust," he said. "Sheila allowed her ego to dominate intuition. It happens to the best of us sometimes. We're only human."

Suddenly, a thought struck me.

"How did you get here?" I asked.

"I beg your pardon?"

"How did you find me? Did you follow me? Did you fly?"

"My dear, you need to understand that you are only *beginning* to understand."

I considered his answer.

"Sheila didn't show up on the FBI's cameras."

"Why do you think that is?"

"I don't understand the mechanics," I said, "but I imagine there is a principle that allows," I waved a hand, "invisibility."

It felt silly saying it out loud.

"And then the others disappeared..." I said, my voice trailing off. Had they teleported away, or somehow disallowed me to see them?

"I know about healing," I said. "I mean, I haven't tried to learn it yet, but I met some healers. One marshal hinted there might be other people like me, us, in custody."

"So what's it all about, then?" he asked. "Flying? Healing? Invisibility?"

I had a lot of ideas, but none seemed right. I relaxed my mind again and looked toward the window.

"Evolution?" I said. "No...that would imply some kind of change. Understanding? Enlightenment?"

"Close. There isn't a good word for it, but those come close. Even evolution isn't bad, though it conjures images of comic book characters with superpowers."

I immediately thought of Mitch and his X-Men comments.

"So it's about realizing potential," I said. "Peeking behind the curtain of the mundane and seeing the fantastic reality behind?"

"That's very poetic. And essentially correct."

Despite my practice of "skimming" the surface of meditation while flying, conversing that way was fatiguing.

"Would you like to walk?" I asked.

"I should go," he said. "I really just stopped by to introduce myself."

He stood and held out his hand again. I took it, and he held mine without releasing it.

"I also wanted to re-invite you to come with us. You're still young, and very much centered in ego, but I like the way you think."

I sighed.

"Tell me this is not where the FBI shows up," I said.

Tseten laughed.

"No. At least I hope not."

He held his hand to his chest in mock anxiety and then smiled.

"I'm not ready to come with you," I said. "I hope that's not 'ego dominating my intuition.'"

"Not *every* choice is life or death," Tseten said, his face serious.

He finally released my hand.

"You're free to make choices and deal with the consequences."

He walked to the door, opened it, and turned.

"I hope we meet again in this life."

That was one of the stranger things anyone had ever said to me.

"Um...me too."

And with that, he was gone.

This brief article describes how freaking cool it is just to be able to fly.

Excerpt from the blog: *Griffin's Flight*

SEPTEMBER 12, 2025

Besides the emergency parachute, I placed bids on an old-fashioned leather flight suit, helmet, goggles, and a silk scarf. I wasn't cosplaying an old aviator, but the gear for open cockpits would help protect me from bugs, birds, cold, and weather. Zippered pockets, fleece, and all the rest would come in handy during the coming winter.

I also began learning about navigation. I ordered a Private Pilot's Ground School course and started learning as much as I could about how pilots navigate and how airspace is organized. Not only did I want to remain unseen, I also wanted to avoid mid-air collisions and other career-ending catastrophes.

Until my new equipment came, I didn't want to risk more bug encounters, but I couldn't resist the temptation to leave the nest.

The night before, I set my alarm to get up early. It was still fully dark when I climbed to the hayloft.

I didn't even meditate first, just flew up and out of the loft through the hay window at the apex of the roof. I landed on top of the barn and gazed around. There were no lights in my parents' house. None in any of the neighbors' houses either. In the sky, there were only lights from distant jets. Swallowing my fear, I began levitating off the roof of the barn.

I flew straight up, not wanting to get lost. I was planning a quick trip straight up, then right back down.

The view was stunning. I didn't get very high before the lights of traffic on the highway became visible. A little higher, and I could make out the lights from the city to the southwest. Below me, all was dark except the lights from a car moving down my road. I kept a constant watch for airplanes, but there were none nearby.

I flew higher.

The silence was intoxicating. No birds up here, no bugs. I could hear the dull roar of machinery coming from town and some noise from the highway. Other than that, nothing.

I went higher.

It was getting light in the east now. I would have to land soon. The moon in the west was nearly full, but waning and on its way down. I bathed in the perfection and beauty of that moment.

The fields fairly glowed in the moonlight. I drifted toward my clearing in the woods. There it was, far below. What a strange feeling to look down at the place where I had learned so much.

A dark shape moved through the clearing. I watched, and then several more followed. They were deer, I realized. I knew deer bedded there, but I had never seen them before.

Looking around for airplanes, I went higher. I was probably twice as high as I had been a few minutes ago. The farmland stretched below me like a patchwork quilt. Moonlight reflected off small ponds and creeks. Radio towers blinked red and strobed white. The moon slid slowly toward the horizon, and the eastern sky continued to brighten.

I hung there, suspended by a force I didn't understand, appreciating the beauty of the world in which I lived. Gratitude for being a part of it overwhelmed me. I was excited to be a member of humanity. Everything in that moment was perfect, with no past or future. I was part of all that was happening.

I turned to the east to watch the sunrise. Even if the rising sun illuminated me briefly, there was little chance anyone would see. I assumed my meditation position, legs crossed, and waited.

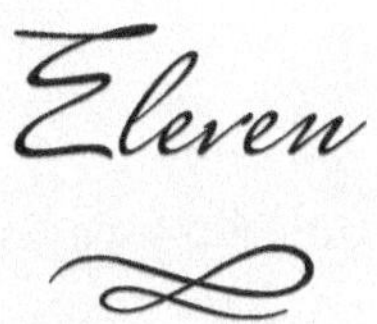

Eleven

When I say, 'he was gone,' I don't mean gone in the sense that he left. I don't mean that he stepped off the porch and drove away, or walked away, or even flew away. He didn't fade out, and there was no flash of light or sound. Tseten existed in the room with me, and in the next fraction of a second, he didn't.

My impulse, nearly undeniable, was to run into the yard and see where he went, to look into the sky or trees, to find him, find an explanation.

"How many laws of physics did you just break?"

Teleportation? Instant transmission? How was that possible?

"How is *flying* possible?" I asked myself as I closed the door.

I had no answers.

I walked to the bed. It was stuffy inside the house, but sometimes that was useful for deep meditation. I took my shoes and socks off. I was already wearing old martial art pants, so they were loose and comfortable, but I untied the drawstring, untucked my t-shirt, and sat down.

To satisfy my brain, I allowed it to review the conversation several times. I thought about the things Tseten had said, about how he appeared to be manipulating me on the one hand, but allowed me the freedom to choose my path on the other.

My ego bristled at words like "manipulate" and "allowed." And while I noticed the ego intrusion, I didn't let it direct my thoughts. Eventually, I could recall the conversation almost clinically, with no emotion. I wondered about their school and what it might be like. Had his departure been an intentional tease? A hook to get me interested in following him?

If so, it was effective. Part of me was deeply curious about what other abilities they taught. Or revealed.

Whatever.

Eventually, I let my thoughts slip away and meditated deeply. During that sort of meditation, I rarely have 'experiences' as such. Time passes, and I have some notion of that, but by limiting and disregarding sensory input, the experience of time becomes inconsistent. That's not the best word. Maybe 'plastic' would be better. At any rate, time becomes inconsistent and is meaningful only in that it will eventually force me to tend to the needs of my body, usually my bladder.

But *this* time, as I meditated, I felt a presence. I didn't feel threatened, but I slit my eyelids and peered into the room. There was no one. I closed my eyes, and it was there again. Not like a body, but I sensed someone to my right, as if their shadow fell over me with my eyes closed. Or maybe like they were a light shining on me. Something like that, but not entirely.

I felt warmth, but not heat, solidity, but no mass. There was no sound of movement, but I sensed amusement as my subconscious processed ideas without words. I relaxed, aware of the presence, but unable to "tune in." The only option was to acknowledge it and move deeper into meditation.

As I did, images came to my mind's eye, images of Gran and Ethan and other friends. Gran tended to a man bitten by a snake. Ethan was worried, Gran confident and at peace. Teri tried to meditate in a white room with bright fluorescent lights. She looked peaceful but tired; her hair hung dirty and limp on the shoulders of a prison jumpsuit.

Mitch was in a similar room. He wore the same color jumpsuit, but he wasn't meditating. Mitch was talking to someone holding a basketball, and he looked angry. I disconnected my emotions from his and tried to watch, curious. I couldn't hear what they were saying, and I couldn't read the words on the jumpsuits.

Eventually, he walked away. The scene shifted, and Agent Stefanie was sitting at a computer, scrolling through screen after screen of text and photos. I couldn't read what was on the screen. A man walked up behind her and began rubbing her shoulders. She rested a hand on his, and then glanced around the room, looking guilty. The other agent, Graham, I thought, took his hands away and pulled up a chair. Stefanie referenced notes on a yellow legal pad. They went back to the screen, and she brought up a new page filled with photos of people I didn't know.

They talked for a while, and then she changed to a screen of younger people, mostly male. Graham seemed satisfied. He briefly rested a hand on Stefanie's knee and then stood and left. I watched her watch him retreat across the room. The look on her face spoke volumes. He wanted more than she did.

Or maybe that was me projecting.

That's when I noticed my bladder. The body brings us back to it, ready or not. I unfolded my legs, wincing as nerves decompressed and restricted blood flow returned.

My bladder was exceptionally full and refused to wait for my legs. I endured pins and needles as I slipped my shoes on, grabbed a light, and headed out to the privy. On my way, I glanced up at the stars. I thought they were bright earlier, in the Appalachians, but here in the Rockies, even competing with moonlight, the sky was simply blazing with stars.

The ones I was used to were there, but it was as if most of the stars had been hidden. There was light everywhere. My bladder nudged me again, so I made my way to the privy.

Back outside, I stood in the yard, looking up, and it wasn't enough. I rose into the air, just clearing the treetops, and the sky opened up. I can't describe the excitement I felt seeing the beauty there. The massive pyramidal mountain, Mt. Ouray, I had learned it was called, rose above me, and I flew up to the summit and lay there. Stars turned overhead, meteors occasionally flashed, and the half moon dominated the sky. I stayed until after the moon set, when I could see even more stars. The Milky Way arched up over the eastern horizon, and it was brighter than I had ever seen in Indiana.

Eventually, I grew sleepy and rose to head back to my cabin. In the dark, I realized I didn't know exactly where it was. I closed my eyes and flew where my gut told me to.

And I found the cabin easily. I slept for several hours and woke around mid-morning.

After a meager breakfast, I was out of food. I debated with myself about where to go next. Colorado Springs was my best bet for having everything that I needed. It was maybe 70 miles to the northeast, over Pike's Peak. But there were maybe a half dozen military installations there. Instinct said no, but intuition was fuzzy.

I shook my head and went back to bed. Perhaps more sleep would help settle the argument.

~

I napped until noon. When I rose, I was more hopeful than I had been in a long time. The conversation with Tseten kept playing in my mind. Should I follow him to his school? Could I learn more quickly there? What about the people looking to me for guidance?

I straightened the cabin and repacked my bags before leaving. I had to go shopping, and I was already hungry. According to the map, Colorado Springs was close, but with all the military bases, being a literal UFO didn't seem like the healthiest choice.

I widened my search and did some basic internet snooping. Eventually, I decided on Grand Junction since there were farmer's markets and other choices for organic food. The problem was that it was over 100 miles away. If my map-reading skills hadn't failed me, there was a river and a system of canyons that would get me there.

I had read that flying in the mountains is dangerous for inexperienced pilots. Even though I didn't worry about aerodynamics and mechanical problems, I was unfamiliar with the weather and air traffic. So, I would take my time getting there and back.

Flying through the mountains on a summer day is indescribably beautiful. Hunger kept me alert. Otherwise, I might have followed some of the more impressive canyons and mountains. I looked forward to exploring the Rockies at some other time.

The flight to Grand Junction took around two hours and was uneventful. I found a decent restaurant and ordered two vegetarian dishes for a late brunch. As I waited, I pondered my next move. I toyed with the idea of flying to Europe and trying to reestablish my site in a country there. Maybe the Pirate Bay would help? They were internet outlaws who were always finding fresh ways to keep their site going despite government interference.

I took advantage of the Wi-Fi and checked my email and social media feeds. My old email accounts were still down, and my new ones had nothing new. It surprised me to find that I could log into my Twitter account.

I hesitated. Could it be a trap to discover my location? Before I tweeted, I made certain to turn all location-sharing off. As I browsed through my Leaders' various feeds, I noted with sadness that there were no posts newer than a week old. Everyone was hiding, in custody, or, God forbid, dead.

My hands were shaking when I hit the "New Tweet" button. And of course, that's when my food came.

I thanked the server who, after being assured that I needed nothing else, left me to my meal.

Despite my hunger, I ignored the food while I decided what to write. Finally, I typed:

Griffin is on the air.

And I set my phone down and began eating.

I ate slowly and meditatively, not for my usual reasons, but because the thought of agents or worse barging through the door with rifles and body armor was terrifying. Meditating controlled the knots in my stomach and allowed me to eat. I had two cups of tea before my food came and then switched to hot water and honey with my meal. My hands were shaking too badly to continue drinking anything with caffeine.

But even though the crowd in the restaurant ebbed and flowed, nobody came crashing through the windows or doors.

Absolutely nobody was interested in me.

Finally, the server came and took my plate. He offered fresh vanilla ice cream made on-site, and I couldn't resist. I asked for a single scoop.

While I waited, I checked Twitter. I had 112 direct messages and over 500 retweets. My heart swelled at those numbers and simultaneously climbed into my throat. The FBI knew by now. Could they force Twitter to reveal my location?

One message was actually from Twitter. They reassured me that my privacy was secure and that I should feel safe using their service. I replied with thanks and took a screenshot of the message. I posted the photo on my feed again with my gratitude.

The ice cream arrived, and I put my phone down to enjoy it. I stopped my server when he brought the check.

"Is it cool if I catch up on some work here? I need to borrow your Wi-Fi for a while."

I handed him three twenties.

"You can keep the change."

He kept my hot water filled for the next hour and a half and brought an enormous bowl of lemon wedges.

I opened my computer and used it to review and respond to the DMs on Twitter. Messages were coming in faster than I could reply, and I couldn't keep up.

Finally, I posted a tweet saying as much. Most of the tweets were positive, with a few inevitable trolls. I received a few strange mentions from a couple of accounts supposedly linked to the hacker group Anonymous. Anonymous is decentralized and anarchical. I wasn't sure whether they were really from the group. The mentions intrigued me because they were offering to help get my site up and keep it running, just to spite the US government.

I chatted with a few of the accounts. The first one I seemed flakey. I responded with something vague about getting in touch later. One finally came in with decent grammar and no exclamation points.

We talked back and forth, and finally they asked for my email address. I was hesitant, but I sent my new email since I wasn't getting anything there anyway. I immediately received this:

Griffin,

I'll start by saying I don't give a rat's arse about your meditation or mutation or whatever. They took your site down, suppressing free speech.

I'm a middle-aged mother living in the UK. I am Anonymous to help people like you whose voices are taken from them, who are oppressed for speaking truth to power.

Send me whatever information you have from your web hosting service, and I'll get you back up. My "friends" and I will host your site and keep the bastards out. You do your thing, and we'll do ours.

Deal?

Anonymous

I've said that I'm not much for conventional prayer, but I said a prayer of thanks right there at that restaurant table.

Three days later, I was back at the cabin, rested and peaceful once again. I needed to move on soon, but the feeling wasn't insistent yet. I was safe for the moment.

I sat in the shade of the front porch working on my computer. While in town, I bought a solar charger for my electronics. It was small and slow, but it got the job done. My website was back up. Yesterday, I posted a new article that brought the timeline up to date. I was very honest about almost everything. I revealed nothing about my web savior, not even that she was Anonymous.

Today I was reading through comments and replying to some of them. And I was cleaning out spam. Even with Anonymous keeping my site up, I still got spam.

I found a comment from someone with the screen name S_Tucciarone. I didn't want to risk a chat session or email, so I replied out in the open via the comment thread.

S_TUCCIARONE

Good to see that you're back in business!

GRIFFIN

Really? I wasn't sure how you would feel.

It took a few minutes before she responded.

Is there a way to talk privately?

Unfortunately, no. The FBI would love for me to try.

Have you seen the news? More federal agents are dead.

No, I hadn't seen that.

She sent a link to a news story. There was a video, too. Apparently, agents had been moving prisoners to D.C. for questioning when they were ambushed. One detainee was shot and killed, along with three agents who had acted to protect their prisoners.

I was furious, but impotent, watching the video.

Are you telling me that those were my Leaders being moved?

I'm uncomfortable discussing this here.

I don't care. I don't trust any of you anymore. To anyone reading this, I'm speaking with Agent Stefanie of the FBI.

Not smart.

Those were my people?

One detainee died. Three Federal Agents. Some would say that's your responsibility.

You rounded them up, that's why they were attacked!

Not true.

She linked two more stories about people shot to death in their own homes.

Those are ones we didn't get to in time.

Why were they in the open? Who knew they were
being moved? Do you have leaks in the FBI?

You can't blame this on us. We're trying to help.

Then catch these bastards!

Come in. Take down this site, so we don't have
to. You're putting more people in danger.

I stopped responding after that. Within a half an hour, Stefanie had deleted all of her comments and erased her presence from the site.

The next day, several things happened.

First, the news sites began talking about me. Not by name, at least not yet. But they referred to me as an 'apparent spiritual leader' with a website where I incited my followers to defy the government. There were several stories from different outlets. None of them gave my web address. Still, the site began getting a lot more traffic.

And I did something I had never done. I posted an article that ended with this statement:

'In a perfect world, I could visit each of you, anyone reading this article. We could meet and interact one on one. I look forward to living in that world.'

I began receiving requests for visits almost immediately.

The news became more biased as time passed. By July, the words "fraud" and "cult" began appearing in many of the stories. They said I was a scam artist, preying on innocent victims.

On the morning of the fourth, I packed my bags. I had spent more time in the cabin than planned. I added another $100 bill to the two on the mantle before I cleaned up and left.

Once again, I had many options. I had money, and I was well rested and healthy. On the downside, I was angry with the FBI almost constantly. Anger is another manifestation of fear and ego, and I wanted to let it go.

I flew through the mountains toward Salt Lake City. The weather was cool, and I had a decent mental picture of the route. I felt good kicking up the speed a little since the visibility was excellent.

In Salt Lake City, I found a park where an Independence Day celebration was in full swing, complete with fireworks and food. I ate a hot dog and even had a beer. It felt normal, almost like I was a tourist. I chatted and relaxed.

I milled with the crowd and found what I hoped would be a decent spot to see the fireworks. Leaning against a wooden fence at the edge of the park, I watched the sun set and the stars come out.

"Mind if I join you?"

It was Sheila. I glanced around, but no one was paying attention.

"Honestly, yes," I said.

"Fair enough. I'll say my piece and be on my way."

My anger and tension levels were rising, so I worked on releasing them.

"Go ahead," I sighed.

"Tseten said that you and he got along well," she began.

"Well enough."

"He said that you are still being stubborn, refusing to come with us."

"Stubborn? Maybe. Refuse, yes. I refuse to have my choices made for me by anyone else. I don't care how spiritually advanced you are. Or claim to be."

"I'm not...we're not trying to make your choices for you," she said. "We just want you to be safe, and to understand the implications of your choices, the consequences of your actions."

"You don't think I'm capable of that right now?" I asked.

"You are, but you're perhaps blinded by the novelty of your discoveries."

"Which is to say you think I'm too immature to handle what I've learned."

"In a word, yes."

I gave the only appropriate response. I stuck my tongue out at her. She laughed, and I smiled, despite my anger.

"I might be immature," I said after a moment. "I won't deny it."

"There's a lot to learn," Sheila said. "You've seen some things my friends and I can do, and most of us didn't start this path until later in life. Imagine what you could eventually do with the head start you have!"

"You're appealing to my ego now?" I said.

"Not ego. Your sense of adventure. And maybe common sense."

There was a muffled BOOM as the fireworks started.

"I'll leave," she said. "Be careful over the next few days."

"What? Why?" I asked.

"They're turning the public against you," she said.

There were more booms and flashes.

"Stay safe," she said, and, like Tseten, was gone.

I sighed.

"I need to learn that one," I said and turned my attention to the show.

There is no growth without risk. But risk doesn't have to be reckless. This article tells how I outgrew my first practice area and found a new one.

~

Excerpt from the blog: *Griffin's Flight*

SEPTEMBER 20, 2025

I now had a parachute, helmet, goggles, and scarf. The only thing I needed daily was the goggles. Protecting my eyes was important, but I wasn't ready for long-distance flights, and the weather was warm.

So, I walked back through the fields, goggles in my pocket, but I left my blanket and cushion in my apartment. I wore jeans, a t-shirt, and tennis shoes. I needed a practice area with more room than the forest clearing, but that kept me hidden.

Dad was working inside the barn, so once hills and trees shielded me from view, I slipped my goggles on and flew up over the corn. The field outside the woods where my clearing was could work, but it was too close to my parents. I flew back another quarter of a mile and did an appraisal.

It looked okay, but I would prefer something more remote. Pushing my goggles up on top of my head, I checked the map on my phone. It showed my location and if I included the satellite overlay, I could get a sense of where I wanted to be.

Finally, I knew where I needed to go. Phone in my pocket and goggles back down, I headed back, skimming the tops of the corn.

It was quiet back there. The vegetation absorbed the sound of the highway. I felt like I was in one of those soundproof rooms, with the spikey insulation on the walls. I rolled over onto my back as I was flying and went farther into the fields.

There were clouds in the sky, but it was reasonably clear. Suddenly, I had an idea. *If I waited until it was overcast, I could fly up above the cloud cover and practice all I wanted without fear of being seen, except by airplanes.* I couldn't believe I had never thought of it before now. I couldn't wait to try it out.

But, for now, I rolled so my stomach was brushing the corn tassels, and crossed a fence into a field that was nearly perfect. It was roughly a mile and a half north of my parents' house. A creek curved around and bordered one side of the field. A small wood and wooded fence rows bounded the other sides. One fence had an opening for a gate, but the gate was long gone. This field was roughly three acres and planted in hay. It didn't belong to my family, but I wasn't worried about using it to practice. They cut hay four or five times a year, and wouldn't interfere much with my training. By farming standards, the field was small, but it was huge compared to my clearing.

I flew to the center of the field and hovered, listening.

Only birds and insects disturbed the silence.

I flew up to the height of the treetops and stopped. I rotated 360 degrees but could see no houses, barns, or roads. Not until the leaves fell, anyway.

I climbed 50 feet above the treetops and looked. Still, I could see nothing.

Perfect.

Now I could get down to business.

I wanted to learn about *speed*. How fast could I accelerate? How fast could I slow down? What effects would it have on my body?

I started by running across the field and timing myself. If I sprinted, I could cross the field at 15 miles per hour. When I flew, I could easily quadruple that speed and feel no effects. No acceleration, no deceleration, nothing.

Interesting.

Later, just for fun, I tried a running launch into the air. Actually, I tried several. It took about 10 tries before I managed it. Timing was key. Once I got the hang of it, though, I got pretty good at it.

There was one spot where the field sloped down to the water. The creek was about eight feet across, with a four-foot bank on the other side. I practiced until I could take a running leap, jumping from one bank to the other.

Again, for fun, I wanted to jump over a tree. I picked the tallest, fullest, black walnut tree in the fence row. I took a running start, gave a big jump, and flew to the top of the tree. At the top of the arc, I tucked and rolled, coming down feet first. I landed and kept running through the next field.

Very pleased, I ran all the way back home. I jumped over all the fences and gates on my way. It had gotten to the point I was no longer sure if I was flying to aid my physical skills or not. Like running, levitation was becoming habitual to me, instinctive.

Twelve

The next morning, I received a message via the website from a member I didn't know. In it was a link to a geocache in Billings, Montana. I packed my campsite by 9:00 am, plotted a course while sipping tea, and was in the sky by 10:00.

As I flew, I kept the usual eye out for other air traffic, but I considered what my next course of action should be. I needed a short-term goal, and I needed to reevaluate my long-term ones.

Obviously, staying free and alive was top of the list, but I needed something else to work toward. I thought about the people in custody for helping me and studying my work. Was there anything I could do?

I thought about Tseten and Sheila. I played the mental images of them disapparating in front of me as easily as Professors Dumbledore and McGonagall would. If I could do that, I could break anyone out of any facility. Could I find out where they were? Could I teach myself to teleport?

Of course, helping people escape from federal custody was itself a crime. A real crime that would allow the FBI to imprison me, legally, for a long, long time.

But if I could teleport, could they imprison me?

It was too much to think about and fly at the same time.

When I flew over Yellowstone, I kept my eye on the scenery below, watching for geysers, elk, bison, bears, wolves, and whatever else I might see. My parents had brought me here as a kid, but I had never been here as an adult.

From altitude, it was hard to make out individual animals, but there were small herds of elk and bison. There were thermal pools everywhere, and vast areas of steam rising into the air. I flew over a lodge and wondered if it was the one near Old Faithful, the geyser that erupts with clock-like regularity. Sadly, there was no time for sightseeing. I mean, the park was enormous. And I wanted to see what was in the cache in Montana. It could be critical information.

I poured on the speed and was over Billings within the hour. I found the landmarks that I had noted earlier and picked a landing spot in a park that I hoped was as empty as it looked from the air.

It wasn't, but I landed unseen. People don't look up very often. I thought maybe I could take off and land on a busy street and nobody would notice.

I kept my pack with me rather than stashing it. The possibility that I was walking into a trap hadn't escaped me, and I couldn't plan on coming back for anything.

Water is heavy, but I kept two bottles in my duffel for emergencies. Trying to save it, I found a park bench near a water fountain. I took my pack off, filtered some water, and rested for a few minutes. After a few dozen squats and push-ups, I made my way to the hidden cache.

I walked a dozen blocks and opened the app. It looked like the cache was in the parking lot between a motel and a bakery. There were hundreds of potential hiding places. If I spent any amount of time here, my bags and strange behavior would surely draw attention. It would be better to get a room and stow my pack before looking.

I hadn't yet been brave enough to try it, but I pulled out my spare wallet. There was a fake driver's license and a credit card that had been in a previous drop. I double-checked the name and birth date before I entered the motel.

The lobby was tiny but clean, and I rang the bell.

"Hi there!" the clerk said, coming around a corner. "How can I help you?"

"Just need a room, Shelly," I said, reading her name tag and setting my bags down.

She was cute, younger than me, but not a kid. She used the mouse and keyboard for a moment.

"Any room preferences?"

"Non-smoking?"

"All our rooms are non-smoking, ma'am," she said, waving at the prominent sign on the wall.

"Perfect."

"Just you then?"

"Yes, um, just me. No pets or…other people."

She glanced at me, took in my rumpled shirt and wind-blown hair, and went back to her computer.

"May I see your ID and method of payment?"

"Here you go. You can scan the card, I think, but I'd like to pay cash, if that's okay."

"You think?" she asked, eyebrows raised.

"What?"

"You said you 'think' I can scan the card. What does that mean?"

"Um…well, I haven't been home for a while," I said hesitantly. "I'm not sure…the bill's paid." My voice trailed away.

"You're what? Hiking across the country?"

"Hiking! Yes, I'm a hiker. I hike a lot."

"Good," she said, eyebrow raised, but all business. "Let's see if your card works."

She swiped it and scanned my license and apparently wasn't instructed to contact Homeland Security because she gave me a key card and told me how to find my room.

"Um, is there someplace to get decent food and a haircut?" I asked.

"Stella's is good," she said, pointing out the bakery across the parking lot, "if you like pancakes and cinnamon rolls."

Shelly directed me to a hair salon accepting walk-ins, and I made my way there after stowing my bags and grabbing a long, hot shower. Despite being busy, it took only an hour to get my hair cut and styled. It made the stylist's day when I asked her to chop my long hair very short.

Afterwards, one of the other ladies in the shop pointed me to a farmers market where I replenished my fresh food.

When I walked back into the hotel lobby sporting my newly shorn do, Shelly didn't recognize me.

"How can I help you today?"

Her bright smile had been a few shades dimmer the first time I was in.

"It's just me, from before. The hiker," I added when she still looked clueless.

"Oh! Hi," she said, smiling again. "Gosh, you look different!"

I grinned. Hopefully, this hairstyle would handle flight (and flight helmets) while looking good. Shelly seemed to approve, at least.

"Thanks," I said, running my hand over my head self-consciously. "I don't suppose there have been any messages for me? Do people still do that? Leave messages at hotel desks?"

"Um…no. I mean, they could, but most people have cell phones, so…" she shrugged.

"Right. Okay, just checking."

"Are…are you busy tonight?" she asked as I turned to leave.

"Busy? No, I'm…not busy," I said, trying to think of what a normal person might say.

"Well, would you like to do something?" She lowered her voice. "Technically, we're not supposed to date guests, but…" her voice trailed off again, and she looked away.

"Um…yeah, okay, that would be great," I said. "I'm not doing anything, so whenever is good for me."

"I should be done by four. Can I pick you up at six?"

"Great, I'll see you then," I said, smiling back at her.

D espite having showered earlier, once in my room, I climbed into the bath and relaxed. An hour later, I was ironing a shirt for my date.

But I hadn't forgotten my reason for being in Billings. Back in the parking lot, I poked around looking for the cache.

There must be a thousand places to hide something, I thought.

Finally, after rechecking the app and decoding a clue, I found a loose brick in a combination flower planter and park bench. I removed the brick and, in the space behind, found a thumb drive. I took the drive and left a piece of red sandstone that I had been carrying around since visiting the Grand Canyon.

My stomach tightened with excitement as I hurried back to my room with the thumb drive. I sat at the desk and opened my laptop, plugged in the drive and ran a virus check. The computer automatically scanned it, but I used another service that my contact with Anonymous had suggested for keeping the government off my computer.

It found nothing malicious, so I looked in the drive's directory. It was password protected. I went back to the message on my site that had brought me here. There was no password. In addition, nothing looked out of place or password-ish. What could it be? Would I give someone a password-protected drive without giving them at least an idea of the password?

Not a chance.

I searched for other posts by the same user.

There it was. Yesterday, a discussion about hacking devolved into a discussion about hacking movies. The user Caterpillar76 had posted only once in the thread.

"Well, we're way beyond birthdays now."

That was a quote from the movie *Clear and Present Danger*, based on the Tom Clancy novel. But what did it mean?

I tried my birthday in several formats.

Nothing.

I tried my parents' birthdays.

Nothing.

I tried combining them like in the movie.

Nothing worked.

"Way beyond birthdays..."

Caterpillar...76.

Rebirth? New beginnings? I tried the date when I first levitated, and that did the trick.

There was a video file in the root directory, plus a folder titled LEAD-ERS. The title of the video was "Watch Me," so I loaded it first.

It used the standard Anonymous talking head in a Guy Fawkes mask and an artificially generated voice.

Ms. Donnelly,

Kudos for finding and opening this drive. Some of us doubted you could follow the clues.

We have compiled a list of your people who are still alive. It's not as long as you might hope. They have murdered many people. You should know that several groups have joined in a loose *alliance* and are operating covertly to kill or capture people connected to you.

You might suspect that Russia is involved, but as far as we can tell, they are not. North Korea has allied with Iran and other fascist Islamic republics. There are also forces formerly associated with Al Qaeda oper-ating and killing inside the United States. The American government has neutralized many assassins, but there is no shortage of replacements.

Most troubling, corporations around the world are helping transport and finance these teams. We suspect that none of this surprises you.

Would it surprise you to know that *American* corporations are involved in the attempts to kill you and the people helping you? Would it surprise you to know that religious organizations are helping?

Anonymous has rallied behind you in an unprecedented fashion. Oper-atives across the globe are working to keep you safe and your message alive. However, you are always in grave danger. You should be very careful before meeting people in person, as you mentioned. It could do more harm than good.

We are working to find these assassins and report them to the authori-ties. The US government is using the information we feed them and either capturing or killing the hit teams. But the people hunting you are like cock-roaches, scurrying from the light as soon as they lose their advantage.

Be safe, Ms. Donnelly. If you are for real, as some of us think you may be, then a different kind of revolution is coming: a revolution of mind and spirit. But if you die, if you allow the nefarious forces allied against you to succeed, that revolution may die on the vine. Please don't let that happen.

We are Anonymous.
We are Legion.
Expect us.

I sat back, stunned.

American corporations? Churches? Allied with fascist governments to kill me? How was that possible?

What should I do? The government is killing or capturing these people, and they just keep coming… "like cockroaches." I didn't panic exactly, but it was scary. I wasn't mentally equipped to deal with hordes of fascist assassins.

And what about Anonymous? Had my plight brought the notoriously nebulous group together? Was that a good thing? Did helping me make them more vulnerable?

I shook my head. What should I do next? I sat up and opened the folder on the drive.

Inside were three spreadsheets labeled "In Custody," "Free," and "Deceased." These people weren't much for subtlety. I opened the one marked "In Custody." I found my parents' names and Mitch and Teri's. They were at the same facility in Dayton, Ohio. I didn't know many of the names, but there was a column for their usernames, and those I recognized. The level of detail they had accumulated was amazing.

I opened the one labeled "Free." There were hundreds and hundreds of names. What was this? Were these people reading the site? Were they all meditating, learning to fly? Or were they just casual visitors? It was as detailed as the first group.

Finally, I opened the file labeled "Deceased." Inside were names I recognized from the news stories, and some of them had screen names I recognized as well. I remembered specific conversations with some of these people. Tears rolled down my face as I read the names on the list.

Part of me wanted revenge. I won't deny it. I think of myself as a good person, but there is a part of me that longed to end the life of every person responsible for a single name on this list. Could I do it? I hoped I would never find out.

I took my time reading through the dozens of names on the last sheet. The longer I spent, the surer I was of my next move. I wouldn't wait around or do any sightseeing. Staying ahead of the FBI wasn't important. Living at Tseten and Sheila's school wasn't even an option.

I was going to ignore part of Anonymous' advice and start visiting people on the "Free" list. Anonymous had given me their names and addresses, but I doubted that anyone else besides Anonymous had them. I copied the lists to my computer and began planning.

Excerpt from the blog: *Griffin's Flight*

JULY 2, 2025

Walking meditation isn't much different from sitting, although the movement and balance issues make it harder to maintain the state of "no-thought" that *is* meditation.

I walked around the perimeter of my clearing four or five times before I tried to levitate. While walking, I imagined the whooshing, dropping feeling in the pit of my stomach.

Nothing happened.

I thought about levitating, pictured myself floating up.

Nothing.

I need more practice.

JULY 8

It's frustrating when nothing happens. But, as I have learned, frustration is a sign that I'm not experiencing "now." I struggle to stay in the moment and not lose myself in thoughts of the future. I try to stay focused on myself and what I'm doing.

This morning, I didn't consciously change anything. I walked, I meditated, and I felt. That was all I knew to do.

When it happened, I was, of course, surprised. I took a step and missed the ground. I thought I was falling and instinctively raised my hands to catch myself. This misstep broke my meditation, and I stepped down hard onto the ground, stumbling.

I kept practicing, bolstered by my success. It's just a matter of time.

JULY 18

Other than actual levitation itself, this is the hardest refinement I have practiced. It's like walking off the edge of a building. My body feels like it's going to fall, and I'm having a hard time convincing it otherwise.

Of course, fear lives in the ego and the future. To bring myself firmly into the present, I put my attention in my breath and my body as I walk. I was practicing mindfulness, meditation, and levitation all at the same time.

Today, finally, I stepped off the ground and into the air with no emotion at all.

What a strange sensation, to float above the ground and yet feel as if I were standing on the ground. I couldn't sense weight in my feet, but I felt secure and not precarious at all. I had wondered if my legs would dangle, as if suspended by my torso, but that wasn't the case. My body was buoyant, not hanging from support, like every cell in my body was levitating.

When I lifted from the ground, I flew right up toward the branches, only a dozen feet above my head. I didn't get the rocketing acceleration I felt the first time I tried to control my altitude, but a slow, gentle ascent.

I reached out to a branch and took hold of it. The smooth toughness of the bark and the solid mass of the limb registered as if I were standing on the ground, but with no sense of weight in my feet. If I didn't think about moving, then I didn't move. I pushed the limb and glided away.

I had imagined feeling my body's mass, and I did. My muscles felt resistance, and Newton seemed to be there when I pushed away from the tree. I looked at the distance between my feet and the ground and remembered Sir Isaac was not exactly in charge here.

I glided up and cleared the tops of the trees, where I stopped. Turning with a thought, my house came into view. Despite the bright sun, the air was cooler above the treetops. There was a slight breeze and lower humidity than among the trees. Cumulus clouds crawled across the sky. On the horizon, they were building into large storm clouds.

Someday, hopefully before the end of the summer, I'll explore the clouds, feel the powerful vertical currents of air and catch hailstones with my bare hands. Not yet though, I'm not ready, and I have no desire to die like Icarus, attempting too much too soon.

So, it's baby steps for me — slow, disciplined progress. I landed and gathered my things. I had to get back to work.

Thirteen

JULY 14

My site was up and running. The government didn't know my location. My parents, if not free, were at least safe. And I... had a date?

It was a weird day.

I wrote the Letter to the World and posted it that afternoon. The response was instant and explosive. News people around the world wrote to the site asking for interviews. Regular people wrote inviting me to visit and teach them in person. The response was overwhelming, and the site's servers couldn't handle it. It went down an hour before my date with Shelly.

I ignored the onslaught of email and turned on the television. I wanted time to think, to consider actions and consequences. Would there would be anything about me on the news?

I sat back to watch and quickly remembered why I hated watching the news. There was little substance to the reporting. A lot of the stories focused on sensational topics chosen to increase viewership rather than to inform. Truthfully, not everything was unimportant, but much of the reporting was shallow. It was as if their goal was to confirm pre-existing bias rather than to inform and educate.

I turned the television off, went down to the exercise room, and began walking on a treadmill. I put some quiet music in my earbuds and meditated while I walked. Before I knew it, it was time to meet Shelly.

I found her knocking on my door.

"Oh, hi!" she said, seeing me coming up the stairs.

"Hello. Wow! You look great!"

And she did. Her professional, pulled back, buttoned-up persona was gone. Her blond hair was down, revealing a streak of green on one side. She wore jeans, cowboy boots, and a loose short-sleeve shirt unbuttoned over a creamy silk cami. I might not have recognized her if I hadn't been expecting her.

"So do you," she said, smiling. "Were you looking for me?"

"No, I was just…walking."

I had just written about taking your practice out into the world with you. Why was I hesitant to mention that I was meditating?

"Oh," she said, apparently puzzled about something. "I didn't plan anything. What would you like to do?"

"Oh, I don't know. I'm always hungry. What about dinner?"

"Sure," she said, and we began walking toward the stairway. "You want to go to Stella's, or someplace nicer?"

"Is there someplace that has organic food? Or something vegetarian?" I asked.

"I'll check when we get to the car. Can I ask you a question?"

"Sure."

"You're here, hiking around the world, and while you're waiting for me, you take a walk?"

Well, hell, I thought.

"Uh, yeah. Look, it might sound crazy, but I needed to clear my mind."

"You don't have to explain."

"The truth is, I am traveling without a car, but I'm not exactly hiking. Not all the way, anyway."

"What, you're hitchhiking? Taking the bus?"

"Hitchhiking," I said, thinking of my time in the back seat of Teri and Mitch's car. "Kind of."

She skipped down the stairs in front of me.

"We'll come back to it," she said, unlocking a giant pickup truck. It was charcoal gray, and I almost needed to levitate to get to the passenger seat.

"I see why you're not wearing a skirt," I said.

She flashed a bright smile and started the truck. The day was hot, and she cranked up the air conditioning.

"Let's see. You're a vegetarian?"

"Not really. But I only like to eat meat raised on pasture, not grain."

"Oh, is that all? I know just the place."

She reversed out of the parking space and took me to a ritzy place called Bistro Enzo. They had grass-fed burgers, lamb, fish, salads; you name it. The food was delicious.

After we had eaten, Shelly and I sipped wine and chatted. It was refreshing to sit and talk with a woman, but also surreal. I mean, people were trying to kill me.

"So, you want to tell me how you're getting around?" she asked.

I puffed air through my cheeks in resignation.

"It will change everything tonight. Are you sure you want to have this conversation?"

She looked at me as if calculating in her head.

"Shoot," she said, not breaking her gaze.

"Okay." I leaned forward.

"I signed into the hotel with a fake I.D.," I said conspiratorially. "My real name is…OUCH!"

Shelly had snatched her dessert spoon and whacked me on the head with it.

"Do NOT say your name out loud!" she hissed. "Are you *stupid?* Don't you realize how many people are trying to keep you safe?"

My head smarted. She had hit me hard enough that it brought tears to my eyes. I rubbed it, but it didn't help.

"What are you talking about? Ouch…who are you?"

"Well, *I'm* smart enough not to answer that question, aren't I?"

My head was swimming. Was Shelly the one who brought me to Montana?

"You're getting there," she said, eyeing me shrewdly. She glanced around. "I'm the one who left the cache."

"What, you? You're Anon…" she raised the spoon, threatening intent apparent on her face.

"Er…you're the one, huh?"

"Yes. One of the ones. I was following your site before everything went tits up."

"Oh. So, then you…. Grf. I don't know. Can we go somewhere and talk? I don't know how to talk about this here."

"Not the hotel," she said. "I'm not convinced they haven't bugged the rooms."

"Seriously?"

"Well, I'm not convinced they have, either."

"So…where?" I asked.

"My place. My partner will be there, but they're involved, too."

"Partner," I said, nodding.

"Sorry. Seriously. You're much cuter than this morning."

"Great. Thanks."

"Let's go," she said.

Shelly and Jake, not their actual names, I'm sure, were good people. Despite the awkwardness of me being on a date with their girlfriend, I liked Jake. They showed me their computers and their work, but they were both cautious to speak in generalities. They never admitted to breaking any laws, only to vague "exploits" and "jobs."

I stayed out late, but I learned a lot. We worked on the design of my site to make it easier to tell who was a "White Hat" and who was a "Black Hat." I wasn't sure I would remember everything they tried to teach me, but I tried.

The White Hats were anyone on either their team or mine. Black Hats were the hackers attacking the site and the mercenaries attacking and killing my team. The Gray Hats were anyone working with the U.S. government, local police, or anyone we weren't sure of. Tseten and Sheila fell into that category.

Jake gave me a couple of new phones and took my old ones. Shelly worked some magic and made new email accounts and a new Geocaching account.

"Shelly and I have your account name. We'll hook you up with whatever you need. Don't hesitate to ask." Jake said.

"Right."

"If you get in trouble," Shelly said, "text 911 to the White Hat number. We'll have your addy and get someone to you pronto."

"Right."

"We can grab a pic from your phone to see what's going on. Our own little virus," Jake said, "Don't use this one for your porn."

"Porn? I don't…."

"Whatever," they said, holding up a hand to stop me. "Just don't. Someone will check in occasionally."

"Good to know, I guess."

"Oh, your server's back up," Jake said, hitting a key and bringing up stats on the site.

"Nice. Over a million hits since it came back up."

"Holy crap. Is that all real, or bots?"

"All real. Sure, there are bots, but we don't include those in the traffic stats. They're trying to take the site down. We're routing them to the North Korean server."

"How on earth did you get a server in North Korea?"

"Friend of a friend," Shelly said, "You don't want to know."

"Grey Jedi exist," Jake said, nodding sagely.

"I don't know if I'm comfortable with that," I said.

"Luckily you don't have to be," Jake said, a hard edge creeping into their voice. "This is our job. Yours is staying alive. You can't do that if you're out there giving your name to every piece of ass you want to ride."

"Look man… er," I fumbled and started over. "Sorry. Look, I appreciate your help and all, but there's no need to be like that."

"I'm just telling you like it is," Jake said. "You can't afford relationships, or even friendships, right now. These are bad dudes after you."

"I get that."

"I'm not just talking about the ones with the guns," they said.

"The hackers they've got working your site?" Shelly said, "Top notch. We've got it bouncing around the world, around the clock, and they've still got us on our heels most of the time. They're really superb."

"Okay. I get it. No romance. No friends. Fine. What else?"

"I don't have to say, 'don't go home,' right?" Jake asked.

"You mean Mom and Dad's house? No. That's been a given for a while."

"Don't even go anywhere you've been before," Shelly said. "By now, they've dissected your life and they're running algorithms to figure out the most likely places that you'll go next. Try not to think like yourself. Think like someone else."

I didn't know how to do that, but I assured them I would try.

Shelly took me back to the hotel.

"Do you even work here?" I asked.

"Yup. Access to information and the occasional credit card," she said.

"Ugh," I said, "I don't want to know."

She laughed, and I unlocked the door.

"See you in the morning!" she said.

We shook hands, and I jumped out.

I used to like to watch movies before bed when I traveled. Tonight, I was simply too exhausted. I dropped off instantly and slept through the night.

In the morning, I got up, showered, and tried to think like someone else.

Where had I never been? The west coast.

There were many on the list who lived on the west coast, but what about safety? I wouldn't consider anyone who requested a visit. I would drop in on people. If they recognized me, I would ask if they wanted to meditate together.

I opened my computer and found the itinerary I had started yesterday. I picked the northernmost name and plotted a course.

I didn't mention dinner when I checked out. I thanked Shelly for her help. Our eyes met and held for a moment, and she smiled and nodded. I sighed, picked up my bag, and left without looking back. The walk to the park seemed longer than yesterday. I suppose I missed human contact. Dinner had been great if you didn't count the hitting and the aggressive partner at the end. But the basic conversation with a lovely woman? It was good.

I found the spot where I landed and suited up. There were occasional breaks in the cloud cover, and I waited for one to pass over. When it was time, I pulled my helmet on, goggles down, hoisted my bags into place and jumped into the air, targeting the slender patch of blue.

The sun dazzled me, as it always does when I break out on top. The air was crisp, and the sunlight reflecting off the tops of the clouds was blinding. I wished for my tinted goggles at times like these.

My next stop was Seattle. I looked forward to seeing the Pacific and the volcanoes, but more than that, I looked forward to meeting people who had read my blog. What would they be like? Would any of them have levitated yet? Would it be possible for them to?

There were too many questions to consider while flying. I put it all out of my head and flew.

JULY 5, 2026

Dear World,

Since you're reading this, you know that I've had help to get my website back up and to keep it up. Some of the smartest, bravest people on the planet are helping me, and I'm grateful. I hope you are too.

The people in my government aren't happy about this. They would like nothing better than to shut me down. Safety is their stated reason, both mine and yours, the people who interact with me online.

The sad fact is that people in power, foreign and domestic, are killing (or trying to kill) anyone who comes in contact with me. They have tried to capture or kill me several times. So far, they've been unsuccessful. Unfortunately, some of my friends haven't been so lucky. You may have heard of the unexplained murders happening around the country. It isn't a hoax or a paranoid delusion. It is a well- planned, well-funded attack on brave people with open minds.

With the help of my new friends, I hope the murders are at an end.

But there are still secrets, things the news and the government aren't telling you.

Many of the missing people are in federal custody. This includes many of my Leaders and my own parents. The government seized their farm, and it is being sold in a ploy to get me to turn myself in.

Despite their stated intentions, another motivator for the federal government is control. I represent freedom that could disrupt the fortunes of many. The wealthy and powerful want to *remain* wealthy and powerful.

The thing is, remember the Sunday school lesson? It's easier for a camel to go through the eye of a needle than for a rich man to enter the Kingdom of Heaven. Flying may not be the Kingdom of Heaven, but it's close.

I don't think you can worry about money and power and discover the ability to levitate and fly. I don't think you can levitate and fly if your purpose is to carry a gun and shoot people, even if your purpose is protective.

Meditation, levitation, flight, healing, and other gifts are about peace. If you aren't at peace, you can't fly. If you aren't peaceful, you can't heal. And yes, I've seen people who could heal. I've seen people who can disappear and, I suppose, reappear somewhere else. That's beyond my abilities so far.

Listen, World, I want to help you. I really do. But I would love it if people stopped trying to kill my friends and me. It would be quite nice if people stopped lying about me, but I can handle that. It's the killing that has to stop.

If you're a friend, could you join me in meditating for peace? I'm going to post some links about the Global Consciousness Project* at Princeton University. Look at the data. In a nutshell, it seems to show that when we watch something, pay attention to it, it changes. If we watch with intent, it changes even more.

So, meditate with me. Meditate on peace, on love, and on goodwill. I don't mind challenges. If it were safe, I would do the talk shows, show people what I do. I would teach and explain and help you move forward. But that idea scares the hell out of powerful people. My mother always says that the opposite of fear is love. So please let's send love to the people who need it most, the ones who are holding us back.

Don't be angry; be peaceful. Don't be afraid; be loving. Practice. Meditate. Meditate in groups, in parks, on street corners, wherever you can. Don't stop people from going about their day, but be honest about what you are doing. Whether you meditate with a mantra, or silently, listening to music, or jogging, I don't care. Just quiet your mind, leave the words and agendas behind. Appreciate stillness and peace. Remember, "the Tao that can be spoken is not the true Tao."

People have been meditating for centuries, millennia even. Only a handful have levitated or flown. Don't make that your goal. However, I believe that this is coming around for a reason, and flight isn't the only gift I've seen. Maybe your gifts lie on another path, or even in everyday life. Please don't be disappointed if that's the case. You're still a better person for making meditation part of your life.

After you learn to meditate in stillness, take your meditation with you

---

* https://noosphere.princeton.edu

into your daily lives. That is where the magic happens, where you transform your life and open to the magic of the lives around you.

"The Kingdom of Heaven is within you!"

Claim that experience for yourself, and I believe that "greater things than these shall you do."

Anyway, World, I'm not here to preach to you. Just because my parents raised me as a Christian and I look at the world through the filter of Christianity doesn't mean that I don't hold other belief systems in high regard. I am very much influenced by the cosmology of my Native American and Celtic ancestors, who revered the divinity of nature. I'm equally in love with the philosophies of Asia: Zen Buddhism and Taoism. As a martial art student, I have learned and internalized a lot of these philosophies, since they go hand in hand with the martial art precepts of peace and nonviolence. I also love the dedication and rigor with which Muslims worship. They truly bring their spiritual practice into their daily lives.

And you know, I appreciate the agnostic and atheistic views as well. They have merit and keep the others grounded. Our atheistic friends remind us that faith is not logical. We can't explain our own spiritual experience, and they are right to doubt the truth of it. If levitation is real, then secular meditation should get you to the same place as religious meditation. If people can fly and heal and teleport, then the phenomenon is real and measurable. If it's not, then it's not.

So, agnostic and atheistic world, try it yourself. Meditate, find the gap, and see what's there waiting for you. Maybe something, maybe nothing, but until you prove it for yourself, you won't know. If your agnosticism and atheism are based on belief and philosophy and not experience, then you, too, are a member of a religion and not a freethinker.

Dear World, I look forward to meeting you someday. I'm trying to find you, but I need you to find me, too. Please meditate for peace, meditate for healing, meditate for love. If you do, we'll find each other soon enough.

Grif

Fourteen

I sat cross-legged on a stranger's floor and meditated as raindrops tapped against the windows and roof. Levitation wasn't my plan. I wanted to start slowly, to meditate with the others. But there was movement in the room. The white noise provided by the rain comforted me and made meditation easy. But the group seemed restless. I opened my eyes to catch the girl across from me peeking, one eye open. When she saw me looking, her eye blinked shut.

"Um…okay," I said, my voice raspy.

I cleared my throat.

"Let's relax for a minute, open your eyes when you want, move your legs a little. Come back to your conscious mind slowly."

Everyone began moving, opening their eyes and looking around. Some had a bleary-eyed look that told me they had fallen asleep, but most of the group seemed alert. I doubted they had managed much meditation, and I thought I knew why.

The group called themselves the Pacific Pacifists, and some of them had been meditating together for years. They occasionally read my blog during group sessions and talked about it during their discussion times. Most of them were young, maybe in their mid-20s. A few were middle-aged, and one lady had to be 80. We were at her house.

"Liv, would you like some tea?"

Two women were passing around glasses and offering iced herbal tea or water. I accepted tea, and when they had finished, spoke to the room.

"So, I think I made a mistake," I began. "I should have addressed the elephant in the room before we started, but I didn't want to lead from ego. It's something that I have to be careful of. The catch-22 is that in attempting to avoid ego, we sometimes blunder right into it."

"What do you want to talk about, Olivia?" Eileen, the owner of the house, asked.

"Not so much 'talk about' as do."

I levitated into the middle of the room, still cross-legged, still holding my tea. The response was almost comical, and I nearly spilled my tea as people scrambled back, hands over mouths. There were shrill shrieks and a few cries of "far out!" I smiled and moved back to my cushion.

"I should have done that at the beginning. Just to…you know, clear the air."

Eileen held her hand over her chest as if afraid her heart might give out. A striking young woman with long dark wavy hair sat with her hand over her mouth, her eyes still wide.

"Not what you expected?" I asked.

She gave two quick shakes of her head, jumped up, and ran from the room. Someone whispered the word "bathroom," and I wondered if she might be ill. I glanced around.

I ran my hand through my newly short hair, self-conscious now.

"Does anyone else feel nauseous?" I asked.

"It's not like we didn't know," a man named Jeff said. "We've seen the videos, read your posts, all that. Just…seeing it in person is like, whoa!"

"Yeah. I felt that way myself."

"Not anymore?" Eileen asked.

"Not so much. I felt some of my old fear of heights recently when I landed on the Willis Tower in Chicago, but I'm reasonably comfortable with the flying stuff now."

"And we're the first ones you've visited?" Jeff asked.

"Yeah, you're my guinea pigs."

I looked around the room. There were smiles and nods, but nobody spoke.

"Eileen," I said, and the old woman looked up at me, "As the hostess, would you like the first lesson?"

"Lesson? You want to teach me to fly?"

I sighed.

"'Teach' and 'fly' are loaded words. I think everyone can probably do it. If so, you'll have to teach yourself. I can help jumpstart you, maybe. Prove to your brain that it's possible."

"What do I need to do?"

Eileen had told me before that she usually meditated on her couch or bed, since she had knee problems. I stood.

"Join me here in the middle of the floor."

I took her hands and placed them on my shoulders.

"Good. Now close your eyes and drop into a shallow meditation."

Eileen and I stood in the center of the room. I watched her breathing slow, and she seemed lightly meditative. I allowed myself to become lighter and willed that sensation to flow into Eileen. Together, we raised an inch, two inches, half a foot off the floor.

Several gasps told me finally that people had noticed our movement. Eileen opened her eyes and looked around the room.

"Oh," she said. Then, "OH!"

She grasped me around the neck with both arms.

I caught her around the waist and brought us gently to the floor. She was shaking in my arms.

"Okay?" I asked.

"Oh, my," she said as tears began filling her eyes, "More than okay! I never imagined that could happen. This is the highlight of my life!"

Ego. You've got to watch out for it. I cleared my throat.

"Who's next?" I asked, so I wouldn't have to address the look on Eileen's face.

"Can we do more than one?" Jeff asked.

I sat amid four members, who all put a hand on my shoulder or back. The woman with wavy hair came back in. When she saw the five of us levitating, she turned and left again.

We did two more group levitations, and finally, everyone had levitated with me, even Melanie, of the weak stomach.

"So that's it. It's meditation, but it's feeling and emotion, and lots and lots of practice."

One of the older women raised her hand, and I nodded to her.

"What about healing? You mentioned you had run into people who could heal."

"Yeah," I said, nodding.

"Is that the same? Meditation and emotion?"

"I don't know," I said, hedging. "My instinct is that it's similar, but I've never done it. I hope to go back and learn someday."

"And the other gifts?" someone asked.

I raised my eyebrows in question.

"You weren't very specific," they said.

"No, I wasn't."

"You don't want us to know what you saw?" Melanie asked.

"Not exactly, no," I said. "It's a little confusing. I just shouldn't talk too much about things that aren't my direct experiences."

Everyone fell silent.

"So, with that out of the way, should we try meditating again?" I asked.

"We still have about 20 minutes," Eileen said.

Everyone got comfortable, and this time, I think most of them meditated easily.

After the meeting broke up, people stood around the house talking. Melanie approached me.

"Thanks for coming," she said.

"It was nice to meet all of you," I said. "I'm happy to be here."

"Do you know where you're going next?"

"Kind of. But kind of playing it by ear, too."

"Do you…well, do you have a place to stay tonight?"

"I hadn't thought about it yet."

"You could crash with Jeff and me. We're not too far from here."

"You and Jeff? Well, uh, sure, that would be great. You don't think he'll mind?"

"No, I'll tell him. He'll be happy!"

She scurried across the room, smiling, and Eileen took her place.

"She's a sensitive girl," she said. "Very spiritual."

"Spiritual how?" I asked.

"Empathic. She's a dog trainer. It's like the animals just want to please her. She's amazing."

"Huh," I said, looking back at the young woman, "I wonder if that's a spiritual gift, too?"

"It wouldn't surprise me. She and her brother, Jeff, live in a house full of cats and dogs."

"Her brother?"

"Yes," Eileen said, putting a hand on my arm and laughing.

I checked in with my intuition several times that afternoon. In shallow meditation, I pondered whether being here was the "right" course of action. "Right" and "wrong" are, of course, relative and have no real meaning. Here, "right" meant a course that would lead to some kind of greater good and not simple ego stroking.

Every time I checked, it felt right, so I stayed.

Jeff and Melanie, and some others in the group, took me to a vegan restaurant. It was a good time.

No, it was a *great* time. The meditation group was a little "hippie" for my taste, but they were terrific people.

Melanie rarely left my side and seemed to consider it her duty to make sure I had anything I wanted. Did I mention my ego? Yeah, it was along for the ride the whole night. Not counting the recent dinner with Shelly, I hadn't been with a girl in a long, long time. My last steady girlfriend had been Holly, who left me when the university kicked me out, before I moved back to Mom and Dad's. I had felt like such a loser.

That night, though, I didn't feel like a loser.

"Where are you headed after this?" Jeff asked as we ate coconut milk ice cream.

"Not positive. A little east, I think. I've always wanted to see Mt. St. Helens and Mt. Rainier. I might have a look at them before I decide."

Melanie grabbed my arm in excitement.

"St. Helens is beautiful this time of year! And they say the Mountain will be out tomorrow. You'll love it. I wish I could go with you, but I have classes."

"What are you studying?" I asked.

"Not studying, teaching — obedience and agility."

"So… teaching young husbands?" I asked.

She punched my arm.

"Eileen told me you have a gift with animals," I said, laughing. "How does it feel when you're working with them?"

"Hmm," she pondered, "Good. I'm happy. Not always laughing, happy. It just feels right. Good, you know?"

"Yeah, I think so."

"They're like people," she said. "Animals like some things and not others, and it's not the same from animal to animal. They like some people and not others. Are you a cat person or a dog person?"

"We always had both as a kid," I said. "The cats were kind of wild. They lived in the barn and kept the mice under control."

"But they weren't friends?"

"Ah, no, not usually. Friendly sometimes, but not friends. Not like a dog."

"Can dogs fly with you?" she pondered, savoring her last bite of ice cream.

"I don't know. Never tried to levitate with a dog."

"I bet they would be scared," she said. "But if they were already your friend and companion, maybe not."

"Let me know when you find out," I said. "You want my ice cream?"

"You don't like it?"

"Too sweet."

She took my dessert, lost in thought.

"Do you think people in our group will learn to fly?"

"Maybe. It's happened before when I've levitated with people. I haven't talked to my mom in a while, but I think she was close."

"It's very sad about your parents," she said, looking up at me with tears in her eyes.

"I had a dream about them recently," I said, eyes misting. "I think they're okay."

"Still, the way they're treating them…"

"I'm glad they're safe, at least."

She took my hand in hers.

"Me too," she whispered.

The party was breaking up as she finished my ice cream, still holding my hand.

This was the day before the epically bad crash in the cornfield. Ironically, I was thinking about landing at high speeds.

Excerpt from the blog: *Griffin's Flight*

OCTOBER 7, 2025

Mom and Dad are spending several days in Chicago for their anniversary, so I have the farm to myself. There's more work than usual, taking on Dad's chores too, but since I can fly through the fields, I saved some time.

After finishing the chores, I practiced landing at speed. I flew to the back of the big field and landed while flying as fast as I dared. When I flew back up to the barn, I accelerated all the way into the yard, and then flipped my body around feet-first and landed right by the door.

It didn't seem possible, but there was no sense of inertia. I felt like I was just flying and then not flying.

Alone in my apartment, I have time to relax and think. It was disturbing to feel no inertia when gravity was already out of the picture. I wrote the words INERTIA and GRAVITY.

What was the connection? What if it were WEIGHT rather than GRAVITY?

Weight and inertia are both properties of mass, which is a quality of matter. Does meditation change the way my body interacts with the rest of the universe? Am I affecting the physical laws of the universe somehow?

There's something to this. The two effects have to be related, but I need more study and more practice.

Fifteen

After visiting Mt. St. Helens, I flew west to the ocean before heading south. The air at 3,000 feet above the surface was fresh. I increased speed and kept the coastline visible on my left. In about four hours, I landed on a beach near San Francisco.

I had the address of a woman, Loretta Fox, who wrote a post several months ago. She talked about how she meditated regularly in the afternoons with her children, who were all young adults and teens. I hoped to crash their meditation time. Using a phone that Shelly and Jake had set up for me, I entered the address and called an Uber.

The driver, after she arrived, was chatty. Shelly and Jake had been clear on the need for secrecy. They told me over and over that anyone could be a source of information, purposefully or inadvertently, to either the Black Hats or the feds.

So, I tried not to talk. I steered the conversation back to her. Did she like driving for Uber? Did she do anything else? Was she from San Francisco? It wasn't conversational artistry, but it filled the 45-minute drive.

I dipped into a meditative state on my way up the sidewalk. Was it awkward arriving on someone's doorstep unannounced, uninvited, with a backpack? Yes. Like…a lot. I dealt with the awkwardness by not acknowledging it. I slid into the gap and erased it from my consciousness.

When Loretta came to the door, she peeked through the Judas window. I smiled and gave a little wave. She frowned, her gaze moving from my helmet hair, down to my rumpled clothing, and to the pack at my feet. The woman met my gaze again, incomprehension written on her face. She called to someone behind her, and a moment later, a young man opened the door.

"Can I help you?"

"Maybe. I think you and your mom follow my blog. I'm on a tour, visiting people."

"You're a blogger? Visiting? I don't understand."

"Oh!" Loretta exclaimed, "I recognize you now! Please come in. David, open the door."

David looked wary, but opened the door.

"Griffin! Welcome! I'm so excited to meet you. I thought about inviting you after your last article, but you must have gotten tons of invitations. Why on earth would you choose to visit us?"

David took my pack as his mother rambled, leading us deeper into the house.

"Can I get you anything?" she asked. I requested to use the restroom before we talked, and David showed me to an elaborate powder room off a hallway. When I came out, there was coffee, hot water for tea, a pitcher of ice water, glasses, and a small dish of sliced lemons.

"Are you hungry?" Loretta asked. "I have some cookies, but I don't think…."

"No, ma'am. Tea would be great, though."

"Of course."

David and three young ladies stood to the side, and I introduced myself.

"I'm Olivia," I said, extending my hand. "Call me Liv."

"Dave Fox," he said, taking mine and giving it a light squeeze, "These are my sisters, Jenna, Catherine, and Amy."

I shook hands with all of them.

"We're so pleased to meet you," Loretta repeated, directing me to a large fluffy chair.

"Likewise, thank you."

As I sat, the chair engulfed me. I felt like I was being attacked by a giant amoeba. The chair made it difficult to stay meditative.

"Um," I said, trying to arrange my elbows so that I would appear comfortable and not spill my tea. "Thank you for your hospitality. I read your post a while back about how you meditate together, and it intrigued me."

"I didn't think anyone saw my posts," Loretta said, smiling. "How are things? You've been having a lot of trouble."

"I'm okay," I said. "Things have been quiet recently."

"That's good to hear."

The girls nodded.

"So, how much do you know about what's been going on?" I asked. "Have you read any of my blogs? Seen my videos?"

The girls nodded noncommittally.

David said, "I've seen the news. They're not very flattering."

"David!" Loretta said.

"No, he's right. What do you think, David? Do you think I'm a fraud?"

One eyebrow flashed up, and his head tilted.

"I'm not sure what to think," he said.

"Well, that's why I'm here. But first, I'd like to ask that you keep my visit a secret for the time being. If people know where I am, there might be trouble, and bad guys might predict where I'll be in the future."

"Certainly," Loretta said, "But are you sure it's safe to be here at all?"

"I have people helping keep things secret," I said. "They're good at what they do."

"How are you keeping your site up?" David asked. "I was sure that Homeland would have killed it by now."

"Again, I have help. I couldn't do it on my own."

Everyone was quiet for a moment.

Finally, the youngest girl, Amy, raised her hand. She looked like she was about 16.

"So, you're the one who can fly, right?"

"Yeah," I said, smiling. I glanced at Loretta, whose face had gone red.

"Can you show us?" she asked. Her sister Catherine nodded.

"Well," I said, squirming, "I might have to levitate to get out of this chair."

I struggled to lean forward and place my teacup on the table in front of me.

"Daddy hated that chair," Jenna said. She was about my age. Maybe a little younger.

David extended his hand. I took it, thanked him, and stood.

"Well, why don't you show me where you meditate?"

We moved into the sunroom. There were cushions on the floor, and we all sat.

"So, what I'd like to do," I said, "is show you that levitation, and eventually flight, is possible…that it's possible for all of you."

"Can you *tell* us how it's possible?" David asked.

"I've written about it," I said. "I don't know all the science, but I believe it's nervous tissue, our brains specifically, accessing higher dimensions of existence."

"I'm sorry, but that sounds crazy," he said.

"I agree," I said. "If you can figure it out and give me a better answer, I'd love to hear it."

With that, I levitated off my cushion.

I was getting used to the shrieking. It didn't bother me much. Loretta was so shocked that she didn't seem to notice her son's outburst of profanity.

I floated about five feet in the air and unfolded my legs horizontally. I flew a circle around the room with my arms extended and did a slow roll back onto my cushion.

David sat forward with his head in his hands. Loretta's mouth hung open, and she seemed to gasp for breath. The girls recovered quickly.

"Are we okay?" I asked, "Do you need a minute?"

"How is that…how?" David couldn't complete the thought.

"Let go of your disbelief. Doubt is healthy, disbelief isn't."

He continued to shake his head as he left the room.

"All true," Loretta whispered. "All of it?"

"Yeah," I said, folding her into a brief hug. "All true."

"Thank God," she said, "And you think everyone can do it?"

"I do. Would you like to try?"

I had her and Amy move their cushions into the middle of the room with mine. As we meditated, they put their hands on my shoulders, and we levitated a foot or so above the cushions.

"Open your eyes," I said.

"Dear lord!" Loretta exclaimed, "Sweet Jesus!"

"So cool!" Amy said.

"Stay in meditation," I said.

They closed their eyes, and after a moment, I took their hands and drifted away. I kept moving until I only our fingertips were touching. Loretta's eyes opened wide when she felt me let go, and she dropped gently to the cushion. Amy put her hand in her lap and hovered in place all by herself.

She was still hanging in midair when David walked back in. I put my finger to my lips to forestall his exclamation. He sat and watched, saying nothing. Eventually, her eyes opened, and she settled gently down.

I clapped along with her family.

"Brava!" I said, "Well done."

Nobody else did as well as Amy, but they all levitated. All doubts were extinguished, and the atmosphere warmed considerably.

"Liv, how long do you think it will be before I can fly like you?" Amy asked.

"Hard to say. It took me a long time, but I didn't have a teacher or people to practice with. Take your time. Don't rush it. Flying can be dangerous."

An hour later, we were chatting in the kitchen.

"Is it just us for dinner?" I asked. Jenna had mentioned her father earlier, but nobody had since.

"Yes," Catherine said, "Dad died a couple of years ago."

"Three," Jenna said.

"I'm sorry," I said, "I didn't know."

"It's okay," Jenna said, "It's part of life. People die."

"It might be part of life, but it's not fun," I said.

"Your parents are still alive, aren't they?" Amy asked.

"Yes," I said, feeling guilty.

David walked in from the back porch.

"Are we ready for the tuna?" he asked.

"Whenever you are," Jenna said, "Can you two serve the salad? I'll get Mom."

David took several thick tuna steaks out of the fridge and outside to grill. I walked out with him.

"Sorry to intrude on your dinner."

"No worries at all. I'm glad you did. Glad you stopped by, I mean."

"How are you doing with this?" I asked.

He set the last steak on the grate, closed the top, and set a timer.

"I'm good," he said. "I don't know how I'll feel after I've slept on it, but for now, I'm good."

"I'll give you my cell number. If you have any problems, you can send me a text. I don't know how long I'll be on the west coast, but if I can come back, I will."

"That's very kind of you, but I'd rather you didn't," he said. "I don't want to be the one responsible for you being caught."

The timer went off, and he turned the steaks and reset it.

"We're almost ready here," he said.

Some of my articles are from my early journal entries, and some of those were fairly short. This article details some of my early frustration with "simple" levitation.

~

Excerpt from the blog: *Griffin's Flight*

NOVEMBER 1, 2024

It's happening faster now. I didn't even notice the next time it happened in late August, only saw it on the video afterward. I raised up from my cushion and then settled back down. It was both exciting and frustrating. Exciting that I caught it and could have missed it, frustrating that I didn't know it happened.

The following week, I levitated outside again. I felt the vertigo that told me I was moving and thought, *I'm doing it!*

Of course, the thought and resulting surge of adrenaline brought me out of meditation. I fell two feet back onto my cushion.

And it happened several more times over the next two months. Eventually, I overcame this instinctive *Whoo Hoo!* response, but it was frustrating.

DECEMBER

I finally experienced the vertigo and watched it happen without reaction. I was levitating, and in the gap. "Time" was the thought that brought me out of meditation. I wondered how long I had been levitating, and I immediately came down.

On reviewing the video, I found I had levitated for almost a minute. I was aware from beginning to end, without the adrenaline response that plagued me for so long.

The following week I levitated again, kept my cool, and watched it happen. This time, though, I ended it on purpose. I "willed" myself back down onto my cushion and stopped meditating. Then I jumped around and patted myself on the back.

So, can I teach someone to levitate? I'm not sure. It seems like a chicken and egg problem. How do you know the feeling if you haven't levitated? And how can you levitate if you don't know the feeling? My only answer is that the feeling and the action are perhaps not linked, but they're related somehow.

One way to meditate is by focusing on feeling your skin. These sensations keep you in the present without thought. Experience, not thought, anchors us to the present moment. Thinking, writing, conversing, teaching, and reading are all bound in the concepts of past, present, and future. By focusing on experience, the sensations of my body, I can be in the moment and remain within the grip of time and space. By focusing on the peculiar "whooshing" feeling in my gut that happens when I levitate, I can rise from the ground.

Sixteen

The next morning, I woke confused. For several moments, I didn't remember where I was. Finally, the day before crystallized, and I relaxed.

I was sleeping on the couch in David's apartment. I had shared a great evening with his family, and now it was time to move on. Spending too much time in one place was dangerous for me and everyone else.

The smell of brewing coffee may have been what woke me up. I rarely indulged in coffee anymore, but once in a while, on special occasions, I did. And this smelled special.

"Costa Rican peaberry, if you're wondering. Dark as sin."

"Smells amazing," I mumbled, stumbling into the kitchen and taking a mug from David. He looked like he had been up for hours.

I sat down at the table and sipped. I felt the caffeine trickle into my brain and reality fell into clearer focus.

I cleared my throat and ran a hand through my hair.

"You a *Star Trek* fan?"

He had served my coffee in a mug with a Star Trek logo and a picture of the Enterprise "D."

"I'm not sure where that came from," David said. "It's left over from college. It showed up at some point and hasn't broken yet. How did you sleep?"

"I have trouble sleeping in strange houses. I miss my apartment, but it's more than that, I think. For a creature of habit, the whole camping and running from the law bit is hard to get used to."

"I believe it. Well, I laid out fresh towels. Take as long as you want, as long as it's only five minutes. We're on water restrictions."

"Dandy."

David turned on the television and switched to a news station.

I thought about getting into the shower rather than watching the news, but decided to enjoy the coffee.

"Liv," David said, his voice sharp.

I glanced up, and he pointed to the television where my driver's license photo was superimposed over an aerial view of a house surrounded by police cars.

"Oh no," I said, "Where is it?"

He fumbled with the remote and turned the volume up.

"…responded to multiple 911 calls reporting gunfire to find FBI and ATF agents already on the scene. We aren't certain of many details yet, including how many people were in the house, how many died, or if there were any survivors.

"The incident is rumored to have involved supposed spiritual leader Olivia Donnelly. Apparently, Donnelly visited the residence several days ago, receiving aid and assistance."

My phone rang, but I ignored it. I felt sick. My head was spinning, and my hands were numb. They were using my picture. Using my *name*.

David got up and fetched my phone. He set it on the table and rested his hand on my shoulder.

"Is there anything I can do?"

I shook my head quickly, still watching the television screen, although it now showed a commercial for antipsychotic drugs. David muted the television and tears rolled down my face.

"Do you recognize the house?" David asked.

I nodded and finally looked away from the screen.

"Seattle. There was a girl… a woman, there," I rasped.

"Is my family in danger?" he asked, his voice brittle.

I looked at him. How could I know? How could anyone know?

"They shouldn't have found me," I said, voice breaking. "Nobody could have known I was there."

I was in shock, and I felt the coffee coming back up. I ran to the bathroom, but I hadn't drunk enough to vomit. So, I dry heaved over the sink. Eventually, I collapsed onto my knees.

David brought me a glass of water and put a blanket over me. He was on the phone with his mother. His voice was raised, angry, but I couldn't tell what he was saying.

Finally, he came back into the bathroom. He turned on the water.

"Come on. If you want a shower, you'll have to get it now. No telling when your next chance will be."

When I stood, it felt like someone else was moving my body. I felt strangely light and out of control as I disrobed and entered the shower. I stood in the shower and gazed around, unsure where I was or what I was doing. Finally, the hot water made an impact. Using David's Ivory soap, I washed my hair and my body as quickly as I could, which wasn't quick. My hands were numb.

I stepped out and was drying myself when the door opened. David and Loretta stepped in with no regard for my nudity.

"Here are your clothes," Loretta said. "We got everything washed and in the dryer last night, thank God."

"Thank you," I mumbled. I held the towel in front of me, stupidly.

"Are you okay?" she asked, putting her hand to the side of my face. "Of course you're not. I'm sorry. I'll leave, and you get dressed. We'll decide what to do when you get out."

David set my coffee on the edge of the sink, and they left.

I looked at the *Star Trek* coffee mug. It seemed inane, pointless. How could I ever enjoy television when people like Jeff and Melanie were brutally murdered?

I sat where I stood, still looking at the coffee mug, and began weeping for a beautiful woman that I barely knew.

By the time I got out of the bathroom, Loretta was gone and David was at the table watching the news. He turned it off when I entered the room.

"Any more details?" I asked.

He hesitated.

"None you want to know."

I sat down and began pulling on socks and work boots.

"Tell me, please," I said, not looking up.

"They're still not giving names, but apparently, several federal agents died."

"You're..." I was going to say, "You're joking," but obviously he wasn't.

"You're sure?" I amended.

"That's what they're saying. Nothing about...anyone else."

"I've got to go. Can you get me to the roof?"

"Not a good idea. Let's leave the city first."

"I don't know how they keep finding me," I said, my voice rising. "Every minute you're with me brings you closer to winding up like... them!" I waved my hand at the television.

"I understand, and I'm scared, but taking off in the middle of the city in the age of smartphones isn't good for any of us."

"Well, call me an Uber then."

"I'll drive you, but Mom and the girls need to be on the road first."

"Where will they go?" I asked.

"Not sure. Also not sure if I should go with them or somewhere else."

I had no answers for him. I finished with my boots and turned on the television. The coffee was cold, but I drank it, tasting nothing.

They were at the point in the story cycle where they were dissecting me, my background, and my motives. I hit the link to my website on my phone, and it loaded, so my Anonymous friends must have been working overtime.

The ticker at the bottom of the screen reiterated the same news over and over. Federal agents killed, reason for original gunfire unknown, casualties unknown, involvement with fraudulent guru suspected. On and on it went.

I turned the television off. My mind told me I should eat, but my stomach felt like someone had replaced it with a rock. There would be no food in my near future.

Melanie….

She had been kind and gentle and beautiful. She hadn't deserved this.

And Jeff. I didn't get to know him very well, but he was funny and protective of Melanie.

The Pacific Pacifists.

Why would they have been targeted? Someone had to know that I meditated with them and showed them levitation, which meant that this entire family was certainly in trouble.

"What are we waiting for?" I asked, suddenly angry that David was just sitting and looking out the window.

"Mom said she would call when they decided where to go," he said.

"Where are they now?"

"Not sure. Heading out of town, I hope."

"Can you find out, please?" I asked.

He took out his phone and dialed.

"Voicemail," he said finally.

Frustration overwhelmed me, and my instinct was to move. But was it fear or intuition?

"Look, it's time," I said. "If you don't want me to fly or get an Uber, we've got to get going."

"Fine," he said. "Let's go."

Downstairs, we stowed the pack in the trunk and jumped in. David drove a Prius, and it barely made a sound as we pulled out of the parking space. He put his phone in a holder on the dash.

San Francisco was entirely new to me, but I didn't pay attention to anything. I was trying to calm myself in case I had to fly, but also so I could better hear intuition.

"Traffic cameras," David said.

"What?"

"Up there," he said, pointing to the traffic lights. Small white cameras took in every angle of the intersection.

Could someone have used traffic cameras to find me?

"You think?" I asked.

"Maybe," he said, "If so, they'd have you from yesterday afternoon until now."

"Damn," I said, "Can I use your phone? I want to try your mom again."

He said nothing, just punched a button on the phone. It rang over the car stereo three times, then a male voice answered.

"Yes? Who is this?" the voice said.

"I'm sorry? To whom am I speaking?" David said. He pulled over quickly.

"This is Sergeant Davis with the SFPD," the voice said.

"Where's my mother?" David said. "What's happened?"

"Calm down, sir. Everyone's fine. We're still trying to sort out what happened. Can I have your name and location?"

Alarm bells went off in my head. I shook my head and hit the mute button.

"Unlock the trunk. I'm out of here," I said. David hesitated and then nodded, hitting a button under the dash.

He unmuted the phone.

"This is her son, David," he said. "I'm in my car. Where are my mother and sisters?"

"Again, sir. They're safe. What's your location?"

"Um… I'm not sure. I just pulled over to talk to you."

"I need your location, sir. I'm sending a car to bring you to your mother and sisters."

"Just tell me where you're located," David said. "I'll drive to you."

Meanwhile, I had jumped out of the car and gotten my bags from the trunk. I strapped everything on quickly and stuffed my goggles and helmet in a cargo pocket.

"Let us help you, son."

"Hang up," I said, "Hang up! I don't think that's the police."

David's face was white as he pushed the button.

"Call the police and ask about Sergeant Davis," I said. "Tell them what just happened. I'm getting out of here."

"But the police? What if they arrest us?"

"Better them than the Alliance," I said grimly.

"My mom?"

"I don't know. Let's hope for the best."

"Why is this happening?" David asked.

I clenched my fists in frustration. I was still trying to answer that for myself.

I sighed and tried to answer.

"This knowledge coming out terrifies some people. That's all I can figure. Apparently, these groups have known about it for a while and suppressed it."

"But...killing? Why?"

"David, I don't know yet. Hold the best thoughts you can and get the police here now. You might not have much time."

He shook his head, took a deep breath, and nodded.

"Police. Right."

"Take care of yourself," I said, turning to go.

"Oh! Hey, wait. Mom left this for you," he said, handing me a cigar box wrapped in brown paper.

"What is it?" I asked.

"Money, a phone, charger, not sure what else," David said.

"David, I can't take this. It will get you into more trouble."

"No, Dad put the money away years ago. It didn't come from any accounts. The phone might be Amy's. I'm not sure."

I stuffed the box into my duffel with a sigh.

"Thank your mother for me. I can't tell you how grateful I am."

I turned and jogged up the alley before he could respond.

I kept a westward heading and stuck to alleys and side roads. David lived in Visitacion Valley, if I remembered correctly. My knowledge of California geography was rudimentary and nonexistent where San Francisco was concerned. I was pretty sure the Golden Gate Bridge was to my north, but beyond that, it was all guesswork.

The geography forced me to angle to the north for a while. Eventually, I found an enormous park where I hoped I could take to the sky unseen.

Signs pointed the way to the Jerry Garcia Amphitheater, so I headed that way. The amphitheater was empty when I arrived. I took out the Anonymous phone and called Jake.

"This is Scarlet," I said, using the code word they had given me. It was short for Scarlet Pimpernel, a favorite literary character.

"Understood Scarlet. Everything is under control."

"How can everything be under control? People are dying!"

"Goddammit, I said everything is fine. Get off the line."

They hung up, and I didn't call back.

Instead, I donned helmet and goggles and did one of my fast take-offs. I didn't want a contrail, so I went slower than in Chicago. But hopefully faster than someone could point a camera or phone. And I didn't stop climbing until I felt the air grow thin and cold.

I started flying west over the ocean and then turned to the south. Maybe I would fly all the way to Mexico. Would there be places that wouldn't mind taking American cash? Would the hotels be picky about identification?

I flew, trying not to think about Melanie and her brother, trying not to wonder about Loretta and her daughters.

The air grew warmer as the sun climbed, then fell. Gulls and other seabirds I didn't know the names of flew below me, small white dots moving over the dark blue of the ocean. There were patterns in the water and realized I was seeing dolphins chasing fish. I checked for air traffic and then slowed and dropped near the tops of the waves.

The dolphins leaped from the water and dove again all around me as I kept pace with them. If I hadn't had my gear on, I would have swum with them. They must be able to see me. The dolphins clustered around, swimming in circles. I slowed and stopped, hovering over the surface of the water, and they swam up to me, rolling over in the water, lifting just their heads out, and even leaping, nearly hitting me.

I began talking to them, the way I did with my dog when I was a kid. They responded by clicking and hissing. I lifted my goggles and took my helmet off. The chittering and clicking intensified.

It was awkward, hovering with my backpack, but there was nowhere to land. So, I hovered and talked to them until suddenly they bolted away. They must have swum deep because they didn't break the surface. For a moment, I wondered if a predator was nearby. Maybe a shark or orca?

I heard the drone of a motor and looked around to see a small military ship approaching. Could it have seen me? Maybe it saw me on the radar?

I slipped helmet and goggles back on and retreated, slowly at first, but gaining speed. At first I tried to mimic the way a boat or seaplane might move, hoping to confuse them, but realized that I wasn't leaving a wake. I changed direction, tracking from west to south again. When they were over the horizon, I poured on speed and climbed out of sight.

I didn't know where I was, and I was okay with that. As the sun dropped toward the horizon, I headed east toward land, but the coast was farther away than I thought. It must have curved eastward at some point. Finally, mountains rose on the horizon, just as the sun touched the water behind me. I poured on speed and landed before full dark.

There was no glow from city lights as far as I could see, but occasional lights dotted the landscape in the oncoming gloom. What were the chances of remaining undetected throughout the night?

I flew in over a narrow rocky beach toward 300-foot cliffs and a deep gorge where a small river flowed into the ocean. It was remote and beautiful. I didn't know about tides or recent weather, so I didn't want to sleep on the beach. I walked away from the beach toward the cliffs as far as I could go without climbing. From what I could tell, I was well above the high-tide line. I shed some clothes, gathered wood, and started a small fire.

Once I had eaten some fruit and jerky, I relaxed. But the events of the day refused to be ignored. My phone had three fairly consistent bars. There was barely enough signal to download news. Nowhere near enough for video.

But it was enough to tell me that my worst fears were realized. They reported Melanie and Jeff to be dead, along with multiple federal agents. Those deaths were being blamed on me and my influence. "Crazed followers with guns doing battle with the federal government" was the gist of the stories. They vilified me, saying that I incited my followers to violence in retaliation for my parents and me being placed in custody.

I couldn't find any news about Loretta and David and their family. Hopefully, they got away. Or maybe they were just saving that story for tomorrow?

So, it wasn't a good night. As tired as I was, I barely slept, and when I did, it wasn't deep. Every sound was someone who wanted to kill me.

What should I do?

Where can I go?

I had thought that Anonymous would keep me safe and, well, anonymous. They had warned me that the hackers were good. They tried to tell me not to involve anyone else. No friends. No lovers.

God. Melanie. She was so sweet. And now she's gone.

And it was my fault.

~

Excerpt from the blog: *Griffin's Flight*

DECEMBER 3, 2024

Why does levitation happen during meditation and not at random times during the day?

That's a pretty good question.

What is it about meditation that allows levitation? What's the process? Is it antigravity? Bending space? Changing the properties of mass?

I have no idea.

The answers might lie in Quantum Physics, but I'm not completely sold on the idea. There are ideas being floated around about Uncertainty, Chaos Theory, and String Theory that are intriguing.

I might need to go back to school.

Questions are never far from my mind. Why is meditation able to cause such a drastic change in physical laws? Does it literally put us "in touch with the mind of God" as Dr. Wayne Dyer wrote?

What does that even mean?

What is "the mind of God?"

Meditation shuts off the logical, verbal left hemisphere of the brain and accesses the artistic, nonverbal right hemisphere. Does something in the right hemisphere write physical laws? Are there other abilities waiting to manifest?

It's hard to imagine ever refining this ability enough to allow me to fly at will, but that's my goal. Now that I have hard evidence, I'm ready to push the limits. If I can learn to fly, I can teach other people.

Maybe it's not about activating the right brain, but shutting down the left. The left brain is the seat of ego, the sense of self. The right brain doesn't care who did what, or how. Left brain is concerned with accomplishments and recognition. Right brain is creative and spiritual.

Of course, the whole left brain/right brain paradigm has limitations. If I decide to go back to school, I'll have to decide between studying physics or psychology.

238

Seventeen

I stayed on that rocky shore for two days before I ran low on food. During that time, I discovered I was on the west coast of the Baja Peninsula. It was the first time I had been outside the United States. The FBI was treating me as a fleeing suspect. I was on their most-wanted list.

When I left the cove, I did what I could to erase my presence. Google Maps said that the nearest town was a few miles up the coast. I walked inland until I found the road and then followed it toward town. The sun was low in the eastern sky when I left the shore, but it was nearly noon before I arrived. I had already drunk all of my water and sweated it back out.

My Spanish was virtually nonexistent. I hoped that the people here were used to tourists and spoke English. Before I entered the town, I walked across a wide, shallow ravine that I realized was a dry riverbed. There were no bridges, so it must not hold water very often. I made my way across, feet dragging, and into town.

I wiped the dust and sweat from my face with a bandana. My plan was to find a market and a place to stay for the night. Though I was ready to blast off at a moment's notice, I didn't want to risk it.

I nodded to a few people in the street, but nobody wanted to talk. Everyone wore hats, and I could see why. The sun on my head was brutal. Still, I left my flight helmet in my pocket.

Finally, I found a gas station. I went inside and bought a Coke.

"Is American money okay?" I asked the cashier.

"Sí," she said, taking a dollar.

"Gracias," I said.

She nodded.

"Can you recommend a hotel?" I asked.

Blank stare.

"Um…hotel…a room for the night…uh…*La Quinta?*"

"No entiendo," she said, shrugging.

"Okay," I said, giving up. "What about a market? Grocery? Supermercado?"

"Si," she said. "Tomorrow, that way."

She pointed into town.

"Tomorrow?"

"Sí."

"Gracias."

Another nod.

I walked in the direction that she pointed and found an open square where they must have an outdoor market. I sipped my Coke and felt the sugar, caffeine, and water hit my system. It helped after the long walk.

"What happened to your hat?"

I turned to see a man sitting in the shade of a tree.

"Um…I don't know," I said. "Must have lost it."

He was older than me, wearing a straw cowboy hat. He looked at me as if I were an idiot.

"How the hell do you not remember losing your hat in that sun? How long you been out there?"

"A while," I said, stepping into his shade. "Do you mind?"

"Help yourself," he said.

"Hey, you don't happen to know of a hotel nearby, do you?"

"No proper hotel here. There's a resort up the road a bit, if that's what you mean."

"No, nothing like that. Just a place to stay."

"I think Silvia still has a room here. The cockroaches aren't huge."

I was too tired to laugh, but forced a smile.

"Is she through here?" I asked, pointing to the door behind him.

"Nah, that's my room. She's around the corner there."

He pointed the way I had come.

"To the left there?"

"Yeah," he said, "Tell her José sent you. I'm Joe, by the way. She calls me José."

I took his hand.

"Uh… Francis," I said, "Fran… Finnegan."

"Pleased to meet you. Get settled and come find me. We can get a beer before everyone settles down for siesta."

"I'll do that."

Silvia turned out to be a large, matronly woman who, apparently, never stopped smiling.

"You come," she said, beckoning me after I had paid her $50 for the next week.

We walked through to a small, run-down courtyard. Joe's room was to the left. She went to the right and opened a door. The screen door stood open, and she had to use her foot to force the door after lifting hard on the handle.

"It sticks a little," she said, her accent thick.

"It's fine," I said.

I heard scuttling as we walked into the room. There was a musty smell. It was probably too dry for mold, but it was vaguely unpleasant.

"Do the windows open?" I asked.

"Sí, just be careful. Don't hit."

"Okay, thank you."

She left, and I sat on the bed. Nothing moved, so that was a plus. I took out my phone. No messages. No relevant news. I checked the website to see if there was anything happening.

The stats showed that traffic was way down from normal. Just a trickle of visitors still coming, maybe to see if I would make an appearance.

I looked through the forums. One of the new messages had a link to a news story. I didn't recognize the user, but I clicked on the link. My stomach clenched as I read.

It was Agent Stefanie. Wounded in a firefight in San Francisco the day I left. How had she gotten there so fast? And what had happened?

Apparently, she had been serving a warrant for Loretta. There had been a gunshot through the front door. She was in the hospital.

Again, I felt nauseous. How was all of this happening? I had been cautious, and yet people were still being hurt and killed because of me! It was insufferable.

If I knew who was behind this, if I had a gun and the opportunity, I believe that I would have killed them at that moment. Melanie, Stefanie, Loretta missing, and all the rest: how could I hide and do nothing?

I stowed my gear in the room. I wrapped my backpack in plastic trash bags. Hopefully, that would keep the bugs out. I stuffed a handful of twenties in my pocket and went to find Joe.

"There you are," he said. "You want to get a hat first? I know a place... hey, you don't look so good."

"No," I said, my voice hoarse with rage and sorrow. "Just got some bad news. Let's get that drink."

"Okay, partner. Whatever you say."

He got up from his chair. He was shorter than I, but probably outweighed me by better than 50 pounds. His jeans strained his suspenders, and he was fighting a losing battle to keep his shirt tucked in. He pulled his straw cowboy hat down in front to shield his eyes from the noonday glare.

I was just wearing work boots, jeans and an untucked t-shirt. I squinted around the square as we walked, not really noticing anything. My eyes were watering, both from the glare and from my anger.

Joe turned off the square and down an alley. Eventually, he opened what looked like the back door to someone's house, and we entered.

"What's your poison?" he asked.

"I'm not really much of a drinker."

"No, I didn't think so. They're fond of tequila around here."

"Sounds good," I said, handing him a twenty.

There were several tables, all unoccupied. I chose the one that looked like it had seen the least violence and sat. Joe came over with a bottle and two glasses. He splashed some pale amber liquid into them and handed me one.

"Cheers," he said, holding his glass up and tossing the liquid into his mouth.

I followed suit and immediately began coughing.

"You weren't kidding, were you, Fran?" he laughed. "Don't breathe through your mouth."

I nodded, and after I recovered, he poured another round. I tossed it back before the burn from the first faded from my stomach.

JULY 25

Despair had been building for a long time. It finally erupted in that small town in Mexico. I had been to parties in college where there was drinking. I usually had a beer or two but had never been falling-down drunk. It had just never interested me.

But now, I drank so that I wouldn't have to think. I didn't want to think about people who hated me so much they would hunt me like an animal and kill innocent people. I didn't want to think about a government that would paint me as a criminal to avoid acknowledging that life was more than making a living, paying your mortgage, and being a good little consumer.

I couldn't stand thinking about all the people who had paid so dearly simply for trying to help me.

Maybe I went a little crazy that afternoon. Joe and I drank a lot of tequila, and I bought tequila for many people that I didn't know. By the end of the night, the bartender and I were old friends. I don't remember his name.

We sang, we drank, and we ate. Someone, maybe the bartender's wife, brought tamales, and I must have eaten a dozen of them and washed them down with the house beer.

After dark, we went back to drinking tequila. I got to where I forgot I didn't speak the language. I gave everyone names, but they seemed to be kind of fluid, sliding from man to man with drunken ease. There weren't many women in the bar, and I'm pretty sure the one that I remember worked there. It's a little hazy.

The patrons of the bar played along. They would answer to whatever name I gave them as long as I kept pouring tequila. We had long conversations about farming, school, martial arts, anything but meditation, and flying. I was never drunk enough to mention that.

"You're a karate chica, then?"

"Not…not karate," I said, slurring my words. "Just call it a martial art. You won't be able to say it right. I probably can't say it right."

He laughed, and I joined in. We toasted our level of intoxication.

"So, you," he said carefully, "are a martial artist. What can you teach me?"

He had pushed his straw cowboy hat back on his head, revealing a bald cranium and a fringe of graying hair around his skull.

"What can I teach you? Tonight, I can probably teach you how to get your butt kicked."

He snorted.

"I can do that just fine on my own," he slurred, waving his glass at me. "What…what would you do if…if I punched you in the face…like this?"

He set his glass down, drew a bead, and punched me right in the nose. I went over backward in my chair, and everyone laughed. Joe was apologetic when he helped me up. The barmaid brought me a towel to hold to my nose, which dribbled blood.

"I'm so…so sorry!" he said, setting my chair up. "I didn't think you'd let me hit you like that."

"Like what? You hit me? I thought…I thought a fly landed on my nose."

We laughed as if it were the funniest thing anyone had ever said. Everyone around us joined in, though I doubt they understood. We sat, and each took a drink.

"So…seriously, what belt are you?"

"I am a brown belt."

"Brown belt? Is that pretty high?"

"Kind of."

"So they haven't covered getting punched by fat old hillbillies in bars yet?"

We both laughed again.

"No, we have. We have. I just wanted to see how hard you could hit," I said, all serious. Joe laughed anyway.

"No, seriously. I've been kicked and hit plenty, but we don't hit each other in the face full force. Not good for business. Nobody wants to go to work with a black eye or broken nose."

I took the towel away and prodded my nose as I said this.

Joe poured two more shots.

"Here's to getting hit in the face!"

After we drank, I punched him in the jaw. I didn't mean to hit him very hard, but he fell out of his chair and didn't get back up.

Everybody laughed, and I finished the bottle by filling several other shot glasses and toasting Joe.

We set him up in his chair. Someone made sure he was breathing, and I spent a few minutes talking to the server. She said little, as I recall.

"Uhh...sorry, must have dozed off. Ouch!"

He worked his jaw up and down and felt it gingerly with his fingertips.

"Sorry. I hit you a little too hard."

"Bitch," he said genially. "I deserved it."

We spent the better part of the night in the bar, eventually stumbling back to our rooms. I fell into bed without getting undressed. I pushed my bags off the bed and passed out.

The room was sweltering when I woke, head throbbing and mouth dry as paper.

I tried to sit up, but my stomach and head both protested. I groaned and closed my eyes. Finally, I felt strong enough to try again. I rolled to my side and used my arms to press myself up into a sitting position.

When I opened my eyes, my belongings were strewn about the floor. Did I do that? Had I been looking for something last night? I couldn't remember.

I got up and stumbled into the bathroom to relieve my bladder. When I came back out, I found my water filter. The top of my head felt like it would explode when I bent over to pick it up. I filled a canteen with filtered water, sat on the edge of the bed, and sipped. I filtered more water, found a pot and boiled it for tea.

Moving was slowly getting easier, but my stomach felt awful. Even the thought of tea was nauseating, but my head needed the caffeine, and I needed to hydrate.

I began picking through the mess, trying to figure out why I had thrown everything about. Despite being more inebriated than I had ever been in my life, I didn't think that I had blacked out. I remembered coming home, pushing the bags off the bed and collapsing. Nothing else.

My backpack was nearly empty.

Computer, phones, and money were all gone.

My atlas was there, along with pens, pencils, and notebooks.

Most of my camping supplies were there. What jerky I had left was gone, dammit. They had picked through my clothes, but nothing seemed to be missing.

How would I get in touch with anyone? How would I live without money? Without a phone?

Whoever had tossed my bags had done a good job. I had a few small caches of $20 bills that they missed. But that was all I had to keep myself alive indefinitely.

I sat at the table and poured tea. I rested my forehead in my hands. Last night had been a mistake. A huge mistake. I felt bad before, but now I was in a worse situation, something that had seemed impossible.

Strangely, I began to feel calmer. I had wanted time, and now I had nothing else. I couldn't write, couldn't read, couldn't watch the news. All I had was myself.

And, of course, the entire universe.

JULY 26

I wasn't surprised to find that Joe left that morning. I had suspected him the entire time I cleaned the room and showered. And I wasn't angry when Silvia, the landlady, told me. I was more sad that he would behave that way.

Sylvia directed me to the market but didn't seem optimistic I would find anything this late in the day.

I wore a battered pair of sunglasses that I found in my bag and made my way down the street toward the market. It must be after noon. The market would close soon, so I hurried as much as my pounding head would allow.

The first thing I found was a stall selling hats similar to what Joe wore yesterday. I found one that fit and bought it, along with some more bandanas. The food vendors were packing up, but I found some avocados and purchased several. I also found some starchy root vegetables and some greens that weren't too wilted. Most veggies around here were hard and had to be cooked for a long time. I was used to things I could eat raw.

I didn't want to buy raw meat, but I hoped to find some jerky. No luck.

At any rate, I had food for the time that I had paid ahead at the hotel. I gathered my bags and ambled back to my room.

Once inside, I began chopping vegetables for soup, since that's all I knew to do with them. Most meals in Mexico, if my experience with Mexican restaurants in the states gave me any useful information, were based on beans, rice, and corn, things that I tried to avoid.

The situation being what it was; I had bought some beans that I set to soaking. If I soaked them for a couple of days, I could tolerate them. Otherwise, they played havoc with my intestines.

With the kitchen chores done, I laid down to my siesta.

When I awoke, my headache had faded to a dull throb. I put the water on for tea, checked the soup, and ate two of the ripe avocados, the first actual food I had tried since last night. They were watery and fibrous, but tasted good and stayed down.

I spent the evening watching television that I couldn't understand and eating vegetable soup with no spices. I found *Smokey and the Bandit* dubbed in Spanish and watched it, because there was nothing else remotely interesting.

I went to bed early that night after washing my dishes, only to be awoken by a frightening thought.

The Alliance and the FBI had been tracking me somehow. They either had a tracker on me, on my gear, or they were, despite Anonymous' help, following my electronic footprints. If it was the latter and Joe tried to use my computer or phones, they would probably find him, question him, or kill him.

I turned on the television, searching for CNN or something similar. There was nothing. I found *Smokey and the Bandit* again, infomercials, and *Gilligan's Island*.

I tried to go back to sleep, but my mind was wide awake. So, I meditated. I sat up in the middle of the bed with a folded blanket under my hips. It wasn't a deep meditation. I think the alcohol was still clearing from my system, and that messes with your deep sleep and meditation. Still, it felt good to meditate. Intuition told me to rest and sleep.

I allowed myself to slip in and out of sleep while I meditated. I didn't try to control it. If you've never been in that place between sleep and meditation, it's hard to explain. You know when you're meditating, but not necessarily when you're sleeping. When you're meditating, you know you've been sleeping, but not necessarily vice versa.

Anyway, I got out of bed again early, maybe around 4:30 am. I visited the bathroom, sipped some boiled and filtered water I had in the fridge, and went back to bed.

This time, I slept soundly for several hours.

When I awoke, it felt like midmorning. I made tea and ate cold soup. After brushing my teeth, I headed out to explore the town. I wasn't really looking for Joe, but thought maybe if I found him, I could help. Maybe he would be grateful and give me some money back. And maybe....

No. He wouldn't be anywhere I could find him.

I couldn't afford to spend money, but I wanted to walk. I might buy something small to blend in. since I had never been outside the US before, I was curious to see how things were different, and how they were the same.

So I walked.

As I got away from the town itself and closer to the highway that bisected it, the stores grew much more commercial and geared towards tourists. I couldn't read most of the signs, but they made it easy to understand by having huge letters and images of what they offered. I didn't see McDonalds and KFC, but there were small mom-and-pop places that sold hamburgers and pizza.

I moved back away from the main road and walked through a residential area. People were poor by US standards, but the children were happy, running and playing in the yards and streets. The adults were unhurried and happy to see each other. Everywhere I went, there were people chatting in gardens, on street corners, on sidewalks. People in cars stopped to talk to each other from the drivers' seats. This was a very gregarious culture. How would an introvert like me survive?

I was back in my room before it got too hot and laid down for a siesta.

When I awoke, I started cooking the beans. They hadn't soaked as long as I like, but I might not be around much longer. Guidance was prompting me, telling me it was almost time to go.

While the beans cooked, I repacked my bags. They were a fair bit lighter without all the phones and the computer. My shoulders would be happy, at least.

Instead of watching television, I asked Sylvia if there was a good place to eat. She directed me to a place I had seen not too far up the road. There was no sign, but tables and chairs were on a veranda with more inside.

I walked there and made my way through the maze of alfresco diners.

Across the dining room, sitting in a booth with a pitcher of water and two glasses, was Tseten.

～

Excerpt from the blog: *Griffin's Flight*

Q: Why did you decide to study karate?

A: I began studying martial art (Karate is a specific martial art, not a general term) for several reasons. If you've read my blog, you know that discipline has been a problem for me. I thought martial art practice would help me with that. Plus, from movies and reading, I knew that meditation and martial art go hand-in-hand. I wanted to get all the help I could with my meditation practice.

So, I found a local school that taught a traditional martial art. ("Traditional" meaning they do things the old way. Think: Not MMA.) I looked for a Chinese martial art, but in my part of the world they are hard to find. In fact, most of the schools near me were more about competition than self-defense and meditation.

The school I joined was kind of peaceful. Weird for a martial art school, I thought, but I liked the atmosphere.

As a new student, I was glad I had already been doing yoga. I was stronger and more flexible than when I moved back to the farm. But from the first day, I knew I would get stronger and faster than with yoga alone.

～

Q: Does yoga help with meditation/levitation/flying?

A: Yoga helps you live in your body. The word shares a root origin with the word "yoke." The idea of union or togetherness is the aim of yoga - bringing local and nonlocal together.

That probably doesn't help a lot.

Yeah, yoga helps me meditate by easing some of the body chatter that distracts my mind. I'm stronger and more flexible, so exertion is less taxing. Landing and maneuvering is easier.

Q: Why can you fly and I can't?

A: Flying was an accident. I didn't mean to do it. I'm no mutant (no gamma rays or pools of toxic waste, at least.) And I'm not special. Heck, maybe I was in the right place at the right time. Make that happen for yourself and let me know how it turns out.

Tseten smiled when he saw me and waved me over. I walked to his table. My brain seemed to have stopped working. How was he here? Could I trust him?

"Hi, Liv. How are you?" he asked, standing and holding a hand out towards me.

I looked at his hand, hanging there between us, then up to his face. I didn't take it. He accepted my choice with a raised eyebrow and sat.

"I didn't expect to see you here," I said.

"Then why are you here?"

"My landlady recommended the place."

"Strange the way the universe works, isn't it?"

"Strange, yes."

"Well, since you're here, you might as well join me. I ordered enough for two."

"Really."

I resigned myself to the conversation and sat across the table from the man.

"Is water okay, or would you prefer tequila?" he asked.

I looked at him through squinted eyes. Did he know about my overindulgence? There was no judgement in his eyes.

"Is the water safe?" I asked.

"Do you want it to be?"

"Yes, I want very much for it to be okay. Dysentery is rather unfun, from my understanding."

He took a sip from his glass.

"It's good."

"Fine."

He signaled to the girl behind the counter.

"So, you've hit another rough patch," he said, nibbling on a tortilla.

I inhaled through my nose, holding my temper.

"Rough patch. People I care about are dying at a record pace, and it's my fault." My voice rose as I spoke, and I struggled to keep my anger under control.

"Rough patch?" I repeated.

"We went through this earlier. How is it your fault if people do evil things?"

"You *know* that's not what I'm talking about. No, I'm not responsible for other people's choices, but I didn't-."

My voice broke, and I stopped talking for a moment. I cleared my throat.

"I didn't have to give them new targets to shoot at," I finished, enunciating each word carefully.

A server brought my place setting and filled my glass. I thanked the girl and took a sip. It wasn't cold, but it wasn't warm either.

"What else is going on besides your friends being shot up?" he asked.

I hated his being so glib about Melanie and Agent Stefanie. My breath was becoming short, and I could feel red creeping up from my collar.

"What else?" I growled, "What else is that someone took all my stuff. Took my phones, my computer, and my money! What else is that I don't have anywhere to go, no one to talk to. What else? What else is there?"

"Listen," he said, leaning forward. "You're angry; furious even! Adrenaline is flooding your system. Can you think? Can you fly?"

I had never seen him so focused and intense.

"Of course I can think," I almost yelled.

"Can you fly?"

My hands balled into fists, and I nearly struck him.

But…could I?

I reached for it as I had learned to do, and it was there.

"Yes," I said, chest heaving. I forced my hands to unclench. "I can."

He sat back, and his demeanor changed instantly, as if someone had thrown a switch.

"Oh, good. Here's our food."

Tseten sat back so our server could place a large platter of beans, tortillas, salsa, and sizzling beef on the table.

"Help yourself," he said, digging in.

His abrupt change in voice and, well, everything, confused me. How could he be so intent and focused on pissing me off one minute and inviting me to share his dinner the next? My hands shook as I reached for a radish.

"You're a martial artist, correct?" he asked around a mouthful of corn relish.

"Yes," I said, voice shaking. I didn't feel like talking.

"Do you spar?"

"Of course."

"I'm sorry?"

"Yes! Yes, we spar."

"What do you learn from it?"

"What do I get from sparring?"

"Yes."

I closed my eyes, clenched my fists, and took a deep breath. This man would not goad me into losing my temper again.

"I learn to trust my training," I said finally. "To allow my body and subconscious to be in control and my mind to rest. I learn about ranging attacks and managing counter-attacks. Targeting, combinations, balance; the list goes on and on."

"Hm," he said, his mouth full of pinto beans. Eventually, he swallowed.

"That's what you learn when you win?" he asked, eyebrows raised.

"Win or lose. I actually learn more when I lose."

Tseten looked up at me, one eyebrow cocked.

"I learn more when I lose," I breathed. I put my elbows on the table and rested my forehead in my hands.

"You have got to be kidding me. I swear, Tseten, if you tell me this is all just some kind of learning game, I might punch you in the face on my way out."

Tseten laughed, holding a napkin to his mouth.

"Olivia," he said, cocking his head to the side and dabbing his mouth with the napkin, "your threats of violence are forgiven."

He became serious again.

"And no, I would never minimize your suffering that way. Your experience is tragic. Your pain is real."

He reached across the table and touched my hand briefly.

"I wept for you when I learned about Seattle and San Francisco. You've made such progress. It's time for us to come out of hiding."

Fury swept through me.

"I think last week would have been about God Damned PERFECT!" I snarled as my left hand slammed down on the table.

Glasses jumped and spilled, plates slid to the floor, and every head in the small room turned towards us - towards me.

My chest was heaving, tears ran from my eyes, and I sobbed, not from sorrow but from rage.

Or maybe both.

"Lo siento," Tseten said to the room at large, holding up both hands. "Lo siento, está bien."

A burly man hurried over to help clean up the mess. I tried, but my hands were shaking too badly. The man looked at Tseten. Unspoken communication passed between them, him asking if he needed help, Tseten saying, Thank you. No, it was under control.

"Sorry," I grumbled to the man as he mopped up water with a towel.

"These things happen, my friend," he said. "May I get you anything else?"

"Just...more water, please."

"Ciertamente, señorita."

He left. I sniffed.

"I'm sorry," I said with a sigh, measuring each word. "Taking my anger out on you isn't fair."

The man returned with the water.

"Muchas gracias," I said.

"You're right," Tseten said after the man left. "But you're also right about us. We should have helped sooner. We sensed the certainty of violence and death, but didn't realize how focused and ruthless these — what do you call them? Black Hats? Yes. We didn't comprehend how swift and brutal the response would be."

"It was that."

"So, what are your plans?"

"Why?"

"I want to work with you."

"I'm not ready to go to your school, to be your student."

"No, I can see that. I'm proposing something else. A sort of partnership."

"How is that…what does that mean?"

"It means that you and I…and Sheila work together."

I bristled at the mention of Sheila.

He raised a finger to forestall my objection.

"I know you don't trust her. But…."

His voice trailed off as he stared at the picture on the wall. He took a bite of steak and chewed thoughtfully.

"Well, let me just say that she has earned your trust."

"How?" I asked, my voice harsh with disbelief.

Tseten looked at me with narrowed eyes, then shook his head.

"No. Not yet. We have work to do, and you don't need distractions."

"Tseten," I huffed, and wiped a hand over my face, "Enough with the games. If I want to, I can leave…I can literally fly out that door and make a grand tour of freaking traffic cameras and security cameras around the country, the continent, heck, the entire world. I don't need your help to get any kind of message out."

"No," he said, sitting back. "I'm aware of that."

"So why are you trying to play more control games with me?"

"Because as good as you are at learning, you don't know everything."

I nodded.

"That's not news. I'm aware of my shortcomings."

"Ignorance isn't necessarily a shortcoming. That's one thing you still need to learn. Don't be so quick to judge ignorance."

My hands had stopped shaking, so I picked up a fork and started helping myself to the meal.

"I was thinking of heading back to the States. Maybe finding another place to hide… camp in the wilderness somewhere," I said.

"Excellent. That's a marvelous idea."

"Why do you say that?"

"No distractions. No electronics. No Black Hats, no Gray Hats, or whatever. Rest. Meditate. Heal. We'll find you when you're ready."

I almost asked, "*How* will you find me?" but decided not to embarrass myself.

I transcribe the rest of this chapter from the journal I kept with pen and paper over the next few months.

8/5

I'm back in Yellowstone. It's reasonably safe up here. I've seen signs of bear and moose, but no wolves. I'm sure they're around, but I doubt they'll mess with me. Hope not anyway.

Tseten left me a field guide to identify edible plants and fungi in the neighborhood. I have the feeling that if I get into real trouble, someone from the School will show up and help me out.

At any rate, I won't starve—for a few months at least. I think snow falls in September or October up here. We'll see. It's hot right now. I'm not cooking during the day. If I have a fire, it's only at night so the smoke doesn't give me away. I'm not camping in the "approved" campgrounds.

8/7

I've been in Yellowstone for three days. I don't remember going this long without showering before. My smell might give me away before anything else does.

I've spent a lot of time meditating. When I'm not meditating, I'm thinking about physics and what's been going on, trying to understand it better.

I believe it has something to do with multiple dimensions, quantum mechanics, and neurochemistry. Physical laws (Newtonian physics) break down on the quantum level. There is evidence of a connection between the nervous system and higher dimensions (albeit evidence not accepted or even recognized in the mainstream. Since the mainstream scientific establishment can't explain my experiences, I'm not too bothered by that.).

So, the thing that brings this puzzle together is meditation. Meditation changes something in the brain (and maybe the rest of the body). It unlocks the potential to interact with higher dimensions. The results of those interactions seem unexplainable and like magic to us, stuck here in just three dimensions (four if you count time).

I remember Dr. Sagan's demonstration on the old Cosmos series of a three-dimensional being interacting in two dimensions. It would have access to information, perform feats that would be unimaginable to the denizens of Flatland, essentially miracles. I think this is something similar.

What we need is a better understanding of the process, and, though it pains me to say it, laboratory testing. And I'm almost willing to do that if I can remain free. But I can't trust anyone to keep me free. I have to take responsibility for it. I won't submit to testing until I'm sure I can maintain my freedom.

8/9

The park is beautiful! I've been staying out of sight. I never know where trail cameras are and I know for a fact that there are cameras in the public areas, so I haven't made any trips to Old Faithful or any of the more touristy locations.

I'm having fun exploring the rim of the caldera, finding and eating wild plants, and making friends with some of the wildlife.

Yeah, when you spend your time in solitude and meditation, you are a real member of the forest, and of nature. Truthfully, it could just be about the smell. I go down to the river and wash off every day, but without soap and deodorant, I smell very "naturey." My hair is growing out again.

Before long, I'll be mistaken for Sasquatch if I'm seen on the trails. That might not be a bad thing.

I've been listening to Guidance, my higher self, God, the Universe, my heart, whatever you want to call it, more and more. I'm beginning to know the difference between my own spirit and that voice. The differences are subtle, but noticeable if you pay attention. Rarely is it words that come across, but usually ideas, pictures, or feelings. When I come across a new plant, I sit and listen, and the answer is there. Of course, I check the field guide to be certain. I'm not batting a thousand, but I'm getting better at understanding.

8/13

Had a visit from Tseten today. We talked about healing. He told me that our bodies are reflections (or maybe projections) of our spirit in three (four?) dimensional matter. The state of our body shows the state of our spirit to a degree. The state of our spirit depends on how connected we are to the Universe around us.

It was good stuff. He never really said anything that I didn't know, but as he spoke, I made connections in my mind that I had never made before.

Yesterday I slipped off a rock when running and scraped my palm. It bled a little, and I was vaguely concerned about infection. Today, after our talk, I looked at my palm and noticed that it was perfect, as if the accident had never happened. Were the two connected, or does my body just heal faster on a natural diet when I'm getting plenty of rest?

8/18

Tseten visited again. He hugged me and told me how strong I was looking. I looked down at my t-shirt with holes under the arms and a rip near the bottom and scruffy jeans with fraying cuffs.

He told me he meant I looked healthy and rested. Being away from stress was good for me.

And he's right. I'm stronger than I have been in a long time. Much more in control.

Tseten talked about healing lore from different cultures around the world. He told me about the Sin Eaters of ancient Israel, Sangoma in African tribes, and more. We talked about how very often healers would use herbs to facilitate healing, not just internally, but externally (burned or just placed in the environment). He talked about healing symbols they would place again, inside a person, outside, or in their surroundings. He talked about singing, massage, dancing, acupuncture, diet, laying-on of hands, essential oils, and crystals. Honestly, there was so much I lost track.

What it came down to, though, was balance. Finding the state of perfection that already exists rather than creating something new, or recovering something old. Perfection of the body exists because that is the state of creation.

Of course, he didn't want to talk about the hard questions like: If we exist in a state of perpetual perfection, then why do we grow old and die?

"That's a question for another day," he said.

We'll see.

Even before learning to levitate, I experimented with lots of variations in my diet. I had learned that eliminating grains and dairy quieted my digestion and gave me tons more energy.

~

Excerpt from the blog: *Griffin's Flight*

JANUARY 13, 2024

My diet goals are:

a. To be as healthy as possible.
b. To remove items from my diet that might interfere with developing the levitation skill.

Obviously, I started with sugar. Eliminating sugar from your diet sounds easy, but let me tell you, it's not. First, I was addicted to sugar. I guess we all are. We are born with that addiction for good reason. There is an evolutionary benefit to being addicted to sweet things like fruit. It keeps us from starving. Good for the plants too, since it aids in seed dispersal.

Food companies and marketers exploit that natural addiction. Not only do desserts and sweets have sugar, but everything from potato chips to canned soup has added sugar. When I started reading labels in the store, I was amazed.

Anyway, I kept some fruit in my diet, but tried to keep it seasonal and local. In the winter, I eat some citrus for Vitamin C and variety, but I keep to dried local fruits in the winter. The summer, of course, was something else.

There are berries in the early summer. Strawberries, raspberries, and blackberries all grow well in my area. There are tons of peaches and nectarines a little later, and then apples and pears come into season. I was never a huge fan of fruit, but as I cut out sugar, I found I appreciated it a lot more.

I tried a strict vegan diet for a while. If you don't know, "vegan" means eating only plant-based foods. It's hard and restrictive, but many people do well. Eating out is difficult, if not impossible. It depends on where you live and what the local offerings are.

Some vegetarians allow things like milk products or eggs. This is easier to maintain, unless you are strict on sourcing your milk and egg products from organic, pastured sources. Then again, any dietary restriction is going to limit your social eating. They call this style of vegetarianism lacto-ovo vegetarianism.

Another thing I tried was the Atkins diet. On this plan, you eat meat and vegetables with very few grains. The goal of Atkins was to keep the blood sugar levels stable, thus limiting insulin release. You accomplish this by eliminating sugar, grains, and fruits. As the body comes back into balance, you can add some carbohydrates (carbs) back into the diet.

I liked Atkins when I did it the way Dr. Atkins intended, but I dropped it. Unfortunately, there's a lot of junk-food carrying his name. It's over processed and not anywhere near organic. Thus, not for me.

After Atkins, I tried several versions of the paleo diet. Very similar to Atkins, the point of this approach is to approximate the diet of our Paleolithic ancestors. The idea is that our genetics favor this diet, which comprises vegetables and meats. It differs from Atkins because it focuses more on fresh, natural food sources. Most people who consider themselves paleo eat organic vegetables and pastured meat, eggs and dairy (if they include dairy). The idea of eating pastured meat (rather than grainfed) is that, just like humans have not evolved to eat grains, cattle and other animals are not either. Cattle, pigs, and chickens are all grazers and foragers. Eating grain makes them fatter and sicker.

Nineteen

Tseten showed up sporadically for the first month, but I hadn't seen him for a while. I had no money to speak of, but I had clothes, a sleeping bag, and a tent. And I could fly.

After several weeks studying my field guides, foraging for greens and fishing, I found I could live indefinitely, as long as I listened to internal Guidance. Of course, I didn't always receive direct answers to questions. I couldn't know or understand what was going to happen next, so I learned to trust the process and take lessons as they came.

That's how, one warm morning in October, I knew something was coming, but I didn't know what. Just in case it was a visitor, I scrubbed my two enameled coffee cups and made a large pot of tea.

My clothes were as clean as I could get them, and I had bathed and washed my hair. I meditated and relaxed while waiting to see what would happen.

I opened my eyes. Someone was standing at the edge of my camp.

"Hello, Liv," Sheila said.

I stood.

"Hello," I said, my voice a little scratchy. I cleared my throat.

"Am I disturbing you?"

"Not at all. I've been waiting for you. Have a seat?"

I waved a hand towards the rock across from me.

"Thanks."

"Tea? It's sage."

"Thank you."

We sat and sipped our tea. It was a pleasant morning, and the sun was climbing above the treetops. We were in a field on the edge of a state forest in southern Illinois.

"This is a lovely spot," Sheila said.

"Isn't it?"

"How have you been?"

"Good. Still on this side of the grass," I said with a grin. "How about you and your students?"

"We're good," she said, but she didn't smile.

I sat and waited. This wasn't my conversation.

Birds sang, crickets chirped, and the occasional horsefly buzzed through camp.

"So," she said with an enormous sigh, "I owe you an apology."

"For what?"

"For everything that happened this summer. Everything."

"You don't owe me. But for what it's worth, I forgave you."

"You aren't angry anymore?"

"No."

And I wasn't. Not that I decided Sheila had been right. She hadn't been. And not that time had dulled my emotions. I still sorrowed for the lives lost and families torn apart. But I had been studying and practicing the lessons on healing, and it was about more than my body. The spirit also sometimes needed to heal. I had worked on myself, and I felt more peace than I ever had before.

"Sheila, you were afraid. In fear, you mistook the voice of ego for the voice of Spirit. It happens to all of us."

She looked as if she were about to argue, then took a deep breath and gazed into the trees.

"You're right. Fear is the opposite of love. I tried to influence you because I was afraid that we would lose you."

"You nearly did. It was a valid concern."

"Yes, but I should have tried to help, not control you."

"Granted."

We sat in silence and sipped our tea.

"This isn't bad," she said.

"Thanks. I gathered the sage in Wyoming."

"Tseten convinced me to leave you alone, for my sake, as much as yours. You seem different. Stronger."

I smiled.

"Being alone will do that."

Silence again.

"So. Any news?" I asked. I've never been one for small talk.

She was looking into her cup and said nothing for a long time. Finally, she nodded slowly.

"Yes," she said, looking up at me. "Not all of it is bad."

"Whenever you're ready."

I probably had a thousand questions, but I would let Sheila tell it however she wanted.

"Your parents are good. We sent some people to the auction with cash. The farm is safe. Some animals, too. A member of the School is there taking care of them."

I was so grateful that I didn't know how to express it. I covered my face with my hands.

"Thank you," I said, my voice hoarse again. I took my hands away, and tears slid down my face.

"It was the only option. Of course, they are still being held in Dayton."

My expression must have changed because she held up a hand, palm toward me.

"They aren't being held in cells. Just under protection. They are on a military base under constant armed guard. We send people in to check on them every so often. They know the farm is safe."

"I know. I mean, I know they are still being held and that they're safe. I've been kind of checking in on them."

"What do you mean?"

"Mentally checking in on them during meditation. I have…visions… sometimes, waking dreams where I see them and other people. I'm glad that the government has been protecting them. Not happy that they haven't gone home yet."

I brought my emotions back to center, took a deep breath, and motioned for Sheila to continue.

"Most of your Leaders are being released. They're going back home. There have been no more murders. Stefanie Tucciarone escaped serious injury. Her body armor protected her from the worst of it - a shotgun blast through a door. She's still with the FBI."

I nodded. This was good news. I had seen Agent Stefanie in my visions a few times, but it was reassuring to get confirmation.

"Who were these assassins, Sheila? How did they get into the country?"

"We think many were already here. Some came from, or were working for, North Korea and China. Some from the Middle East - oil countries."

I shook my head in disbelief.

"Why?"

"Transportation? Freedom? What you were teaching people might mean the end of reliance on oil. It would also be hard to control people if they could literally fly away from oppression."

"Freedom is intrinsic to humanity. You think that's what it's all about?"

"Yes."

"And now they've won. The governments, religions, and corporations have won another round, keeping the masses stupid and uninformed."

"Not necessarily," Sheila said. "They may have won the first round, but it's time for round two. And we're going to be in the fight this time."

"What does that mean?"

"It means, my dear, that you are no longer alone."

"**B**ut what can we do? Start over? Land on the White House lawn?"

"No. We're not all into flying, for one thing. But we are led to support your mission. You began by yourself, and you didn't do badly. With our help, we think you'll succeed."

"And by 'we' you mean...?"

"Me, Tseten, other instructors, students. Everyone."

"Can I ask you a question?" I said.

"Why didn't we support you earlier?"

"Yes. Tseten and I started this conversation in Mexico. It didn't go well."

"I heard. Liv, I wish I had a better answer. We felt the time wasn't right. Maybe it wasn't. Maybe something has changed that will stack the odds in your favor. I don't know. Many of us…most of us, felt the timing was wrong."

"So, it was a self-fulfilling prophecy. Since you didn't help, the time wasn't right. Now that you want to help, you think the time is right."

"Don't be like that," Sheila said, setting her cup on the ground. "Don't be angry. You have every right to be, but please don't. That's why I'm here: because we were wrong. We were wrong, and people died."

A remnant of the old anger flashed through me. Sheila was right. I was angry that people had died, at the injustice, but it hadn't only been on her head. I was angry with myself, too. I should have seen what was happening, known better than to lead the Black Hats to innocent victims.

I needed to move, so I stood and paced around the campsite.

"I don't know, Sheila," I said, after a minute, "I don't think I can do this again."

"Why?"

"Why? Why can't I put innocent lives at risk? Seriously?"

I turned and stopped, staring at her.

"I'm telling you, it won't be like that this time," she said.

"Because I'll have you and your X-Men behind me?" I scoffed. "Look, Sheila, I don't mean to be insulting, but I'm not sure how you can help."

"They're not expecting you. Nobody knows what happened to you, whether you're still alive, or what. And we won't meet people personally. Not yet. Nobody but us will be targets, and *we* can be rather hard targets to hit."

"So I'll go back to blogging? Posting videos?"

"Why not? It worked last time."

"No. It's too passive. I need to be active, take charge of the situation."

"What are you thinking?"

I squatted and poured more tea. What *was* I thinking? The adrenaline rush was dwindling, leaving me feeling deflated and shaky. I sat back on the stone across from Sheila and took several calming breaths.

"Look, to be honest, I don't know what needs to happen. I'm not comfortable being passive. Not because these people pissed me off, but they've made mistakes, broken laws. The world needs to know the truth. The systems that allowed this to happen need to change.

"If you commit to helping me bring that change, then I'll accept your help. If you commit not just to going public, but to changing the world, I'll...be your student."

Sheila held her cup in both hands, looking at me over the rim, then up to the puffs of clouds riding a few thousand feet above our heads. Finally, her gaze dropped back to the metal cup, and she swirled the tea a few times and sighed.

"Yes, I think you're right. That was the delay. This is about more than a spiritual and scientific revolution. It's also about social change and responsibility."

She stood and held her hand out to me. I rose hesitantly and took it.

"It will take a lot of work. It won't be easy."

"I understand."

"So, for the record, I officially reject your offer to be my student."

"Sorry, what? That's what you've wanted all along. Why?"

"Several reasons," she said, releasing my hand and walking to the edge of the camp.

"First, because it's not that kind of school. Everyone comes to us as a master of something. But also because *we* need to change, too. We're pretty progressive, but none of us ever had the guts to put everything on the line for our principles like you did.

"You were fearless."

"Ha! I was petrified!"

"Okay, maybe relentless, then. Whatever the adjective, you didn't back down, didn't give up. You wrested the ability to fly right out of the aether. You figured it out, and you showed the world what was possible.

"My people could learn a few things from you. Even Tseten and me."

Her praise was embarrassing. I could feel my face coloring.

"Well, maybe," I said, looking at the ground. "Still, I want to learn more. Tseten and I were talking about healing."

"Yes. But that's not what I'm getting."

I paused. Not what she was getting? I asked my internal voice what I should learn next. It was silent.

Usually, Guidance was quiet when I asked the wrong question or I had already made my mind up and was looking for reassurance.

"Yeah. I'm…not sure," I said.

Over the past few months, my inner spiritual voice had grown, or maybe I had just become used to listening to it. I spent my days in nearly constant meditative silence. I turned toward the trees, quieted my mind, and opened it to every possibility. Then I listened again.

Working with Sheila was the right thing to do. Now was the time. Not that healing and teleportation weren't on a list somewhere, but continuing to make people aware and broadening their horizons was more pressing.

"Back when I was traveling with my friends Mitch and Teri, we talked about making camera raids," I said. "We never did it, but we talked about finding security cameras and flying in front of them. Some footage would inevitably leak to the internet. Word would get out."

I turned back to Sheila.

"What do you think?"

"Think bigger," she said, nodding.

This is the article that accompanied that famous viral video. Many of you read it on the blog, but more will have seen the video elsewhere.

Excerpt from the blog: *Griffin's Flight*

OCTOBER 11, 2024

Discouragement has stalked me for the past month. I have been recording, viewing and deleting files from my video camera for nearly five months. It's beyond old, but I can't think of a better way to avoid missing a brief levitation.

My parents wonder about all the time I spend alone. They worry but don't pry. At the end of my first year, Dad's pleased with my work but suggested that I need more time with other people.

Mom and Dad tease me sometimes about the time that I spend alone, wondering if I'm secretly talking to friends from yoga or martial art classes. I go on dates from time to time. Mostly, I work, practice, read, meditate, and watch meditation recordings.

The walk to the woods has become a sort of pre-meditation meditation. As I'm walking, I intentionally let my worries go, and leave all thoughts of levitation behind. I focus on meditation and not on levitation. I don't want my ego involved and try to remain very conscious of everything I do, every movement, every choice on the way.

Finally, yesterday, my patience was rewarded. The light differed from that day back in May, but the spot was as familiar, just as friendly. Meditation doesn't require the stillness and connection to nature I am blessed with, but I would be a fool not to acknowledge how much easier it made things for me. If not for my parents and their life choices, I wouldn't have the peace and clarity that I have.

On entering the clearing, I stopped short, stunned by a thought. If I hadn't flunked out of school, I wouldn't be here. If Holly hadn't left me, I wouldn't be here. Right now was perfect, and that meant everything leading up to it had been perfect as well, even the hard times.

I spread my blanket, sat, and followed the train of thought.

Every event in my life has led me here. Everything in my parents' lives brought me here, right now. I looked around. The present moment was important, not the setting, but being present in whatever circumstances I found myself.

Learning about health, meditation and yoga all came from being present and engaged in what was happening now. I closed my eyes and thought about times that had seemed less than perfect. Ideas of past or future, failure or success occupied my mind. The ideal moment was beyond labels. I needed to be present in every moment, not just when I meditated or did yoga or martial art.

I thought about Zen masters sitting on a mountaintop somewhere. Even a few hundred years ago, it had been easier to be in the moment away from the clutter and noise of society. They proved what was possible, but didn't put it into meaningful action. For any esoteric teachings to make sense, they had to work when applied to daily life.

I opened my eyes and looked around the clearing. The clearing was my mountaintop. I would have to come off it someday. Hopefully not soon.

Not today, at any rate.

As I prepared for meditation, I began taking deep breaths into my diaphragm. I set up my camera, double-checked it was recording, took off my shoes, left my socks on, sat on the cushion and began.

My breathing regulated and conscious thought ceased. I sat up straighter and felt a sinking feeling in my abdomen. I didn't think in words, just flashes of sensation, brief ideas. Letting all thoughts go, I allowed my eyes to creep open so I would remain conscious and not fall asleep.

As my eyes opened, there was a disorienting feeling, something like riding in a fast elevator. I could see the blanket, but not as it should have looked.

Holy crap, I thought, *I'm doing it again!*

And with that thought, I wasn't. I had only been a foot above the ground, but as soon as I left the meditative state, I was falling, not levitating. I hit my cushion and immediately jumped to my feet.

"Holy crap! Holy crap! That was it! I'm not crazy!"

I began running around the clearing, jumping into the air, fists above my head, whooping and yelling at the top of my voice.

My jubilation lasted only a couple of minutes. Honestly, it was more relief than anything. Some part of me, whether I acknowledged it or not, was concerned I had hallucinated the event. What I just experienced was real, without a doubt.

Remembering the camera, I trotted back to my blanket. I never watched the video on the small screen, but I had to see it. I watched myself prepare the blanket, the cushion, settle down and become still.

After just a few minutes, I watched myself rise slowly, rather majestically, I thought, into the air. It was a smooth motion, and I could understand why my brain had likened it to an elevator ride. My mouth fell open as I watched from an observer's point of view. My head swam, and I felt dizzy and a little nauseous.

"Oh, my god."

Suddenly, I didn't feel good at all. I got up and started pacing around the clearing.

"Oh. My. God."

Reality hit me like a physical blow. I felt chilled. Was I going into shock? I picked up the blanket and put it over my shoulders. I didn't know what to do. Something momentous had happened… was happening. I needed to think. I needed a plan of action. I needed to meditate.

Meditate. That's funny.

I laughed. I laughed even though I didn't feel like laughing.

This is not healthy, I thought, and laughed even harder.

In the movies, someone always slaps the person who can't stop laughing. I pinched myself hard instead.

And that helped.

I wasn't laughing anymore, but I felt weird. And I didn't want to be alone.

I picked up my things, put the cushion, camera, and tripod in the backpack, threw the blanket over my shoulder, and headed back to the barn. I would spend the afternoon with my parents. Maybe see if they wanted to catch a movie, work in the garden, or do anything ordinary.

I'll think again tomorrow.

For now, I needed to reconnect with "ordinary."

Twenty

After Sheila visited, I started making my way west. She next found me in Utah and invited me to their island for a strategic planning session. She left a pack with water and a new GPS, already programmed with the island's coordinates. Two days later, I was in the air over the Pacific Ocean, somewhere southwest of Hawaii. The sun was bright, the sky flawlessly clear and blue. I had strapped the new GPS to my wrist and was closing on my destination, a dot on the screen to my west. Nothing but waves were visible on the ocean surface below. I passed a pod of orcas a few hours ago, but had seen nothing but a few ships since. When the device finally said I had arrived, there was nothing but water below. I would have to get a closer look.

I stopped flying and fell toward the surface. Now, textbooks say that a human body accelerates to about 120 miles per hour in free-fall before air resistance stops its acceleration - terminal velocity. But I will tell you that falling toward a wall of water at 120 miles per hour is an almost surreal experience. I've mentioned before that sometimes when you're flying, your perspective slips, and reality becomes hard to be sure of. This was one of those times.

I stopped my fall when I could no longer tell how high I was. As soon as I began slowing, the surface of an island popped into existence. Where before there had been blue water as far as I could see, now there was a curving beach bordering lush vegetation. I was only about 300 feet above the treetops, but I was already slowing quickly. I allowed myself to fall right onto the sand at the edge of the trees, dropping to one knee in a perfect superhero landing, spraying sand for several yards in all directions.

"Well done!" a voice said. There was clapping. I stood and slipped my goggles up, looking around.

"Welcome!" Tseten said, opening his arms and coming in for a hug.

"Hi," I said, taken aback by the greeting.

"We were expecting you. Allow me to make introductions."

A dozen men and women stood in a loose group. They were all wearing light-colored clothes. Light to reflect the sun, I assumed. Most of them looked my parents' age, at least. Many had gray hair and beards. Some wore glasses; most had the same healthy glow and vibrant strength as Sheila and Tseten.

I shook everyone's hands. I was too surprised to remember names, though there were familiar faces from Chicago. It quickly became warm, and I shed helmet, flight jacket, and silk scarf.

When I was down to jeans and a t-shirt, someone took my bag, and Tseten took my arm and led me down a path, deeper into the island. We strolled along, and I took in the different plants, birds, and insects.

"No Sheila?" I asked.

"Shopping. She'll be right back."

"Shopping," I repeated. Tseten nodded and held my arm tighter.

"It's so good to see you. We were worried."

"Sorry. Why did you stop coming?"

He wagged his head from side to side.

"It was the right thing to do. You needed time and space to heal, not babysitters."

He laughed as he said the last, and I smiled.

"I could have used a babysitter once or twice. Or at least someone to share a meal with."

"You won't have trouble with loneliness here. Not unless you want to, that is."

"Well, you're right. Spending time with myself was good. I learned to listen to and trust my inner voice."

"Yes," he said, beaming, "That's why we could finally come back, I think. You were ready, and so were we. Now, we'll see what's next."

We had come upon a group of buildings. The first ones to my left were palm huts, as I expected. But just to the right was a brick, two-story house that might have been plucked from American suburbia. Farther inland, a stone farmhouse that resembled ones I had seen in a documentary on Scotland. As I walked, there were Japanese-style houses, chalets, tents, and a split-level ranch.

The eclectic mix was jarring at first, but as I walked among them, I felt a sense of balance in the community's design. How did they get the materials here? Or the labor force? I didn't ask.

"What do you think of our village?" Tseten asked.

"Lovely. Which is yours?"

"We haven't seen it yet. It's a cozy English cottage with vegetable and herb beds all around."

"Nice. You live there by yourself?"

"Usually. A young man is staying with me at the moment. He joined us only recently."

I looked at Tseten's face, creased with lines and softened by age. How old could someone be and still seem "young" to him?

"No significant other in your life?" I asked.

"Heavens, no! I've been a widower for quite some time now."

We were coming to a large open area. It wasn't a lawn, really, because it was mostly bare patches of sand. But coarse grass and other herbs grew in the shady boundaries. Was this the center of the village? We stepped into the square and walked toward an old brick one-room school building.

"Here we are," Tseten said, waving a hand.

"This? This is your school?"

"School, town hall, church. Whatever it needs to be."

"Church," I said, more to myself than him.

"Some of us are believers. Not all."

I glanced to see if he was making a joke.

"Seriously," he said, "What?"

He released my arm and stood back.

"Well, I mean, how could someone be here and not be a believer?"

"You might be surprised, I think. Most of us acknowledge some infinite intelligence, or perhaps consciousness, but not everyone."

"I don't understand."

"Do you come from a religious background?" Tseten asked, walking around the edge of the park toward the school.

"Kind of," I said, following. "Not religiously religious, if you know what I mean, but we were believers."

"And what about now?"

"Um… kind of the same," I said. "I haven't found a religion that comes very close to explaining what I've experienced on my own."

"So, this evolving experience over the past few years hasn't changed your worldview much?"

"No."

I saw where he was going.

"But I'm surer than ever that the cosmos couldn't have simply evolved from nothing. I mean, we can't *only* be a product of chance and evolution. There's some sort of organizing intelligence."

"Again, most of us agree. The ones who don't are much like you. Their experiences with all of this," he waved a hand to encompass the village and the island, "have reinforced their previous beliefs."

I couldn't wrap my head around it.

"Liv! Olivia!"

Sheila was hurrying from the center of the park towards us.

"Hello," I said. Her dark clothes seemed strange. She had several bags in her hands.

"Have you met everyone yet?" she asked.

"No, not yet," Tseten said. "Come on inside. You'll roast in that." I could see perspiration beading on Sheila's forehead already.

"I got you some traveling clothes," she said. "There's a phone and a laptop, too. We'll get everything set up tonight."

"Thanks," I said. I looked down at my clothes. I had been living in them for the past couple of months. Washing in mountain streams, hiking through deserts and mountains, forests and plains had left their marks. My boots, new less than a year ago, were barely holding together. In fact, sand was working its way through my socks and between my toes from the hard landing and the walk through town.

"I got sneakers, not boots," Sheila said. "I hope that's okay."

"Fine," I said. "Do they still call them 'sneakers'?"

"What do you call them?"

"Just…shoes, I think. Tennis shoes? I don't know."

"Oh, I'll stick with 'sneakers.' It's fun to say."

Tseten laughed.

"Let's get out of the sun," he said, climbing the steps into the building.

I followed. Inside, dozens of wooden folding chairs were facing a raised dais at the front. There was no cross or other religious symbol. Sheila set the bags down on a table.

My footsteps echoed in the single room as I strolled to the dais.

"Olivia," Tseten said, "before we get started, we have something of a surprise for you."

"What's that?" I asked, turning.

Beside him, standing in the open door, was a young woman. I couldn't see her face, but the sunlight shining through her dark, curly hair made the breath catch in my throat. I stopped, not understanding.

"Hi," Melanie said shyly, stepping forward and giving me a little wave.

"Melanie?" I whispered.

I looked at Tseten and then Sheila, who both nodded, beaming.

"Melanie? How?"

Suddenly I was holding her, squeezing her. Her arms were around my neck, I was breathing her hair and crying, and I had never felt happier in my life.

I tried to be angry with Tseten and Sheila for not telling me sooner, but I couldn't. I was too happy. Melanie and I walked, hand in hand, to a beautiful sandy beach and talked.

"It started with the FBI. At least, that's who they said they were. But when they came into the house, they didn't seem like FBI agents should seem, you know?"

"I think so."

"I just thought that they were too angry or something. They were looking for you, of course. But we wouldn't tell them anything."

I smiled and kissed the side of her head.

"I can't believe how brave you were. What happened after that?"

"Cerberus wouldn't stop barking, of course."

Cerberus was a little mop of a dog - a mutt that Melanie and her brother had rescued.

"That's when things got weird. They made Jeff and me sit on the couch while they searched the house. Cerberus was on my lap, and he was scared. He wouldn't stop barking, no matter what I said. The agent who was watching us wasn't a dog person. Probably not an animal person at all. He kept telling me to shut Cerbie up. I was terrified, and that's when I saw Sheila standing behind him."

"What did she do?"

"I'm not really sure. She just kind of touched his neck and knocked him out."

"What…like a Vulcan nerve pinch?"

"No. More like a gentle ninja chop. Right there," she said, reaching up to touch a spot on my neck just under my jaw.

"Ah. I see," I said, shivering a little at her touch.

"Then she said, 'Let's go,' and she held out her hands. Jeff hesitated, but I took her hand right away. And then ZAP! We were here!"

"You teleported?"

"I guess."

"That's cool!"

She squeezed my hand.

"I'm sorry you thought we were dead for so long. They let us call our family, but not you."

"It's okay," I said. "Some old guy stole my phone anyway."

"That sucks," Melanie said.

She convinced me to take my boots off to wade into the water, but I wouldn't take my jeans off.

"Trust me, wearing the same underwear for months should be a private thing."

She laughed.

We spent an hour there, talking. It was still warm, though the sun was setting on the other side of the island.

"Let's go get your clothes changed and watch the sunset," she said, jumping up and pulling me to my feet.

I carried my boots, and we ran back to the school building. Tseten and Sheila were still there, but gave me privacy to shower and change into the light-colored island clothes they all wore.

After watching the sunset together, Sheila, Tseten, and I settled down in the School to talk. Tseten and Sheila had stepped in to fix the worst of my mistakes at great personal risk. They really were like superheroes.

The Fox family was here, too. Melanie's brother Jeff came to talk at one point, and the Fox family, too. Catherine and Amy, the youngest girls, bounced into the room, all excitement. Their older sister, Jenna, was more reserved, but still seemed happy to see me. The tropics agreed with all of them, and they were tanned and fit.

Whenever people stopped by that night, they brought refreshments. We tried to talk serious strategy, but we kept getting interrupted. Finally, I gave in to the inevitable, and everyone told the stories of their escapes, the fake FBI agents, and how scared they had been. I met the other members who had helped rescue everyone. I heard their stories, how they came to find the school, all of it.

And Melanie never left. She didn't hover, but seemed happy to play hostess, organizing food and drink, making sure everyone had a place to sit. She brought in candles and everything else we needed. When not flitting around organizing, she sat with me, sometimes holding my hand.

Finally, at midnight, we went to Tseten's house for a late supper. Jeff was there cooking. He was Tseten's houseguest and, despite nibbling on fruit and cookies all evening, we ate well.

The next morning, Cerberus and I were reacquainted. As the lone dog on the island, the entire population had adopted him. He went pretty much where he wanted when he wanted, coming home to Melanie most nights.

I really got to know David and the rest of the Fox family. I broke into tears a few times just looking at them. You see it in the movies, people coming back from the dead. When it happens for real, it messes you up. Or it did me, anyway.

By the end of the first whole day, I had finished crying. The second day I rested, swam, and recovered emotionally. Not counting my midnight cruise ship encounter, I had never been to the tropics. Our island wasn't huge, but there were coconuts, papayas, tropical birds, white sandy beaches, and plenty of other things to keep my attention.

Meaning Melanie, of course.

We weren't *really* in a relationship. Prior to being reunited on the island, we had spent one magical evening together. Then, as far as I knew, she had been murdered.

I spent the second morning with Mel on the beach. I was trying to meditate, to get in touch with the tides at the junction of sky, earth, and sea. Melanie in a red bikini was distracting.

"How are you ever going to tan if you don't wear fewer clothes?"

I was sitting on a towel in a lotus position, wearing shorts and a t-shirt, hands in my lap.

"The farmers' tan is a sacred thing. We wear it like a badge of honor."

"Even Jeff has a better tan than you," she said, giggling.

"What's that supposed to mean?"

She sat up and climbed into my lap, forcing me, *forcing me* to wrap my arms around her.

She whispered in my ear.

"When you're on a tropical island and a computer programmer from Seattle has a better tan than you, it means you're wearing…too… many…clothes."

Very distracting.

Later, David's mother, Loretta, came to my rescue. She was fair-skinned, a redhead, and had some natural sunscreen she shared with me. I wasn't on the island long enough for my legs to catch up to my forearms, but I made progress.

I had been in paradise for four full days. By the fifth day, I started getting restless. After a long, lazy morning, I found Tseten in his lettuce patch.

"Hey there," I said, ambling up the path.

"Hi," he said, nodding. "How are you getting on?"

"I'm good. I've just about wrapped my head around everyone being alive."

He nodded and glanced at me, eyebrow cocked.

"Thank you again for that."

"You are very welcome again."

"Can we talk about what we do next?"

"Anytime."

He stood and moved his equipment one box to the right, kneeling again.

"Can I help with anything?" I asked.

"The beds pretty much take care of themselves. I'm thinking more than weeding, really."

I kneeled across from him and looked for weeds.

"Did you have a plan? I mean, in terms of what to do next?" I asked.

"Sheila said you want to go public. Again," he said, glancing up at me.

"That's what we talked about."

"Is that what you're still feeling?"

I reached inside for guidance. Did it still apply?

"Yeah, it's still there. But being here is right for now. Something is about to happen."

"Is it?"

I laughed. But he didn't join me.

"Wait. You don't feel it?" I asked.

"No," he said, sitting back on his haunches, arms on his knees. "Tell me."

"It feels like working on a problem and the solution is around the corner."

"Like anticipation?"

"Like certainty."

"Oh."

He gazed at me intently for a few moments, smiled, and went back to the lettuce.

"Give me an hour or two. I'll gather some friends."

"Okay."

Did he seem sad? Or hesitant maybe?

"On second thought, meet me at the school at four. We'll have some tea. And conversation."

"Right."

"Just you, though."

He looked back up at me, but I didn't reply.

"Or bring her," he said. "We're not keeping secrets. Not anymore."

"We're not joined at the hip," I said. I was curious about his attitude.

"Okay," he nodded. "You decide. See you then."

Feeling dismissed, I stood and made my way out of the garden. I glanced back, and Tseten was tending his lettuce beds as if I had never bothered him.

Mel and I went for a barefoot run around the beaches, chasing Cerberus through the surf, and trying to get our heart-rates up. Since we kept stopping to look at pretty flowers and fish, and to throw shells and driftwood for the dog, we really didn't get much exercise.

"I'm meeting with Tseten and Sheila and some others later today," I said, throwing a stick for the soggy dog.

She sighed.

"I knew it wouldn't be long," she said, tucking hair behind her ear and looking out over the ocean.

"Yeah," I said, nodding.

My parents were still being held, not to mention all the others. I had to do something, no explanations required.

"I wish I could stay here…with you."

She nodded.

"I know."

Melanie glanced at me, and then down over my swimsuit. I was too lean and hard to give her any competition in a swimsuit, but I had tried with a blue one-piece that Sheila picked out for me. It looked strange with my dark arms and white legs. Melanie brushed some sand off my shoulder.

"You're getting pink. We should go in."

"Mel," I said, taking her into my arms. "I don't want to go. You know that?"

"I know. You need to go. I just got used to not worrying."

She shrugged, and I felt her sobbing quietly. Cerberus sat beside us with his stick dangling expectantly.

"How are your parents?" I asked eventually, trying to find a neutral subject.

She sighed and pulled away, wiping her face.

"They're fine."

She glanced at me, shrugged, and kneeled to throw the stick for the dog.

"They want us, Jeff and me, to come home."

That thought sent a spike of fear through me.

"Will you?"

She waded into the water and sat, letting the surf flow around her. She could have been a mermaid there, the sun on her damp curls. I followed, entranced, but wary.

"I don't know what to do. We're imposing on your friends here. But those men...."

Her voice trailed away. I got it. She hadn't dealt with the trauma of that night.

"You're not a problem. Having young people around is good for these old guys."

That got a smile from her as Cerberus barked from the beach.

"Well, if you want to know what I think," I said, "you should stay here and give us all one less thing to worry about."

"Give *you* one less thing to worry about, you mean?"

"Yes," I said. "I'm being selfish. That's exactly what I mean."

I picked her up and kissed her, flying out of the water to land in the shade farther up the beach.

I sat on my sneakers in the shade, legs crossed, hands in my lap, and slipped into the gap. The air was fresh and zingy with energy. I could hear the surf, feel the breeze against my face, ruffling my hair. Fragments of conversation drifted across me, and all of it helped nudge me deeper into the gap.

I felt the bones of the island beneath my legs. My spine was a conduit of energy from earth to sky. The water all around me was connected, molecule to molecule, to the running water of home. Every person around me was connected, DNA molecule to DNA molecule to every other person on the planet.

Connections rippled through me, like the surf on the beach. Energy, knowledge, and power lapped at the shores of my consciousness.

You are about to learn something troubling, someone told me. Or maybe, I told myself. It didn't matter.

What is it? I asked.

No answer. Wrong question.

How will it affect me?

Nothing.

Will it change anything?

Nothing real.

Thank you.

My skin felt like an electric current was passing through me. I felt huge and tiny. I was infinite and free, yet confined.

I breathed deep, smelling the freshness of the island, allowing the feel of air in my nostrils, the sensation of my expanding diaphragm, and the sound of the surf to bring me up and out of the gap.

I moved my face, then my head, then shoulders and arms. Slowly, I got used to the sensations of my body again.

I glanced at my watch. It was time for the meeting.

Excerpt from the blog: *Griffin's Flight*

MAY 16, 2023

What do you do after levitating for the first time? Probably just what I did. When I got back to my apartment, I searched online for human levitation.

If it were real, what could the mechanism be? What made it possible? There were lots of questions, lots of possibilities.

Aside from several dubious ones, the only levitation videos I found were magic tricks. Real levitation wasn't high on the list of things most people believed in.

I found historical figures who claimed to have levitated. Some levitation events had witnesses. There were loads of Christian and Hindu saints who allegedly levitated.

There was a lot of information about the various meditation practices. But only one method, Transcendental Meditation, held advanced classes in levitation. I found videos of meditators apparently popping up off the floor for a moment before landing again, sometimes several feet away. That didn't seem like what happened to me.

Several Christians allegedly levitated during the "rapture" of intense prayer. Some levitated in private, but most had multiple witnesses, including popes and cardinals, priests, and nuns. That was more like it, but I wasn't praying. I was meditating.

What would cause a person to levitate? *If* it were possible, then *how* was it possible? I was trying to stay open about the experience. But the most likely explanation, and the one I would suggest if someone brought this story to me, was that I had fallen asleep.

But I hadn't felt like I was asleep. I knew what it was like to fall asleep while meditating, and this wasn't it. I had been meditating nearly every day for over eight months and had fallen asleep a lot in the beginning. It still happened, but not as often.

I could see several possibilities. First, I had been dreaming. Second, I was crazy. Third, I was hallucinating.

The least likely explanation was actual levitation.

I bought a small camera with a tripod, and another tripod for my phone. I scheduled a doctor's appointment to make sure there was nothing medical that would explain the hallucinations or other problems.

I had to prove to myself I wasn't crazy, hallucinating, or dreaming. Once I did that, I could move forward. Until then, there was nothing to do but go on with life as if nothing had changed.

Twenty-One

They had folded the chairs and stacked them against the walls. One long table sat in the center of the room. Pitchers of tea, a plate of cookies, and various fruits and cheeses were arranged artfully on a linen tablecloth.

Tseten and Sheila were there, along with two others. The man reminded me of a professor. He was quiet, but well-spoken. The laugh lines and crows feet on his face nearly disappeared when he was listening, but burst into full relief when he smiled.

The woman, shorter and curvier than Sheila, seemed just as robust. Her hair was long and dark, shot with silver. Today she wore it up in a bun held with a pin through a woven cage.

"Olivia, you remember Will and Sophia?" Tseten said, greeting me as I came into the room.

Everyone was barefoot, with sandals lined up at the entrance. I added mine and entered, greeting everyone. Sheila handed me a cup, and I served myself. Hibiscus tea and two ginger cookies.

We sat and chatted for a few minutes. The cookies were good, and I was tempted to refill my plate. Just then, Tseten brought up the subject of the meeting.

"Liv and I were speaking about her situation earlier," he said, leaning back in his chair, sitting cross-legged as if he were on the floor. "While we wait for our other guests, Liv, can you tell us what you are thinking?"

I set my cup down and brushed crumbs from my hands.

"I've been hiding for what, four months? Physically and emotionally, I've been healing. I've learned a lot. It's time to get things back on track."

"Things?" Will asked.

I glanced at Sheila. She held my gaze but didn't offer encouragement.

"The revolution Sheila and I spoke of in Chicago."

I felt resistance from the four of them. What was going on? Weren't they on my side now?

"Tell us what that would look like," Sophia said. Her voice was gentle and delicately accented.

"The revolution? Easy. We give people the opportunity to open their eyes. As things stand, the Alliance is keeping the truth from them. We don't have to allow that."

"What do you know about the Alliance?" Will asked.

"Not much. Only that they're kind of dicks and they keep trying to kill me."

Will's eyebrow went up at my language, but Sophia and Sheila smiled. Tseten leaned forward.

"Olivia, you need to understand something. The Alliance is...nebulous. They aren't a single group with a unified agenda."

I nodded and picked up my cup, forgetting it was empty. Before I could set it down, Sheila moved the hibiscus tea within my reach. I nodded thanks and turned my attention back to Tseten.

"The Alliance wasn't trying to kill you," he said.

"What do you mean?"

"Some *members* of the Alliance were. But the Alliance isn't an evil empire."

He glanced around at the others.

"In point of fact, many principals in the Alliance were students at one time."

I froze, my cup halfway to my mouth. I put it down, mental wheels spinning.

"Excuse me?"

"Liv, hang on," Sheila said. "We aren't *with* the Alliance. We're not *against* you, okay?"

My breathing was already speeding up. Anger rose like a wave.

I closed my eyes and went into the gap. I collected my emotions and examined them. The anger wasn't justified. It was ego, nothing more. My pride had been wounded last year, and anger was a way to make itself feel better.

I opened my eyes and walked to a window, looking out onto the lawn. The sun was sinking toward the treetops on my right. An elderly woman was sitting in a chair on her lawn and throwing a ball for Cerberus.

I centered myself again before turning.

"Okay," I said, "Tell me more."

"I told you I had been in business before," Sheila said.

I nodded, taking my seat again.

"Now I'm here. People come to us from everywhere. They 'wake up' for lack of a better term, and we find them. Or they find us."

"Or, they don't," Will said, "Or they do, and leave us to join the Alliance later."

"It's not black and white," Sophia said.

"Do they know about this island? Do they know I'm here?"

Tseten and Sheila glanced at each other.

"Yes, they do," said a voice from the doorway. I turned. Agent Stefanie stood there, slipping out of her shoes.

You know that phrase, "you could have knocked me over with a feather?" That was the moment I learned what that phrase meant.

My mind whirled, and I lost my balance. Even seated, I was dizzy and nauseous. I was also scared, angry, and betrayed.

"Stay with us, Liv," Sheila said.

She leaned forward to put a hand on my shoulder, which was a mistake. I broke her nose without a thought.

"Liv! Olivia!" Tseten shouted as Sheila fell back onto the floor.

I whirled on him, standing, hands up, ready to fight. I backed toward the wall, trying to keep them all in my field of vision.

"Liv, try to calm down," Agent Stefanie said, coming into the room, hands raised, palms out. "Nobody's here to hurt you. We're all your friends."

The tea and cookies made their way back up. It's hard to think about defending yourself when you're throwing up, but I did my best.

Sophia was glaring at me and helping Sheila to her feet. Tseten and Will stood between me and the other women, protecting them, apparently. That almost made me laugh. Protecting *them* from *me*.

I spat and dragged the back of a hand over my mouth. Then I took a deep breath, shuddering.

"Is Melanie in on this? The others?" I asked.

"Olivia, there is *nothing* to be 'in on'. We aren't your enemies," Tseten said.

"You're not part of the Alliance? None of you?" I glanced at Agent Stefanie but didn't allow my gaze to linger anywhere. I kept my eyes bouncing around the room, alert for danger.

"Yes," Agent Stefanie said. "You're right that I'm with the Alliance, but it's not what you think. Or...not *only* what you think. Please let us explain."

Sheila's chair had broken, so Sophia set it aside and gave her mine. Blood and tears streaked her face, and bruises were blooming under her eyes. I tried to feel good about that. I didn't.

Anger and fear at the intensities I was feeling made it nearly impossible to get into the gap, to touch Guidance. I had to calm myself to find my spiritual center, my connection, and determine what was happening here.

"Liv," Tseten said, getting my attention, "Liv, let me get you a chair. You need to sit down before you fall down. Okay?"

Without waiting, he moved to the wall and got a chair and brought it to me, unfolding it beside me. I said nothing, but sat after he moved away.

"Good," Will said, tension easing from his shoulders, "Good. Shall I get someone to help with...."

His voice faded away, but he waved a hand that took in both Sheila's battered face and the vomit on the floor.

Sophia frowned.

"Healing isn't my specialty, but I'm trying. Towels and water would be good."

Tseten and Agent Stefanie contemplated each other, but said nothing.

I was feeling nauseous again. I leaned forward, an elbow on my knee, and massaged my forehead, trying to breathe.

"I'm glad you're calming yourself," Tseten said from across the room. "Let me know when you're ready to talk."

"Jesus…the nerve. Just shut up, Tseten. Stop talking."

Will came back in with towels, a mop, and soapy water. I took five seconds to wonder how they got and disposed of water here. I had seen no water treatment facilities.

"Olivia? Can I get you anything?" Sophia asked.

I tried to think of something clever, but my brain wasn't there.

"No, Sophia. But…let's talk. You must have had a plan here. I'm curious. What did you *think* would happen, bringing her here like this? Telling me you're in bed with the Alliance?"

Sheila struggled to sit up straight. They had cleaned the worst of the mess from her face, but her nose was swelling.

"Liv," she tried to say, but it came out as "Lib."

She shook her head, but apparently that hurt, and she winced.

"I haven't had a broken nose in a while. I forgot how much it stings."

The injury muffled her words, but she was understandable.

"Liv, we are on your side. *We* didn't hurt you. We helped you and the people you care about, remember?"

"But why? Why did you 'help' me, Sheila? Was it just to gain my trust? To control me?"

"Would you get over yourself?" Tseten nearly shouted, "Olivia, don't you see? We are your friends, but we are teachers, after all. You need to understand what you don't understand."

I squinted at him. My ego, which I could hear just fine, was screaming at me to leave. Grab Mel and the dog and put these creeps in the rearview. Get over myself?

But by now I was calming down. I could feel the touch of Guidance as well. I needed to be here to listen and learn.

I took the mop from Will. I needed to move, and it was only right that I clean my mess.

"Okay," I grumbled. "Somebody talk. I'll be here getting over myself."

Agent Stefanie made her way to the other side of the table.

"Olivia, 'Alliance' isn't a synonym for 'assassin.' Yeah, there are some tough, scary old people involved. Most of them want to control the knowledge that you're trying to share. Their power *depends* on people not knowing, not believing what they are capable of."

She leaned against the far wall and crossed her arms, and I glanced up at her. She frowned, giving me time to process and question if I wanted.

I went back to mopping.

"The Alliance's only shared goal is keeping information controlled," Will said.

"Right," I said, pausing. "Explain why that's a good idea for you folks. What's the upside for the School?"

"We get to operate without interference," Sheila said. "If we were out there teaching and recruiting, they wouldn't approve. We keep a low profile, help from time to time, and they leave us alone."

"Help?" I asked, anger spiking in my chest. "How?"

"By snagging people like you," Agent Stefanie said, coming off the wall and jabbing a finger in my direction. "You have to disappear, end of discussion. You disappear, or we all do."

That stopped me.

"It's not *quite* as dire as all that," Tseten said, holding up a hand to Agent Stefanie. "Yes, we help guide emerging talent, encourage discretion. Bring them here when the time is right. Our collaboration with the Alliance keeps us in the loop."

"It keeps us relevant," Sophia added.

"I need to wash my hands," I said, standing the mop in the bucket.

I walked through the door at the back of the room and washed my hands and face in the utility sink. The water had a metallic taste, but I felt better after rinsing my mouth. I took a clean hand towel from the stack and returned to the main room.

I reached inside and listened. I didn't receive Guidance to leave, which I would have if there were danger.

Nodding to myself, I went back to the table and poured more tea. I glanced at Agent Stefanie, who was still scowling, and held the pitcher out to her in invitation. As I set it down, she heaved herself off the wall and came over.

For the next hour, we talked about the various groups that made up the Alliance. It surprised me that so many of the powerful churches were active. Corporations too. I suspected big oil, but also tech companies, social media giants, retail outlets. They all profited hugely from the status quo.

"There's big money in keeping people poor," Will said.

"How can you go along with that?"

Tseten and Sheila both started talking, but I interrupted them.

"Okay, okay, I get keeping the wolves from the door. I get it. But that's short-term survival. Long-term? How do you justify it?"

"Hold that thought," Tseten said. "Excuse me for a moment. I'm afraid Master Kim overslept."

He stood, slipped his sandals on, and left.

Who is Master Kim?

I frowned after him, but nobody else said anything. Sophia checked Sheila's nose and clucked her disapproval.

I looked away, feeling guilty. Unfortunately, I looked right at Agent Stefanie, who was looking at me.

"Good to see you," she said. "You okay?"

"Well enough. You?"

"Good."

"I heard you got shot in Seattle," I said.

"Kind of. It was a shotgun blast through the door. Small shot. The vest took most of the splinters and lead. Got a few in the face and neck, nothing serious."

She turned her head and showed me. The dark skin of her neck was pink in a few spots, leading up under the curve of her jaw.

"Could have been bad," I said. "You got lucky."

She glanced away and shrugged.

"I...forgot my helmet in the excitement. I knew they were going to shoot through the door. I was trying to keep my team safe."

"Your team? You...arranged...."

"No. No, Liv. I had been trying to catch these guys all summer. I felt them getting ready to shoot. My tactical team was in trouble, so I pushed to the front. I just forgot my helmet."

I put a hand to my forehead and tried to breathe.

Was she being truthful?

"I thought you meant you were working with them. Sorry."

"I wouldn't kill people. The Chinese hired those guys, I think. Maybe the Iranians."

"Chinese? Why do they want me dead?"

"Seriously? Liv, how do you control 1.4 billion people if they can just fly away? That's no way to run a dictatorship."

I gazed out the window, lost in thought. Then I realized she had made a joke and was attempting to lighten the mood. I glanced back, but the moment was past.

"Sorry," I said anyway, "I should have known."

"Maybe," she said. "But it's okay."

I caught a whiff of her perfume from across the table. I thought of that day in my apartment when she and Graham had arrested me. It seemed ages ago.

"Liv," Tseten said from the door.

I turned, surprised when everyone stood. I followed suit, trying to see around Tseten.

Kim, the old man from the truck-stop, ambled up the steps and through the door. He stopped just inside and bowed slightly. Everyone but Agent Stefanie bowed from the waist.

"Hello, Master Kim," they said, nearly in unison.

Master Kim?

"Hello," Kim said, kicking off his shoes and lining them up with the others. "Sorry I'm late. I fell asleep."

I looked around at the group. They continued to stand respectfully, waiting for something.

"How are you, Olivia?" he asked.

"Mr. Kim? It's good to see you. I'm fine. How are you?"

"Just 'Kim.' I'm fine. Please, everyone sit."

They did, embarrassed to sit while he still stood.

"Did you save me any gingersnaps?"

"Please allow me, sir," Sheila said, standing.

"Sit," he said. And she did. No argument.

He sighed.

Tseten brought a chair and set it near mine while Kim helped himself to tea and cookies.

"Liv," Tseten said, not looking at me, "you were asking a question, I believe."

Was I?

I tried to remember the conversation before Tseten left.

"Um…yeah. Yes. How long has the School been cooperating with the Alliance?"

"About 200 years, give or take," Kim said without hesitating.

He and Tseten sat.

"Two hundred years, give or take," he repeated.

"Before the Civil War in the United States, there was a lot of anger. Lots of people wanted to *control* lots of other people. Not just that. They wanted control over the story, over how people thought and what they remembered."

Agent Stefanie leaned forward, elbows on the table, paying rapt attention to Kim.

"We, the School that is, had just migrated to the US from France. That's a beautiful spot in the countryside near Provence. Anyway, the School was moving. With all the turmoil, it made sense to look for new members—people who showed ability."

He ate a cookie and grunted approvingly. Nobody else spoke.

"I was maybe 25 or so when my father began his apprenticeship. Long story short, he went to Tennessee. Fifty years later, he was the principal teacher. The steel companies and railroads approached him shortly after that."

My mind boggled.

"Wait a minute. You're 200 years old?" I asked.

Everyone but Kim looked at me like I was an idiot. Kim laughed.

"Older, yeah. Old dude, remember?"

"So…wow. Okay. Your dad, then? Wow."

While my mental wheels spun, Tseten turned to Kim.

"If I may, Olivia brought up a good point earlier. Working with the

Alliance seems like a good short-term solution. Do you know what your father's long-term plans were?"

"Don't know. He died suddenly, not long after establishing a working relationship."

His gaze drifted, and he wandered into memory for a moment.

"Oil company, I think. Coal maybe? Someone wanted the land they were on. My father was Korean and had no real social status."

He glanced at me and nodded slightly.

"Most people thought he was Native American. Everyone else thought he was Chinese. Either way, most white people looked down on him and the rest of us."

I gazed around the room. Some were nodding, others lost in their own thoughts.

"I'm sorry," I said. "Was it them?"

Kim glanced at me and shrugged.

"It was someone. Don't know who."

"So…what? You just got used to working with the Evil Empire? You capitulated, and the world lost a couple of centuries of progress?"

"Liv," Sheila winced when she spoke. "Are you going to work with us or not? I need to put some ice on this and get it looked at. If we're wasting time, I'm leaving."

"Sheila, wait," Tseten said. "I'm sorry. I know you're in pain, but the girl's hurting as well."

He turned to me.

"This is difficult, but reach inside and find your peace. We can't move forward if we can't relate to each other."

I didn't acknowledge him, but I turned my face to the window and thought about my meditation session earlier. Meditation on the island had been especially deep and restful the past few days. Mentally, I reached for it and felt the calm rise through me like water into a plant's roots. I breathed it in, allowing it to heal my nerves and hurt feelings. My ego, always ready to jump up and protect my sense of self, lay down and slept in the presence of so much peace and love.

I nodded to Tseten, finally. He flashed a half-smile and glanced back at Sheila. She acknowledged him with the twitch of an eyebrow and turned away.

"Anyway," Kim began again, standing and walking to the table, "my opinion about the situation doesn't really matter anymore. Work with the Alliance or tell them to flip sand. Not my problem."

He stacked more cookies on his napkin and glanced at Sheila.

"Perhaps not, but, as ever, we appreciate your guidance," Sophia said, bowing her head slightly.

"As ever," Tseten agreed.

Sheila said nothing.

Kim reached out and rested his hand on Sheila's head for a moment, eyes closed and head tilted.

"Thank you for the cookies. Now," Kim continued, walking toward the window, "if I *were* offering guidance, I would say that you need to listen to the kid."

He raised a hand toward Sheila preemptively.

"I know. She has a lot to learn. She's rash, quick to anger. But her heart's in the right place."

Sophia and Will looked at me with fresh interest.

"She's a leader. Not *your* leader," Kim said, again glancing at Sheila, "but *a* leader. They have heard her voice, and the time is now."

Kim walked around the table, briefly resting a hand on my shoulder as he passed. He continued around the table as everyone else stood. He stopped in front of Agent Stefanie, who stood. Kim held out a hand.

"It's a pleasure to meet you," he said as she took it.

"Likewise," she said, inclining her head, "I've…heard stories."

Kim grinned.

"People like to tell stories."

Who is this guy? I asked myself.

"I'll see you around, Olivia. Thanks again for the cookies, Sheila."

Kim waved and turned toward the door, but couldn't be bothered to walk all the way there before he vanished. It was the first time I had actually seen it happen in full daylight.

"Okay," I said, plonking down in my seat again. "There's obviously a…story…there. Someone spill."

"Another time," Tseten said briskly. "Master Kim gave advice."

"I've never heard him do that," Will said.

"You're right," Sheila said, touching her nose. The swelling was down, and the bruises under her eyes appeared less livid. She turned to me.

"We've already agreed that we'll work with you. Fight with you if need be. We'll also cease cooperation with any members of the Alliance.

"Unfortunately, that will include the United States government," she said, glancing at Agent Stefanie.

"If you shut me out, I won't be able to help her anymore," she said, rising. "This is a mistake, Sheila."

"Sophia, could you show Agent Tucciarone out?" Tseten asked gently.

"Liv, I'm not your enemy. Believe that," she said as she turned toward the door.

There's nothing revelatory in this brief anecdote. It's about the day I moved back home. I was depressed and Dad lifted me up with a simple gesture.

Excerpt from the blog: *Griffin's Flight*

JULY 17, 2023

The crunch of tires on the gravel outside caught my attention. I looked out the barn door and saw Dad pulling into his parking space. He came in and hung the spare keys in their spot over his workbench.

"I got some keys made for you," he said. "There's one for the truck, the Ford tractor, the barn, and a few others. That'll make all of our lives easier."

He handed me the key ring.

"Thanks, Dad."

"Look, Liv, we had some words last winter…."

"No worries, Dad. You were right."

"Maybe, but I still shouldn't have…. Anyway, I just wanted to say, I'm glad you're back. We missed you," he finished in a raspy voice.

I looked down at the ground, then to the back of the field, cleared my throat, and when I thought my emotions were under control, I met his eyes.

"Thanks, Dad. I'm glad to be back, too."

Impulsively I hugged him with both arms, something I hadn't done in years. He hugged back briefly.

"Okay," he said, patting my back and sniffing. "Enough with this Oprah stuff. Why don't you get cleaned up and we'll see what we can do for dinner before your mom gets home."

Twenty-Two

B ack in the States, I avoided cities, towns, and interstates. I flew low, avoided security and traffic cameras, groups of people, and anything government owned, including state and national parks.

I had been doing a lot of reading in the past week. Lots of people had written about me, but the reporter out of Las Vegas, George Kemp, still intrigued me. I had turned down tons of interview requests back in May, including his. Even so, he had been fair and open-minded in his reporting since then. He came across as skeptical, but willing to be convinced. I respected that.

Reporters rarely tell you what to think. Not directly, at any rate. Skilled writers and editors can direct stories in almost any way they want. And the lead-in bits that seem ad-libbed? The editors craft those for a desired spin.

Kemp had talked about me several times on the Las Vegas news. Not just about me, but the stories around me over the past few months. If he couldn't sell a story to the station, he put it on his blog. The tone wasn't much different, but he could devote a lot of space to detail and context on his blog.

Kemp wasn't afraid of controversy. He was brave and smart.

Would he still want to interview me?

~

After several weeks of travel and research, I found what I was looking for. Glenrio was a sort of ghost town on the border between Texas and New Mexico on old Route 66. There were several abandoned buildings where we could mount cameras, record meetings, and everything anyone said and did.

Sheila, Tseten, Sophia, Will, and I had planned at length and it was now time to make contact. I flew east to Lubbock, Texas, where I found a cafe with decent food. I didn't order coffee, just hot water with lemon wedges, bacon, eggs, and a big salad. After eating, I checked my website.

It was still up.

The stats had stayed high through the end of the summer and then dropped. There was little traffic now.

So, I wrote a new article for the blog. I apologized for being gone for so long. I told the story of being attacked by assassins, attacked by the government, robbed, and spending months in the wilderness. And I wrote about the people I had visited and how the Alliance of governments, religions, and corporations had viciously attacked them.

I explained that coming out into the open again would certainly set more bad guys on my trail. And I promised it would be over soon.

Finally, I invited George Kemp to reach out again. I hoped he would be brave enough to bring a small crew and conduct my first ever interview.

After I posted the article, I hung out on the site. I didn't think it would take long to hear from someone.

I was right.

The first one to message me was ANON_GRL, my old friend Shelly from Billings. We chatted briefly, and I thanked her for keeping the site up. She was unconvinced that I was who I claimed to be, despite providing the ridiculously complicated site password and the correct response to her challenge phrase, so I agreed to Skype briefly.

"Hey, girl! You look good!" she said.

"Thanks! I like the purple hair."

"Oh, yeah. Kind of flashing back to middle school. It was fun. So what's new?" she asked.

"I'm waiting for the FBI to call," I said. "Should be any minute."

"Call?"

"Well, message me on the site. I don't think they have my phone number yet."

"Cool. Good luck with that. Look us up if you get back this way."

Ten minutes later, Blue_Eyes_90 messaged me.

GRIFFIN

Is this Agent Stefanie?

BLUE_EYES_90

Yeah. Surprised you didn't catch on earlier.

I thought I might know you. Mistook you for a friend.

Ouch. Look, about what happened on the island…

Yeah.

I didn't want you to find out that way.

Okay.

It's just…complicated.

Fair enough.

Graham knows nothing. You need to know that.

Not hard to believe.

He's not so bad, you know. He's a good guy.

Okay. I'll take your word for it. Can I ask? Short version?

What? My story?

Yes.

Started with my mom. She was a dancer connected to the mob in St. Louis.

Whoa.

Yeah. Eventually we moved away to Sedona, got into the spiritual stuff there.

I was near there earlier in the year. Beautiful country.

Powerful. I showed talent, similar to yours.

Similar how?

I levitated when I was 15. Just a few seconds. The right people heard about it and I was off to school in Europe.

Fifteen? You must have been terrified.

A little. I haven't told this to anyone else, Liv. I hope you'll keep it between us.

Of course.

Anyway, between Mom's connections, and those at my school, getting a job as an analyst at the FBI wasn't hard. My unofficial job was keeping an eye out for people like you.

You were looking for me?

People like you, yes.

Was Air Force One the first you knew of me?

Um....

It wasn't?

I have an algorithm running that correlates Amazon and eBay purchases with search history and library usage.

You were watching for a while.

And Graham doesn't know?

There's a lot he doesn't know.

And you'll keep this conversation from your
bosses? All of them?

Like it never happened.

Agent Stefanie, you keep surprising me.

Well, I do like keeping people on their toes.

I had to focus. My feelings were going to give me whiplash if this
kept up.

Okay, look. Neither your federal nor "other"
bosses are going to be happy if things go
according to plan for the next few days.

You need to think, Liv. I don't want to see you get
hurt.

No, me neither. But, like you said, "It's about
freedom."

Me and my big mouth. Good luck, Liv. I hope we
meet on the other side of this.

S heila organized our team into crews. Several were in Glenrio, setting
up cameras and other equipment. Besides regular cameras, they
installed sensitive listening devices, infrared cameras, and other gear to
ensure that nobody could sneak into town without us knowing about it.

Our people left shortly before dark. I was torn between spending the
night at the hotel with the crew from the School or camping in Glenrio. I
flew up to the roof of the old cafe. They had probably built it in the thir-
ties. It had a steeply pitched roof that was rotten in spots. I could see and
barely hear the interstate to the north. I made my way east to the abandoned gas station. The roof was flat and fairly sound. I looked out into the
clear night and wondered about tomorrow.

George Kemp would be here at noon with a camera crew. In deference to my requests, they would wear bulletproof vests. We hoped to do the interview, complete with video of me flying through the ghost town and maybe levitating with Mr. Kemp.

As I stretched out to relax and gaze at the stars from the gas station roof, my phone vibrated. I took it out, held it under the sleeping bag to block the light, and turned it on.

It was a text from Agent Stefanie: *Can I call you?*

Sure, I replied.

The phone buzzed, and I answered, still under the sleeping bag.

"Hello," I said.

"Good to hear your voice," she said.

"You too."

"Are you sure about this?"

"Yeah, I'm sure," I said. "Why? How do you know about it?"

"They have eyes everywhere," she said. "You know that."

The fear in her voice surprised me.

"Why are you afraid?" I asked. "What's going on?"

"Graham is on his way there now. He's been on this case for nearly two years, ever since you came onto our radar, so to speak."

"Wait, are they listening now?" I asked.

"No, we're alone."

"Okay, well, that's a long time. How do Graham's bosses feel about him failing to catch me?"

"It hasn't been pretty, but he can handle it."

I remembered my vision of the two of them in a relationship.

"I'm sure he can," I said. "Are you two still a thing?"

"What? Why would you ask that?"

"I don't mean to pry," I said. "It's none of my business, but I'm wondering who it is you're worried about tomorrow."

There was silence for a moment.

"Both of you," she whispered. "They murdered so many people...they could have gotten me."

Her voice broke.

"I'm sorry."

"Wasn't your fault," she replied, her voice flat. "There's nothing for you to feel sorry about. Can you tell me, what's your plan for tomorrow? What's the payoff?"

"Vindication."

"What? How?"

"There are going to be reporters here. If the Alliance shows up and tries to kill me, at least we'll get it on camera."

"That's the dumbest thing I've ever heard," she said, nearly shouting. "You're using the media to get back at the government?"

"Not at all. This isn't about my ego. It's about people knowing the truth; that there's more to reality than they're allowed to know. That the people in charge know the truth and are hiding it."

"Christ!" she swore. "I cannot believe you're doing this on purpose. I had hoped you were just innocently stupid."

"It's fine," I said.

Despite what I had learned, her insults hurt.

"I've taken measures to keep everyone safe," I said.

"Oh, you've taken measures. *You've* taken measures. Tell me, *007*, what *measures* have you taken?"

"There's no need to be nasty. The only reason I've had to do anything is that the feds couldn't handle the job!"

"Couldn't handle...? Agents died trying to keep you safe, sister. I could have died!"

"Well...that's what happens when you play both ends against the middle!"

It was hard to stay cooped up under the sleeping bag with the adrenaline rush that I was feeling. Hard to keep my voice under control.

I took a deep breath, let it out slowly, and willed my body to calm itself.

"Okay, look. I'm sorry. I appreciate the work, all the effort that you've put into keeping my family and me safe."

She said nothing. I sensed the same struggle for civility on her side of the line.

"These people are pretty good with electronics. They've wired the town with motion detectors, infrared, audio, and video. We'll know whether anyone shows up early. In fact, I'm here now."

"You're at the meeting spot? Dammit, Liv, that's not smart. Are you alone?"

"Yeah, just me and the scorpions," I said, trying to laugh.

"There's a team inbound," she said. "Feds. They're supposed to be in place before dawn."

"Oh," I said. That was a surprise.

"Um, what…or who…is their target?"

"I can't tell you. I've already said too much."

"Maybe I have too," I said. I was sorry that I had told her where I was. Would she tell her bosses?

"Look, just get out of there. Come back at noon, like you said. Or don't. That would be better."

"No, I'm seeing this through," I said. "I have to."

"Please, Liv, be safe. Don't put yourself in harm's way."

"I don't plan to. I like life, and I still have a lot of work to do."

"Are you going to tell Graham that we talked?" I asked.

"No," she almost whispered, "This is between you and me."

"Thank you," I said.

I believed her.

"I need to get going. I'm going to suffocate under this sleeping bag." She laughed and sniffed.

"Okay, Liv. Call me when you can. This phone is secure."

"I will. Thanks, Agent Stefanie."

We hung up, and I turned the screen off. I pulled the bag off my head but left the phone under the cover. It was good to breathe the cool night air again. I gingerly rested my back against the facade of the building. It seemed sturdy.

I watched the stars for a while. The ghost town was a mile south of the interstate that had killed it so many years ago. I could hear the roar of passing traffic muffled by distance. Headlights and billboards obscured some of the starlight, but several large meteors flashed across the sky over the next 30 minutes. Venus sat low on the western horizon. I remembered watching the phases of Venus as a kid with my small telescope in the backyard. I wished I had a telescope with me now. Despite the light pollution from the highway, the stars were beautiful.

I dozed off sometime around midnight. I had checked my phone every few minutes, but there had been no alarms. When I awoke, it was still fully dark, but something had changed. My brain was slightly fuzzy, but something had woken me.

I felt under the sleeping bag for my phone and unlocked it. It was 5:30 am. There were three alerts on the screen. My stomach clenched.

I dove under the bag and checked the first one. It was from an hour ago, motion detected at the west edge of town. The next one was 20 minutes ago, thermal detected to the south. The last was the one that woke me two minutes ago, motion detected in my building.

I stuffed the phone in my pocket, grabbed my helmet and goggles and lifted quietly into the air and down over the facade. Was this the Alliance or the feds? No way to know yet. Whoever they were, I had to assume they had thermal detection of their own. I hovered there as I pulled my helmet on and wondered what my best move would be.

I reached inside and checked with my Guidance. Staying put felt good for now, but I kept the connection open. It was rather like listening to instinct, but I had to stay focused. My phone buzzed in my pocket, but checking the screen felt wrong.

A layer of clouds had moved in. It was patchy, but probably thick enough to mask the light from my phone if not my thermal signature. I dropped my goggles over my eyes and flew up, quick but silent, right over the tops of the clouds.

No gunshots rang out, no shouts of *"There she is!"* I flew right over the cloud deck and hovered, waiting. There were no further pings, and I saw and heard nothing else. Maybe it was safe.

Intuition told me to check my phone. The latest ping was thermal detection from the east. I opened the app that would allow me to communicate with the cameras. What I saw sent a chill through me.

Two men had stalked through town. Neither of them were feds, judging by their lack of military uniform and headgear. The first one, responsible for three pings, was now on the roof of the gas station. The second was coming in from the other direction. Another ping told me he was in the cafe by the hotel.

I hovered over the clouds for the next 30 minutes, waiting to see if either man moved, but they seemed happy with their positions. The next question, with the condition of that building, was it safe to land back where I had been?

"No," I mumbled to myself, verbalizing the glaringly obvious answer from intuition.

There was another abandoned building west of the hotel. I had traveled east a few thousand feet, just by hovering over the clouds. I zipped west and dropped below the clouds. There were a few cars on the highway to my left, and a dark smudge in front of me where the abandoned town sat. I quickly got my bearings.

I dropped to a hundred feet above the ground and flew in. I wished I had thought to ask for personal night vision goggles. All things being equal, I was happy with internal Guidance from the Universe. I trusted intuition to bring me in safely.

And then I flew past the building in the dark. It was a small square building obscured by overgrown vegetation. I pulled up hard as it flashed under me and I looped back over, landing on the roof.

I sat for a moment, listening with both my ears and my mind. Shutting off the rational part of the mind and operating on instinct was nearly meditative. Finally, I opened my eyes and lifted my head to have a look around. There was a ping on my phone as I tripped the motion detector on the roof.

It seemed safe enough. I would wait here for the feds to show up. I hoped I could get word to them about the location of the assassins.

I didn't realize it as it was happening, but this was the last major practice session in my little clearing in the woods. It's funny how some endings hurt, even though we see them coming. Others, even if they are bittersweet, are more melancholic in hindsight.

Excerpt from the blog: *Griffin's Flight*

AUGUST 13, 2025

"Aerobatics" is the term used to describe the acrobatic maneuvering of aircraft. It could also apply to birds, insects, and soon to people. I began practicing today by hovering in the center of the clearing. My camera was on a tree to give a wide viewing angle.

Last week's footage was terrific. Even though I was the one in the video, it was exhilarating to watch. It's exciting to think about what this could mean for humanity. But I have to put those thoughts out of my mind. The things I'm ready to learn are dangerous.

Aerobatics in an airplane depends on the interaction of lift, drag, thrust, and weight, all of which depend on the power of the airplane, its shape, and the speed it can achieve. None of those forces matter to me. I can do the movements at much lower speeds and pull much lower "G-forces" than airplanes.

When I was ready to have fun later, I could try them at higher speeds. Fun, but dangerous too. I do not know what will happen.

I started by flying in a circle around the edge of the clearing, nice and slow in the beginning, but accelerating headfirst. I didn't have any way to gauge my speed, but I must have been going 15 to 20 miles per hour. Almost immediately, I took a bug hit to my left eye. My face exploded with pain, and I rolled to the inside of the clearing, holding both hands to my face. I landed softly and fell to my knees. I felt gingerly around my face, but the bug was gone.

There was no blood. I couldn't tell if it had stung me. I went to my camera and turned the screen so I could see my face.

A red welt was forming immediately below my left eye.

"I guess that makes me lucky."

I spoke to the camera as if I were addressing an audience.

"That bug could have taken my eye out."

I reset the camera and went back into the clearing. I sat down and tried to get back into the gap. Soon, I was levitating. I unfolded and extended my legs, looking up. I flew up towards the tops of the trees, and as I neared the open sky, I arched my back and curved back down toward the ground. There was a brief sense of vertigo, but I squinted my eyes at the rushing air and continued flying back down towards the ground. At about 10 feet above the surface, I changed direction to fly parallel to it. I headed toward the oak, flipped at the last second like a swimmer turning in a pool, rebounded off the tree, and headed in the opposite direction.

Instead of flying straight, I extended my arms and rolled clockwise the entire width of the clearing. When I got to the other side, I slowed, reached out to the tree, and closed my eyes, trying to resist the nauseous feeling. It subsided, and I stayed in the air.

I flew straight up and curved back toward the opposite side of the clearing. When I got there, I was heading straight down. I arced down toward the middle of the clearing, my back brushing the grass as I completed the bottom of the loop and curved back up to where I started. This was an "outside loop," one of the hardiest aerobatic maneuvers in an airplane because of the power required. For me, it was effortless.

I began playing in the clearing's airspace, almost dancing in the air. There was no plan, and I moved in slow motion. I simulated hammerhead stalls, barrel rolls, chandelles, vertical rolls of all sorts, and some things airplanes couldn't do. I hovered, reversed course, did both outside and inside loops feet first, perched on tree branches and dived off, and did cartwheels in the air. Finally, I tried forward rolls, followed by dives and climbs. It was a lot of fun, and I was sweating hard by the time I finished.

I sat down to rest for a moment before I headed home. While I sat there, I took out my phone and made a list. I would need some things to continue my training. I had purchases to make and studying to do.

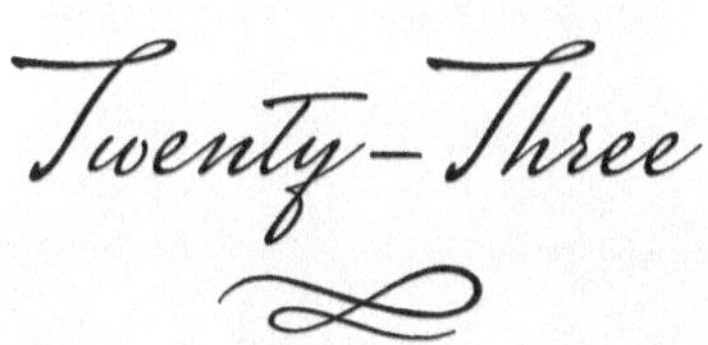

Twenty-Three

Dawn came and went, but there was no sign of federal agents. Confident that they were in the neighborhood, I kept my head down. Unlike the gas station, there was no facade on this roof, and I was completely exposed.

At 8:00 am, I risked a phone call to Agent Stefanie.

"Hello?" she answered. She sounded tired, but alert.

"Didn't sleep much last night either, huh?" I asked.

"Not at all," she said, her voice hushed. "What's wrong?"

"Black Hats. They snuck up on me while I was sleeping."

"Are you okay?"

"Fine. Any chance you can get word to the feds? I can give you their locations."

"Maybe, but they'll know I've been in touch. Can you post it on your site?"

"Can't get back to my computer," I said, then stopped. "Wait, I can post from my phone. Give me a minute."

I hung up and held the phone above me. This would be awkward. I wrote quickly and gave it a quick proofread:

Dear Federal Agents,

While preparing for my meeting today, I noticed that I have unwanted guests. They are at the gas station and on the roof of the hotel. (These "guests" and their ilk are the ones responsible for the tragedies last summer.)

If you're in the neighborhood and willing to help, I'd be obliged.

Sincerely,

Griffin

I attached screenshots from the infrared cameras, showing the intruders and their cowboy hats and rifles, and posted the article.

I closed the apps and called Stefanie.

"Done," I said when she picked up.

"I see that. Your friends really came through, didn't they?"

"They did."

"I've already forwarded this to the team. Where are you?"

"Building on the west of town. Safe for now."

"Stay there. If you move, you're likely to get hurt."

"I value my hide. I'll stay here until the smoke clears."

After she hung up, I put away my phone and lay still, listening to the daybreak.

About 20 minutes later, things began to happen. First, my phone started pinging almost nonstop. I had set it to vibrate, but the buzzing sounded loud coming from my pocket. I pulled it out and powered it down, just to be safe.

Suddenly, there were shouts from the east, then automatic gunfire. I couldn't hear anyone moving nearby, so I crept to the eastern side of the roof and looked over the edge. Nothing. After checking with intuition, I felt like there was nobody else on this side of town. I scooted back to the west and began sitting up, moving slowly until eventually the hotel and gas station came into view.

There was someone on the roof of the gas station. They were wearing what appeared to be a ghillie suit (thank you, video games). This must be one of the feds. I watched him creep to where I had hidden. He rummaged briefly through my stuff. He might have sensed me watching because he turned toward me. I dropped back onto the roof and stayed there.

After 3 or 4 bursts of gunfire, everything was silent for about 15 minutes. I pulled my phone out and powered it on. I scanned the notifications and saw that the feds had moved in, but about five minutes ago, there had been more movement on the edge of town, both behind me and to the east. Who was this? More feds?

I closed the phone and put it in my pocket. I was getting nervous. There were a lot of serious guys here, and it wouldn't bother any of them if I ended up dead. Some of them wanted exactly that.

Recognizing my fear woke me up. I had been falling into the dream of apparent reality. I remembered that none of this mattered. None of this affected anything real.

I stayed where I was, but I took out my phone again and called Agent Stefanie.

"Hey there," I whispered, "How are you?"

"How am I? What the hell are you doing on the phone?"

"I'm fine, thanks. Hey listen, can you ask the feds not to shoot me, please?"

"They know where you are. Stay there."

"No, I am. But more Alliance assassins are coming into town. Things are about to get scary, and I just want to be sure."

"More Alliance? You're sure?"

"Yeah."

"I'm sure we…the feds have their own cameras in place by now," she said.

"Good. But these guys started moving in five minutes ago and haven't stopped. There's a boatload of them."

"Shit! Goddammit, stay where you are," she snarled and hung up.

I rechecked the app, and the pings were almost nonstop. Suddenly, the crack of supersonic sniper rounds filtered over my hiding place. A body hit the ground nearby.

Gray Hats or Black? I didn't know.

With eyes closed, I meditated. I saw federal agents, police, and military — I imagined them waking up, seeing the mysteries of the world, and accepting them. I watched ordinary people reading my blog, watching the videos on the news and realizing that it was for real, not a hoax.

And the Alliance operatives, the Black Hats, whoever they were, waking up to the realization that they were holding humanity back. They were as bad as the corporations and religious leaders, manipulating people for personal gain.

I saw myself, spiritual and whole, flying down the street, giving Black Hats and Gray Hats alike a glimpse of reality, a peek behind the curtain, a chance to wake up and make a difference. I opened my eyes and found that I was already levitating six feet above the rooftop. At that moment, I knew bullets couldn't touch me; I wasn't a physical body. My body was the manifestation of Spirit, and that couldn't be harmed. I flew to the east, about 100 feet above the ground all the way past the edge of town, then did a kind of reverse Chandelle, turning 180 degrees and dropping to just 10 feet above the ground.

I flew west down Old Route 66, past every building in town. Gunfire ceased. There were shouts. Then I was past, rising into the sky, looping back around to the east. I held the vision in my mind and flew past again slowly, this time at 50 feet above the ground.

Still, no one shot at me. But when I landed on the gas station roof, the agent in the ghillie suit I had seen earlier lay in an unmoving heap. Sorrow and rage assaulted me, shattering my vision. He was dead, and there was nothing I could do. I kneeled for a moment in grief, then grabbed my computer bag and left.

More death, senseless and tragic, but ultimately meaningless. The Cosmos didn't care.

I kept telling myself that as I flew south over the desert, tears of rage and frustration streaming down my face. Laughing at an abstract concept on a mountaintop was one thing, but when a dead soldier lay at your feet, it was quite another. I had only glimpsed his face when I felt for a pulse, but he had been about my age.

My phone kept buzzing for a few minutes after I left, so I turned it off. Eventually I found a hilltop that was bare rock and landed. I was tired and thirsty, but I left my water and other supplies back at Glenrio. Still, I needed to rest.

Swiping my helmet and goggles from my head, I tossed them onto my bag. I hadn't been this frustrated since last summer. I should have been able to keep everyone safe. With enough preparation and personnel, things shouldn't spiral out of control.

I threw myself down and sat, elbows on knees, head in hands, and tried not to scream.

"When your emotions are out of control, go back to your breath," my martial art teacher had taught. "Breath is the key to hacking the limbic system. Control your breath, and you can control your fear or anger."

So I slowed my breathing, holding the negative breath as long as I could, allowing the feeling of oxygen starvation to linger a moment or two longer than was comfortable. My heart rate slowed as the rage faded. I crossed my legs to meditate.

I reached for the vision and saw the Black Hats and the Gray Hats fighting, each trying to kill the other. In my mind's eye, I poured love into both parties. I couldn't allow them to kill each other. If I were trying to raise the consciousness of humankind, that had to include both groups. I wanted them to wake up, to stop killing each other, to see what was happening, to see their potential.

Again, in my mind's eye they woke up, reached out, ceased hostilities and began working together. Was that real? Was it possible? Was it rational to think it could happen?

"You just flew away from a gunfight without a scratch," a voice said.

I opened my eyes. I recognized the voice, recognized the man in front of me. A quick glance around the hilltop showed me he was alone, sitting cross-legged like me.

"I did."

"Was that real? Possible? Rational?"

He cocked his head.

"Yes, obviously, and probably not," I said. "How are you?"

"I'm well. Sheila asked me to look in on you to see if you needed help."

"So, Mr. Kim, you can…read thoughts?"

"Just Kim. And in a manner of speaking, yes. Are you reading my thoughts?"

"No," I said, confused.

"Then how can you know what I'm thinking?"

"I only know what you tell me."

He nodded.

"I only know what you tell me, too."

He smiled as he said this. I thought for a moment.

"You're saying that mind reading is a kind of, what, communication?"

"Yeah. The better you are at communicating, the more it will seem like you're reading people's minds."

"Huh. I never thought about it."

"I know," he said, laughing. "You're not very good."

"I don't like to talk much," I said defensively. "I'd rather read or watch movies or something."

"Communicating and talking are two different things. Related, but very different."

We were way out in the country. Part of me wanted to ask him how he found me, where he had been hiding, but it didn't matter.

"I'm sorry. Is this important right now?"

"Not especially. What would you like to talk about?"

"Do you have any water or food?"

He tossed me a canteen from around his neck.

"No food, but I can get you something."

"No, this is good, thanks."

"So, you like flying, huh?"

After taking a deep drink, I capped the bottle and handed it back.

"Yeah, I do. Do you fly?"

"Not much. I can levitate over a fence, maybe stop myself from falling too hard. That's about it."

"Why? Don't you like seeing the world fall away from you? Being in control of where you go and how you get there?"

"Oh, I can travel wherever I want. Traveling and flying are kind of like communicating and talking."

"Huh."

It irked me that he didn't seem to enjoy flying.

"It's not that I don't like flying. I just never took the time to learn like you did. Don't take it personally."

"I think I'd prefer it if you didn't read my mind."

"I'm not reading your mind. You're projecting your thoughts."

"Projecting? How am I projecting?"

"You're thinking in words. That's one way. If you don't want people to hear you, then don't think in words."

"You mean like in meditation? Think in concepts and pictures?"

"Kind of. But you're also very judgmental. That always comes across, whether or not you think in words."

"I am not judgmental."

"So, it's your opinion that you're not judgmental?"

"Yes."

He laughed.

"If you keep doing that, I'll keep hearing it."

"Okay, look. Thanks for the water, Kim, but someone else just died. I need to decide what to do."

"More judgment. Okay, I'm down for it. What do we need to decide?"

I remembered Kim's claim to be over 200 years old. His ethnicity made it hard to tell, but he definitely didn't look over 70 years old. Probably much younger. There were crinkles around his eyes, but his hair was only slightly gray. He was nowhere near as trim as Tseten or Sheila, probably because of his rate of cookie consumption.

"Remember, I'm half-Korean. My father's side. My mother was Apache."

"Oh," I said, embarrassed.

At any rate, I didn't think he would be much help in dealing with federal agents and Alliance assassins. I had to go back, but I wasn't looking forward to it.

"Why do we need to go back? Didn't you do what you wanted?"

I clenched my fists in frustration, then sighed.

"Yes and no," I said. "Tseten can pull the data any time he wants, as long as there's cell signal. But there's a reporter coming. I told him I would do an interview. And I still want to help Graham and his agents. I haven't seen them yet."

I looked at the sun climbing toward its zenith.

"It's coming up on 10:00 am."

"Right. Well, thanks for the water, but I should head back."

"Wait here for a minute. Tseten's on his way."

"Oh, you called him?"

"We communicated. And no, I don't have a phone."

"Nice place!" Tseten's voice said. I turned, but I couldn't see him at first. Finally, his head and shoulders appeared, rising over the edge of the hill. He was on a trail coming up the side, walking stick in hand.

"It is," Kim said. "The kid found it."

Tseten shrugged a small pack off his shoulders and sat down. He dug inside and tossed us intricately folded paper parcels. I opened one and found it filled with granola. I started eating, and he passed me a full canteen.

"Thanks."

Tseten and Kim watched me as they ate. Were they trying to communicate as Kim had done? I listened mentally, but I couldn't hear anything.

"How do you fly?" Kim asked. "How does it work?"

I didn't answer. He was addressing my thoughts and didn't necessarily want or need a reply. So I thought about the answer. I meditated. That's how it started. Then I focused on my feelings, sensations, and emotions.

But with communication, how would that work? To meditate, I shut off my conscious "babbler" as one teacher named it. Then what? How did communication feel? Understanding? Connection?

I cleared my mind, closed my eyes, and slipped into meditation. Then what? I tried to imagine hearing Kim's voice. Nothing. Tseten's? Nothing.

"If you're trying to hear my voice, that won't work."

I let go of my meditation.

"You can't tell what I'm trying to do?"

"Not when you're in the gap. The idea is there, but it's hushed. Like a whisper in a cathedral, I can tell something's there, but can't understand."

"Interesting. If I don't listen for your voice, what then?"

"You *feel* the connection," he said. He reached out and touched the center of my chest. "The heart is where communication happens, not the brain."

I nodded, closed my eyes and tried again. The spot on my sternum still tingled where Kim's fingers had touched. I focused there and felt my heart chakra open, then tried to imagine the same of Kim, his heart opening and touching mine.

And there you are, Kim said.

I am?

Yes, you're communicating with me.

I reached out to Tseten as well.

Yes, I'm here too, Tseten said.

Well, son of a gun, I said.

I opened my eyes. They were both smiling at me.

"That's wild. Was it real?"

"Yes, you're a quick study."

He turned to Tseten.

"D'you think that comes from her learning so much on her own?" he asked Tseten.

"I don't know. Most of us learn a lot on our own. I did before you found me."

"Wait, he found you? You found him?" I asked, turning to Kim.

"Yeah. Old dude, remember? You're probably right about me not being much help in a fight."

"Yeah, but if you found him," I nodded at Tseten, "then how come you're not in charge?"

"I don't like the tropics?"

I frowned. I was missing something.

We need to focus, Tseten said.

Or thought. Or something.

"Okay, okay. Is the plan still viable? Can we still do the interview? Have you downloaded the data?"

"Not yet," he said. "It's up to you. Do you want to keep your appointment with Kemp?"

"I think so. I'd like to talk to him."

"Why don't you call Stefanie first?" Kim asked. "She's dying to hear from you."

"Okay. Poor choice of words, but you're probably right."

I stood and walked to the edge of the hilltop, turning on my phone.

"Oh, thank God!" she said when the line connected.

"How is everyone?" I asked.

"We lost two agents," she said. "Ten of the...others, the Black Hats? Ten of them died. The rest fled."

"The feds didn't follow?"

"They did. Graham's in charge. I haven't had an update recently."

"Does he still want to arrest me?"

"Yes, he does. But he's busy at the moment."

"Hm. Well, let's hope he stays that way."

"Take care, Liv," she said. "I can't believe the stories they're telling me. The Black Hats...I mean, they didn't even try to shoot you?"

"No," I said. "I think they were waking up."

"Waking up?"

"We'll talk later," I said. "I need to get in the air."

"Be careful."

I left my pack with Tseten, taking only the water and stowing my phone in a pocket.

"Good to see you again, Kim," I said, shaking his hand.

"Until next time," he said.

"I'll see you soon," I said, turning to Tseten.

"I'll be waiting."

I jumped off the edge of the hill and soared into the sky. I fastened the buckle on my helmet as I flew and lowered my goggles into place.

I got up to about 3,000 feet above the ground and willed myself to go fast. For once, stealth didn't matter. Everyone knew where I was and where I was going. I pulled my scarf around my mouth, pictured my destination, and imagined *speed!*

The air thundered in my ears. Even the fluttering of my jacket and trousers was loud. I could barely see where I was going, but I felt minor course changes happen. Was I somehow avoiding obstacles? Soaring vultures or something?

Whatever they were, the flight that had taken me more than an hour took less than 15 minutes. I slowed without thinking and saw the ghost town of Glenrio below.

I flew low over the town, but saw no one. The gas station roof was empty except for my sleeping bag and duffel. Someone had recovered the dead agent. I landed, took off my flying gear, and began packing. There was no sense in leaving everything behind.

My phone buzzed with an incoming text.

GEORGE KEMP

Leaving the rest area. Be there in 10 minutes.

The December wind was picking up, and it was chilly on the roof. I jumped down and dug into my pack until I found some jerky. Gnawing, I leaned against the glass bricks at the front of the cafe and thought about what to say. Why did I even agree to this?

I calmed myself and began to relax. My goal was to remain mindful during the interview, not worried and tense. I sipped water and waited. My mind wandered to Melanie and what she was doing. I missed her. But if she were here, I would worry about her safety. Safe is better in this case.

Stress tried to creep back into my stomach. I put the jerky into my pocket and drank another mouthful of water. I walked into the road and sat down. The sun warmed me, and I closed my eyes, going deeper into the gap.

I heard the car pull up, and I opened my eyes. As I stood, I realized I didn't know what I looked like. I must be a wreck.

I'd never been the lipstick and mascara type, not every day at least, but who doesn't think to shower and comb their hair when they're going on TV?

George Kemp opened the passenger door and stepped out into the brisk desert air.

"Olivia, I presume?" he asked, walking to me and extending a hand.

"Yes, sir. Mr. Kemp?"

"Call me George," he said with a smile. He took my hand and looked into my eyes briefly.

"I…forgot to comb my hair," I said, running my fingers through it. "Also, the cops could be here any time. Feds actually."

His eyebrows shot up as I blasted him with information and insecurity.

"Ah...well, let's see," he said, glancing around. "I doubt there's water, but there's probably a mirror inside the cafe, if you can get the door open."

Not only was the front door locked, but there were trees growing out of the threshold. I walked to the back, and the door was already open. Someone from the School had been here to set up cameras earlier.

I walked in while Kemp was talking to his crew. I navigated a narrow hallway, past the kitchen and into the dining room.

There were still tables and chairs, but the place was decaying slowly. Dust was everywhere, and little light made it through the glass-bricked wall that paralleled the highway in front.

There was movement behind me as the news crew entered.

"Wow," Kemp said. "You don't see places like this much anymore."

"Thank God," the camera operator said.

I found the restroom. Using the light from my phone, I got my hair under some kind of control. It was barely long enough to get back into a ponytail again. I splashed the last of the water from my canteen over my face and put on my cleanest, blackest t-shirt.

Back in the dining room, the crew was busy with the camera, microphone, and lights.

"I thought we'd take advantage of the...er...ambience," Kemp said, waving an arm to take in the mummified dining room.

"What about the feds?"

"Hopefully, they won't arrest us for trespassing," he said, smiling.

I didn't smile. I was worried about their safety.

"My producers are on the phone now," he said. "We've got contacts in the FBI. Hopefully, they'll let us finish before they come in."

"Okay, up to you," I said. "They want to arrest me, though. And I don't see Graham letting us finish."

I glanced around the room.

"I can't exactly escape from here the way I normally do."

"What can I do?"

I sighed.

"Nothing, I guess. Let's get to it. Do I look okay?"

Kemp introduced the crew. Denzel was on the camera, and Tiffany was doing sound. They did something with the lights so that

I looked less like a corpse, and we got set up by the glass brick wall.

"So, I'll pretty much let you talk," Kemp said. "I have questions prepared and I'll ask one now and then, but this is your chance to tell your story. Okay? Questions for me?"

"No. Just a little nervous."

Kemp laughed.

"Everyone is at first. Just be yourself."

I nodded.

Finally, we started recording.

"Good evening. This is George Kemp, on location in Glenrio, New Mexico, or is it Glenrio, Texas? That's another story. I'm here today with Olivia Donnelly, who you might know better as 'Griffin,' the blogger who stunned the world with her story of learning to fly. Thank you for sitting down with us, Olivia."

I cleared my throat.

"My pleasure, George."

"You've had quite a year. Would you care to tell us about it?"

And so we talked. I told my story. I told how I accidentally touched Air Force One, how the DoD found me, and sent US Marshals and the FBI to arrest me. How I escaped assassination and incarceration, and how I had been on the run for months.

"And as we speak, the government knows where you are, right? They're coming to arrest you?"

I put my hands in my lap to camouflage their shaking.

"That's right."

"All because you touched the president's airplane?"

I tried to laugh, but I think I just looked ill.

"Well, George, they say they want to keep me safe from the bad guys," I said. "While that's true enough, the real reason is they don't want my message getting out."

"And what message is that?"

"That the 'reality' we know, that we live with every day, isn't all there is to know."

Tears sprang to my eyes. I shook my head, hoping to collect myself.

"I'm sorry. It's just… people keep dying. Another agent — two actually

— died this morning. Along with many of the Alliance, the group that's trying to stop me."

Tears were streaming down my face now.

"All of them are dying so the people in charge can keep you from knowing, keep us fighting amongst ourselves."

I reached into my heart center as I looked into the camera.

"Listen, please. This isn't just about right and wrong. It's about control, who has it and why they want to keep it. I don't have those answers."

I glanced back at Kemp.

"That's actually more your area of expertise," I said, again sniffling and trying to smile. "I'm just a farmer."

Kemp sat, arm over the back of a chair, a finger over his upper lip, head tilted to the side. He blinked at me several times, then shook himself and sat up.

"Olivia, can you give us an idea of the nuts and bolts of this? Can you tell us how you fly? You say everyone can do this, right? How? How does it work?"

So, I talked about the connection between neural tissue and higher dimensions, how thinking itself, any creativity, is a trans-dimensional activity. I talked about multidimensional physics and an aware and intelligent Universe.

"Just a farmer, huh?" Kemp asked, grinning.

"Well, a farmer with a hobby."

He laughed at that, then became serious again and made a throat-cutting gesture to the crew.

"Take a moment," he said, leaning in. "I want you to tell me everything you can about this 'Alliance.' Can you name names?"

The only name I knew was Agent Stefanie, but I couldn't give her to him.

I looked away.

"No," I said finally. "I...don't know any names that I can give you."

I glanced back.

"But it's everywhere. The Alliance isn't permanent; it doesn't have offices. And they don't even seem to agree on much. A team of their soldiers was here this morning. Many of them died. That might be a place to start."

Kemp was taking notes furiously.

"Right," he said. "I don't know if I'll be able to get anything on them. Depends on the agencies. And this Deputy Marshal Graham? Is he connected?"

"Not directly. Not that I know of, at least. Just doing his job."

Kemp nodded, gazing into the glass brick, lost in thought for a moment.

"Well, what do you say we go outside and get the money shot?" he said finally.

The crew broke down what they would need, and we headed outside.

My rapid progress that summer led me to think about taking the spring semester off. I had a feeling, an intuition, that something was on its way.

Excerpt from the blog: *Griffin's Flight*

JULY 22, 2025

My progress this summer has been quicker than I expected. All the time I put into practicing, sitting still and not moving is paying off. I'm not ready to go off into "the wild blue yonder," but I can see it happening someday.

I attached my camera's tripod to a tree branch at the edge of the clearing. I sat and slipped into the gap. The space between thoughts is always there, ready for me, and the more time I spend there, the easier it is to enter. I began with no ceremony, but sat and enjoyed the stillness briefly.

When I was ready to practice, I flew into the air and opened my eyes as soon as I lifted off. As I neared the treetops, I slowed so as not to pop above them and risk being seen. I picked an altitude a good 10 feet below the treetops as the ceiling for my exercise.

As I straightened my legs, I moved toward the center of the clearing. I felt like I was standing, but my feet were still five feet in the air. Now for the part I had never done before. I held an image in my mind of me lying on my stomach.

Nothing happened.

I saw the branch I had broken earlier in the summer, still attached to the tree. I moved toward it idly, no real goal in mind, just practicing.

As I began moving, I reached out toward the branch and my body rotated, so I was flying, superhero style, toward the tree with the broken limb. I made it there with my right hand extended. I laughed at the silliness and turned to where my camera was filming.

I reached one hand out to my camera in a fist, and pulled the other back to my side, in a fist with the palm up. As I flew toward the camera, my feet out behind me, I bent a knee and extended the other leg directly behind me.

It was silly, but it worked. I flew right to the camera, body horizontal. I landed and had a good long laugh at myself. As ridiculous as it was, the position was comfortable.

I composed myself and launched back into the air.

Picking a tree on the opposite side of the clearing, I reached for it with both hands. I was aiming for a spot about halfway up with no branches and a broad expanse of trunk. As I neared the tree, I turned and hit it with both feet. My legs compressed, and I sprang back into space, targeting a tree on the other side.

I flew faster this time and hit a little harder, but my ankles and knees were tough from martial art and running practice. I rebounded off the tree and back into the clearing.

This time, I aimed for a large oak with big, sturdy branches. I reached with both hands, aiming for a spot between the branches. I flew between them and curved in a tight arc around the trunk of the tree and rocketed back into the clearing.

What a rush! Despite my exultation and pleasure, I didn't fall out of the air. I was learning to separate emotions from thoughts. I could feel the thrill and pleasure of flying without my ego latching onto the feelings and connecting them with the future or the past.

Back in the open, I rolled over onto my back and stopped. I floated, feeling as if I were lying on a bed or a sofa. I looked up at the sky and folded my hands over my abdomen.

I tried floating up towards the ceiling of the clearing in this position. It was easy. Then I rolled over face-down, and rotated, so my head was pointing down. I hung there, suspended 80 feet in the air. It was scary and uncomfortable.

Well, that was what I had expected. It was only scary because things looked different. I didn't feel like I was falling. I didn't feel blood rushing to my head.

Was my blood levitating too?

I flew straight down and stopped a few feet away from the ground, reached, plucked a blade of grass and then reversed, soaring feet first back toward the sky.

Again, it was a strange sensation. I flew 50 feet into the air, feet first, looking toward the sky past my feet. As I slowed to a stop and rotated, I experienced mild vertigo and queasiness in my stomach.

I descended slowly to land feet first beside the tree with my camera.

As I walked through the fields to my apartment, I pondered. By next week, I might be ready to leave my "nest." The clearing had been the perfect place to learn, but I had outgrown it. Today's practice had gone better than I hoped. Despite the mild motion sickness, I could maneuver my body however I wanted.

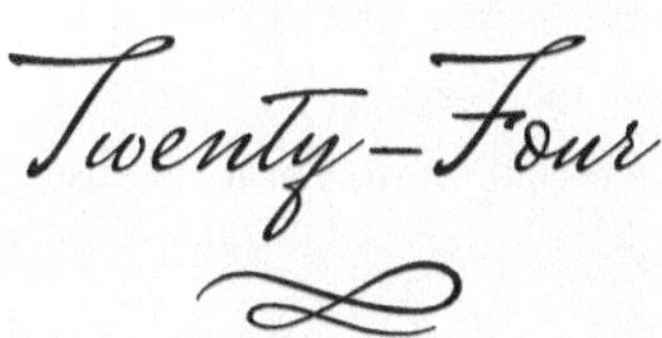

Twenty-Four

I got the go-ahead from Kemp and walked to the middle of the road. Camera and sound were ready, and he gave me a thumbs up.

I turned and lifted into the air, crossing my feet under me in a lotus position. I floated 20 feet into the air, and as I turned back around, both Denzel and Tiffany were staring, open-mouthed. Kemp had a hand on his head and was slowly shaking it back and forth.

He spoke, but the wind was kicking up, and I couldn't understand him at this distance.

I landed and walked over.

"That is just the damndest thing," he said.

Both of the crew's eyes were huge, and they looked scared.

"I know; it's weird," I said. "You can check me for wires."

"Wires? What would they connect to?" Tiffany asked. "There's nothing above us!"

They walked toward the road and got shots of everywhere a crane might hide.

"There's just nothing here," Denzel said.

"I know. That's one reason I picked this place. There are trees and old buildings on this side of the highway, but nothing else."

"Are you still rolling?" Kemp asked.

"Yeah, boss. Never stopped."

"Let's try again without the chatter."

Sound and camera both gave an apologetic thumbs up, and I walked back to the center of the highway. This time, I jumped into the air, flying straight up about 100 feet above the ground. Denzel struggled to find me, then to focus. I waved and pointed to the ground.

I dropped, not quite in freefall, but when I landed and kneeled to absorb the energy of the fall, a small cloud of dust went up and floated on the breeze.

"Is that okay?" I called, "What else do you want to see?"

"Give me the boom," he said, not looking at the tech.

"What? Why?"

"I want you to fly with her," Kemp said.

"No way, boss. I'm scared of heights. I can't just…no. Sorry, but no."

"Don't even ask," the camera operator said. "That's why you get the big bucks."

Kemp looked a little green but seemed to accept his defeat. He took a deep breath and began walking toward me.

"You said that you could fly with one of us. That still hold?"

"I said I've done it in the past," I hedged. "We can try, for sure."

He shook his head and grumbled something I couldn't understand as he closed the distance.

"Your insurance paid up, boss?" the cameraman quipped.

"That's funny stuff. Let's close in a little. Tiff, can you hear me with this wind?"

The sound tech made some adjustments.

"Again…" she called.

"Check. Test."

She flashed him a thumbs-up.

"Why am I doing this?" Kemp asked.

It didn't seem like he wanted one, so I didn't answer.

"Ready?"

He just nodded, uncharacteristically mute.

"Close your eyes and breathe. Slowly in, hold, then slowly out and hold."

I took his hands, and we went through the meditation procedure. He was shaking, but I said nothing.

I don't think he noticed when we levitated. Not at first. We had gotten to nearly 30 feet, about even with the tall peaked roof of the cafe, when I heard the SUVs. I looked to the west, and four of them were barreling towards us on the gravel highway.

~

D*amn.*
"Mr. Kemp, open your eyes, please," I murmured, hoping he wouldn't freak. "Try not to talk, and *really* try to stay calm."

He opened his eyes and looked around. I didn't release his hands, and he didn't stay calm.

"Oh, God," he said, looking down. "Oh, my god!"

"Shhh. We're going down now."

"Down! Yes!"

The crew below were focused on us and didn't know about the SUVs. The gentle descent was agony. Not physically, of course. I wasn't carrying Kemp with my physical strength. But for every foot we descended, the feds were 100 feet closer.

Finally, we touched down, and Kemp promptly fell as I let go of his hands.

"Sorry!" I said, kneeling there with him. "Are you okay?"

"Good," he muttered, struggling to catch his breath. "Dizzy."

"He'll be okay," I said to the crew. "It can be rough at first."

I looked up. The dust plume was visible, but I couldn't see the cars from down here.

"Look, the feds are coming," I said to the crew. "Can you protect your tapes, or whatever? Don't let them take them."

"Feds?" Kemp said, climbing to his feet.

"Yeah, they're close."

"Legally, they can't take our stuff without a warrant."

"What about illegally?"

They glanced at each other and at the dust plume.

"Switch 'em out," Kemp ordered. "Hurry."

They ran to the trunk of their news truck and began working as fast as they could.

"What about you?" Kemp asked.

"They won't catch me unless I let them," I said, pulling out my cell. I needed the crew from the School to download their data before the feds got here.

There was no signal.

"I've got no cell signal. You?"

"Nothing," Kemp said, checking.

"I need to contact my friends," I said, glancing around for a moment. I had less than a minute. The black SUVs were visible now, coming down Old Route 66. No time to sit and meditate. I had to reach out to Tseten.

Kemp asked another question, but I closed my eyes and held up a finger for silence. I quieted my thoughts, went as deeply into the gap as I could, and opened my heart. I reached for Tseten, or Kim, or Sheila, or anyone else who might hear me.

Help! I need you to come get your footage before the feds steal it! Somebody come!

It was all I could think of. I kept reaching out, trying to stay in the gap and think in images. Thirty seconds later, Tseten walked into the street beside me.

"Hello, Liv. We're here."

"Whoa," Kemp said with a start. "Where did you come from?"

"Thanks, Tseten," I said. The government vehicles were pulling up 20 feet away.

"No time for introductions. Thanks Mr. Kemp. It was a pleasure meeting you."

"Likewise," Kemp said, looking around dazedly. Tseten had just vanished.

I glanced over at the news van, where Tiffany and Denzel had just finished their frantic switching. Agents were surrounding them and shouting commands. Their hands were on their weapons, but they stayed holstered for now. Denzel was talking to someone inside the van, but there were no windows. I couldn't see who he was talking to.

Deputy Marshal Graham was shouting at me not to move.

"If I leave, will you be okay?"

Kemp looked at me. He stamped a booted foot on the ground.

"Gravity's working again," he said, a crooked grin breaking across his face. "I can deal with the government."

I nodded, jumped into the air, and flew east as fast as I could. Once out of sight, I circled around and landed on the roof of the cafe. It was too steep to stand, so I levitated, looking over the peak just in time to see Kemp and his crew in handcuffs, forced into the backs of the SUVs.

Graham stood in the highway, looking around and talking on a radio. I knew they could probably see me by now. They had a satellite, or a drone, or some other technology in play over Glenrio. They may have seen Sheila's team come in to download the information.

There was nothing more I could do for Kemp and his crew. I had to trust in Graham's integrity. I snatched my pack from behind the restaurant and flew away.

How did Tseten and Sheila find me? After some thought, I reached inside and searched for the link we'd had when we communicated.

I felt them; they were close. Tseten and Kim were having a late lunch. I paused, got my bearings, and was there in 20 minutes. I landed a block away and walked to the restaurant.

They were sharing a bowl of tamales and had tall glasses of beer on the table.

"May I join you?"

"Please," Kim said, kicking out a chair.

"How did it go?" Tseten asked, removing the husk wrapping from a tamale.

"Good, I think. The feds arrested the reporter and his crew. But I think everyone is safe."

"Will swiped their memory devices," Tseten said. "It's all sitting on Kemp's desk, waiting for him."

I laughed.

"There's a future in package delivery if you're interested," I said. "We could make a fortune."

Kim snorted around a tamale. Tseten just shook his head and pushed the tamales toward me.

"Hungry?" he asked.

"Ugh," I said, "Not for that. They smell good, but I can't eat like that and fly."

"Maybe that's my problem," Kim said, rubbing his round belly.

"Look it up, man. Gluten gives you brain fog. Doesn't anyone read my blog?"

"What's a blog?" He asked seriously.

"Never mind."

When the server came over, I asked for a lot of water and a plate of raw vegetables. She walked away shaking her head, but in a few minutes brought a large lettuce salad with radishes, cucumbers, cilantro, lemons, limes, and bell peppers.

I gave the peppers to Tseten but dove into the rest.

"Can I have my computer, please?" I asked.

He reached down, grabbed my bag, and pushed it toward me.

"I want to go to Mexico until we hear from Kemp."

"Mexico? Why? Why not come home with me?"

"I want to write. Tell my story so people will understand. Even the ones who don't watch the news or read blogs."

I turned to Kim.

"You read books, right?"

"You mean scrolls?"

I laughed and continued eating.

"Your ID and cards will work," Tseten said. "No limits."

"Thanks," I said, "I won't take advantage."

"It's not a problem," he said. "Have fun."

They hung around while I finished, and we left together.

"Thanks for your input this morning, gentlemen," I said. "It really helped."

I reached out with my heart as I thanked them and felt them respond in kind.

"Good luck!" they both said as they embraced me together.

I walked down the road until I was out of sight of the restaurant, took off, and headed south.

One final article from early on. I had been at the farm, working on myself for nearly a year, eating right, exercising, and meditating. I was gaining self-confidence and body-wisdom as the whole levitation thing started. I understood that my strength was fragile. I gave it time to mature before I tested it too strenuously.

Excerpt from the blog: *Griffin's Flight*

APRIL 7, 2024

I am writing in earnest. Getting everything down in order seems important. I want to record my feelings and emotions, my thought processes. I was going to start a blog, but I've had second thoughts.

If I blog everything right now, whoever reads it, if anyone actually does, will immediately call for proof, and the only proof I have, a couple of quick videos, will be easy to dismiss as fakes.

I need proof. I need to be good, *really* good, before I share with the world. So I'll write my articles but not publish them. Not yet.

Will it be considered dishonest or manipulative if I'm caught taking liberties with the timeline? Maybe, but I look at it as self-defense. By waiting to publish, I'll be giving future readers the best possible information, without exposing myself to ridicule.

I'm using the pseudonym "Griffin" to stay anonymous when I do finally start publishing. The time may come when I trade invisibility for truth. But who knows? Maybe everyone will think I'm a fake, and nobody will read it.

Twenty-Five

An instructor at my martial art school told me once about his honeymoon in Cabo San Lucas. He talked about how beautiful it was and how much there was to do. So I found a resort online that served decent food, and I flew down. I landed on a beach at night and waited until mid-morning to walk up to the desk.

Getting a room was no problem. A young man took my backpack and duffel to my room. I tipped him $20 and asked him to bring a lot of bottled water, and he ran off.

I got settled and, after a call to Melanie, I caught up on sleep and rest. For the next two days, I slept, ran, swam, practiced martial art forms, and ate. I kept an eye on the Las Vegas news. Even though Kemp was back on the air, my story wasn't. I was concerned, but intuition was silent.

On the third day, I started writing. I worked four or five hours a day, sometimes in my room, sometimes on a porch, watching the seabirds fly back and forth to the beach and the waves rolling in.

I had been in Cabo for over a week when I got a text. Agent Stefanie told me to go to The Guardian's website in the UK.

There was the story of that day on the border between Texas and New Mexico. There was video footage from Tseten's cameras, cut together with that of Kemp and his crew. Along with my interview,

Kemp told the story of the massive incursion of mercenaries hired by religious groups and foreign governments working together to kill me, my family, and my friends in vivid detail. The FBI had captured some of the mercenaries, and Kemp had actually interviewed Graham about it. The mercenaries told stories of family members held for ransom, vast fortunes promised for success, dire consequences for failure.

There were U.S. government stamps on some of the videos, which meant that either Graham or Agent Stefanie may have helped somehow. They showed my slow passes in the morning where the assassins let me fly by without shooting, and the subsequent lightning fast departure. The video and story together proved, once and for all, that I was real.

The week after that story broke was nothing short of amazing. I was completely vindicated. The U.S. government issued apologies, and they released my friends and family still in protective custody. They promised mercenary squads leniency if they turned themselves in. The government released my email accounts.

But I was still cautious. I was outside the country, and I had a sense that security in Mexico might be more lax than in the U.S. I left my email alone. Aside from the call to Melanie and the text from Agent Stefanie, I didn't contact anyone.

I kept working and resting for a solid month after the story broke, ignoring all attempts at contact, requests for interviews, and all the rest.

Finally, I wrote a blog to let everyone know I was okay. My mom had written a post telling about her and Dad's adventures over the past year, how some kind soul had bought their farm at auction and donated it back to them.

It was good to know they were home. I can't tell you how grateful I am to Tseten and Sheila and the rest for saving the farm.

After the blog, it became impossible to ignore the pleas for more information. Finally, I gave in and asked Agent Stefanie for my parents' new phone number.

"Hello?"

"Hi, Mom!"

"Olivia?"

"Yeah! How are you?"

"Good! Oh, it's so good to hear from you! Your father is out in the barn. Hang on."

"No, it's okay, Mom. I'll call him in a minute."

"I'm so glad to hear from you. Where are you?"

"Can't tell you. It might not be safe yet."

"Oh, Livvie. Are you still in danger?"

"No, Mom. Just being cautious, being careful, like you always tell me."

"I'm so glad to hear your voice," she said, tears in her voice.

"Yeah," I choked, "You said that. Me too."

"Last summer, I was worried…."

She stopped, unable to go on.

"I know. But I'm safe."

"All those poor people that you tried to help…."

"I know, Mom," I said. I didn't want to discuss that. "Can you talk while you're walking? Take the phone and go find Dad."

"Hang on," she said. "While we were gone, I forgot how steep these steps are."

The steps from the kitchen to the back door were steep. As they got older, both Mom and Dad were having trouble with them.

The screen door slammed.

"It's good being back on the farm," she said. "Though I miss my chickens, at least we're home."

"The FBI didn't let you keep chickens there?" I asked.

"Ha! They barely let me have eggs. Couldn't cook, couldn't garden, couldn't sew. Couldn't even teach. I read and watched television. Well, and meditated."

"Really? You meditated?"

"I did. Your father, too. We're both getting pretty good."

A brisk wind could have knocked me over.

"Liv, are you still there?"

"Uh…yeah! Just surprised."

I heard a faint clanging sound in the background.

"Ah, here he is. Walter?"

No answer. More clanging.

"Walter!"

The clanging got louder.

"WALTER!"

I heard my dad's voice, "Huh? What's wrong?"

"It's Olivia!"

"Oh!"

Shuffling.

"Liv? How are you, kid?"

"Good! I'm good, Dad. What are you working on?"

"Oh, those government bastards sold my tractor. I bought a new one, but I have to rig some cultivators. They aren't original."

"Sounds like a pain."

"Yeah, well, give me pains like this over the past year anytime," he said. "How are you? You okay?"

"Yeah, I'm…well, I can't say *where* I am. But I'm good."

"Yeah, we're good too. Okay, here's your mother again. Take care."

"You too, Dad."

In the background, Mom whispered, "That's it?"

I heard Dad sniffling and blowing his nose.

"Well, a man of few words, I guess," she said.

"Yeah, you know Dad. Any chance for your garden this year?"

"Do you know it's already started? The Smiths and Hardins got some lettuce and flowers started for me. They took care of the hay last year, too."

"That's very kind of them! Can you thank them for me next time you see them?"

"I will, but won't you be coming home soon?"

"I will, but I have work to do. I'm trying to get this down before I forget," I said.

"But surely you could do that here?"

"I could. And I will. It just might take a while."

"Well, we miss you, Livvie."

"Miss you too, Mom. I'll call back soon, okay?"

"Okay. We love you so much."

"I love you too. Take care."

After that, it was harder to focus on writing. More and more, I thought of home, of Melanie, and of Agent Stefanie. Yeah, her. But not *that* way. I mean, kind of, but I felt like we had unfinished business. I was attracted to her at first, but now she was on my mind for other reasons.

I toughed it out at the luxury vacation resort for another week before I realized that what I was feeling was Guidance prompting me to leave. While living in the wilderness, I had grown accustomed to listening to Guidance all the time, even during sleep. Here in civilization, it was easier to ignore.

Once I realized what was happening, I phoned the desk to tell them I would check out. I showered, packed my things, and left. I felt uneasy as I stepped into the hallway. By the time I entered the lobby, my skin was crawling. I stood in line behind a family waiting to check out, and it was one of the hardest things I've ever done. I wanted nothing more than to blast through the front doors and into the sky.

Finally, it was my turn at the desk. I answered questions as politely as I could, but didn't encourage the young man's small talk. My ears were buzzing. I looked around the lobby, down the hallways, and into the driveway outside the doors. Everything seemed normal.

Until it wasn't.

Three men entered the room at the same time. One from the hallway to my left, another through the doors behind me, and another from the restaurant on my right.

"Get down! Behind the counter!" I hissed at the desk clerk.

He gave me a faint smile, head tilted to the side. I dropped my bag, vaulted the counter, and kicked him hard as the first gunshots rang out. Single shots from handguns, probably.

I didn't have time to check on the clerk, other than to scan for obvious gunshot wounds. He looked okay, but was out cold. I ducked into the hallway behind the counter and began weaving my way through a maze of desks and office equipment. Women looked up as I passed.

"Under your desks!" I shouted as men burst into the room behind me.

I jumped into the air, thinking if I flew, they might aim high, hopefully away from the civilians. I flew to a door that should have led, if my memory of the hotel was correct, to the pool area. There would be people, but also access to the sky.

The door had a knob, and it opened into the room. I lost a couple of seconds getting it open and didn't hear the shot, just felt the slug slam into my shoulder. I fell into the door and then through the widening gap before I got my feet under me.

Breathing hurt. But escape was still possible.

The pool was on my right. Two men were coming through the room behind me, and I felt another closing from my left. I closed my eyes, took a breath, and flew down the hall to my right. There were screams from somewhere, and I nearly vomited from the pain.

I tucked my feet under me and hit the glass door feet-first. It shattered, and I slipped through. Jagged teeth of tempered glass dragged at the flesh of my arms as I passed. I landed on my feet, crouched, and looked around.

There was still screaming somewhere behind me. Men were shouting. Several shots rang out. My body was shaking, and I realized I was going into shock. I was unarmed and unprepared to help anyone, but I had to try, didn't I?

I didn't even have my flight gear. My leather jacket, helmet and goggles were back with my bag in the lobby. I was wearing jeans and a t-shirt and carrying a pocket knife.

I could die here, trying in vain to save people, or I could flee, hopefully draw their fire and get them to leave the resort. A gunshot behind me shattered glass, and I leaped forward, over a plant border and into the air.

Shouts followed me, more gunshots. Screaming.

They shot me with a cannon. It knocked me out of the air and slammed me into a wall before I slid to the ground. A shotgun blast had hit my abdomen. Blood bloomed crimson across my T-shirt. Breathing was no longer possible. Neither was thinking.

Gravity skyrocketed to Jovian levels. I tried to hold myself up, but my arms shook. I wasn't angry, which surprised me. Normally if someone knocked me down, I'd get back up, fighting mad. But not being able to breathe or hold myself up struck me as funny. Even the pain spreading through my body was so intense that it was absurd. If I could, I would have laughed.

I saw the man in front of me walking slowly, gun held high. Smiling, I held up a blood-covered hand, trying to share the joke. I coughed, and a spray of blood left my mouth.

He was emotionless, hard, but when he saw me smile and gesture down at my body, his face seemed to fall. As he watched me, anguish washed over his features. The gun came down. He closed his eyes and crossed himself. Gravity dragged at my eyelids now, but the man with the gun dropped to a knee.

He said something, but I couldn't understand. Maybe it was an apology.

Then he was standing and yelling. There were screams, but they registered only dimly. In a moment, I would lose consciousness, slide down the wall and die.

Do you want to die?
Want to? No. No, but it's okay. No choice now, really.
That bad, huh?

I looked at my abdomen.

Yeah, looks like it.
Not possible to do anything about it?
No. Not possible.

I tried to sigh, but it hurt too badly.

That's too bad. Impossible things are like that. Impossible.

Frowning hurt too. The sun felt good, though. It shone through my closed eyelids.

If only you knew someone.
Knew someone?
Yeah, someone who could do impossible things. They might know what to do.

Opening my eyes hurt. Frowning still hurt.

I don't have time. Even if I could fly, I don't have time. I don't know where the
hospital is. Or....

You're right. Not possible. See you around.

Oh God DAMMIT, do not *play that game with me!*

Are you swearing at me, chica? I ought to come down there and kick your
butt.

I snorted. Blood came out of my nose.

I could see Kim in my mind's eye. He was in Albuquerque. I'd never
been.

I needed to go.

Suddenly, I was a thousand feet in the air, arcing into the sky like a
missile. I don't remember the trip. Actually, I remember it for what was
absent. There was no sense of acceleration, no wind, and no sound. The
ground moved beneath me so fast that I couldn't pick out individual
features or landmarks.

And there was a squarish vehicle below with a cross painted on top.
An ambulance! They could tell me where the hospital was.

I landed and somehow kept my footing. I held onto the ambulance's
mirror and dragged my other hand up, moving my finger in a circle to get
the driver to open his window. He sat, mouth hanging open.

His partner, however, was quicker. She was out the door, around the
front, and caught me before I hit the pavement.

When I woke up.... Well, I didn't just "wake up." There was a
foggy in and out transition from mostly dead, to nearly dead, to
touch-and-go. I remember lights and tunnels, stressed voices, interminable
beeping. You know, someone really needs to do something about all the
beeping in hospitals. What is it with that?

Anyway, when I awoke, Ethan was there beside my bed. He was
standing, one hand hovering over my head, the other over my
abdomen. His face was relaxed, but his hands moved with intent, occasionally making circular movements, sometimes closer, sometimes
farther away.

I closed my eyes and let him work. I tried to feel loving and open towards him, not sure if it would help or not.

"Olivia?" he asked.

"Hey," I said.

"Croaked" might be a better description.

"You should feel pretty awful right now," he said.

I tried to nod, but that set off fireworks in my skull.

"Thank you," I managed to grate out before I tipped back over the edge of unconsciousness.

People faded in and out of my awareness. My parents were there. Tseten and Sheila. Melanie was there a lot, holding my hand. They had me on some intense pain meds, which made thinking and remembering very fluffy activities. Meditation was impossible.

I went with it. It was okay. I was okay.

So, as far as I'm concerned, that was the end. Or maybe the end of the beginning. People all over the country, all over the world, believe that there's this crazy lady out there who can fly. She can fly, not because she's special, not because God chose her, but exactly the opposite.

I can fly because I'm *ordinary*. I'm like everyone else out there. I'm just like you.

Don't believe the people who tell you we are meant to suffer. Don't believe that you are somehow defined by how much crap you can take from life. Be the one who steps up and says *No!* when the authorities, whoever they are, try to sell you those limiting beliefs.

Be strong, and if you don't feel strong, that's okay. Just keep *being*, keep trying. Choose to change, and then keep making that same choice every day, every hour, every minute if you have to. That's the only way to change.

I believe in you. I believe you can fly! I believe you can heal, communicate, be invisible. I believe you can do whatever you want to do.

And who knows?

Maybe someday I'll meet you out there.

I'll look for you.

Don't make me wait.

Scan or click to find your retailer to leave a review.

Acknowledgments

Even though much of the writing process takes place in solitude, it does not take place in a vacuum. This book simply would not exist without many of the people mentioned here, and all of them shaped it somehow. They all have my unending gratitude.

When I started writing, maybe a dozen years ago, my wife Krystal supported me and gave me the space I needed. Sometimes, it was a lot of space. Thank you is not enough.

It's hard to remember that far back, but I think my kids were all still living at home with us then, so all of them would have made sacrifices. Leo, Chip, Kat, and Kris, I love you all and appreciate your help.

Of course, I wouldn't be who I am without the support of my parents and grandparents. Since I came to writing later in life, most of them aren't around anymore, but the genesis of this book came from a conversation with Mom. My parents created a safe space for reading when I was a kid, and they supported their strange, quiet son without fail.

Since I don't make friends easily, I treasure the relationships that have lasted years. Throughout the writing process, I asked my friends for input. And they never failed to respond with helpful, thoughtful, advice.

Eric Ballenger edited a very early version of the manuscript many years ago. I think some of his work even made it into the finished product, despite it being drastically different. His advice certainly did.

Brent Clevenger, and Michelle and Douglas Rockett have given invaluable feedback on more recent versions.

C.J. Farley and Lisa Harkrider-Farley are always enthusiastic and never fail to answer odd questions at odd times.

Greg Ledet and Rory Gentry gave expert advice that made the text better.

Angela Cox, Vanessa Stephens, Lindsey Cox, Ann Alton, Kathy Feeney, Sarah Klein Ratekin, and Mary Hammons have all answered questions and given feedback that, while helpful, forced me to think and evaluate my thought processes rather more than was comfortable. Many, many thanks.

Jen Ward has been embarrassingly supportive and liberal in her praise of my work.

There are many people in the World Kuk Sool Association that I should thank, but I'll just mention a few. First, thanks to my instructor, Master Ben Mitchell, who accepted me as his foster student when I was in need. And even though we haven't spoken through the pandemic years, Master Daniel Middleton has been a quiet source of inspiration since learning that I was writing. Master Caroline Hurst and Instructor Sally Runnacles helped me more than they will ever know by taking on the weight of the *I Love Kuk Sool Won* page so that I could focus more on writing. I (and the entire Kuk Sool Won community) owe them many thanks!

Several editors have helped over the past year. Olivia Batker Pritzker helped immeasurably. I'm sure that I didn't take enough of her advice. And Lorna Timmerman and Annabeth Butler did the final proofreading and editing. Of course, any typos you find are still my fault. (Let me know of any you find.)

Irene Martinez created the fantastic cover. One reason I decided to self-publish was so that I would have control over the cover art, and I'm glad that I did.

There are many people that I've never met who shaped this novel. Most notably, Richard Bach. I read and reread *Jonathan Livingston Seagull* and *Illusions* more times than I can count as I was growing up. In fact, this novel is, in some ways, a retelling of *Jonathan*, based on an idea in *Illusions* - that there is a principle, waiting to be discovered, that people can fly without airplanes. Thank you.

I've read and studied spiritual books my entire life. The collective works of these authors, and more, have helped shape my view of the cosmos, and thus, this book. If you want to know more about the science of meditation and spirituality, you should definitely check out Deepak Chopra, Wayne Dyer, Eckart Tolle, Joe Dispenza, Lynne McTaggart, Gregg Braden, Rhonda Byrne, and Pam Grout.

As far as healthy diet and lifestyles, Abel James, Mark Sisson, Pavel Tsatsouline, and Scott Sonnon have all taught me a lot.

I owe thanks and apologies to George Knapp, on whom I shamelessly based the character of George Kemp. I have the *utmost* respect for Mr. Knapp and meant the character as an homage. I hope if he ever reads this that he's pleased.

Facebook has become a useful tool for writers. I specifically want to thank the folks at the following groups: SPF Genius, Scrivener Users, SPF Community, and Rachel Payetta and *The Creative Writing Collective*. These folks are welcoming and supportive, and always willing to answer questions and offer support.

A special thank-you must go to Mur Lafferty and her podcast *I Should Be Writing*. If it weren't for her, I simply wouldn't have continued writing. Besides expert advice and interviews, her compassion and constant cheerleading of "wannabe fiction writers" kept me going. Also, to all the Inkstained Fabulists on the Discord, *thank you!*

In the past year, since I decided to self-publish, I've become addicted to a couple of podcasts specifically geared toward independent authors. Thanks to Mark Dawson and James Blatch at *The Self-Publishing Show*, and to Joanna Penn at *The Creative Penn*.

Before the pandemic, I used to leave the house to write. I wrote or edited much of this book at The Guardian Brewing Company and at The Downtown Farmstand (which is owned by my brother and his family), both here in Muncie, Indiana.

Finally, I haven't been in a while, but thank you to the folks at the Midwest Writers Workshop. Ever since my grandmother attended back in the '80s, I've thought about becoming a writer. You helped make that happen.

And, as usual, I'm sure I'm forgetting important people, places, authors, and projects. This book, and future books in the series, are a product of everything in my past. My fascination with science, spirituality, self-defense, and fitness has shaped me, and my writing.

Author's Note

When I decided to become an author, I knew I wanted to write about Important Things. Of course, as an independent author, the choosing of the Important Things is up to me. And the writing and editing. Everything.

That's a lot of responsibility.

After the decision to write, I had to learn *how* to write. If you've gotten this far, you'll know I'm still working on that.

But… Important Things.

Big Pictures.

I grew up in a spiritual family. We went to church for many years. Both grandmothers were religious. I have everything from Quakers to Christian Scientists to Brethren in my background.

But none of those traditions ever really answered my questions. So I read a lot. In second grade, I picked up a paperback book of ghost stories that my mom left on the couch. I probably didn't understand it all, but it left me with questions.

Around the same time, my dad would spend evenings listening to the police scanner, hoping to hear reports of UFOs. There was a lot of that sort of thing in our area at the time (remember Richard Dreyfuss wearing a Ball-U t-shirt and looking for Cornbread Road in *Close Encounters of the*

Third Kind? That was here in Muncie.) Several times, I remember, they piled us into the back of the station wagon and went racing into the night, hoping to see lights in the sky. We heard a strange mechanical sound once, but I don't remember ever seeing anything.

As I got older, I continued to be intrigued by strangeness. In fifth grade, I found the work of Dr. Kenneth Ring (no relation, as far as I know) on the Near-Death Experience (NDE.) I read as many of his books as the library had, then started branching out.

I loved the idea of Sasquatch, large animals living among humans, without leaving a trace. I read books, watched television shows, and talked to anyone who would listen.

I've realized, the thing that intrigued me the most about ghosts, UFOs and cryptids wasn't whether the stories were true, but belief itself. Why did some people believe while others refused? And why did the two kinds of people argue with each other?

Half a century on, there's still no universally accepted evidence for ghosts. We have lots of security camera footage, interesting work on Electronic Voice Phenomena (EVP,) but not enough to convince the skeptic. Same for Bigfoot. NDEs and UFOs (now UAPs) are more widely studied, but are still firmly in the "fringe" category for most people.

Since elementary school, I've continued to read, continued to be fascinated by the strange. During my teen years, I loved Richard Bach's work. I mentioned in the Acknowledgments that I lost track of how many times I read *Jonathan Livingston Seagull* and *Illusions*. Similarly, I read and reread and re-reread *Bridge Across Forever* and *One* when they came out. I owe a lot of my personal cosmology to Mr. Bach.

In early adulthood, I found Whitley Strieber. I've never been a fan of horror as a genre, but like many, I found the figure on the cover of *Communion* compelling. It struck a chord, somehow. In fact, my baby sister saw it on a grocery shelf, reached for it with both hands and said, "Grandma!"

Weird.

I followed Mr. Strieber through all the books in that series. It was a wrenching experience. He clearly believed what he was saying, but again, there was no hard evidence. In *Breakthrough* Mr. Strieber presented evidence enough to prove the reality to himself, I doubt it made much difference to skeptics.

Two authors kind of owned my spiritual space in the '90s: Neale Donald Walsch and James Redfield. Walsch's book *Conversations with God* broke paradigms like nothing else I'd ever seen. His bold assertion "Hitler went to Heaven" angered almost everyone I knew. I liked that.

Redfield's book *The Celestine Prophecy* was also polarizing. Instead of physics, he focused on psychology and the spiritual interplay among individuals and groups. It's interesting stuff. Beyond the subject was the format of the book. Back in college, many of the textbooks were tedious at best. I wondered if authors might be more effective if they approached teaching with fiction. The addition of a story, any story, would make the subject easier to follow and increase engagement. Mr. Redfield did a good job of that throughout the series.

I've read many books on eastern mysticism and philosophy over the years. Deepak Chopra is a prolific writer and I love all of his stuff that I've read. Probably the first piece of his I encountered was a booklet on addiction. I was studying for a paper on exercise addiction and found it insightful and moving. It inspired me to look up more of his work. Now, I can't find the booklet, but he has a *ton* of outstanding work on religion, meditation, and health.

Wayne Dyer is the one who finally taught me Zen. I'd studied meditation for a long time, but aside from a brief instance while sitting on a swing in the second grade, that moment of *no-thought* eluded me. Dr. Dyer's book *Getting in the Gap* changed that. It uses the Lord's Prayer, words that most of us know without having to think about them, as a tool to get to that space between thoughts. It's powerful stuff. Of course, he wrote a lot of books before he died and I have most of them. I regret that I never got to see him in person.

Michael Talbot had already passed by the time I found *The Holographic Universe*. That book was transformational in my understanding of reality. And it led me to Lynne McTaggart, who continues to do outstanding work in understanding intention and how we affect the universe. I loved *The Field* and *The Intention Experiment*.

Rhonda Byrne made old ideas new again with her book and video *The Secret*. Of course, many people dismiss it as wishful thinking. That's easy to do. But there was a lot of interesting stuff there and she highlighted a lot of interesting teachers.

One of those is Fred Alan Wolf. Similar to Carl Sagan, he is great at breaking down the science and making it accessible. Rather unlike Dr. Sagan, Dr. Wolf is unabashedly refreshingly enthusiastic about his subject. Dr. Wolf was also in the *What the Bleep Do We Know?!* movie, which also led me to many more authors.

One of those was Joe Dispenza. I read *Becoming Supernatural* after I had already completed several drafts of this novel, but I would still say that it was influential to the final version. Dr. Dispenza has some excellent aids for meditation, besides his outstanding books.

I could go on and on about various authors who have influenced me and my work. I'll just mention one more. Gregg Braden, again, has written many books and continues to speak and write. I think the first book of his that I read was *The Divine Matrix,* and it continues to influence my understanding of the cosmos and the connection between science and spirituality.

We're all living in a stew of information and relationships. Through books, we get both. I sometimes feel like I've developed relationships with the characters, or the authors. And sometimes both.

Perhaps I've written this book as a thank you to these authors, and many more.

K.G. Ring is the author of *Flight*, Book One of the *Ordinary*^{Super} Series. Besides this series, he is working on a Science Fiction series and a Young Adult Martial Art/Fantasy mashup series.

He lives in Muncie, Indiana, where he has taught traditional Korean martial art for over fifteen years.

facebook.com/KennethGRing

x.com/ring.kenneth

instagram.com/kenneth_ring_author

tiktok.com/k.g.ring

goodreads.com/kgring

First paperback edition February 2022

Cover design by Irene Martinez

ISBN (paperback)
979-8-9856209-0-0
ISBN (ebook)
979-8-9856209-1-7

www.KGRingAuthor.com